Gothic Stories Within Stories

Gothic Stories Within Stories

Frame Narratives and Realism in the Genre, 1790–1900

CLAYTON CARLYLE TARR

McFarland & Company, Inc., Publishers
Jefferson, North Carolina

ISBN (print) 978-1-4766-6748-5
ISBN (ebook) 978-1-4766-2820-2

Library of Congress cataloguing data are available

British Library cataloguing data are available

Front cover image: Limbird's British novelist engraving for *The Mysteries of Udolpho*, London, 1826

Printed in the United States of America

McFarland & Company, Inc., Publishers
Box 611, Jefferson, North Carolina 28640
www.mcfarlandpub.com

Table of Contents

Introduction 1

1. A "frame of uncommon size": Ann Radcliffe and the Sublime Real 21

2. Go Forth and Prosper: Mary Shelley's Monsters Unbound 45

3. Loose Ends: *Melmoth the Wanderer* and *Confessions of a Justified Sinner* 63

INTERLUDE. The Fabric of Reality: *Sartor Resartus* 83

4. The "science of human brutality": *Wuthering Heights* and *The Tenant of Wildfell Hall* 91

5. The "romantic side of familiar things": *The Old Curiosity Shop* and *Bleak House* 109

6. The Descent of Man: *Jekyll and Hyde* and *Dracula* 130

CODA. Glory in a Gap: *The Turn of the Screw* and *Heart of Darkness* 153

Chapter Notes 165

Bibliography 191

Index 205

Introduction

> I show Rabelais in the history of realism. Perhaps I am mistaken, but I believe that I have added a new page to the history of realism. The term "Gothic realism" did not previously exist in French or Russian literature. Nobody would be able to cite any examples of anybody, anywhere, at any time writing about Gothic realism. I have enriched the history of realism.
>
> —Mikhail Bakhtin[1]

On 15 November 1946, the Academic Council of the Gorky Institute convened in Moscow to hear Bakhtin defend his dissertation, "Rabelais and the History of Realism." The meeting was famously contentious, and Bakhtin was ultimately conferred the degree of Candidate rather than earning the higher rank of Doctorate. One of the many points of debate concerned the suitability of Bakhtin's "Gothic realism." At the insistence of the committee, Bakhtin revised the term to "grotesque realism," which, together with his model of the carnivalesque, became the focus of his 1965 book *Rabelais and His World*. In spite of the revision, Bakhtin's concept of the grotesque remains intimately connected with the Gothic. He argues that the Romantic grotesque is a "terrifying world, alien to man. All that is ordinary, commonplace, belonging to everyday life, and recognized by all suddenly becomes meaningless, dubious and hostile. Our own world becomes an alien world. Something frightening is revealed in that which was habitual and secure."[2] Bakhtin suggests that the grotesque triggers a supernatural terror that destabilizes perceptions of reality. The Gothic accomplishes the same effect, but to an even greater degree. From its inception with Horace Walpole's *The Castle of Otranto* (1764), the Gothic novel accessed hidden psychic realms—what Bakhtin calls the "*interior infinite* of the individual"—and revealed the supernatural hidden in the natural world.[3] Perhaps most important to this study, however, is Bakhtin's claim that "form and content in discourse are one."[4] For the distinctive thematic effects of the Gothic novel are, in great part, the result of the genre's formal attributes—namely its prevalent and dynamic narrative frames.

The Gothic has often been considered reactionary anti-realism, an attempt to counter "things as they are" by imagining "things as they are not." Yet, from the beginning, the Gothic aligned itself alongside realism, rather than advertising its opposition. Walpole, for example, famously writes that *Otranto* was an "attempt to blend the two kinds of romance: the ancient and the modern. In the former, all was imagination and improbability; in the latter, nature is always intended to be, and sometimes has been, copied with success."[5] Similarly, the initial title of William Godwin's Gothic thriller *Caleb Williams* (1794) was "Things as They Are," and Wordsworth and Coleridge's *Lyrical Ballads* (1798, 1800, 1802, 1805) was, according to the latter, to be "composed of two sorts": "persons and characters supernatural" and "incidents of domestic or ordinary life."[6] In Bakhtin's words, "[t]wo types of imagery reflecting the conception of the world here meet at crossroads."[7] Indeed, Bakhtin's distinction between "classical realism" and "grotesque realism" demonstrates that several genres share "Realism Road."[8] For the principal discrepancy between realism and the Gothic is a matter of differing perspectives on what is "real." Whereas realism shows the world reflected *in* a mirror, the Gothic looks *through* a glass darkly to suggest the hidden realms of the human experience. This effect—the unveiling of an alternate "reality" and the horror that comes with it—is reliant on the formal properties and distinct function of narrative frames.[9]

Gothic novelists have long employed framing devices both around and within their novels. In a manner similar to what Jacques Derrida conceptualized with his model of the parergon, Gothic frame narratives blur narrative and cognitive boundaries, producing a destabilizing effect that challenges rational epistemology and suggests a deeper "reality" than the realist novel can possibly achieve. This "reality" can be understood through both Immanuel Kant's realm of *das Ding an sich* ("the thing in itself") and Jacques Lacan's concept of the Real, the chaotic welter of presymbolic life that dissipates all forms of logic. Although Gothic novels can never represent the Real, they do suggest its existence through horrifying, yet attractive figures—monstrosities that can be articulated through symbolic devices that are best explained by Julia Kristeva's theory of abjection. These implications of the Real draw readers closer to a deep reality while simultaneously screening them from the horror that is at the core of being. I argue that they achieve their distinctive and disturbing status in Gothic novels as a result of the dynamic process through which the central narratives interact with their frames. Although Gothic frames seem to serve as boundaries, they in fact function as thresholds between the central narrative and the reader's reality, which are often articulated by objects like veils. When monstrous abjections transgress narrative frames, the novel's narrators and readers are forced to face the horror that they have worked to reject. This argument has several steps, and I will make them more coherent below both by expanding on theoretical concepts and by engaging literary examples, which conclude with a brief reading of Walpole's *Otranto*—the first text to call itself a "Gothic Story."

But first, it is prudent to address not only the aims of this book, but also to acknowledge its potential limitations.[10] Scholarship on Gothic literature, in all its forms, is rich and rewarding, perhaps more so than any other genre. Due to the deep, complex nature of the Gothic, critical approaches line the theoretical spectrum.[11] To propose a reading of Gothic literature based primarily on psychoanalytic principles, whether inspired by Freud, Lacan, Kristeva, or others, is not a new approach. In fact, the productive history of such readings only continues with two recent, equally invigorating, contributions, and no doubt there will be many more to come.[12] This book, however, does not attempt to supply comprehensive psychoanalytic readings of canonical texts. Nor does it aspire to consign authors, characters, or even readers to the analyst's couch. Rather, it engages select psychoanalytic models to articulate one distinct set of formal attributes pervasive to Gothic fiction. And it does so not only with assistance from other theoretical approaches, including deconstruction and narratology, but also with the backing of contextual documents, ranging from letters and journals to records and reviews. No text is placed in a psychoanalytic vacuum. And no author is subject to posthumous diagnosis. But this does not mean that I wish either to disparage psychoanalytic approaches or to undermine my own readings. For the Gothic and psychoanalysis are so closely intertwined that to unravel them would be not just fruitless, but potentially irresponsible.[13] Writing of Sigmund Freud's relation to the Gothic, William Patrick Day observes:

> The Gothic is not a crude anticipation of Freudianism, nor its unacknowledged father. Rather, the two are cousins, responses to the problems of selfhood and identity, sexuality and pleasure, fear and anxiety as they manifest themselves in the nineteenth and early twentieth centuries. The Gothic arises out of the immediate needs of the reading public to escape from conventional life and articulate and define the turbulence of their psychic existence. We may see Freud as the intellectual counterpart of this process.[14]

Gothic literature and psychoanalysis are cooperative, though sometimes combative, participants in the human drive to unlock the secrets of the mind, to explore uncharted psychic regions, to understand the unconscious disturbances that trigger our conscious desires. Rather than employing psychoanalysis to diagnose authors, characters, and settings, this book uses theoretical models to articulate the extraordinary cognitive impacts of Gothic form. The frame narratives that ubiquitously appear in Gothic literature, though often critically ignored, play a crucial role in the way that the genre develops and deploys its horror.

Gothic Framing

> Forthwith this frame of mine was wrench'd
> With a woeful agony,
> Which forc'd me to begin my tale
> And then it left me free.
>
> —Samuel Taylor Coleridge (1798)[15]

Coleridge's "The Rime of the Ancient Mariner" provides a particularly useful model to articulate the narratology of Gothic frame narratives. The poem opens with an unnamed, omniscient voice that describes a scene in which the titular Mariner detains a wedding guest. The opening stanzas constitute an extradiegetic narrative layer, the frame that surrounds the Mariner's central, diegetic tale that follows. At the conclusion of the Mariner's tale, the poem closes with a return to the scene at the wedding. Thus, the Mariner's diegetic narrative is framed at either end by the anonymous narrator's extradiegetic voice.[16] Werner Wolf argues that narrative frames are "integral parts of the respective verbal representations which are located on a logically higher (diegetic) level. As narratives (or at least narrative fragments) they in addition partake in the narrative nature of the entire artifact."[17] Thus, frames are not ornaments that can be ignored, but rather are vital components of the entire fictionality of the text. To ignore the frame narrative of "Ancient Mariner" means to miss crucial aspects of the poem and perhaps to misunderstand it entirely.

The narrative layering in "Ancient Mariner" becomes more complicated when we consider the revisions Coleridge made for his 1817 collection *Sibylline Leaves*. In its initial form, the poem was composed with antiquated spellings—most evident in its title, "The Rime of the Ancyent Marinere." In the 1798 "Advertisement" to *Lyrical Ballads*, Wordsworth writes that the poem "was professedly written in imitation of the *style*, as well as of the spirit of the elder poets."[18] By 1805, however, Wordsworth had overseen two modernizations of the poem. In *Sibylline Leaves*,

Coleridge introduced a new marginal gloss, which, Paul H. Fry notes, "makes the poem seem like a rare manuscript and thus has the effect of reintroducing much of the archaic atmosphere that Wordsworth had wished to dispel."[19] This revision also complicates the narrative structure of the poem. As Jerome McGann points out, the prose gloss, which often incorporates antique spellings, differs from the anonymous voice that composes the extradiegetic frame.[20] Thus, Coleridge introduces another narrative layer, an extra-extradiegetic commentary that frames the extradiegetic narrative.[21] "Ancient Mariner" presents a fascinating series of narrative frames—dependent, of course, on which text one reads. In the 1817 version, the Mariner's diegetic tale is framed by the anonymous narrator; the prose gloss; the epigraph from Thomas Burnet; and Coleridge's preface to *Sibylline Leaves*.

The many potential frames that make up "Ancient Mariner" seemingly shield readers from the horrors of the Mariner's tale, which include water-snakes, the ghost ship of Death and Life-in-Death, and even the undead crew. Yet Coleridge expertly undermines the narrative boundaries he has introduced. As Elizabeth MacAndrew has argued, a "narrative method" such as this one "places the reader in the same relation described as the listeners of the tale."[22] The wedding guest, who "cannot chuse but hear," functions as a proxy figure for the reader, who is drawn into the Mariner's tale of physical and psychological suffering.[23] The supernatural horror of the Mariner's narrative taints the commonplace festivities of the wedding party and spreads its contagion into the reality of the reader. We share in the wedding guest's fate that closes the poem: "A sadder and a wiser man / He rose the morrow morn."[24] Coleridge sets up the poem's many narrative layers only to collapse them by paralleling the wedding guest's listening of the tale to the reader's reading of it. In a 30 January 1801 letter, Charles Lamb writes that the "feelings of the man under the operations of such scenery dragged me along like Tom Piper's magic whistle."[25] While the wedding guest sits mesmerized by the Mariner's "glittering eye," readers are similarly drawn in by the anonymous narrator's hypnotic rhyme, with the result that, as the tale begins, they "cannot chuse but" read.[26] This effect blurs the borders between the extradiegetic, everyday world of the wedding party and the reader's reality, which draws readers into closer narrative proximity to the diegetic horrors of the Mariner's tale.

The most disturbing narrative effect of the poem, however, is the prose gloss that Coleridge added to the 1817 version. As John Spencer Hill observes, "[a]t certain points in the supernatural parts of the story … the gloss adds details that are not in the poem itself."[27] Readers are assailed, then, by explanations, if not outright additions, of supernatural elements that are not explicitly manifest in either the Mariner's diegetic tale or the poem's other extradiegetic layers.[28] For the framing device of the prose gloss does not merely highlight the supernatural; it raises the otherworldly figures of the Mariner's tale and relocates them in a paratextual space, while simultaneously introducing new elements of horror through the pretext of editorial explication. Although meant as a criticism, David Pirie's assessment of the gloss as "perverting" is nonetheless accurate.[29] The gloss fundamentally alters the poem, twisting its meaning through a supplemental narrative authority that introduces new horror in an extra-extradiegetic space. The multiple frames in "Ancient Mariner" draw out the horror of the diegetic tale and place it systematically closer to the everyday world of the reader that the editor inhabits. Perhaps most important, what had, over the last two decades, become Wordsworth's lyrical ballad was newly reformed as Coleridge's Gothic story.

The Force of Frames

> But let the frame of things disjoint.
> —William Shakespeare, *Macbeth*[30]

In "The Philosophy of Composition" (1846), Edgar Allan Poe describes his process for choosing the "locale" for his haunting poem "The Raven" (1845): "a close *circumscription of space* is absolutely necessary to the effect of insulated incident:—it has the force of a frame to a picture. It has an indisputable moral power in keeping concentrated the attention."[31] Without borders, the textual canvas would spread indefinitely and become too varied and unruly to elicit the desired environmental effect. Yet the frame of Poe's chamber, which is meant to shelter the speaker, ultimately permits the access of the raven, the symbolic reminder of lost love, whose shadow traps the speaker's soul to "be lifted—nevermore!"[32] The "force of a frame," then, "radiates in two directions simultaneously," pulling together that which it purports to separate.[33] Frames occupy a space that is part of both the central, fictional narrative and of the outside, real world, so the frame narrative is closer to the world of authors and readers not only in terms of its primary and terminal positions in the text, but also because it merges into that world, uniting reality and fiction prior to the appearance of the embedded narrative. This effect is even more evident—

and disturbing—when applied to Poe's "The Fall of the House of Usher" (1839).

Although the tale appears to be a straightforward diegetic account (following Poe's other stories of the macabre), it actually features an unusual frame narrative, in which the anonymous narrator's musings outside the titular house frame the horror that is apparently sequestered within. In the opening frame, the narrator approaches the House of Usher and notes the discomforting atmosphere of the edifice and its environment: "I looked upon the scene before me … with an utter depression of soul which I can compare to no earthly sensation more properly than to the after-dream of the reveler upon opium—the bitter lapse into everyday life—the hideous dropping off the veil."[34] The nightmarish prospect—which is intensified by its inverted reflection in a pool—not only foreshadows the horror inside the house, but also suggests that what is inside the walls has already seeped into the narrator's extradiegetic world. The narrator notes that the "fabric gave little token of instability," but does observe a "barely perceptible fissure."[35] This ominous fracture can be examined through Jacques Derrida's definition of the "conceptualization of totality" that is the hallmark of structuralist theory. "Structure is perceived through the incidence of menace," Derrida writes, "at the moment when imminent danger concentrates our vision on the keystone of an institution, the stone which encapsulates both the possibility and the fragility of its existence."[36] Gothic frame narratives routinely demonstrate the uncertainty of structure and the ambiguity of boundaries. Textual architecture in Gothic novels is never more than a cracking façade, a house of cards poised to topple.

In his *Critique of the Power of Judgment* (1790), Immanuel Kant briefly draws attention to objects that are "detrimental to genuine, uncorrupted, well-grounded taste."[37] Kant labels these "charms" or "ornaments" as parerga—frames, columns, or clothing—"not internal to the entire representation of the object as a constituent," but only associated with it "externally as an addendum."[38] Kant elsewhere argues that "foliage for framework or on wall-papers, etc., have no intrinsic meaning; they represent nothing … and are free beauties."[39] In *The Truth in Painting*, Derrida questions the very capacity for intrinsic art by exploring the charged interstice at its boundaries. He contends that a "parergon comes against, beside.… [B]ut it does not fall to one side, it touches and cooperates within the operation from a certain outside. Neither simply outside nor simply inside."[40] Simultaneously part of the work and the environment (milieu) outside the work, the parergon blends into both: "With respect to the work which can serve as a ground for it, it merges into the wall, and then, gradually, into the general text."[41] It is a "hybrid of outside and inside."[42] In "Usher," the narrator enters a "Gothic archway" within the house that designates the frame between the outside world and the inside horror. Once inside, he makes note of the "insufferable gloom" of the surrounding environment, and is "ushered" through "many dark and intricate passages" before he arrives at the "chamber" that is the heart of darkness of his decaying friend.[43] Thus, the house's precarious frame pulls together the worlds it appears to separate, as the central horror bleeds into the reality outside. What is more, the structure of "Usher" demonstrates that frame narratives do not necessarily require distinct chapter-like separation to achieve the particular effects examined in this study. As will be demonstrated in Chapter 1, Ann Radcliffe's *The Mysteries of Udolpho* (1794) features a distinctive framing device that relies on geographic borders rather than formal spacing. To be sure, *Udolpho* and "Usher" focus their energies on the fearsome diegetic interiors of their titular structures, but the enduring horror of both texts lies in the supernatural effects that have invaded the familiar natural frame that surrounds them. The texts' narrative parerga, in other words, are delineated by environment and architecture, but are no less significant than those formed by textual divisions.

One of the principal aspects of Derrida's parergon is that its very status requires the existence of a lacuna, a lack in the ergon, an effect that constantly pulls the frame and the embedded work together: "What constitutes … *parerga* is not simply their exteriority as a surplus, it is the internal structural link which rivets them to the lack in the interior of the *ergon*."[44] The most enduring horror in "Usher" may be that the lack that has driven Roderick Usher to madness, the life and survival of his sister Madeline, is filled by the narrator who arrives from the frame. The narrator admits: "I personally aided him in the arrangements of the temporary entombment."[45] When Roderick hears Madeline escaping from her vault, he shrieks: "*We have put her living in the tomb!*"[46] Madeline's entombment was a collaborative undertaking. Indeed, Roderick's letter to the narrator, "in its wildly importunate nature, had admitted of no other than a personal reply."[47] He requires an accomplice, one fit to help him bear the body into its coffin, to close the "immense weight" of the vault's iron door, and to ignore the "faint blush upon the bosom and the face" of the alleged corpse.[48] Although perhaps not as guilty as Poe's homicidal narrators in "The Tell-Tale Heart" (1843) and "The Cask of Amontillado" (1846), the narrator in "Usher," the figure we trust with objective authority, is ultimately complicit in the crime. And as the house bifurcates and disappears beneath the tarn, he walks away with impunity. The narrator's collusion in the crimes blurs the boundaries between the frame and the embedded scenes within the house, and the unspoken horror of incestuous desire, which would have been buried, instead clings to the narrator, who in turn infects readers.

The Gothic Real

> And what if all of animated nature
> Be but organic Harps diversely framed,
> That tremble into thought, as o'er them sweeps
> Plastic and vast, one intellectual breeze,
> At once the Soul of each, and God of all?
> —Samuel Taylor Coleridge,
> "The Eolian Harp" (1795)[49]

Coleridge's image of a harp "Placed length-ways in the clasping casement" to be plucked by a "desultory breeze" arguably serves as the foundational metaphor for Romantic-era poetry. Yet it is potentially more disturbing than comforting, as the subjective mind becomes a passive instrument activated by outside stimuli. The poetic imagination, if not basic cognition, relies on the labor of unknowable, capricious forces. Percy Shelley would elaborate on the harp metaphor in his "A Defence of Poetry" (1821) by arguing that "[m]an is an instrument over which a series of external and internal impressions are driven."[50] Thus, in what could suggest a nuanced reading of Kant, Shelley argues that the functioning mind depends on the interaction between outside sensations and inside "principles."[51] In his *Critique of Pure Reason* (1781), Kant posits that what we conceive of as reality is actually a cognitive construct made up of representations that are gathered from the frenzied fusion of subjective sensations and *a priori* categories. Through the process of synthesis, our understanding attempts to frame this teeming manifold—what Wordsworth might call the "mighty sum / Of things for ever speaking."[52] Yet this chaotic multiplicity not only highlights the disturbing limitations of our cognition (where time and space become mere "forms of thought"), but also implicates the presence of the unknown and unknowable elements of the universe—the leftovers that escape the framing process.[53] Stephen Houlgate clarifies this concept by noting that Kant "insists that we can never know whether there is actually anything to things beyond what we experience of them, but he maintains that we can and indeed must entertain the *thought* that there is."[54] Of most significance is Kant's concept of *das Ding an sich* ("the thing in itself"), which exists in an unknowable realm outside the reach of our senses. In a 7 August 1783 letter, Kant explains: "All objects that can be given to us can be conceptualized in two ways: on the one hand, as appearances; on the other hand, as things in themselves."[55] We may only comprehend of *das Ding an sich* in the negative sense, Jonathan Bennett notes, as "facts about our experience which impose limits on what we can meaningfully say."[56] The "realist," Kant writes, "changes mere representations into things in themselves," but the truth is that we can never know the "inside pertaining to the object in itself."[57] The distinctive form of the Gothic novel intimates the existence of inaccessible realms and suggests the presence of the impossible, frightening "things" that structure our reality. In so doing, it challenges the hegemony of both rational empiricism and aesthetic realism.

Kant's model of a deeper, unknown world, (in)articulated through the "residuum of reality" that is *das Ding an sich*, in many ways resembles Jacques Lacan's concept of the Real.[58] The foundation of Lacanian psychoanalysis concerns the relationship between three registers—the Real, the imaginary, and the symbolic—which are linked in all human constructions of self and world, and roughly correspond to the stages of human development.[59] The symbolic order marks our entrance into the systems of language (the complicated, fluid, and antagonistic associations between signifiers and signified) that structure our reality. The Real, on the other hand, is made up of pre-symbolic elements and resists representation in the symbolic order—hence Lacan's famous formulation: "the [R]eal as the impossible."[60] Lacan writes that the "[R]eal is that which always lies behind the automaton," the networking chain of signifiers that make up our known reality.[61] For Slavoj Žižek, the Real invades our constructs of reality through the "fundamental deadlock" of social antagonism.[62] Culture "attempt[s] to limit, canalize—to *cultivate* this imbalance, this traumatic kernel, this radical antagonism," but its irrepressible resolve inspires the uprising of totalitarian regimes that are driven by the "aspiration to abolish it."[63] Circulating and conflicting ideologies that emerge in the processes of social antagonism—and which are thereby analogous to Kant's chaotic manifold assaulting the senses—blur together at the point of the Real. "This immediate coincidence of opposite or even contradictory determinations," Žižek writes, "is what *defines* the Lacanian Real."[64] Through the blurring and synthesizing function of its frame narratives, the Gothic novel became the site where ideological antagonisms (gender, race, class, nationality, and religion) could "[m]ix ... together," to borrow from a 1797 reviewer, "in the form of three volumes."[65]

The Real also makes its appearance in our reality—encounters that are termed moments of *tuché* by Lacan—in both mundane disappointments ("the fact that things do not turn out all right straight away") and far more traumatic moments and memories.[66] "The trauma reappears," Lacan writes, "frequently unveiled. How can the dream, the bearer of the subject's desire, produce that which makes the trauma emerge repeatedly—if not its very face, at least the screen that shows us that it is still there behind?"[67] Žižek describes the function of this screen, which simultaneously conceals and implicates the Real: "Lacan's fundamental thesis is that a minimum of 'idealization,' of the interposition of fantasmatic frame by means of which the subject assumes a distance vis-à-vis the Real, is constitutive of our sense of reality—'reality' occurs insofar as it is not (it does not come) 'too close.'"[68] When the Real does make intimate contact, however, it "shatters the symbolic co-ordinates of the subject's horizon of meaning."[69] Gothic novels present readers with these dream-screens, these fantasy idealizations, in the form of monsters, ghosts, and other supernatural or otherwise extraordinary figures. Jerrold E. Hogle observes that "Gothic monstrosities ... keep us from beholding that level of the Thing directly because their references to the Real are re-presented by fake, and thus half-comforting, symbolizations."[70] As the Real "remains essentially ungraspable by any representation," it can only be suggested by figures that symbolize what we have repressed, the abjections that disturb our sense of identity and reality.[71]

In *Powers of Horror*, Julia Kristeva argues that the abject is located at the point at which "meaning collapses" and is defined as that which "disturbs identity, system, order. What does not respect borders, positions, rules."[72] In Kantian terms, abjections are the things that are framed off from the manifold of senses during the process of synthesis and that store the frightening multiplicity that reality denies. Thus, the abject also suggests the existence of the Real by exhibiting what we "permanently thrust aside in order to live."[73] As Joan Copjec remarks, "[t]o constitute ourselves, we must ... throw out, reject our nonselves."[74] One experiences the abject during confrontations with bodily secretions and, especially, with corpses, which remind us of the base horror of our existence—the object-materiality that we must deny ("throw off") in order to conceive of ourselves as "I" in opposition to "others." Hogle expertly describes the process of abjection as it relates to our formation of identity:

> [A]n "I" can exist in particular contexts or definite combinations of them only if a "primal repression" disallows some potential and contradictory relations.... Some order of discourse must limit the subject's relational options and consign all excluded ones (including most erotogenic memoirs of the birth state) to an unnamable, taboo status. These castoffs, to seem completely "other," must be covered over

> by a symbol of what the "I" seems *not* to be (a "devil," for instance) that helps to declare the "I" a specific entity separate from that opposite.[75]

Abject monstrosities are both repulsive and attractive; they simultaneously suggest the existence of the Real that we desire to grasp and yet function as fantasy screens to keep us from being overwhelmed by it. The revulsion of the abject is the result of facing Kant's "thing in itself," of coming "too close" to the Real and butting up against the dark chaos of pre-symbolic existence that we can neither control nor even grasp. Kristeva writes that "literature may ... involve not an ultimate resistance to but an unveiling of the abject."[76] And Žižek points specifically to the Gothic novel as site where these horrors are unveiled:

> [The] catastrophic consequences of the encroachment upon the forbidden/impossible domain of the Thing are spelled out in the Gothic novel: it is by no means accidental that the Gothic novel, obsessed as it is with the motive of the Thing in its different embodiments (the "living dead," and so on), is contemporary to Kant's transcendental turn. We could even risk the hypothesis that the Gothic novel is a kind of critique *avant la letter* of the Kantian insistence on the unsurmountable gap between phenomena and the transcendent Thing-in-itself: what are the specters that appear in it if not *apparitions of the Thing*, if not points of a "short circuit" at which the transphenomenal Thing invades the phenomenal domain and disturbs its casual order?[77]

The Gothic novel forces us to confront the horror of what we have tried to discard in order to seem coherent to ourselves. The particular dynamic of its parergon-like frame narratives permit the Real—the things, antagonisms, and traumas "ejected beyond the scope of the possible, the tolerable, the thinkable"—to come "too close."[78] The monstrosities that assail readers are, as Žižek argues, "*Things that think*" (220), impossible made possible, repressed emerged, Real reality, Gothic realism.

Frame Breaking

> One gate there only was, and that looked east
> On th' other side: which when th' Arch-felon saw
> Due entrance he disdained, and in contempt,
> At one slight bound high overleaped all bound
> Of hill or highest wall, and sheer within
> Lights on his feet.
>
> —John Milton, *Paradise Lost*[79]

There is perhaps no more disturbing transgression of boundaries in literature than Satan's leap into Eden in *Paradise Lost*. Rather than wage war on Heaven, the fallen figures of Hell decide to enter Earth, God's favored new creation, to corrupt its founding couple. Satan volunteers for the task, and eventually arrives at the border of paradise, where he is impeded by a coppice, "so thick entwined, / as one continued brake."[80] With "one slight bound," however, he overcomes the obstacle—like a wolf "[l]eaps o'er the fence" and a thief "at the window climbs."[81] His unsettlingly easy entrance takes him from a demon-realm of shadows into a human-world familiar to readers. Satan's invasion could be considered not only as the archetype of a "cast off" abjection resurfacing in an idyllic world, but also, in Lacanian terms, as the Real penetrating symbolic reality. Milton's epic is an origin story of the Real, a narrative of original sin as conceived through a desire for what the symbolic order denies. This reading is especially enticing if we include Satan's amorphous, incestuous progenies, Sin and Death, in the equation. Perhaps most important, in the frame-breaking power of its anti-hero, *Paradise Lost* could be canonized as one of the pioneering texts of the Gothic.

While frame narratives in other genres demarcate and contain the central narrative, making embedded content less threatening to readers who are fully isolated from the fiction, Gothic frames exploit the more devious formal possibilities of the device, making readers victims as much as voyeurs.[82] Gothic frames also achieve distinctive effects that other Gothic novels cannot claim. They establish seemingly conventional worlds that rely on verisimilitude to draw readers into the text before the diegetic narrative begins. We are meant to share in the wedding guest's hypnotized horror in "Ancient Mariner" and to identify with the first-person narrator in "The Fall of the House of Usher." However, Gothic novelists subtly work to taint the everyday, extradiegetic narrative with the horror that lurks within. Coleridge's famous account of the genesis of *Lyrical Ballads*, to some degree, parallels this process. Tasked with composing the supernatural poems in the collection, Coleridge sought "to transfer from our inward nature a human interest and a semblance of truth sufficient to procure for these shadows of imagination that willing suspension of disbelief for the moment, which constitutes poetic faith."[83] The extradiegetic frames in Gothic novels mimic "human interest and a semblance of truth" before the diegetic supernatural reveals the "shadows of imagination." In spite of Wordsworth's disdain for "sickly and stupid German Tragedies," his project was ultimately no less Gothic than Coleridge's.[84] His set of poems promised "to give the charm of novelty to things of every day, and to excite a feeling analogous to the supernatural."[85] To do so required Wordsworth to dispel the "film of familiarity," to lift the veil of reality in order to represent the truth that the senses concealed. This effect is what Thomas Carlyle would later call "natural supernaturalism." This is Gothic realism.

Gothic frame narratives also rely on the same dynamic that Derrida attributes to the parergon. By being both "inside" and "outside" the diegesis, Gothic frames in fact reveal what they would appear to conceal. What they attempt to "other," to abject from the synthesizing labor of the Kantian manifold, leaks into them. This process includes the social antagonisms that Žižek points to as indicators of the Real. In Poe's "Usher," for example, the anonymous narrator is disturbed by the ominous landscape well before he encounters the horror within the house. He seems immediately unable to control the frightening multiplicity of sensations that assail his mind: "nor could I grapple with the shadowy fancies that crowded upon me as I pondered."[86] Thus, the Real that the "mansion of gloom" appears to contain, which is evidenced by blurred boundaries within (generations of inbreeding, culminating in the incestuous mingling of the twin brother and sister; the merger of inmate and house, of life and death, of reality and representation), becomes part of the house's unsettling exterior, and then escapes entirely as the framework of the house splits, sinks, and disappears.

Even more disturbing are the many occasions when figures from the central or embedded narrative invade the frame—events that often seem inspired by the "slight bound" of Milton's Satan. The diegetic narrative's monstrous abjections become horrifying "found manuscripts," buried entities that resurface in the extradiegetic frame to challenge the borders between fiction and reality. The extraordinary capacity of Gothic monstrosities to move between narrative frames is a process known as metalepsis, the "metaphorical usage resulting from a series or succession of figurative substitutions" (OED).[87] Debra Malina observes that metalepsis "has the power to endow subjects with greater or lesser degrees of 'reality'—in effect, to promote them into subjectivity and demote them from it."[88] When characters transcend their status as fictional figures, they become disturbingly subjective and potentially dangerous to the shrinking authority of the narrator, the author, and the reader. Coleridge's Mariner survives his ordeal within the world of the supernatural and trespasses the reality of the extradiegetic wedding party. His experience with the poem's implications of the Real invades the reality of the reader by becoming part of the paratextual elements that appear to contain them. The gap in the symbolic reality of the wedding party—whatever unknown family tie or misaddressed invitation that grants the Mariner's attendance—allows the emergence of the Real. Readers experience the result of the poem's diegetic horror, which is physically manifested in the "loon" Mariner's "glittering eye" and "skinny hand," before we know the cause.[89] Through the process of metalepsis, Gothic abjections are raised from buried narratives so that they come "too close" to readers. As Malina argues, "[m]etalepsis dramatizes the problematization of the boundary between fiction and reality endemic to the postmodern condition."[90] Gothic novels anticipate such constructions, with the added touch of horror. For the blurring of ontological boundaries made possible by the metaleptic transgressions of Gothic figures not only challenges our understanding of reality, but also suggests the existence of the Real, an effect that destabilizes—and has the potential to dissolve—our identity. The Gothic novel, like Kristeva's abject corpse, "beckons to us and ends up engulfing us," as our reality becomes a disjointed narrative, our minds unhinged by unknown and unknowable forces.[91]

The Gothic Veil

> Lift not the painted veil which those who live
> Call Life; though unreal shapes be pictured there,
> And it but mimic all we would believe
> With colours idly spread,—behind, lurk Fear
> And Hope, twin Destinies; who ever weave
> Their shadows, o'er the chasm, sightless and drear.
>
> —Percy Shelley (1818)[92]

Shelley's sonnet suggests that what we perceive as reality is indeed an artificial image, a fantasy representation of what we have been conditioned to believe. Yet the speaker urges his audience to resist venturing behind this imaginary screen, for what it reveals refuses to provide answers.[93] The poem rather overtly recalls the famous veil scene in Radcliffe's *The Mysteries of Udolpho*, in which Emily St Aubert "went towards the picture, which appeared to be enclosed in a frame of uncommon size, … [and] with a timid hand, lifted the veil; but instantly let it fall—perceiving that what it had concealed was no picture, and, before she could leave the chamber, she dropped senseless on the floor."[94] At the novel's dénouement, Radcliffe reveals that a wax effigy of a decomposing body was hidden behind the veil. Emily's initial terror prevents her from returning, and she remains as ignorant of the truth as Shelley's "one who had lifted it // a Spirit that strove / For truth, and … found it not."[95] Part of what provokes her terror is that the singular frame supports "no picture," but rather encases an "unreal shape"—an uncanny object with dimensions and depth.[96] Like Jane Austen's Catherine Morland in *Northanger Abbey* (1817), Emily believes—indeed, wants—it to be an actual corpse, and she projects this desire onto the waxen form.[97] Thus, the answer that Emily seeks does not lie behind the actual veil, but rather "lurks" behind the metaphorical "painted veil" that represents reality. Lacan writes that "if the Thing were not fundamentally veiled, we wouldn't be in the kind of relationship to it that obliges us, as the whole of psychic life is obliged, to encircle it or bypass it in order to conceive it."[98] Emily's traumatic encounter intimates the presence of the Real, the abjected level where the difference between life and death disappears. The veil and the "frame of uncommon size" (if not "the chamber") function as fantasmatic screens between the reality of Udolpho and the horrifying Real of Emily's unconscious desires—her morbid drive to unveil the corpse, the "utmost of abjection."[99]

Discussing a similar literary device, Bakhtin observes that in Romanticism the mask "hides something, keeps a secret, deceives.... A terrible vacuum, a nothingness lurks behind it."[100] We might be here reminded of Poe's "The Masque of the Red Death" (1842), in which the mysterious guest is revealed to be "untenanted by any tangible form."[101] The Gothic novel is filled with veils, masks, and tapestries, many of which function as permeable objects that screen the portal between reality and unknown worlds. Throughout this study, I would like to conceive of frame narratives not only through the metaphor of pictorial framing, but also through the image of veiling that Shelley and other writers employ. When we read framed novels, we lift veils as we pass through the layers of narrative. To open the Gothic book, to turn its pages, is to encounter the "unfathomable fold" of the Real, the horrifying realm that lies beyond our perceptible reality.[102] Gothic frame narratives typically introduce us to a familiar world, the "painted veil" of reality, but when we proceed into the embedded narrative(s), we enter another world, a deeper level of reality where we experience the abject monstrosities that suggest the Real.[103] Through the effects of metalepsis, however, Gothic frame narratives ultimately demonstrate that the everyday world (and by implication the "reality" outside the fiction) is not as ordinary as it seems. In Arthur Symons's words, "the visible world is no longer a reality, and the unseen world no longer a dream."[104] Through the distinct properties of the framing devices in his "Gothic Story," Horace Walpole made the horrors of his personal dream confront the reality of his readers.

Framing Otranto

> [Y]ou have with the most singular art displayed the talents of my two departed friends to the fullest advantage; and yet there is a simplicity in your manner, which, like the frame of a fine picture, seems a frame only, and yet is gold.
> —Horace Walpole, 27 November 1773
> letter to William Mason[105]

The preface to the 1764 first edition of *The Castle of Otranto* reports that the manuscript was "found in the library of an ancient catholic family in the north of England. It was printed at Naples, in the black letter, in the year 1529."[106] The title-page indicates that the text was translated by "William Marshal, Gent" from the Italian of "Onuphrio Muralto," which juxtaposes the translator Marshal, an enlightened English gentleman, against the author Muralto, a superstitious Italian priest. Peter Garrett argues that the supernatural scenes in the novel "can be set within the ideological frame of 'the dark ages of Christianity,' which encloses the actors of the drama but not necessarily its implied author or audience."[107] Marshal's preface, Garrett continues, "offer[s] readers the opportunity to distinguish themselves from vulgar minds and enjoy the satisfactions of enlightened superiority."[108] This paratextual frame functions as a narrative layer that promises to separate readers from the supernatural mayhem of Muralto's text. Marshal speculates that the "author's motives" may have been to challenge the Protestant reformers, who "dispel the empire of superstition" by "turn[ing] their own arms"—letters—against them.[109] With the novel's second preface, however, Walpole turns letters against his own readers, making the supernatural a force of the present rather than a relic of the past. He becomes, in a sense, his own "artful priest," whose novel has "enslave[d]" far more than "a hundred vulgar minds."[110]

Walpole brought out a new edition of *Otranto* just four months after the first printing, and included a new preface in which he revealed himself as the author. Of his initial guise as translator rather than author, Walpole admits: "diffidence of his own abilities, and the novelty of the attempt, were his sole inducements to assume the disguise."[111] The second preface renders the first spurious and appears to transform what was quasi-textual fiction into paratextual truth. The problem with this later revelation is that Marshal—and his preface written from the perspective of enlightened English readers—has disappeared. Furthermore, the title page has undergone a transformation: the second edition is a "Gothic Story" rather than just a "Story." Readers of the first edition had been duped into thinking that they were safely removed from the text's supernatural forces. The *Monthly Review* admonished Walpole for "re-establishing the barbarous superstitions of Gothic devilism!"[112] Initially to his acquaintances and eventually to the public at large, Horace Walpole—the son of the late Prime Minister and himself a member of Parliament—had all the while been both Marshal and Muralto, both Protestant and Catholic, both reforming realist and superstitious zealot. That is, the H. W. who signs the second edition is perhaps as much a fictional construct as the "new species of romance" he blends together.[113] This narrative subterfuge is the greatest achievement of Walpole's prefaces: the outright fiction of the first should make us cautious to accept the claims of the second. Walpole's willingness to deceive renders him a double of his own character Manfred, whose rule at castle Otranto relies on a fake document—a "fictitious will."[114] If the author H. W.—the initials with which Walpole often signed his letters—becomes part of the novel's formal fictionality, then readers must begin to question the authority of their own reality.

In *The Rise of Supernatural Fiction*, E. J. Clery makes many crucial observations about the impact of Walpole's dual prefaces and the historical exigencies that played a part in the author's ruse.[115] Since the absence of the supernatural in many ways defined the rational, enlightened society in which *Otranto* appeared, then "modern supernatural fiction is unthinkable, let alone unreadable."[116] Through the unveiling process of the second preface, the diegetic story that is littered with the hyperbolic supernatural becomes the product of a contemporary mind, rather than a vestige of antiquity long ago discredited or even abjected. In this sense, the horror of the Real confronts readers who inhabit the same modern world as Walpole. Clery elsewhere argues that the novel's "theme is evoked not by *blending* the marvelous and the natural, but rather by utilizing the gulf between them to dramatic effect."[117] We might also think of this "gulf" in terms of *Otranto*'s two settings (the castle and the Church of St Nicholas) and the subterraneous passageway that connects them. As Žižek writes, "the Real is *nothing but* the gap or antagonism that thwarts the symbolic from within."[118] In *Otranto*, the subterranean passage that Isabella uses to escape, and the "gap" through which Theodore breaks free from under the enormous helmet, are the tears in the tissue of reality that thwart Manfred's power.[119] Žižek further writes that "spectral apparitions emerge in this very gap that for ever separates reality from the [R]eal."[120] The novel's supernatural objects and entities, which range from the giant pieces of armor to the fleshless hermit skeleton, travel through the gap between church and state, emerging from the antagonistic abyss between two symbolic constructs; they are abject suggestions of the Real that invade the reality of Otranto and its denizens.

These abjections are able to come "too close" to readers, however, only through the narrative gap formed by the contradiction of the novel's two prefaces. As Clery observes, "[o]n the basis of the difference between the first two editions of *Otranto*, a shock metamorphosis, a new stage in the career of the supernatural was publicly initiated."[121] Whereas the first preface attempts to distance readers from the supernatural, the second admits that the novel is a product of a contemporary author. But even after the Catholic influence is removed from the manuscript's origin story, we are still forced to confront the horror that the novel's supernatural elements inspire. The second preface does nothing to dispel the threat of the supernatural, but rather enhances it by failing to account for its existence. Walpole's editor writes in the first preface that "[m]iracles, visions, necromancy, dreams, and other preternatural events, are exploded now even from romances," but the second edition of the novel proves that this is definitively not the case, as it revitalizes dormant horror.[122] The inability of *Otranto*'s second preface to resolve the problems of the first creates a gap in the symbolic order through which the novel's supernatural entities confront readers. This effect is a novel type of narrative metalepsis in which embedded, diegetic elements actually bypass the now ineffectual extradiegetic layer of paratext and permeate the reader's reality. The giant helmet that crushes Conrad within the first few pages of the novel might cause us to glance upward with apprehension and horror.[123] But the image that best defines the novel's structure is the portrait of Manfred's usurping grandfather that "quit[s] its pannel, and descend[s] on the floor with a grave and melancholy air."[124] Representation escapes its frame and enters the characters' reality in much the same way that the medieval supernatural becomes an element of the eighteenth-century present for Walpole's readers.

The most significant effect of the *Otranto*'s dual prefaces is that they allow its social antagonisms, the residue of the Real, to leak into—and potentially escape—the frame. Clery points to the novel's interest in "[m]obile property," which threatened the "system of heritable wealth."[125] But there are myriad other conflicting ideologies available in the compact narrative—eighteenth-century empiricism and medieval superstition, Enlightenment rationalism and Romantic imagination, Protestant and Catholic, reality and representation, life and death, subject and object. And the blurring of each these antagonisms implicates the Real, which escapes the novel's diegetic boundaries through the particular dynamic of its dual frames. As Clery remarks, *Otranto* "extend[ed] the limits of what could be felt by the reader as 'real.'"[126] Over a decade before Kant explored the inaccessible realm of *das Ding an sich*, Walpole promoted the existence of a mysterious world outside the purview of reality. What is more, as Žižek writes above, Walpole's Gothic suggests that the allegedly impassible, if not impossible, gap between the Kantian realms of phenomena and noumena is, in fact, "surmountable" by the monstrosities that implicate the Real. When Walpole named his "new species of romance" a "Gothic story" in the second preface, he forged an enduring connection between the Gothic novel, frame narratives, and the Real. This book will examine the ways in which subsequent Gothic novelists adapted Walpole's example to interrogate exigencies attendant to their time.[127] Thinking of the Gothic novel as a storehouse for unstable ideological energies fails to do justice to the lasting fear that the genre inspires. For its frame narratives permit the horror of the Real, the "things," traumas, and antagonisms that were abjected by the symbolic world, to enter reality, where they continue to challenge our ideological perspectives and to shatter the tenuous structures of our identities.

1

A "frame of uncommon size"

Ann Radcliffe and the Sublime Real

> But this whole hour your eyes have been intent
> On that veiled picture—veiled, for what it holds
> May not be dwelt on by the common day.
> This prelude has prepared thee. Raise thy soul;
> Make thine heart ready with thine eyes: the time
> Is come to raise the veil.
>
> —Alfred, Lord Tennyson, "The Gardener's Daughter" (1842)[1]

> Have you never looked through an archway … and seen the landscape beyond as bright as a lost paradise? That is because there is a frame to the picture.... You are cut off from something and allowed to look at something. When will people understand that the world is a window and not a blank infinity; a window in a wall of infinite nothing? When I wear this hood I carry my window with me. I say to myself—this is the world that Francis of Assisi saw and loved because it was limited. The hood has the very shape of a Gothic window.
>
> —G. K. Chesterton, *The Return of Don Quixote* (1927)[2]

Over the course of her brief but prolific career, Ann Radcliffe legitimized and popularized the Gothic novel by making the formal elements she borrowed from Horace Walpole expected and accepted. Of these elements, the "found manuscript" is perhaps most prominent. Walpole's fictional editor in *The Castle of Otranto* (1764) explains that the manuscript "was found in the library of an ancient Catholic family."[3] Radcliffe appropriates and embellishes this aspect of Walpole's framing device as the passive "was found" of *Otranto* becomes the active "who" and "how." Unlike Walpole, whose framing devices are explicitly labeled as paratexts, Radcliffe never wrote a preface. Instead, her frame narratives either appear in the interstitial space before the first chapter, or are structured, as is the case in *The Mysteries of Udolpho* (1794), through geographic features that are demarcated within the diegetic plot. In either case, Radcliffe's frames seem to provide aesthetic boundaries for the limitlessness of nature, a textual picturesque that soothes readers into believing in the frameability of the human experience. Yet she engages these structures only to challenge them through the powerful force of the sublime—itself a frame that suggests the horror of the Real.

In his 1826 memoir of Radcliffe, Thomas Talfourd describes the author's "pictorial powers" and argues that the whole of her works makes up a "prodigious painting."[4] Radcliffe's critics routinely understood her novels as textual canvases that adapted landscapes painted by Claude Lorrain, Salvator Rosa, and Gaspard Poussin. Walter Scott notes that Radcliffe "knew how to paint Italian scenery, which she could only have seen in the pictures of Claude or Poussin," and observes that there are "descriptive passages," which "approach more nearly to the style of Salvator Rosa."[5] In this sense, Radcliffe's textual landscapes cover the spectrum between the sublime (Rosa) and the beautiful (Lorrain).[6] In 1819, however, William Hazlitt argued that Radcliffe's word paintings fall somewhere outside these categories: "Her descriptions of scenery, indeed, are vague and wordy to the last degree; they are neither like Salvator nor Claude, nor nature nor art."[7] In refusing Radcliffe categorization, Hazlitt implicitly evokes the picturesque, an amorphous aesthetic mode that insists, in David Marshall's words, on an "uncanny wavering between art and artifice, between reality and representation."[8] Hazlitt was not the first to observe Radcliffe's attention to the picturesque. In an essay on Radcliffe's *A Journey Made in the Summer of 1794*, the *Critical Review* notes that her "language … is in some respects peculiar and unfamiliar, but it is the language that has been formed by all writers who have made picturesque description a study."[9] William Gilpin, author of the celebrated and influential *Observations on the River Wye* (1782), defined the picturesque as "that peculiar kind of beauty, which is agreeable in a picture."[10] In so doing, he sought to "revise the theory of seeing that had dominated the eighteenth century."[11] Responding to Gilpin's work, Uvedale Price redefined the picturesque as a category that "appears to hold a station between beauty and sublimity," but is "more frequently, and more happily blended with them both."[12] The picturesque, then, is a liminal aesthetic, a threshold mode that resembles Jacques Derrida's sense of Kant's parergon, the interstitial site where extrinsic and intrinsic, extradiegetic and diegetic, and reality and representation meet and blur together.

Radcliffe explores the vibrant aesthetics of framing most prominently in the formal composition of her novels. I argue that Radcliffe's frame narratives establish the picturesque by introducing an idealized representation of reality, one that is simultaneously familiar to readers, yet exotic enough to warrant attention as an aesthetic product. However, Radcliffe routinely challenges the efficacy of such limiting devices to contain the horror of the sublime. Whereas the picturesque offers detachment, the sublime forces immersion. Radcliffe's novels alternate between these two states, ushering readers from the comforting reality of frames to the horrifying Real of the indefinable, the inconceivable, and the infinite. The homogeneity she restores at the conclusion of her novels, which has been pejoratively titled the "explained supernatural," appears to ground the sublime in the everyday world. But the enduring horror is that this "reality" has been infiltrated by the Real, which is often legible in the dark desires of characters and readers alike. In her 1797 review of *The Italian*, Mary Wollstonecraft asserts that the "delusions of the imagination" conjured in Radcliffe's novels are "glistening bubbles," which burst and leave readers with "aching sight searching after the splendid nothing."[13] The Real is this "splendid nothing." Radcliffe frustrates the desire for the unknown, and in so doing suggests that the Real existed all along as part of the reader's unconscious rather than on the novel's pages. Radcliffe's frame narratives are textual veils, tantalizing screens that offer readers a sense of security from the horrors they introduce. But they ultimately undermine this effect through the process of metalepsis, in which sublime objects from the diegetic narrative become part of the extradiegetic, picturesque world.

In *A Philosophical Enquiry into the Origin of Our Ideas of the Sublime and Beautiful* (1756), Edmund Burke defines the sublime as "[w]hatever is fitted in any sort to excite the ideas of pain, and danger, ... whatever is in any sort terrible, or is conversant about terrible objects, or operates in a manner analogous to terror."[14] For Burke, the sublime is the "strongest emotion which the mind is capable of feeling," because it promotes the sensation of pain, which is more intense than pleasure.[15] Experiencing the sublime is stimulating and disturbing because it suggests the existence of a deeper level of reality that is analogous to both Immanuel Kant's *das Ding an sich* ("thing in itself") and Jacques Lacan's Real. In his *Critique of the Power of Judgment* (1790), Kant argues that we can only locate the sublime "in ourselves" because natural objects are merely the "presentation of a sublimity that can be found in the mind; for what is properly sublime cannot be contained in any sensible form."[16] This crucial revision not only suggests that the true sublime exists beyond our symbolic reality, but also promotes the objects and the scenes that we might before have considered sublime (for Kant, an expansive, stormy ocean) as instead mere implications of it—disturbing, to be sure, but not the actual, inaccessible sublime. The sublime is, in Slavoj Žižek words, "our suprasensible nature," the indicator of the Real that is untenable in and denied by reality.[17]

In *Powers of Horror*, Julia Kristeva writes that the "abject is edged with the sublime."[18] In this sense, the sublime acts as a frame that allows the subject partly to experience the Real without being overwhelmed by it. For Kristeva, the "sublime triggers ... a spree of perceptions and words that expands memory boundlessly. I then forget the point of departure and find myself removed to a secondary universe, set off from the one where 'I' am."[19] The immensurable sublime object produces sensations that demonstrate the failure of symbolic reality and serves as a horrifying, yet alluring, reminder of the chaos of pre-symbolic life. Žižek defines the sublime as the "permanent failure of the representation to reach after the Thing."[20] The sublime object "evokes its Beyond by the very failure of its symbolic representation."[21] Objects in nature that implicate the feeling of the sublime function as fantasmatic frames that ultimately keep the Real from coming "too close"—for what "constitutes reality is the minimum of idealization the subject needs in order to be able to sustain the Real."[22] The true sublime is the unceasing, unsuccessful grasp to represent the unrepresentable, which suggests the limits of our reality, the gaps in the symbolic network. Žižek writes that the "[R]eal object is a sublime object in a strict Lacanian sense—an object which is just an embodiment of the lack in the Other, in the symbolic order. The sublime object is an object which cannot be approached too closely: if we get too near it, it loses its sublime features and becomes an ordinary vulgar object."[23] Since representations of the sublime, both natural and aesthetic, only hint at its existence, they might be considered as analogues to the supernatural figures that appear in other Gothic novels—fantasmatic screens that simultaneously suggest the horror of the Real and keep us from being overwhelmed by it. While Radcliffe has long been recognized, and indeed criticized, for her use of the "explained supernatural," the ubiquitous presence of the sublime in her novels ultimately upsets the balance of reality in ways that are just as disturbing as floating portraits and falling helmets.

Žižek asserts that the sublime object is best understood through the "symbolic deadlock" of social antagonisms. The traditional argument is that antagonisms demonstrate the impossible co-existence of conflicting ideologies, each of which "prevent[s] the other from achieving its identity with itself, becoming what it really is," but the truth is that the subject can never achieve a full identity because "identity is already in itself blocked, marked by an impossibility," which we "project" and "externalize" (or even "abject") onto our antagonists.[24] Social antagonism only shows the lack within one's own ideology, the impossibility of realizing a complete identity: "the moment of victory is the moment of greatest loss."[25] During the sublime experience, which suggests the existence of a world denied by reality, these antagonisms embrace, dissolve, and reemerge through supernatural representations. For Žižek, reality "conceals the [R]eal of an antagonism, and it is this [R]eal, foreclosed from the symbolic fiction, that returns in the guise of spectral apparitions."[26] The sublime object similarly draws attention to the gaps in the symbolic order and suggests the dissolution of identity experienced during pre-symbolic life. Radcliffe, in some sense, anticipates these effects not only by making the sublime the principal Gothic horror of her novels, but also by regularly equating it with the blurring of conflicting ideologies (Protestant and Catholic, reality and representation, life and death, subject and object), which takes place via her novels' distinctive formal dynamics. Although Radcliffe's frame narratives appear to create a picturesque boundary that contains diegetic horror, the picturesque frame collapses through the metalepsis of sublime characters and themes; the Real invades reality.

In the frame narrative of *A Sicilian Romance* (1790), an anonymous and un-gendered traveler in Sicily stops at some ruins to contemplate human mortality: "Thus ... shall the present generation—he who now sinks in misery—and he who now swims in pleasure, alike pass away and be forgotten."[27] By using the enduring ruins to reflect on the transience of human life, Radcliffe connects the seemingly disparate worlds of the frame and the central narrative. Although spanning centuries, all of humankind bows to the unyielding hand of time. As the traveler admires the scene, he spots a friar, who "formed no uninteresting object in the picture" (1). That the friar is an "object" suggests that he has become part of the traveler's picturesque view, which transforms nature, including its subjects, into representations fit for a painting. The friar remarks: "A solemn history belongs to this castle ... which is too long and intricate for me to relate. It is, however, contained in a manuscript in our library" (1). The manuscript falls into the hands of the traveler, who becomes an editor through the act of "arrang[ing] ... the following pages" (2). After the central narrative closes, the frame returns with a moral:"Here the manuscript annals conclude. In reviewing this story, we perceive a singular and striking instance of moral retribution. We learn, also, that those who do only THAT WHICH IS RIGHT, endure nothing in misfortune but a trial of their virtue, and from trials well endured derive the surest claim to the protection of heaven" (199). The editor secures the definitive word in the novel and provides a pithy moral for readers who have been quickly transported from sixteenth-century Catholic Italy back to the present perspective of Protestant England. This formal move to close the frame, to embed the central text into the world of an English traveler, seemingly disassociates the romantic, yet dangerous, foreign world from the novel's readers.

In the opening frame, however, the editor calls the "situation" of the surrounding natural environment "admirably beautiful and picturesque," and then notes the "sublimity and grandeur of the ruins," and describes the "air of ancient grandeur, which … impresses the traveler with awe and curiosity" (1). The friar explains that a "singular instance of the retribution of Heaven" caused the castle to be "forsaken, and abandoned to decay" (1). We should be reminded of not only the giant, intact statue of Alphonso in *Otranto*, which causes the collapse of the titular castle, but also Poe's bifurcated House of Usher. When the editor of *A Sicilian Romance* speaks of the "protection of heaven" given to the virtuous, he suggests that supernatural forces punished the story's villains and destroyed the symbol of their power, the castle Mazzini. While the Italian landscape is picturesque, the castle's ruins are decidedly sublime—"resound[ing] with the voices of the dead" (1)—and are a testament to the power of the Real that escapes the novel's narrative and endures in the editor's frame world. But it is not just the ruins that suggest a connection between the past and the editor's present: the monk who "collected and recorded" the events of the diegetic narrative is a "descendant of the noble house of Mazzini" (1–2). When Ferdinand, the son of the iniquitous marquis realizes with horror that he is the "descendant of a murderer" (54), we ought to recall that the surviving monastery in the opening frame might still house members of the bloodthirsty family. Thus, just as the supernatural events of *Otranto*'s narrative were all along the product of Walpole's eighteenth-century imagination, the "barbarous superstition" (117) of past ages becomes part of the reader's present. The story's horror is not contained by the frame, but rather empowered by it.

As we will see dramatically and memorably echoed in *The Mysteries of Udolpho*, Radcliffe employs the metaphor of the veil in *A Sicilian Romance* to articulate the boundaries between reality and the horror of the Real.[28] After she escapes from her father's clutches, Julia enters a convent where she must choose between two evils—either marry the cruel

Duke de Luovo or become a permanent member of the church. In spite of the wrath of the domineering Abate, Julia refuses both prospects. Cornelia, Julia's only ally in the church, relates her troubled history and describes the sensations that followed her ceremonial taking of the veil. Through her "irrevocable vow," Cornelia claims that "all conspired to impress my imagination, and to raise my views to heaven … and elevated my soul to sublimity" (121). Passing behind the painted veil, as it were, transports Cornelia to a divine world that is concealed from reality. The sublime object of complete religious sacrifice gives its subjects access to the Real. In addition, Radcliffe constructs the convent as a sanctuary for the Real, not only for otherworldly meditations, but also for secrets that are too disturbing to exist in symbolic reality. In *A Sicilian Romance*, Radcliffe establishes a trope that she continues to mine in subsequent novels: the clergy must "observe a religious secrecy upon all matters entrusted to them in confession" (139). The secret always comes to light, however, and escapes the boundaries of both the church and the diegetic story, as it enters the time and ideological purview of the frame.

Radcliffe also engages the veil as an architectural metaphor in *A Sicilian Romance*. The Mazzini siblings are magnetically drawn to investigate the curious lights and sounds that emanate from the sealed-off portion of the castle—the gaze and voice that Žižek calls the "remnants and leftovers of the Real."[29] We learn early on that a "veil of mystery enveloped that part of the castle" (12), and that Ferdinand possesses an "irresistible desire to penetrate the secrets of this desolate part of the fabric" (37). Radcliffe's word choice here is telling as the "fabric" not only represents the edifice of the castle, but also sets the stage for Ferdinand's means of passing into this structure: "He removed the tapestry, and behind it appeared, to his inexpressible satisfaction, a small door" (39). Ferdinand's horror arises in great part because "beyond this door were chambers of considerable extent" (46), and his "fruitless search" (47) suggests that the truth remains inaccessible in his reality. Joan Copjec notes the liminal nature of the "forbidden room in Gothic fiction" and argues: "by withdrawing itself from the rest of the house, it marks the limit that allows the house to constitute itself as a whole—but a whole from which this room is absent."[30] In this sense, the many allegedly uninhabitable rooms in Gothic novels, which include Rochester's attic in Charlotte Brontë's *Jane Eyre* (1847), are spaces of the Real in which madness thrives. In *A Sicilian Romance*, Ferdinand fails to reach the "recess of horror" (176), but Julia stumbles upon it via an accidental subterranean escape. There she confronts a shocking form of abjection—"the pale and emaciated figure of a woman" (175)—but then returns to reality once she identifies the figure as her mother. The forbidden Real transforms into accessible reality; the ghost becomes the mother; the history of kidnapping and imprisonment fills the gap in the symbolic order.

Radcliffe expertly establishes tension in the moments preceding the reunion of mother and daughter as Julia's earlier movement through subterraneous passages reveals a far more gruesome and disturbing suggestion of the Real. During their flight from a band of banditti, Julia and Hippolitus enter a series of labyrinthine vaults, and eventually approach an iron door.

> They now entered upon a dark abyss; and the door which moved upon a spring, suddenly closed upon them. On looking round they beheld a large vault; and it is not easy to imagine their horror on discovering they were in a receptacle for the murdered bodies of the unfortunate people who had fallen into the hands of the banditti.... Their situation was the most deplorable that can be imagined; for they were now inclosed in a vault strewn with the dead bodies of the murdered ... [which] exhibited a spectacle too shocking for humanity [165–66].

Radcliffe places Julia and Hippolitus among piles of rotting corpses, what Kristeva would call the "utmost of abjection."[31] Not only do the corpses represent the lovers' potential fate at the hands of the banditti, but they also signify the base materiality of human existence. In the "dark abyss" of abjection, Julia and Hippolitus come "too close" to the Real, which shatters their symbolic reality by being literally "too shocking for humanity." This encounter with the Real is the extreme of the editor's "trial of their virtue," and it also casts a shadow on his opening words concerning the "present generation" who "alike [shall] pass away and be forgotten" (1). The horror of the "mansion of the murdered" (167) becomes the reader's horror through the editor's equation of human mortality. The narrative metalepsis in *A Sicilian Romance*, in which the horror of the diegetic becomes part of the extradiegetic frame world, occurs through the connective strand of universal materiality. The unavoidable truth of death, decay, and ruin is the sublime Real that passes from the central text into, and indeed beyond, the traveler's frame.

Neither of Radcliffe's next novels features an explicit formal frame narrative.[32] However, in *The Mysteries of Udolpho* (1794), Radcliffe does employ the technique of geographic framing to surround the sublime environs of Castle Udolpho.[33] In so doing, Radcliffe establishes an alternate set of rules for framing that many subsequent Gothic authors would follow. For example, the frame narrative of Edgar Allan Poe's "The Fall of the House of Usher" (1839) is demarcated by the narrator's entrance into the titular edifice. And in *Jane Eyre* (1847), Charlotte Brontë constructs a geographic (or even architectural) frame narrative, as Jane's schooling at Lowood and retreat with the Rivers family bookend her residence with Rochester at Thornfield Hall. As Walter Scott writes, "[e]verything in *The Mysteries of Udolpho* is on a larger and more sublime scale"—and this includes the frame narrative.[34] Although Emily's imprisonment at Udolpho proves the most cited and celebrated portion of novel, it occupies only the central third, and is surrounded by lengthy accounts of Emily's adventures outside Montoni's grasp. The titular castle is "framed at either end," Elizabeth Bohls observes, "by hundreds of pages of picturesque travelogue."[35] Thus, the sublime castle is seemingly contained within the frame of the picturesque. Terry Castle urges readers not to divide the novel into "two ontologically distinct realms," but rather to see in the "frame-world" examples of the "displaced" supernatural.[36] What is more, the many overlooked elements of the supernatural that appear outside Udolpho undermine the standard argument concerning Radcliffe's "explained supernatural." In what Castle calls the "supernaturalization of everyday life," the seemingly "ordinary parts of *Udolpho* may begin to look increasingly peculiar."[37] Elements of the supernatural in the environments outside Udolpho ultimately demonstrate that the novel's geographic frame is easily transgressed by Gothic horrors—from "spectralized language" and "recollected 'presences,'" to the disturbing introduction of banditti, Montoni, and Agnes (Lady Laurentini).[38] In this sense, the sublime invades the picturesque, and the Real seeps into Emily's reality—the familiar world of Radcliffe's readers.

After the death of Emily's father, Montoni makes arrangements to travel from La Vallée to Castle Udolpho. The trip requires a passage over the Alps, which "guard the entrance of Italy."[39] Emily grieves over her geographic separation from Valancourt: "those tremendous barriers! would rise, and whole countries extend between the regions where each must exist!" (151). Only Emily's imagination, "piercing the veil of distance, brought that home to her eyes in all its interesting and romantic beauty" (120). As they travel east, Montoni's ruthless spirit awakens: "[his] eyes lost their sullenness, and seemed instantaneously to gleam with fire" (171). Not surprisingly, Radcliffe introduces yet another frame through which Montoni's power seems to strengthen: "There," he ominously declares, "is Udolpho" (226). Emily surveys the picture: "Silent, lonely, and sublime," the castle "seemed to stand the sovereign of the scene, and to frown defiance on all, who dared to invade its solitary region" (227). The personification of the foreboding edifice parallels the "vacant eye-like windows" of Poe's House of Usher, and its transmission of power to Montoni resembles Bram Stoker's *Dracula* (1897).[40] Anticipating the introductory frame to *The Italian*, the imposing entrance into Udolpho functions as a metaphor for the similarly transformative threshold for readers of the novel:

> The gateway before her, leading into the courts, was of gigantic size, and was defended by two round towers, crowned by overhanging turrets, embattled, where, instead of banners, now waved long grass and wild plants, that had taken root among the mouldering stones, and which seemed to sigh, as the breeze rolled past, over the desolation around them. The towers were united by a curtain, pierced and embattled also, below which appeared the pointed arch of a huge portcullis, surmounting the gates [227].

The "curtain" that stretches between the gateway towers functions as the first of several veils that Emily must lift in this middle third of the novel. Since the commanding appearance of Castle Udolpho comes at approximately thirty-three percent of the way through the novel, it seems certain that Radcliffe carefully planned its place in the narrative. Emily is finally able to escape the "dreadful gates" (451) of the castle at sixty-seven percent of the novel, almost exactly two-thirds through. Thus, remarkably, Emily's confinement at the castle is framed equally on both sides, which makes the central portion appear even more like a painting, but one whose sublime power forces its way beyond the limits imposed by the mountain frame. This effect is best evidenced by the ghostly images that haunt Emily outside Udolpho. Castle observes that the "breakdown of the limit between life and death … lies at the heart of Radcliffe's novel."[41] The dead live on through Emily's memory, and the living inhabit her dreams: "her eyes glancing a second time on the arm-chair … the countenance of her dead father appeared there" (102). Valancourt, especially, consists mostly of disembodied sounds and visions in reverie. Ultimately, the novel shows that the dark core of Udolpho is an architectural representation of the true horrors that exist within Emily's psyche. The novel's implications of the Real are not the castle's material sideshows, but rather the traumas that she carries within.

In the novel's most memorable scene, Emily finally satisfies her desire to discover what lies behind a veiled picture in one of the castle's obscure chambers. She finds that the "frame of uncommon size" (248) borders "no picture" (249), but rather encases something "horribly natural" (663), an object whose dimensions and depth indicate that it is not a portrait, but rather something far more ominous. We might feel relief at the end of the novel when Radcliffe reveals that the veil hides a wax effigy, but this explanation fails to account for the fact that Emily's horror causes her to participate in the same "penance" required of an earlier monk, who was forced to look on the figure that "serv[ed] as a memento of the condition at which he must himself arrive" (662). Emily recommences the act that descendants of this monk had long since ceased practicing—but to a literal end. For her the figure *is* the moldering remains of Lady Laurentini and thus a horrifying harbinger of her fate inside the castle under the murderous reign of Montoni. In *Barchester Towers* (1857), Anthony Trollope writes: "When we have once learnt what was that picture before which was hung Mrs Ratcliffe's [*sic*] solemn curtain, we feel no further interest about either the frame or the veil. They are to us merely a receptacle for old bones, an inappropriate coffin, which we would wish to have decently buried out of our sight."[42] Indeed, what is significant about the scene is not what ultimately lies behind the veil, but rather how Emily reacts to the unveiling, a horror that continues to haunt her outside Udolpho. The removal of the veil momentarily exposes Emily's unconscious, a space of horror, a glimpse of the Real.

The black veil scene in *Udolpho* can be further investigated through Kant's concept of *das Ding an sich*. For the true essence of the "thing" behind the veil is not the reality of the material effigy, but rather the inaccessible realm of Emily's unconscious desire. Given this connection, we might also examine the encounter through Lacan's *objet petit a*, the "something from which the subject, in order to constitute itself, has separated itself off as organ."[43] It is a remnant of the Real, the thing that we abject to formulate our identity, yet also what we long to repossess, to assimilate into our symbolic reality. For Žižek, the *objet petit a* "stands simultaneously for the imaginary fantasmatic lure/screen and for that which this lure is obfuscating, of the [v]oid behind the lure."[44] Thus, the *objet petit a* in *The Mysteries of Udolpho* is both the veil that entices Emily's curiosity and also the potential that what lies behind it is nothing but the horror of Emily's "desire of the Other."[45] Žižek elsewhere argues that the *objet petit a* "finds its best correlation in the film trope of the MacGuffin, the object of "pure pretext whose sole role is to set the story in motion but which is in itself 'nothing at all.'"[46] Although the black veil is the principal mystery in the novel, and certainly its greatest source of narrative momentum, it only exerts its power through Emily's cognitive transmutation. In reality, it is a material object "made to resemble a human body ... after death" (662), but it is transformed into a sublime object, "the point of the Real in the very heart of the subject which cannot be symbolized," through the refashioning properties of Emily's unconscious desire.[47]

As it turns out, the woman Emily imagined was murdered and ensconced behind the veil was instead an accomplice to a more disturbing crime—one that took place outside the confines of Udolpho and in the everyday world of Emily's reality. The murder of Emily's aunt, the Marchioness de Villeroi, occurred at Chateau-le-Blanc in southern France, well beyond the Alpine frame that demarcates the novel's narratives. The true horror of the novel is located within its seemingly ordinary frame, not only in its central murder mystery, but also all along within Emily's own mind. In her dying throes, Lady Laurentini ominously warns Emily: "you have passions in your heart,—scorpions; they sleep now—beware how you awaken them!" (574). The embedded narrative at Castle Udolpho receives the most critical attention because it gives substance to the specters of the Real that populate the frame that surrounds it, the haunting images that readers who identify with Emily can locate within themselves. This effect is wonderfully represented in Jane Austen's *Northanger Abbey* (1817), in which Catherine Morland is "wild to know" what lies behind the veil: "I know it must be a skeleton, I am sure it is Laurentina's [*sic*] skeleton."[48] Emily and Catherine are drawn to abjection. They project their desire for death onto the effigy and the page, respectively, demonstrating a psychological horror that does not stay within the confines of Udolpho or *Udolpho*. Death comes to Pemberley, indeed.

In 1796, two years after the unprecedented first-printing success of *Udolpho*, Matthew Lewis published *The Monk*. The novel's open exploration of sex and violence, among its myriad other scandalous subjects, made Lewis a problematic celebrity. Equal parts repellent and beguiling, *The Monk* features a complex, multi-layered narrative, which follows the sensual and sanguine adventures of the titular monk Ambrosio. Seemingly in response, Radcliffe crafted the most intricate and experimental plot of her career in *The Italian* (1797). As with *A Sicilian Romance*, the frame narrative of *The Italian* begins immediately after the title page and concludes before the central narrative's first chapter. It is a virtuoso performance, which two of the period's most distinguished critics celebrated. "Nothing can be finer than the opening of this story," Anna Laetitia Barbauld writes in *The British Novelists* (1810): "This prelude, like the tuning of an instrument by a skilful hand, has the effect of producing at once in the mind a tone of feeling correspondent to the future story."[49] Barbauld's astute reading not only expresses the significance of the frame as a striking introductory chord, but also suggests that there are crucial thematic links between the extradiegetic and diegetic narratives that might blur the formal and temporal boundaries between them. In 1824, Walter Scott similarly observes:

> Most writers of romance have been desirous to introduce their narrative to the reader, in some manner which might at once excite interest, and prepare his mind for the species of excitation which it was the author's object to produce. In *The Italian*, this has been achieved by Mrs Radcliffe with an uncommon degree of felicity, nor is there any part of the romance itself which is more striking, than its impressive commencement.[50]

For modern critics, however, *The Italian*'s frame has proved divisive. E. J. Clery has called it a "small masterpiece of ideological self-consciousness and formal dexterity," and Rictor Norton argues that it exemplifies Radcliffe's "dazzling technical proficiency."[51] Yet others find it disjointed from the central narrative. Liz Bellamy sees the frame as "entirely irrelevant to the plot of the novel," and Cannon Schmitt locates a "lack of direct plot connection between prologue and tale."[52] In spite of these reservations, I argue that the frame proves indispensable to the thematic core of the novel. The manuscript we become privy to in the space of *The Italian*'s frame provides a foundation for the main narrative's themes of secrecy and duplicity. We access, together with the familiar English travelers, a story that should have remained secret—the history of a troubled figure, which was confessed with the promise of divinely appointed confidentiality.

Most significant, the frame introduces and undermines the confessional, the paradoxical space where secrets too horrific to remain hidden are revealed. We might consider the frame narrative in *The Italian* as a confessional screen that appears to provide a boundary between the horror of the confession itself and the reader who plays the role of the confessor. But this permeable partition is hol(e)y, so to speak; it neither confines the disturbing secrets nor protects the listener from their horror. Michel Foucault remarks that the confession "became one of the West's most highly valued techniques for producing truth," and that it represents the "infinite task of extracting [the truth] from the depths of oneself."[53] We might also think of the confessional through Žižek's definition of the *objet petit a* as a "fantasmatic lure/screen," for it attracts clients through unsubstantiated promises.[54] Perhaps more important, the *objet petit a* stands for both the obfuscating screen and the "void behind the lure."[55] The inner truth that the confessional exposes in *The Italian* is the horror of the Real, the acts of passion that are motivated by unconscious desires for abjection, which take the form of the uncontrollable emotions of envy and lust. These antagonisms that materialize in the diegetic space of the novel enter the everyday world of the extradiegetic frame through the promise of divine absolution that accompanies the confession of sins. Individual horrors become a collective concern as the religious structures purported to contain them only support the necessity of discourse, the "institutional incitement to speak."[56] The subject may only be granted divine forgiveness by exposing his sins, by making the violent, implacable implications of the Real a matter of reality.

The central narrative of *The Italian* is a drama of concealing and revealing, of interruptions and continuations, of traps and fissures. And the novel's subtitle, "Confession of the Black Penitents," demonstrates the significance of the confessional as a symbolic apparatus that fosters and blurs these conflicting states. In fact, the ominous confessional that the travelers observe inside the church "consist[s] of three compartments, covered with a black canopy" (3), which seems implicitly to symbolize the three-volume novel complete with the veiling frame narrative. This confessional space proves permeable, however, and its secrets become exposed for publication. It appears that the "shield of the church" (173) cannot control the sublime power of the novel's horror. Although Schedoni, the troubled villain of the central narrative, "wished to throw an impenetrable veil over his origin" (34), his principal secret cannot stay contained: "the enormity of the sin seemed too big for utterance, yet the penitent appeared equally unable to endure the concealment of it" (338). Similarly, the vague details of Schedoni's story are, for Vivaldi's servant Paulo, "somewhat too big to rest within [his] brain" (73). The eventual revelation of Schedoni's secret resembles the lifting of the veil in Radcliffe's previous novels. Schedoni's crime, the murder of his brother, cannot be concealed by a religious order founded on the sanctity of brotherhood. It is no surprise, then, that Schedoni's secrets come to light through a betrayal by his former confidant Nicola di Zampari. Indeed, the novel's two conflicting factions are paradoxically cut from the same cloth. Although similarly motivated by Catholic doctrine, the novel's monks attempt to contain secrets, while its officers of the Inquisition work to see them revealed. When these forces collide at the novel's conclusion, Real horror emerges accompanied by Schedoni's murder of Nicola and his subsequent suicide. And this grisly dénouement is the culmination of a series of previous crimes, including fratricide and the attempted murder of his wife, which have transformed Schedoni into a figure of abjection, a specter of the Real. But the enduring horror of the novel, the passage of diegetic Real into extradiegetic reality, relies on the performance of the narrative frame, which gathers the disturbing secrets and reveals them to readers. And the unprecedented 2,000-copy first-printing of *The Italian* meant that this horror reached the hearts of many who would identity with the frame's "English travelers in Italy."[57]

The novel's frame opens upon a party at the portico of an ancient Neapolitan church in 1764. The narrator remarks that the church is unique to the area: "The interior of this edifice had nothing of the shewy ornament and general splendor, which distinguish the churches of Italy, ... but it exhibited a simplicity and grandeur of design, considerably more interesting to persons of taste, and a solemnity of light and shade much more suitable to promote the sublime elevation of devotion" (2). In its muted magnificence, the church appears to uphold Protestant aesthetic values—an effect that serves to connect the novel's English readers to the foreign, Catholic environment. In addition, the frame's 1764 setting might refer to the publication year of Walpole's *Otranto*, the first novel that blended these religious and ideological antagonisms through the interplay of framing devices. Jerrold E. Hogle observes that Radcliffe "re-establishes" in *The Italian* the "fundamentals of the Gothic as they appear" in *Otranto*, especially as they are defined in Walpole's second preface.[58] When Walpole undermined his "found manuscript" device of the first preface by making the supernatural a product of the mid-eighteenth century, "[c]hronology was confounded."[59] Radcliffe similarly blurs temporal and ideological boundaries through *The Italian*'s distinctive formal dynamic in which the confessional becomes a symbolic structure to channel horror from the hidden depths of the troubled subject into the ordinary world of the novel's readership.

Like the gateway to the castle in *The Mysteries of Udolpho*, the portico in *The Italian*'s frame serves as an entrance into the unknown for the novel's characters and its readers. Clery observes that "[w]e share the travellers' visual perspective, first as they admire the architecture, then as they examine closely a loitering figure of singular and menacing appearance. Seamlessly, we are made complicit with their ideological viewpoint."[60] Upon passing the threshold, the party is accosted by a friar from an adjoining monastery, who points out "objects in the church, which were most worthy of attention" (1). The friar quickly disappears, however, during a conversation between an Englishman and an "Italian gentleman, who was of the party" (2). It is this Italian, rather than the friar, who is in possession of the manuscript "written by a student of Padua"—a story detailing a singular and horrifying confession, which "became public" (4). That the subject-matter of the confession has already transgressed its sacred boundaries within the church to be studied and disseminated partially absolves the players in the frame from their culpability in further publicizing the secret. Yet the Englishman translates, we must assume, the student's Italian prose into English (a foreshadowing of an environmental transformation that occurs at the end of the novel), and then forms it into a novel to be consumed and circulated by curious readers. As in *A Sicilian Romance*, the diegetic narrative becomes a threat to the novel's readership through the editorial work of one of their countrymen. That the English traveler readies the text for consumption makes him an agent in the transfer of horrors from foreign representation into domestic reality, yet he remains less complicit than the mysterious Italian who initially brings the manuscript to light.

Before the manuscript story passes hands, the Englishman's attention is excited by a man "too singular in his conduct, to pass unnoticed" (1). This "tall thin figure," with an eye "expressive of uncommon ferocity" (1), Radcliffe ingeniously (and disingenuously) casts as an uncanny double of Schedoni, who is also "tall, and … extremely thin," with a "large melancholy eye, which approached to horror" (34–35). Radcliffe not only makes this opening figure resemble Schedoni, but also characterizes him as an "assassin"—in spite of the Italian's dubious claim that he "has no relation, with what I am about to mention" (3)—which establishes a novel-long uncertainty about whether Schedoni survives. Furthermore, since the confessional of the Black Penitents is used by both Schedoni and the mysterious monk in the frame, we are meant to speculate throughout the majority of the central narrative whether these figures are the same person. While the assassin in the frame "glid[es]" and "disappear[s]" (1), Schedoni "glid[es]" and "vanishe[s]" (105). Since the frame narrative is set only six years after the central action, unlike Radcliffe's other frames that set present-day visitors against ancient ruins, Schedoni becomes a potential part of the extradiegetic frame.[61] He is an implication of the Real, with his clandestine history of monstrous crimes, who invades the narrative world that lies closest to the reader. Only after a "livid corse was all that remained" (404), just two short chapters from the novel's conclusion, are we assured that the mysterious figure in the frame is not Schedoni.

Although we might take solace in Schedoni's death, we must remember the Italian's assertion in the opening frame that the assassin "is by no means … uncommon" (2). As Talfourd observes in 1826, Schedoni gradually "melts from demon to man," but this provides little comfort when measured against the myriad assassins that evidently populate Italy.[62] It also ignores "the Italian" who dominates the opening frame—in great part through arrogant replies to the Englishman's questions. Clara McIntyre has commented on the "unsatisfactory nature" of the novel's title because "all personages of the story were supposed to be of that nationality."[63] Indeed, the title most obviously reserved for Schedoni could belong to any number of other characters. Vivaldi routinely confuses monks and officers of the Inquisition, whose movement and costume make them all appear like potential assassins. Most significant is the villainous monk Nicola, who stalks Vivaldi's steps in the novel's opening chapters, "gliding" with a "strange facility" (19) that resembles the otherworldly movement of the assassin in the frame. Yet there is only one "the Italian" ever referred to in the novel: the ominous figure who furtively trespasses into a party of English travelers; who knows so much about the whereabouts and rights of assassins; who markets a manuscript confession as if it is public property; and who only appears in the frame. This "Italian" might be the novel's true antagonist, the prime agent through which the horror of the central narrative permeates the everyday world of the frame. That the monk who hears Schedoni's confession was never again "properly himself" (81) suggests that readers will be similarly transformed by its horrors.

Perhaps the most enduring horror of the frame is that it is left unresolved. Indeed, *The Italian* is the only of Radcliffe's novels with a missing terminal frame. We never return to the world of 1764; instead, the closing voice comes from Vivaldi's faithful servant, Paulo, a skeptic of the supernatural who possesses the "archness of [a] dark, penetrating eye" (84). Echoing the closing frame of *A Sicilian Romance*, Paulo rhapsodizes: "you see how people get through their misfortunes, if they have but a heart to bear up against them, and do nothing that can lie on their conscience afterwards; and how suddenly one comes to be happy, just when one is beginning to think one never is to be happy again!" (414). So close is the frame temporally to the central narrative that we are to imagine Vivaldi, Ellena, and indeed Paulo still residing "a few miles distant from Naples" (412) at the very moment the English traveler visits the church and reads their history. We rejoice alongside our reunited lovers and revel in Paulo's repeated cries of "O! giorno felice!" Happy days, indeed, are these for our protagonists—but what of the Englishman and *his* party? As Clery observes, he "vanishes into" the central narrative, "never to re-emerge."[64] Similar to the novel's mysterious monks, he disappears, as his own story proves unable to contain the force that it introduces.

In *The Italian*, Radcliffe refuses to go back to the future. As we look over this happy valley and exalt with a triumphant Paulo, we are but subjects in the author's most remarkable execution of the sublime. No closing boundary to form the picturesque—only measureless, un-frameable horror—a distinctly ominous contrast to the moralizing conclusions of *A Sicilian Romance* and *The Mysteries of Udolpho*. The *Anti-Jacobin* makes a remarkable observation: "Thus we proceed, till the development takes place. But then, we never see the veil of mysteriousness drawn aside to our perfect satisfaction. Something supernatural still remains: and, at the close of the story, we look back, through the whole, as through a moon-light haze; as through the coloured atmosphere of a Gilpin."[65] It is when "we look back" that we see the tints of the picturesque, remembering the horror of the central narrative and the tense atmosphere of the opening frame. The Gothic horror of *The Italian* rests in the fact that the narrative remains unresolved, sprawling, and sublime—an event horizon wherein time itself collapses. To see the picturesque frame, one can only look back; but it is an obscure view of the past, stained by the uncertainty of the present and the infinite, ungraspable future.

Gilpin argues that nature "works on a *vast scale*," while an artist is "confined to a *span*" and must adhere to "*principles of picturesque beauty*, merely to adapt such diminutive parts of nature's surfaces to his own eye, as come within his scope."[66] The incomplete frame of *The Italian* removes the artist from the equation: there are neither references to the manuscript transcribed by the "student of Padua" in the main narrative, nor are there any editorial interruptions. We are left, instead, among the party in the sprawling "pleasure-grounds," close enough chronologically to the year of the opening frame (as it has probably been the "several years" that separate them) that the narrative worlds collide; the picturesque, detached world of the English traveler is engulfed by the vast and unending narrative he reads. Kant argues that the sublime can be "found in a formless object insofar as limitlessness is represented in it."[67] Without a terminal frame, *The Italian* loses its limits. As in Walpole's *Otranto*, chronology blurs, as the time gap between the extradiegetic and the diegetic worlds is displaced. Radcliffe's manipulation of time blends the narratives to the point that we cannot be comforted by a separation between England and Italy, between frame and framed, and, most disturbing, between reality and the Real. We are left in a world where any clandestine figure could have "an assassin's heart shrouded by his garments" (224).

The monumental success of *The Italian* confirmed Radcliffe as the bestselling novelist of the 1790s. At the height of her powers, however, she went silent. The few remaining details of her life come from her private journals. In 1802, Radcliffe and her husband William journeyed through Leicester and Warwick, stopping off at Kenilworth Castle. A great part of the description that she recorded appears, sometimes verbatim, in *Gaston de Blondeville*, which was published posthumously in 1826. Rictor Norton argues that the novel was not withheld from publication, as has been the popular belief, but rather "withdrawn (or possibly rejected) late in 1803."[68]

Critics generally agree that *Gaston de Blondeville* is a poor follow-up to *The Italian*. Contemporary reviewers considered it to be "less complicated," "slight," and "simple."[69] Norton regards it as such a "weakening of Ann Radcliffe's imagination" that it must have been a "joint effort between husband and wife."[70] Indeed, *Gaston de Blondeville* marks a sharp departure from Radcliffe's previous novels: it is set entirely in England; it contains minute and painstakingly researched historical annotations; and, most important, it is the first of Radcliffe's novels to feature an unexplained supernatural entity, what one reviewer calls the "advantage of a *ghostly* aid."[71]

What *Gaston de Blondeville* does share with its predecessors is a frame narrative—the most ambitious and elaborate of Radcliffe's career. As Norton has observed, Radcliffe returned to the novel three times over the course of a decade, and it appears that she added the frame narrative during the latter part of this period. Unlike her previous novels, this frame is presented through the paratextual labels "Introduction" and "Conclusion," but I am hesitant to attribute this formal move to Radcliffe, especially since her trustees felt the freedom to manipulate the frame by cutting out a portion of it for an essay that they titled "On the Supernatural in Poetry." Providing the frame a paratextual distinction seems to be a posthumous editorial maneuver, similar to a modern edition of *The Italian*, in which "Prologue" was added to the frame "for the sake of convenient reference."[72] As in her previous frame narratives, Radcliffe constructs this extradiegetic narrative in the picturesque mode. In this case, however, the sublime Real of the central narrative permeates the "reality" of the frame by way of the frame's disturbing lack of authority, which Radcliffe establishes through the bumbling negligence of her fictional editor.

The frame introduces two English travelers, Willoughton, an antiquary, and his friend, Simpson. They pass through the forests of Arden, where they discuss Shakespeare and mortality, and then proceed onto the grounds of Kenilworth Castle. There they meet an intrusive and garrulous stranger, who, like Schedoni and his frame-narrative double in *The Italian*, is "tall" and "thin."[73] The stranger reveals that he is in possession of a chest, dug out of the ground, which contains "old parchments … and some old books" (15). Among them is an illuminated manuscript, titled a "Trew Chronique," which purports "to be an account of what passed at Kenilworth, when Henry the Third there kept the feast of Saint Michael, and some wonderful accident that there befel" (18). Willoughton pays for the manuscripts, and the pair sets off for Warwick. That night Willoughton acts as an editor, translating and deciphering, in accord with the "modern style" (27). What follows is a story of cunning deception and supernatural redemption. In contrast to *The Italian*, the narrative frame closes as it returns to Willoughton, who muses on the validity of the manuscript and contemplates working through another specimen from the antiques he purchased. The terminal frame, however, is dominated by the thoughts of an extradiegetic narrator, the voice that has heretofore described Willoughton's frame-narrative thoughts and actions.

In the opening frame, Willoughton is momentarily skeptical about the true age of the manuscript. The stranger explains its remarkable condition: "what made me wonder most was to see it look so fresh, after it had laid all that time in the ground; to be sure it was well wrapped up in parchment, and the trunk was thick enough" (15). The stranger also reveals that he "took out some of the best of the books" from the chest, but then placed the "trunk in the earth again" (15). Thus, Willoughton never sees the chest or the other decayed materials inside it; he is allowed access only to the materials the stranger has selected. When Willoughton gets a chance to analyze the text, he is surprised to find that the illustrations "were traced, with more knowledge of perspective and more attention to proportion, than [he] expected" (18). The narrator reveals that Willoughton, "long before he had finished … had some doubts, as to its origin" (205). Yet, because he has the "enthusiasm of an antiquary," and not the skeptical rationalism of his friend Simpson, Willoughton ignores the manuscript's "contradictory circumstances" (205). For the narrator, however, the manuscript is apocryphal:

> Perhaps, one better versed in antiquities would have found out, that several of the ceremonies of the court here exhibited, were more certainly those of the fourth Edward, than of the third Henry, or the second Richard, and would have assigned the manuscript to a later period than that of the title, or than that afterwards alluded to in the book, whether written by monk or layman. And though that same title said this chronicle was translated from the Norman tongue, by Grymbald, a monk of saint Mary's Priory, it said nothing of its having been composed by one; and the manuscript itself seemed to bear evidence against such a supposition, by the way in which some of the reigning superstitions of Henry the Third's time and of the monastic life in general were spoken of [205].

In questioning the authenticity of the central text with such force in the terminal frame, Radcliffe challenges the assumptions of all "enthusiastic antiquaries" who pervade the period's fiction and culture. Critics, it appears, were fooled into reading the frame too literally. A reviewer for the *Port Folio* derides the "tedious introduction" and accuses Radcliffe of employing an outdated formal device: "This threadbare story has long ceased to deceive any body."[74] And the *London Magazine* criticizes Radcliffe's "affectation of antiquity."[75] But in *Gaston de Blondeville* it is not the supernatural that is explained away, but rather the text itself. By adding the frame narrative to a "Trew Chronique," Radcliffe in fact parodies the "found manuscript" trope. When the narrator questions Willoughton's judgment and asks for "one better versed in antiquities" (205), we must call into question not only the events of the central text—historical *and* supernatural—but also those of the opening frame.

Willoughton's slippery status in the text demonstrates his potential unreliability. When he appears without warning in the central narrative, as he "laid down the manuscript, and went to a window of his chamber" (102), he momentarily becomes a character trapped inside the manuscript that he is editing, and the novel experiences a metaleptic rupture. We become aware that Willoughton's actions to this point have been part of the novel's diegetic world—a demotion that implicates the events of the introductory dialogue—and that the central story is in turn hypodiegetic, a tale (literally, in the case of the manuscript) buried within a tale. Thus, Willoughton descends from editorial agent to fallible character under the omniscient sway of the extradiegetic narrator. Even worse, the consummate English aesthete is left ignorant of his own disturbing credulity. That Willoughton will never know the error of his ways demonstrates his "lack of epistemological authority," in Castle's words.[76] As with *Udolpho*'s Emily, who remains unaware of the wax effigy behind the veil, Willoughton's firm position in the novel's diegetic world prohibits him from accessing the omniscient knowledge of the extradiegetic narrator. It is a fitting end for Radcliffe's last novel, for as it undermines the figure who seemingly occupied the narrative level closest to the time, space, and perspective of the reader, it questions all textual authority.

Similar to the effect of the two prefaces of Walpole's *Otranto*, Radcliffe makes us doubt the authenticity of the manuscript, and urges us instead to consider it as a product of a contemporary writer—perhaps the stranger who cunningly markets it to overeager antiquaries, and remarks that "[p]eople are always conjuring up strange tales when they have nothing better to do" (13). If this is the case, then the supernatural becomes an enduring concern of the present rather than a fleeting remnant of the past. In the central narrative, the ghostly figure of the murdered knight exacts his revenge on Gaston de Blondeville. But this is not the novel's only ghost, for in the opening frame the stranger describes the ghost of Queen Elizabeth haunting the ruins of the castle, and insists that he "saw a man standing with a mask on his face ... with a drawn sword in his hand" (13). The latter, like the shadowy monk in *The Italian*, is an uncanny harbinger of the masked ghost that wields a sword in the central narrative. As with the supernatural forces that appear in the ordinary frame-world of *The Mysteries of Udolpho*, the breakdown of narrative frames in *Gaston de Blondeville* suggests that the Real was always part of reality. The supernatural is not confined to ancient manuscripts, but instead is a persistent threat of the present.

Perhaps most significant, *Gaston de Blondeville* ultimately draws attention to the desire all readers have for the supernatural, the drive we have to access the horrors of the Real. Not only is Willoughton duped into believing in the authenticity of the manuscript, but so are readers. For the "unexplained supernatural" in the novel is the product of a disingenuous character, not Radcliffe. In other words, any argument that the novel demonstrates a change in Radcliffe's presentation of the Gothic ignores the fact that the manuscript is more than likely a fake, a brilliant ruse (along the lines of Macpherson and Chatterton) that plays on the hopes and fears of readers, penned by a mysterious stranger. This hoax ought to make us question Radcliffe's other "found manuscripts." Perhaps the true villains in her novels, the implications of the Real, have been located all along in the frame as the duplicitous figures (the friar in *A Sicilian Romance*, the Italian in *The Italian*, and the stranger in *Gaston de Blondeville*) who work to disseminate narratives of horror to willing audiences. In a sense, we must work backwards to account for the horror in Radcliffe's novels. The results are manifest in the diegetic narrative, but what is most significant is how they got there and what made it possible. Žižek writes that "[t]he Real is an entity which must be constructed afterwards so that we can account for the distortions of the symbolic structure."[77] Following Walpole's lead, Radcliffe demonstrates that horrors cannot be contained through either historical separation or narrative frameworks when they are already, and always were, products of the here and now—the chaotic, disturbing Real of the universal human experience.

I would like to conclude, through similar lines, by interrogating the authenticity of Radcliffe's "On the Supernatural in Poetry." In spite of the fact that some descriptive passages from the frame are direct transcriptions from Radcliffe's diary, it should not be ignored that the essay was originally part of a dialogue whose participants are undermined by the narrator. Dale Townshend goes as far as to claim Willoughton as "Radcliffe's mouthpiece," but the former is often little more than an excitable comic foil to Simpson's indolent rationalism.[78] Since the narrator is suspicious, to say the least, of Willoughton's authority as an antiquarian editor, we cannot, in turn, trust that Willoughton's opinions on Gothic effects are also Radcliffe's. While Norton argues that "[n]either the essay nor the Introduction suffer any disjunction by this severance," there is, in fact, a profound problem when we transform a fictional conversation *in* a Gothic novel into a non-fictional treatise *on* the Gothic novel.[79] The fact is, Willoughton cannot be trusted, and his critically definitive bifurcation of the Gothic into terror and horror is the opinion of an incompetent editor who gradually becomes a character—and a foolish one at that. This slippage of states, on both linguistic and ontological levels, is suggestive of a series of antagonisms that implicate the Real. *Gaston de Blondeville* blurs lines, complicating and obfuscating critical attempts to categorize or even to diagnose. It fundamentally frustrates, which makes it a Gothic masterwork and a fitting end to Radcliffe's monumental career.

As a final note, the tendency of critics to promote Willoughton's words as proof of Radcliffe's desire to separate her version of the Gothic from Matthew Lewis's is irresponsible. For neither Lewis nor his 1796 thriller *The Monk* are referred to in the essay. There is, to put it bluntly, absolutely nothing in "On the Supernatural in Poetry" to suggest that Radcliffe had Lewis in mind. Certainly, Willoughton seems to support terror over horror, as the former "expands the soul" while the latter "contracts, freezes, and nearly annihilates [the faculties]."[80] Yet his closing words on the subject suggest that there is something unique about the sensations that the mode of horror imparts. Willoughton addresses the difference between obscurity (horror) and confusion (terror): "Obscurity leaves something for the imagination to exaggerate; confusion, by blurring one image into another, leaves only a chaos in which the mind can find nothing to be magnificent, nothing to nourish its fears or doubts, or to act upon in any way."[81] Confusion, in this sense, strikingly resembles the chaotic manifold that Kant examines in the *Critique of Pure Reason* (1781). The blurring together of the multiplicity of sensations, rather than confirming the authority of our perceived reality, in fact undermines it altogether by implicating the existence of a deeper realm populated by *das Ding an sich*. Willoughton argues that "neither Shakespeare nor Milton by their fictions, nor Mr Burke by his reasoning, anywhere looked to positive horror as a source of the sublime," but this is potentially the case because Radcliffe falls more in line with Kant.[82] In his *Critique of the Power of Judgment* (1790), Kant writes that the experience of the sublime is a negative, "namely a feeling of the deprivation of the freedom of the imagination."[83] This cognitive deprivation that the sublimity of horror provides may be just the ingredient that pulls us out of reality and into the Real. Willoughton's recipe for this experience, one that may be linked to the unexplained supernatural in *Gaston de Blondeville*, has escaped the limits of the novel's frame narrative and entered the critical, non-fictional realm of the 1826 *New Monthly Magazine*. Indeed, Willoughton's dialogue concludes with his recollection of standing on a platform at Windsor Castle, "which there projects over the precipice," and being disturbed by a sentinel, who "moves a shadowy figure at his foot."[84] The lasting horror of Radcliffe's final published writing is that the ghostly Real has been abjected from both the novel and its frame and has invaded the reality of the periodical's readership.

2

Go Forth and Prosper

Mary Shelley's Monsters Unbound

But for those obstinate questionings
Of sense and outward things,
Fallings from us, vanishings;
Blank misgivings of a Creature
Moving about in worlds not realized.
—William Wordsworth, "Ode: Intimations of Immortality" (1807)[1]

Something there is that doesn't love a wall,
That sends the frozen-ground-swell under it,
And spills the upper boulders in the sun,
And makes gaps even two can pass abreast.
—Robert Frost, "Mending Wall" (1914)[2]

In Mary Shelley's *The Last Man* (1826), Lionel Verney records: "I remembered the dark monk, and floating figures of 'The Italian,' and how my boyish blood had thrilled at the description."[3] Stirred by the surviving classical grandeur of Rome, the world's last man in 2099 ultimately recalls Ann Radcliffe's 1797 novel.[4] Although Shelley's Gothic discards several familiar Radcliffean tropes—castles, historical settings, the explained supernatural—it not only maintains, but also promotes the formal energy of the frame narrative. Like Radcliffe, Shelley typically locates her introductory frame narratives between the paratext(s) and the first chapter, but she experiments with the device by introducing first-person storytellers rather than reproducing third-person manuscripts. Thus, Shelley's frames and the tales they embed are often disturbingly intimate portraits of motivations, mistakes, and miseries. Yet the personal ultimately becomes universal; the decisions of individual characters have potentially global consequences.[5] The distinct dynamic of Shelley's frame narratives may reveal her anxiety over making private despair a public concern, as she permits her demons to "go forth and prosper." Rather than functioning as barriers between representation and reality, Shelley's narrative frames allow embedded horrors to escape diegetic boundaries and to enter the extradiegetic world closest to the reader. In *Frankenstein* (1818), Robert Walton "cannot bear to look on the reverse side of the picture," but the painted veil ultimately lifts, and he dramatically confronts the creature, a disturbing implication of the Real, that lurks behind.[6]

Shelley experimented with narrative frames throughout her career. In *History of a Six Weeks' Tour* (1817), she provides not only a preface to explain the text's genesis and to apologize for its faults, but also an introductory account of the group's arduous passage over choppy waters from Dover to Calais. This short entry serves as the opening frame for the chapter-like divisions by country that are terminated by four lengthy letters. Percy Shelley's "Mont Blanc" closes the text and provides a final introspective account of the implacable power of nature, which bookends the unforgiving waters in the opening narrative. Shelley followed *History of a Six Weeks' Tour* with three Gothic novels: *Frankenstein*, *Mathilda* (written in 1819 but not published until 1959), and *The Last Man*.[7] Each of these texts features an elaborate and fundamentally distinct framing device that authorizes embedded horror access to a narrative world that exists on more intimate terms with the novel's readership. The penetrable frames, in other words, permit the proliferation of monstrous forces, which range from abject creatures to apocalyptic contagion. Slavoj Žižek urges us to "conceive [of] the monster as a kind of fantasy screen," through which "we communicate with the 'suprasensible' virtual universe to be found nowhere in reality."[8] When these monstrosities move into the frame, they not only elevate their subjectivity through the transformative passage from diegetic to extradiegetic narratives, but also bring the horrors of the Real into closer proximity to the novels' readers.

Frankenstein presents a complex system of narrative frames—from paratexts (Percy's 1818 Preface and Mary's 1831 Introduction), to Walton's opening and terminal letters, and finally to the creature's and Safie's embedded stories.[9] Walton's storytelling letters to Margaret transform into his edited journal of Victor's story, which pauses when Victor commences the creature's narrative—and so on. Exploring *Frankenstein*'s frames reveals a stunning example of *mise en abyme* (place into abyss). Each narrator that Shelley introduces mirrors the one previous with complicated and uncanny results. Mieke Bal's preference of the term "mirror text" does not do justice to the framing in *Frankenstein*, for readers, in a sense, do enter an abyss. The Gothic horror of the novel is the inscrutable, immeasurable Real that the creature suggests, the urgent destructive force that authoritatively appears in both sides of the narrative that frames him.[10] If the creature can jump authoritatively between frames, then how safe is Margaret (or the novel's readership) outside the frame?

Walton's frame narrative puzzled early reviewers. "The story begins at the end," the *Literary Panorama* observes.[11] And the *British Critic* asserts: "In a sort of introduction, which precedes the main story of the novel, and has nothing else to do with it, we are introduced to a Mr Walton, the Christopher Sly of the piece."[12] That the reviewer links the novel's opening letters to Sly's drunken frame in *The Taming of the Shrew* implies that the story Walton hears is at best dubious, if not a ruse altogether.[13] Readers are still at odds over the function of *Frankenstein*'s frames. Some critics focus on how the narrative levels foster unreliable narrators, while others read the frames as barriers that separate Shelley from her "hideous progeny." "[T]he narrative strategy," Mary Poovey argues, "permits Mary [Shelley] to express and efface herself at the same time."[14] And Anne Mellor contends that the frame "builds a series of screens around [Shelley's] authentic voice."[15] Critics also claim that the many frames shield English readers from the horrors within. Beth Newman argues that the frames "mark the exclusion of Mrs Saville—and the reader as well—from the horror of the narratives they contain."[16]

I argue that the effect is quite the opposite. The force that *Frankenstein*'s frames impart is not in containing, but rather in reaching in two directions and pulling representation and reality into disturbing proximity. As Jacques Derrida submits, "the parergonal frame stands out against two grounds, but with respect to each of those two grounds, it merges into the other."[17] Walton's frame acts as a portal between two worlds more than it does a barrier. Criscillia Benford observes that the "creature's visit to Walton's narrative level subverts the narrative hierarchy that would privilege Walton, calling into question any reading that proceeds from the assumption that Walton is more 'real' than the creature."[18] In fact, the creature is an implication of the Real, the kernel of horror that disturbs our symbolically structured reality. Victor's death erases the narrative boundary between the creature and Walton so that Walton's ship becomes the vessel for the creature's passage from the embedded narrative into the world of the reader. Mellor has noted that "nine months enwomb the telling of the history of Frankenstein, bringing Mary Shelley's literary pregnancy to full term," and Marc Rubenstein reads "the entire novel, [as] a womb."[19] Since the creature jumps from Walton's ship and is "borne away by the waves"

(191), then the novel's conclusion is a rebirth, not a death; the creature's promised self-immolation is to be promethean fire, not ashes.

Walton establishes close proximity with readers not only through the location of his narrative, but also in the way that he opens his letters—an effect that creates more narrative intimacy than Victor ever achieves. Walton's opening and terminal frames both begin with a resounding call to the readerly "You." He is addressing the silent interlocutor Margaret, of course, but as Walton's writing moves increasingly from letter to journal, the second "You" that opens the terminal frame appeals more directly to the reader. When measured against Victor's opening, "I am by birth a Genevese" (18), and the creature's "I expected this reception" (77), Walton's frame comes into close proximity to any reader of the letters. But this intimacy is uncomfortable, and possibly dangerous, as the creature's "powers of eloquence and persuasion" (188) dominate the terminal frame. When the creature enters the ship, Walton portentously declares, "I am interrupted" (186). This narrative disturbance marks the point at which the frame narrative is consumed by the embedded story. Victor and the creature are permitted to tell their tales with no breaks. Both say "Listen to my tale" (17, 78), which puts their audience in a trance, much like the effect of Coleridge's Ancient Mariner on the wedding guest.

The creature's status as a horrifying implication of the Real is related to the structure of Walton's frame letters. When Victor collects the materials for his experiment, he encounters a problem of proportion: "to prepare a frame for the reception of it, with all its intricacies of fibres, muscles, and veins, still remained a work of inconceivable difficulty and labour" (35). He decides "to make the being of a gigantic stature" (35), which echoes Shelley's project of supplementing her original tale with enough matter to produce a novel—a process during which she no doubt also "spent some months in successfully collecting and arranging ... materials" (35–36).[20] Shelley produced Walton's letters to be the "frame for the reception" of her own secret and shocking work. Percy urged Mary to add parts to her original tale, but it was Mary who ultimately continued the process. The 1831 Introduction is, in Mary's words, an "appendage to a former production" (192). Joseph Lew points out that in it "we find yet another set of frames."[21] In the Introduction, we first encounter the creature, looming ominously in Shelley's description of her dream. Perhaps more important, because this new introductory frame was published in Henry Colburn's *Court Journal* nine days before the novel appeared in print, the creature escapes even the boundaries of the novel, and invades new generic and physical realms.[22] It is in this introduction that Shelley "once again" allows her "hideous progeny [to] go forth and prosper" (197).

Victor's horror originates from the fact that the creature's "yellow skin" can barely contain the "work of muscles and arteries beneath" (39). Although Victor had "selected [the creature's] features as beautiful" (39), he admits his aesthetic error: "I gazed on him while unfinished; he was ugly then" (40). The creature has a "deformity of its aspect" (56), is a "blot upon the earth" (96), and a "filthy type" of human, "more horrid from its very semblance" (105). In his suggestions for revision, Percy carried it even further, scratching out "am the devil" and writing above the famous "am an abortion."[23] The creature does not have a place in our symbolic reality; his uncanny appearance makes him incapable of interaction.[24] Žižek writes that "what is ugly is ultimately the brutal fact of existence (or the [R]eal) as such," and observes that ugliness is the "excess of the interior stuff that threatens to overwhelm and engulf the subject."[25] The repulsiveness of the creature is the result of the viscera of charnel houses suggesting an escape from the bodily frame; the horror of the Real is close to consuming the reality of Victor and Walton (and Margaret and readers). We might consider the creature's taut skin not only as a fantasmatic frame that is perilously on the verge of allowing the Real to come "too close," but also as a symbol for the novel's frame letters, which are constantly in danger of permitting embedded horrors to burst through.[26]

Walton's narrative ultimately succumbs to the creature's force in the novel's terminal frame, but this invasion of the Real happens only after Walton abandons his own project, the failure of which is mirrored by the unfulfilled ventures of Victor and the creature. In the opening frame, he reminds Margaret of his unsuccessful early plans to be a poet: "You are well acquainted with my failure, and how heavily I bore the disappointment" (7). Flights of fancy give way to more material endeavors, such as finding a passage through the North Pole. But the latter enterprise is still motivated by the resources of an unchecked imagination: "the pole … ever presents itself to my imagination as the region of beauty and delight" (5). In the 1831 edition, Shelley makes Walton's passion obsessive rather than speculative: "love for the marvelous" is enough to "sacrifice my fortune, my existence, my every hope, to the furtherance of my enterprise."[27] The misgivings and near mutiny of his crew force Walton again to bear disappointment and to head back south. Victor's objectives are arguably more realized, as he is successful in bringing life to dead matter. Like Walton, Victor's education blends the imaginative (what he digests from the alchemy of Agrippa, Magnus, and Paracelsus) and the scientific (books from Krempe and lessons from Waldman). Once Victor sees the creature stir, however, he recalls: "the beauty of the dream vanished, and breathless horror and disgust filled my heart" (39). Victor eventually embarks on a new mission, to destroy the creature, but he fails, and his "task is unfulfilled" (177). As Joan Copjec asserts, "Frankenstein's invention did not go awry, as the standard reading claims, it *failed*."[28] Lastly, although the creature concludes, "My work is nearly complete" (190), his last promise is to travel farther north (perhaps to realize Walton's dream) and to burn himself alive. If the creature is a double of both Walton and Victor, however, then we must not assume that he finishes his work. This ambiguity in some sense defines the Gothic mode, as the dead, Benford notes, "do not always lie quietly in their graves."[29]

The horror of the creature's ambiguous fate is intensified by the novel's own lack of finality. Walter Scott considered the ending "an uncertainty," and even Walton remarks: "How all this will terminate, I know not" (183).[30] Garrett Stewart notes that because the novel "never arrives at a *narrated* destination" its terminal frame "functions ... as an open bracket."[31] What should provide tight closure prompts more questions about the fate of its living actors. In her analysis of the novel's letters, Mary Favret deftly explains the indefinite conclusion: "Walton's missive never ends, and something monstrous escapes."[32] Walton's terminal frame fails to conclude; no "affectionately yours" appears to assure Margaret and the readers of his safety. Shelley ends the text on a "mortifying negative" (195). The creature's final disappearing act reflects Shelley's anxiety over the "blank incapability of invention" (195) that she admits to in the 1831 Introduction. For what Victor creates, both as physical body and as oral tale, fades into nothingness, disappears into the ice at the poles of the earth and into the white pages at the poles of the novel. It is a new beginning for the creature, as he is "borne" (191) from the womb of Walton's ship, Walton's frame narrative, and Shelley's novel, and allowed to "go forth and prosper" (197).[33]

Whereas *Frankenstein* in great part concerns the application and the interaction of frames, the drama of Shelley's next novel is the result of a fundamental reframing of vision and genre. The first version of Shelley's *Mathilda* featured a frame narrative that was most likely inspired by Mary Wollstonecraft's unfinished manuscript "The Cave of Fancy."[34] Shelley initially titled the text "The Fields of Fancy," but eventually discarded the opening framework. Elizabeth Nitchie, the first editor of the *Mathilda* manuscript, calls "The Fields of Fancy" frame "unrealistic and largely irrelevant."[35] Subsequent editors have chosen not to include it. However, examining the effect of the original frame is vital to understanding the ultimate impact of Shelley's controversial novel. As Margaret Davenport

Garrett observes, the "revision indicates a change in her fundamental intentions for the story."[36] Shelley's decision to excise the opening frame does not suggest that she wished to abandon the effects of framing that she employed with such success in *Frankenstein*. Rather, the initial frame served too effectively to mitigate the force at the novel's Gothic core. The horror of the embedded tale softens in its passage through the frame instead of growing in virulence. By removing the original framing device and drawing attention to a new, more intimate frame, Shelley sought to highlight the central horror—the Real desire of incest—and to transform the text from a comforting didactic affirmation into a disturbing Gothic confession.[37] The complexity of this formal transformation is perhaps best expressed by Mathilda's rhetorical question: "What am I writing?" (151).

Readings of *Mathilda* tend to be heavily autobiographical, and most see the text as both a reaction to Shelley's grief over the loss of her children, Clara Everina and William, and a response to suppressed (or perhaps repressed) emotions about her husband and her parents.[38] In these readings, Mathilda is Shelley, the unnamed father is Godwin, and Woodville is Percy. Since it appears that Godwin blocked the publication of Mary's text, it is possible to infer that he suffered great anxiety over the potential publication of such scandalous themes, especially if he saw himself represented in it as a father with incestuous desires. More recent studies have attempted to lay aside autobiographical readings in favor of examining *Mathilda*'s curious thematic and structural elements. Still, in these formal readings, frames have remained largely ignored, and the effect of the abandoned frame on the novel's overall design has not been sufficiently explored. The monstrous Real that lies at the heart of *Mathilda* is brought to light with disturbing immediacy precisely because Shelley decided to remove the didactic frame and to highlight an alternate frame that intensifies, rather than diminishes, its force.

In May 1820, Shelley commissioned Maria Gisborne to deliver the manuscript from the Shelleys' residence in Italy to Godwin in England.[39] Shelley hoped that her father would use his influence to see it published. It appears he refused, however, as he ignored Shelley's repeated attempts to have the manuscript returned. Although we have no direct explanation from Godwin, Gisborne does provide some clues, noting that he thought the "subject ... disgusting and detestable."[40] Nevertheless, Godwin did suggest (according to Gisborne) that *Mathilda* required a preface "to prepare the minds of the readers, and to prevent them from being tormented by the apprehension from moment to moment of the fall of the heroine."[41] An 1818 review of *Frankenstein* makes clear the power of a preface to soften potentially harmful material: "This is a very *bold* fiction; and, did not the author, in a short Preface, make a kind of apology, we should almost pronounce it to be *impious*."[42] Shelley's decision to discard the frame, to remove the moderating influence of a didactic ethos, is curious. We can only speculate on Godwin's reaction to the manuscript had Shelley decided to keep the framework intact. For "The Fields of Fancy" effectively distances readers from the story by transforming a personal horror into a moralizing tract, a quasi conduct manual that concerns the search for happiness through self-discovery. By removing the original frame and adding a new one, Shelley transformed *Mathilda* from being conventionally certain to radically inconclusive, from universal to personal, from comforting to horrifying, and—paradoxically—from supernatural to Gothic.

In "The Fields of Fancy," an unnamed narrator is visited by a spirit Fantasia. The narrator, who initially refuses to follow Fantasia, falls asleep and finds herself in the Elysian Fields. Fantasia explains to the narrator that she will see the part of Elysium where the dead reside, who, while living, "wished to become wise & virtuous by study & action," but who now "endeavour after the same ends by contemplation."[43] The narrator comes upon a group huddled around Diotima, a "woman about 40 years of age," whose "eyes burned with a deep fire and every line of her face expressed enthusiasm & wisdom" (110). Diotima hopes to guide those who in life were "misconducted in the pursuit of knowledge" (111)—rhetoric that appears to cast the text as a conduct manual in which Diotima is the sage teacher and the dead are her students. Among the party in Elysium is an unnamed woman, "of about 23 years of age in the full enjoyment of the most exquisite beauty" (111), who turns out to be Mathilda. After professing that the only way to achieve true happiness is to seek knowledge through the "study of [one's] own heart" (115), Diotima urges Mathilda to tell her story as a therapeutic release that may allow her to join her dead loved ones in the afterlife. Eventually, Mathilda begins her "tale" of "dark and phre[n]zied passions" (117).[44]

Removing "The Fields of Fancy" allowed Shelley to compose a more intimate frame in which the horror of the central narrative threatens the reader's reality. The opening four paragraphs of the revised text establish Mathilda's lonely disposition and morbid motivation for writing: "it is in this persuasion that I begin to write my tragic history" (19). Although she claims that her secret is better kept untold, she nevertheless resolves to record her narrative: "there was a sacred horror in my tale that rendered it unfit for utterance, and now about to die I pollute its mystic terrors"

(20). Mathilda's duplicity here is the key to understanding how the horror of the secret makes its way out of the boundaries of the text. "There was too deep a horror in my tale for confidence," she later writes: "I was on earth the sole depository of my own secret" (68). Yet she records her story, which contains the details of the "deformity of sin" (57), for Woodville, whose trade as a writer suggests that he will make the story public as a literary commodity. Mathilda surmises as much, if not implicitly dictates what she desires: "perhaps he is already planning a poem in which I am to figure. I am a farce and play to him, but to me this is all dreary reality: he takes all the profit and I bear all the burthen" (89). The opening frame of the novel, then, might be considered as an introductory passage meant to inform Woodville of her impetus for writing, the "hideous necessity" (20) of revealing her secret to the public. Since she resolves to recount her tale "as if I wrote for strangers," she seemingly intends to "unveil the mystery" (20) to a wider audience than just Woodville. The Real horror of the story becomes part of reality because it has been "depicted upon paper" (104) and addressed to a man whose work was "hailed by the whole nation with enthusiasm and delight" (78).

Mathilda claims that her impending death has motivated her to write. Yet, as in *Frankenstein*, Shelley leaves the terminal frame steeped in ambiguity. We have only Mathilda's promise that she is dying when her text concludes, which is especially dubious as she earlier had admitted to faking her own death. In this sense, Mathilda mirrors the creature, whose pledge of self-immolation might be mere lip-service to relieve Walton of the burden of murder. But the connections between *Frankenstein* and *Mathilda* are even more complex. Mathilda is the creature of her father, of course, but the lines between creature and creator are regularly blurred. Upon learning her father's secret, Mathilda swoons, and her father intriguingly channels both Victor and the creature:

> [S]he is alive! Oh, Mathilda, lift up those dear eyes in the light of which I live. Let me hear the sweet tones of your beloved voice in peace and calm. Monster as I am, you are still, as you ever were, lovely, beautiful beyond expression. What I have become since this last moment I know not; perhaps I am changed in mien as the fallen archangel. I do believe I am for I have surely a new soul within me, and my blood riots through my veins: I am burnt up with fever. But these are precious moments; devil as I am become [51–52].

Like the creature, Mathilda's father remains nameless, and when he suggests traveling "to some fertile island where we should live at peace for ever" (34), he echoes the creature's fantasy life with his mate in South America. Charlene Bunnell observes that Mathilda "constructs" her father's "image from a picture, a letter, and some history."[45] He exists for sixteen years as nothing but a letter of farewell and a miniature—which she wears "exposed" (30) on her breast, anticipating the scandalous revelation of the secret. Eventually, Mathilda's father begins to blame his daughter for his wretched existence: "Why do you bring me out, and torture me, and tempt me, and kill me" (50). Yet Mathilda also suffers from being an outcast: "I believed myself to be polluted by the unnatural love I had inspired, and that I was a creature cursed and set apart by nature" (95). Mathilda's physical pursuit of her father, the scene that Godwin thought "the finest part of the whole novel," further blends the roles between creature and creator that Shelley constructed in *Frankenstein*.[46]

This effect challenges any reading that would consider one of the novel's characters as an explicit implication of the Real, for in *Mathilda* the Real is the secret itself, the inexpressible horror of incest, the implacable residue of pre-symbolic life.[47] Mathilda's father claims that he has made "every effort to cast it off," but his incestuous desire nevertheless "clings closer" (60). The "monstrous passion" (57) that should have been abjected during his passage into the symbolic order remains and triggers his psychosis, a return to the "perpetual chaos" (40) of primordial life. We might regard the novel, then, in respect to other prominent literary treatments of incest. The Oedipus myth is most obvious, of course, especially as it serves, in some ways, as the foundational text of psychoanalysis, through its depiction of a literal act of incest between mother and son. The other is *Hamlet*, which intensifies the psychic violence of the act because the "incestuous wish is repressed and displaced."[48] The familiar psychoanalytic reading maintains that Hamlet's oedipal desire for his mother motivates the events of the tragedy. His encounter with his father's ghost, his jealousy of Claudius, and his rejection of Ophelia are all manifestations of the incestuous antagonism that takes place in his unconscious. Lacan argues that

> incest law is located as such at the level of the unconscious in relation to *das Ding*, the Thing. The desire for the mother cannot be satisfied because it is the end, the terminal point, the abolition of the whole world of demand, which is the one that at its deepest level structures man's unconscious. It is to the extent that the function of the pleasure principle is to make man always search for what he has to find again, but which he never will attain, that one reaches the essence, namely, that sphere or relationship which is known as the law of the prohibition of incest.[49]

The desire for an incestuous encounter is the subject reaching after the impossible Real, the inaccessible pleasure of *jouissance* that is prohibited in reality. Shelley explores the Real of incestuous desire in *Mathilda*, but transposes the actors by presenting a father's sexual love for his daughter—an illicit desire that has its foundation in his upbringing and life events. Mathilda's father lost his own father at an early age and was raised by a "weak mother" (21), who appears to have satisfied his every indulgence. As a child, he developed a deep bond with Diana, a "favorite with his mother" (23), who eventually becomes his wife, but then dies shortly after childbirth. It is as if Shelley designed the novel to be read with a psychoanalytic lens. Diana serves as a replacement for the father's mother, and after Diana's death he finds a further replacement for her in Mathilda. His words to his daughter on continuing Diana's reading are telling: "you shall go on where she left off" (43). But thereafter he is even more disturbingly explicit: "Diana died to give her birth; her mother's spirit was transferred into her frame, and she ought to be as Diana to me" (60). When he returns to his daughter, all is relatively normal until she receives attention from a suitor in London. His jealousy reignites the embers of his suppressed desires, which become unmanageable. Yet he understands that the relationship is forbidden, the Real cannot exist in reality, and he chooses flight and suicide.

Thus, the monstrous antagonist in the novel is not Mathilda's father, but rather the Real of his unconscious that he cannot contain. Žižek argues that "in order for social reality to establish itself … something must be primordially repressed. Something cannot be symbolized, and the spectral apparition emerges to fill up the gap."[50] But the virulent horror of *Mathilda*, which is perhaps unmatched in the Gothic genre, is the result of Shelley initially providing no such "spectral apparition," no fantasmatic screen, to cover the gap in the symbolic network. The revelation of the secret, the loaded phrase "I love you!" (51), emerges with shocking force, and only after it is exposed does Mathilda's father become "Monster as I am" (51). As he steals away from the house, he becomes an "unlaid ghost" (55), and then appears as part of Mathilda's dream, "pale, and clothed in flowing garments of white" (56), only to escape her clutches and to plunge down a precipice. The next she sees him, he is dead, "something stiff and straight … covered by a sheet" (66). Thus, the incestuous desire of Mathilda's father, the gap in the social order, the fissure in symbolic reality, is filled retroactively by his "spectral apparition," which prevents the Real love of father and daughter, literally, from coming "too close." However, the father's disembodied state following his confession might suggest the dissolution of his identity. Žižek notes that coming "too close" to the "fantasmatic kernel" of one's being causes an "aphanisis of the subject," in which "the subject loses his or her symbolic consistency, it disintegrates."[51]

When the Real admission of incestuous desire irrupts in reality, he disappears, and his secret becomes the sole property of Mathilda, who implicitly works to see it published—to "go forth and prosper."

In the opening frame, Mathilda provides instructions for the horror to pass from her father's unconscious to the novel's readership, directives that are disguised by the disingenuous question, "What am I writing?" (20). It appears that she fully acknowledges that her writing not only satisfies her own desires for dramatic infamy, but also might give Woodville fodder for his own literary dreams to "be fulfilled" (105). That she records her story in writing and sends it off to Woodville is but her "last task" (20) in gaining the secret and exposing it for public consumption. The whole novel, then, might be considered as Mathilda's ploy to ensure that her solitary, eventless life becomes a "tragic history" (19) to captivate and consume readers. Charles E. Robinson observes that Mathilda "conceives of herself as a tragic actress who has played a dramatic role not only in her life but also in the very narrative that she constructs for Woodville and thus for her audience."[52] The only thing left is to construct a frame that both justifies her work and makes the unsubstantiated claim that she is dying. In so doing, she remains guiltless: "my faults may be easily pardoned" (20). When she reveals, "I gained his secret and we were both lost for ever" (46), we must think about the illicit secret that we, as readers, have gained as well—all via Mathilda's frame-narrative notes to Woodville, the de facto editor of this "found manuscript." Her remark that "[o]thers will toss these pages lightly over" (19) is insincere, if not roundly duplicitous, for she has made certain that the Real horror of incest circulates in reality.

In "The Fields of Fancy," Shelley evokes the framing device featured in Boccaccio's *The Decameron* (1353).[53] The frame narrative's idyllic setting, in which storytellers are huddled around Diotima in the haven of Elysium, moderates the revulsion of Mathilda's story in much the same way that Boccaccio's aristocratic asylum blocks the speakers from the Black Death raging in Florence. Shelley's final Gothic novel, however, most explicitly does not engage the formal possibilities of narrative sanctuary, but it does borrow *The Decameron*'s thematic horror—the plague. In *The Last Man*, Shelley adapts Radcliffe's found manuscript model to apocalyptic ends. As in *A Sicilian Romance* (1790) and *The Italian* (1797), the frame of *The Last Man* features English travelers who stumble upon a manuscript. But this manuscript is prophetic, not historical; it is a warning for a cataclysmic scourge that will wipe out the species. The inexorable spread of plague in *The Last Man* is the effect of the fantasmatic frame of reality collapsing entirely. As Barbara Johnson writes, the plague is "at once that which stops all systems of meaning from functioning and that against which those systems are necessarily erected."[54] The devastation of apocalyptic contagion is the unfettered Real wiping out the illusion of reality.

Readings of *The Last Man* range from examining its status as a *roman à clef*, to engaging with its political implications (as a reaction to its turbulent historical moment) and its representation of epidemic (as a novel about nationhood, population, emigration, and human rights). Others have found the structure of the novel's main narrative troubling. The tale of Lionel Verney and his domestic circle occupies the majority of the first volume. This personal history quickly spirals into national and global intrigue as the plague grows in virulence. The plague eventually takes center stage, and becomes the novel's central and most absorbing character. As Charlotte Sussman notes, "the novel necessarily describes the gradual unraveling of that net," the systematic collapse of everything Verney constructs in the first volume.[55] More recent discussions of the novel examine its perplexing frame narrative. The fictional introduction follows Radcliffe, but complicates the "found manuscript" device via a complex network of temporal layering and editorial intervention. Mark Canuel observes that the frame demonstrates "*how* the work acquires a meaning: not by seeking to perpetuate a consciousness but by seeing the author's work as dependent upon the reciprocation from other persons."[56] In this sense, *The Last Man* adapts the dynamic transmission of stories that constitutes *Frankenstein*. To access the creature's narrative requires passing through the editorial frames of both Victor and Walton (if not the writers of the 1818 Preface and 1831 Introduction). In *The Last Man*, this transmission disrupts chronological time; to read Lionel Verney's account of being the world's last man involves the paranormal power of an ancient prophet and the passionate curiosity of a contemporary traveler.

In the opening frame, two travelers in Italy ignore the warnings of their guides and explore the depths of a secreted cave. They eventually find themselves "at a wide cavern with an arched dome-like roof," where "leaves" of written text are "strewed about" (3). As several critics have pointed out, the travelers enter a sort of womb that fosters the productive transformation of hidden manuscript into public novel. The travelers come to find that they have entered the cave of the Cumaean Sibyl, who has recorded prophecies on the leaves. As the Sibyl stories go, the papers are loose and unarranged. "We made a hasty selection of such of the leaves, whose writing one at least of us could understand," the narrator explains, "and then, laden with our treasure, we bade adieu to the dim hypaethric cavern" (6). The narrator returns several times to the cave to collect more of the remains, the leaves of which require editorial work: "Scattered and unconnected as they were, I have been obliged to add links, and model the work into a consistent form" (5). In not only editing the "obscure and chaotic" sheets, but also in reconstructing them into "their present form," the narrator becomes a second Sibyl, whose work as a "decipherer" (6) is ultimately as important to shaping the text's final meaning as the prophet herself.

The main narrative is set in the late twenty-first century and consists of the first-person account of Verney. Although born of humble means, he ominously portends his future importance: "I was born for something greater than I was—and great I would become" (19). Once wild and undisciplined, Verney transforms under the influence of Adrian, the frail yet passionate son of the abdicated king. Adrian teaches his new companion the wonders of reading and the arts. "I was at once startled and enchanted by my sudden extension of vision," Verney recalls, "when the curtain, which had been drawn before the intellectual world, was withdrawn" (31). It is a transformation that alters his very conception of his surroundings: "I had lived in what is generally called the world of reality, and it was awakening to a new country to find that there was a deeper meaning in all I saw, besides that which my eyes conveyed to me" (31). In order to cultivate and to express these new perceptions, Verney passionately devotes himself to writing; he yearns "to penetrate the last veil of nature and her God, and to display the highest beauty in visible expression to the understandings of men" (158). In a sense, Verney gets what he desires: his obsession with removing the veil is realized to vast and catastrophic proportions when the Real horror of the plague spreads and unravels the fantasmatic veil of reality.

The pestilence makes its sinister entrance in volume two—"[t]hat word.... PLAGUE" (175)—first erupting in Constantinople and then moving relentlessly westward. Although England proves to be the world's last untainted refuge, it eventually "become[s] a wide, wide tomb" (248). In spite of the plague's effects, some brave souls (including Verney) continue to practice the arts. In need of emotional release after experiencing the "banqueting hall of death" (281) in London, Verney finds himself at Drury Lane, and he enters a staging of *Macbeth* at the commencement of its fourth act. "The curtain drew up," he writes, "and the stage presented the scene of the witches' cave" (281). Verney's claim that the "supernatural machinery" of the scene "was a pledge that it could contain little directly connected with our present circumstances" (281) is a colossal underestimation. Ross's equation of Scotland as "our grave" (4.3.166) and Macduff's grief over his family killed with "one fell swoop!" (4.3.218) mesmerize the playgoers who have experienced similar loss from the plague.[57] Perhaps most important, what the play reveals is not fiction, but rather a suggestion of the Real:

> The extreme darkness of the stage, whose only light was received from the fire under the cauldron, joined to a kind of mist that floated about it, rendered the unearthly shapes of the witches obscure and shadowy. It was not three decrepid old hags that bent over their pot throwing in the grim ingredients of the magic charm, but forms frightful, unreal, and fanciful. The entrance of Hecate, and the wild music that followed, took us out of this world. The cavern shape the stage assumed … permitted the imagination to revel [281–82].

The witches are represented as supernatural entities, who "look not like th' inhabitants o' th' earth, / And yet are on't" (1.3.41–42). Whereas late-eighteenth-century productions of the play, especially those starring siblings Sarah Siddons and John Philip Kemble, chose to humanize the witches through the application of Scots attire, the version Verney attends makes their otherworldliness explicit. It seems that this version has more in common with William Davenant's Restoration-era adaptation, which featured "Machines, as flytngs for the Witches; with all the Singing and Dancing in it."[58] This effect not only escorts rapt audience members from reality into an unknown world, but also suggests that their reality has become the horror of the Real. What is more, the obscurity of the scene calls to mind Edmund Burke's definition of the sublime: "To make any thing very terrible, obscurity seems in general to be necessary."[59] Since the sublime suggests the horror of an unknown world, it is no wonder that Lionel forgets the reality of his situation and loses himself in the Real—until, "absorbed by the terrors," he "rushe[s] out as from an hell of torture, to find calm in the free air and silent street" (283). Yet the world outside has been transformed: "Free the air was not, or the street silent" (283). Drunkards revel and corpses lie in piles; even Westminster Abbey becomes a den of horrors. Žižek observes how fantasy

> sustains the subject's "sense of reality": when the phantasmic frame disintegrates, the subject undergoes a "loss of reality" and starts to perceive reality as an "irreal" nightmarish universe with no firm ontological foundation; this nightmarish universe is not "pure fantasy" but, on the contrary, *that which remains of reality after reality is deprived of its support in fantasy.*[60]

The dissolution of the arts as a consequence of the plague suggests that fantasy, the "screen that conceals something quite primary," breaks down and causes the Real to spread into Verney's reality.[61] "Farewell to the well-trod stage," he remarks, "a truer tragedy is enacted on the world's ample scene, that puts to shame mimic grief" (322). The Real that was confined to traumas and dreams becomes reality, and the horror of the supernatural becomes the everyday natural. The world governed by plague in *The Last Man* is Gothic realism.

The witches cave in *Macbeth* also serves as an analogue to the "gloomy cavern of the Cumaean Sibyl" (3) in the opening frame, for both function as sites where chronology blurs. In the play's "cavern," a recess framed by the stage and veiled by a curtain, the witches conjure images of the future that Macbeth wishes to know, but the apparitions ironically show him the circumstances of his demise rather than the conditions of his survival. Macbeth's death is predetermined, and his efforts to endure only serve to seal his fate. What he believes impossible nevertheless occurs—an enemy not "of woman born" (4.1.80) and the movement of "Great Birnam wood to high Dunsinane hill" (4.1.93). The Real of the apparitions' prophesies becomes part of Macbeth's reality. In some sense, Shelley makes Verney a twenty-first-century Macbeth—as both are "[s]omething wicked this way comes" (4.1.45) when they enter the play. Yet Raymond is perhaps the more fitting echo of Macbeth: both are driven by hubristic ambition; both ignore cryptic warnings that foretell devastation; and both die on the battlefield. Verney is more of chorus-figure, a narrator seemingly immune to the plague's effects. For this reason, he remains the sole survivor of the human tragedy. Peter Melville calls him a "*bona fide* freak of nature, a man whose immunology is monstrously disproportionate to all those around him."[62] Thus, Verney joins Shelley's other Gothic protagonists (Frankenstein and Mathilda), as his existence might be as monstrous as the creature he faces. The plague simply realizes, with the most devastating results possible, Verney's desire "to penetrate the last veil of nature and her God" (158).

The global devastation of the plague is most threateningly forecasted by women in *The Last Man*. Indeed, following the connections to *Macbeth*, the witches in novel are the Cumaean Sibyl and the frame narrator, and the apparitions who foretell the future are Evadne and Perdita. Morton D. Paley observes that the plague is "represented as female," and that it "finds vehement expression" in Evadne, whose death from a war wound is an ominous harbinger of subsequent plague suffering: "her dry, hot hand ..., and her brow and lips burned with consuming fire" (181).[63] In the throes of death, she presages Raymond's demise: "Fire, and war, and plague, unite for thy destruction.... [T]here is no safety for the!" (181). It is Perdita, however, whose emotional anguish proves to be a warning of the global cataclysm that is to come. Spurned by Raymond, Perdita becomes a shell of her former self, which is embodied in a crucial scene of self-recognition:

> She stood before a large mirror—she gazed on her reflected image; her light and graceful dress, the jewels that studded her hair, and encircled her beauteous arms and neck, her small feet shod in satin, her profuse and glossy tresses, all were to her clouded brow and woebegone countenance like a gorgeous frame to a dark tempest-pourtraying picture. "Vase am I," she thought, "vase brimful of despair's direst essence" [135].

The outward charms of Perdita's body and clothing frame the dark pain of her psyche. We might be reminded of the "frame of uncommon size" in the *Mysteries of Udolpho* (1794), which encases the Real horror of Emily's desires.[64] If we consider Perdita's image in the mirror as a symbol for the novel's form, we see that the beauty and the safety of the opening 1818 narrative frames the horror of Verney's embedded tale. "[T]he painted veil of life is rent," Perdita asserts: "I sit for ever shrouded in darkness" (139).[65] She becomes a receptacle for suffering, a recess of horror framed by thin drapery. She ultimately chooses death rather than "appear[ing] to live—while I am—dead" (134). Yet her drowning is met with the same objective indifference as Leila's death in Byron's *The Giaour* (1813).[66] After Lionel hears a "splash in the sea," a shipmate assumes that "something has been thrown from the aft cabin" (214), but it is Perdita, dead at twenty-eight, the same age as Shelley when *The Last Man* was published.

The frame narrator's work in adding "form and substance" (7) to Sibyl's scattered leaves echoes Victor Frankenstein's assembly of the creature. If the creature is not only rudely stitched-together pieces of other bodies, but also words to be transcribed by Walton and letters to be reconstructed by Margaret, then what the narrator accomplishes in *The Last Man* is to bring to life yet another "hideous progeny," a creature that realizes Victor's fear of the "race of devils" who will threaten the "existence of the whole human race" (138). The plague in *The Last Man* is "[t]hat same invincible monster, … that fiend more cruel than tempest, less tame than fire" (221). This "modern Prometheus" is in fact an unbound anti–Promethean force that extinguishes rather than illuminates, destroys humanity rather than giving it the spark of life. But the enduring horror of the novel is that the introductory narrative frame, as in Radcliffe's *The Italian*, has no terminal counterpart. Lionel is afforded the novel's closing words—"the LAST MAN" (470)—a final emphasis that the world of the frame will not return. If an opening frame synthesizes the world of the novel's readers with its embedded representation, then the disappearance of a closing frame, in a sense, traps readers in the representation. Readers are left with no concomitant perspective, no moralizing voice to help them come to terms with the apocalyptic future, to ease them out of the plague and back into the relative safety of their present. We should heed the advice of Shelley's epigraph to the novel: "Let no man seek / Henceforth to be foretold what shall befall / Him or his children."[67]

3

Loose Ends

Melmoth the Wanderer *and* Confessions of a Justified Sinner

> She left the web, she left the loom,
> She made three paces through the room,
> She saw the water-lily bloom,
> She saw the helmet and the plume,
> She looked down to Camelot.
> Out flew the web and floated wide;
> The mirror cracked from side to side;
> "The curse is come upon me," cried
> The Lady of Shalott.
>
> —Alfred, Lord Tennyson (1842)[1]

> "And mind ye recommend weel that them 'at brake t' bits o' frames … suld be hung without benefit o' clergy. It's a hanging matter, or suld be; no doubt o' that."
>
> —Charlotte Brontë, *Shirley* (1849)[2]

Tennyson's embowered Lady of Shalott weaves a "magic web with colours gay" (l. 38) from images reflected in a mirror. Eventually, however, she grows tired of these "Shadows of the world" (l. 48)—especially after Lancelot makes his dazzling appearance—and decides to gaze upon the actual scene outside her window. Released from her loom, she flies from the tower and boards a boat, but is cursed to die before she reaches Camelot. Tennyson draws explicitly on the Gothic through the poem's engagement with the blurring categories of reality and representation.[3] On the surface, "The Lady of Shalott" reverses the stakes of Percy Shelley's "Lift not the painted veil" (1818): whereas the painted veil represents the "cobweb of semblances" that conceal the horror of the Real, Tennyson's poem seemingly juxtaposes the danger of reality against the safety of representation.[4] However, the Lady of Shalott sees shadows because she weaves from the dark side of the tapestry.[5] In this sense, she is an implication of the Real breaking through representation and penetrating reality—Shelley's fear and hope "who ever weave / Their shadows, o'er the chasm."[6] Although her living stay in reality is brief, she remains as a "gleaming shape" and a "dead pale" corpse to haunt the city's denizens: "And they cross'd themselves for fear, / All the knights at Camelot" (ll. 156–67). Most important, the Lady of Shalott's gamble is a destructive act: the mirror cracks, and the frame of the loom disjoints to allow the Real to pass through the loose threads of representation and to flow into the space of reality.

In Gothic novels, suggestions of the Real enter symbolic reality through a similar destruction of frames. The creature's authoritative jump into Walton's narrative in *Frankenstein* (1818) provides the foundation for even more disturbing frame-breaking by Gothic characters who followed. The titular protagonists in Charles Robert Maturin's *Melmoth the Wanderer* (1820) and James Hogg's *The Private Memoirs and Confessions of a Justified Sinner* (1824) similarly transgress narrative frames, but the characters' spectacular energies also blur spatial and temporal boundaries. To the confusion and frustration of editors and readers—both fictional and actual—Melmoth and Robert Wringhim defy definition and resist form. The narrative frames that are featured in both novels might be imagined through the metaphor of a weaving loom; the outermost frame that encases the threads of representation is under constant threat of being dismantled by the narrative force of figures from within (and perhaps behind). As in "The Lady of Shalott," the horror in *Melmoth* and *Confessions* emerges when the narrative web is allowed to "float wide"—when fictional creatures enter frames of reality, and dead threads become loose ends.

In his 1954 preface to *Melmoth the Wanderer*, André Breton writes: "One must wait until 1820 for a new meteor to detach itself from the ritual framework of the Gothic window and suspend its endless rain of ashes."[7] Maturin's novel "will consume, in flashes of great spiritual scope, all the power that remains in a genre that continues to falter at the hands of mercenaries."[8] Breton anticipates many critics by assigning *Melmoth* a distinctive, if not terminal, position in the history of the Gothic.[9] But most intriguing is his metaphor of framing. Modern scholars have generally failed to consider *Melmoth* through the image of frames, but the effect was not lost on contemporary reviewers. The *London Literary Gazette* blasts Maturin for "out-Byroning Byron" and contends that "he might and ought to have avoided the monstrous framework in which he has exhibited this picture, or rather series of pictures."[10] The *Eclectic Review* similarly asserts: "Such is the frame-work of Mr Maturin's inventions, and such the foundation on which he has rested a strange and fantastic fabric."[11] *Melmoth* might be considered, following the early reviewers, as an intricately woven tapestry that presents a series of interacting vignettes, all precariously encased within a fragile narrative frame.[12] In the novel's largest embedded tale, the Spaniard Monçada compares monastic life to the "wrong side of tapestry, where we see only uncouth threads, and the harsh outlines, without the glow of the colours, the richness of the tissue, or the splendour of the embroidery, that renders the external surface so rich and dazzling."[13] This metaphor recalls Walton's fear in *Frankenstein* over encountering the "reverse side of the picture."[14] The novel's tapestry is Monçada's tale—the text that meets the frame at both ends. Rather than seeing the "glow of colours," however, Maturin places readers immediately and irrevocably on the dark side of the tapestry and into the Real horror that is woven by the figure of Melmoth. "[T]he facility with which [Melmoth] has been observed to pass from region to region" is an extraordinary example of metalepsis: from tale to tale he moves, "knowing all, and known to none" (397), until he enters the space of the frame, and perhaps escapes beyond it.

Melmoth is built on an elaborate network of framed tales, which are almost always unstable, fragmented, or otherwise incomplete. Maturin's framing aesthetic intensifies Radcliffe's sublime to the end that characters, environments, and even plot are veiled in an ominous obscurity that rarely seems contained by any structure.[15] Victor Sage notes that the novel "cultivates a labyrinthine form without a centre."[16] Indeed, the passageway through Monçada's central narrative is a labyrinth of blind alleys and dead ends, yet Maturin provides no Ariadne to challenge the mazes, and the ball of thread simply keeps unwinding. Where negotiable, or even tangible, the plot concerns the shadowy movements of Melmoth, who made a Faustian pact for a cryptic set of powers that include partial immortality. In hopes of relieving his burden, Melmoth supernaturally appears in such restricted spaces as a madhouse and the dungeons of the Inquisition to market his powers to desperate customers. "When they are plunged in the lowest abyss of human calamity," he boasts, "*they are sure to be visited by me*" (45). The novel's most complete feature is—paradoxically—its inscrutable protagonist, who looms large yet remains frustratingly abstract. Melmoth's "charmed life, 'defying space and time'" (66), allows him to wander freely (though not unencumbered) through the novel's complex architecture. He breaks narrative frames, bores through physical boundaries, and penetrates delicate psyches to affect and to infect every action, every word. Melmoth's power, rather than establishing form, leaves it crumbling in his wake.

Initial reactions to *Melmoth* were generally hostile.[17] Most critics were left perplexed and annoyed by the novel's form, which was "singularly clumsy and inartificial," as its tales appeared to be "unconnected with each other" or "very inartificially connected."[18] Several reviewers accurately saw the novel's disparate narratives as possessing only one link, that of Melmoth himself. A remarkably prescient piece in the *Quarterly Review* observes that the novel's narratives are "contained one within another like a nest of Chinese boxes; but instead of being the effect of nice workmanship, Mr Maturin's tales are involved and entangled in a clumsy confusion which disgraces the artist, and puzzles the observer."[19] Imagining the novel as a framed tapestry might resolve some of its structural complexity, especially as an example of *mise en cadre* (to set within a framework). As in Radcliffe's novels, the outermost frame provides the circumstances for an ancient manuscript to be brought to light. But this narrative is so fragmented and incoherent that we must return to the initial frame to reestablish narrative coherence. Maturin thereafter introduces the novel's principal storyteller, Alonzo di Monçada, whose "Tale of the Spaniard" hosts several other narratives, each framed by the one preceding it. We travel, in confounding fashion, backwards and forwards through time, beginning in 1816; moving to the late seventeenth century in the initial manuscript; jumping back to the early nineteenth century; and then revisiting the seventeenth century for a series of tales before the frame returns. At the conclusion of all this chronological maneuvering, Maturin is obliged to remind us of his initial protagonist, "whose name perhaps the reader has forgot" (534).

Melmoth traverses these narratives with remarkable alacrity as "[o]ne whom these walls can never exclude" (155). Perhaps more significant, he is "independent of time and place" (44), able to disregard the cognitive categories that define our experience of reality. In the *Critique of Pure Reason* (1781), Immanuel Kant asserts that "space and time are only forms of our sensible intuition, and therefore only conditions of the existence of things as appearances."[20] By transcending these categories, Melmoth seems to exist outside experiential reality, what Kant would call the noumenal realm, "the domain beyond the sphere of appearances."[21] As such, Melmoth intimates the existence of an inaccessible and unknowable world that is analogous to Jacques Lacan's concept of the Real. He seems, in fact, to be carrying the burden of the Real; the power that allowed him to escape reality only showed him the horror that lies beyond the symbolic register. In this sense, Melmoth mirrors Percy Shelley's "one who had lifted" the painted veil: "A splendor among the shadows, a bright blot / Upon this gloomy scene."[22] Marketing his powers to only the most desperate customers, namely those in their "dying hour" (116), gives him the best opportunity to relieve himself of his burden. His subjects have the opportunity to escape reality, to break the bonds of time and materiality, but to do so would require living through the unspeakable horror that lurks behind the veil.

Edgar Allan Poe's 1842 comment that Melmoth "plots and counterplots ... for the entrapment of one or two souls, while any common devil would have demolished one or two thousand," ignores the level of horror that Melmoth hosts.[23] Time and again his temptations fail, for the glimpse of horror that he reveals proves too disturbing for even the most wretched subjects. Perhaps the most desperate of all is Walberg, whose family faces overwhelming poverty caused by a misplaced will. "He has offered, and proved to me," Walberg recalls, "that it is in his power to bestow all that human cupidity could thirst for, on the condition that—I cannot utter! It is one so full of horror and impiety, that, even to listen to it, is scarce less a crime than to comply with it!" (427). In a horrifying revision of the biblical story of Abraham and Isaac, Walberg nearly strangles his wife and children, rather than accept Melmoth's proposition. But the fortunate coincidence of his weak hands and his restored will ultimately prevents the murders.

The lengths that Walberg is willing to go to refuse the curse should motivate us to reconsider the terms of Melmoth's own pact. Whatever happened to the latter during his "travel[s] abroad" (26) was evidently more disturbing than any of the other characters' fates chronicled in the novel. Unlike the mythic plight of the Wandering Jew, or even the egomaniacal bargain of William Godwin's St. Leon, the terms of Melmoth's power are never revealed. However, the descriptors "assigned" (397), "commissioned" (435), and "accorded" (538) suggest that it may not have been a choice. The untold circumstances that caused him to accept the pact, in other words, might be the novel's most disturbing unresolved horror. In the 1820 preface to *Melmoth*, Maturin writes: "I cannot again appear before the public in so unseemly a character as that of a writer of romances, without regretting the necessity that compels me to it. Did my profession furnish me with the means of subsistence, I should hold myself culpable indeed in having recourse to any other, but—am I allowed the choice?" (6). It appears that Maturin was also compelled to accept a dark pact—the burdensome power of the Gothic novel. Indeed, as Robert E. Lougy argues, Maturin "almost certainly" modeled Walberg's wife, Ines, after his own wife, so the story of pecuniary hardship and supernatural temptation applies to both families.[24] While the fictional Walberg refused the panacea, however, Maturin sold his soul to "convers[e] with the visions of another world."[25]

Although Melmoth's mysterious power affords him the ability to "defy space and time," it nevertheless expires after a period of approximately 150 years. Thus, the supernatural spreads from the pre–Enlightenment era of the seventeenth century to the post–Napoleonic world of 1816, which comes precariously close to the novel's 1820 readership. "It must be remembered," one character remarks of the seventeenth century, "that at this period, and even to a later, the belief in astrology and witchcraft was very general" (26). Since Melmoth's appearance in the 1816 frame as the confirmed subject of the 1646 portrait provides proof of his supernatural powers, the contemporary world cannot separate itself from its irrational ancestry. This effect implicitly echoes the principal horror of *The Castle of Otranto* (1764), in which Horace Walpole's second preface reveals that the medieval monstrosities contained in the diegetic narrative were all along a product of an imagination located firmly in the enlightened world. With this in mind, we might also acknowledge the potential influence of yet another frame in the novel, the apparent editor whose explanatory footnotes dot, if not mar, the text. Victor Sage astutely observes that these footnotes "break the frame ..., and sometimes initiate jarring and even contradictory relations between text and context, fiction and historical fact, often creating further horror rather than authenticity."[26] For all of Melmoth's "defying space and time" in fact parallels the machinations of the intrusive editor. Twice in the novel footnotes admit to "anachronism," and the second qualifies this disclosure with the defiant "n'importe" (475). This note crucially suggests that "any" evidence in "The Lovers' Tale," if not in the novel as a whole, could be historically inaccurate. As in Radcliffe's novels, these anachronisms blur chronological boundaries—an effect that is mirrored and intensified through the distinctive performance of *Melmoth*'s narrative frames.

The novel's opening frame begins in 1816 as a young John Melmoth enters the grounds of his dying uncle's neglected and crumbling property: "He approached his uncle's gate. The lodge was in ruins, and a barefooted boy from an adjacent cabin ran to lift on its single hinge what had once been a gate, but was now a few planks so villainously put together, that they clattered like a sign in a high wind" (9). In contrast to the formidable gateway to the castle in Radcliffe's *The Mysteries of Udolpho* (1794), the estate's entrance functions as a symbol for the disintegrating frame of the opening narrative: "There was not a fence or a hedge round the domain: an uncemented wall of loose stones, whose numerous gaps were filled with furze or thorns, supplied their place" (9). The house itself is replete with broken frames that represent the novel's constant deconstruction. The "dismantled frame" of a window, for example, provides young Melmoth a decidedly un-picturesque view—if not a glimpse into the horror of the Real—of the "most cheerless of all prospects, … the garden of death" (25). The ominous landscape of Tennyson's "Mariana" (1830) comes to mind here, with its "clinking latch" and "glooming flats," which externalize the melancholy of the perpetually waiting title character.[27] The nightmarish environment in *Melmoth* demonstrates that much of the novel's horror is located in its frame, especially when it is contrasted against the lush ecosystem of the centrally located "The Tale of the Indians." As in Poe's "The Fall of the House of Usher" (1839), moreover, the precarious edifice draws a "harsh outline" (9), which foreshadows the disturbing scenes within. Young Melmoth's entrance into the house reveals the horror of his miserly uncle's final hours, as he slowly fades surrounded by a harem of obsequious, shadowy women, including a "withered Sibyl" (10), who is the novel's first storyteller. At his uncle's request, young Melmoth enters a secreted closet, which resembles the room in which Adeline finds her father's manuscript in Radcliffe's *The Romance of the Forest* (1791): "There was a great deal of decayed and useless lumber, such as might be supposed to be heaped up to rot in a miser's closet; but John's eyes were in a moment, and as if by magic, riveted on a portrait that hung on the wall" (17). In his dying gasps, young Melmoth's uncle assures his nephew that the figure in the painting is still alive, even though the portrait is dated 1646, and he reveals the existence of a manuscript that is connected to the curious painting. Although his uncle's will cautions that young Melmoth "had better not" read it, like many a Gothic character before him, "the wild and awful pursuit of an indefinite object, had taken strong hold of his mind" (22).

The heavily fragmented manuscript is penned by Stanton, an Englishman whose "incessant and indefatigable" (59) search for Melmoth eventually leads him to a madhouse, where Melmoth turns the tables and now stalks the den of desperation in hopes of passing his burden. At the conclusion of the manuscript, we return to the frame world of young Melmoth. The horror of the tale prompts him to heed his uncle's wish to destroy the portrait: "He tore it from the frame with a cry half terrific, half triumphant" (60). We might consider this scene as a metaphor for the novel's form. Young Melmoth's separation of the painting from its frame signifies his attempt to keep the embedded figure of Melmoth from entering his narrative space. But the painting becomes animated during this action: "as the wrinkled and torn canvas fell to the floor, its undulations gave the portrait the appearance of smiling," and young Melmoth "felt horror indescribable at this imaginary resuscitation of the figure" (60). This scene implicitly echoes an event in Walpole's *Otranto*, in which a portrait "quit[s] its pannel, and descend[s] on the floor with a grave and melancholy air."[28] There is little imaginary about the vitality of the portrait's original, however. Young Melmoth has already seen the figure in the portrait at his uncle's deathbed, and had been informed of its existence by an elderly servant, who "in her terror cried, 'Stop him,' but nobody minded her" (23).

After he disposes of his ancestor's relics, young Melmoth nearly drowns while witnessing a nearby shipwreck. During the chaos, he spots the figure in the portrait standing above him: "the object of his daily and nightly dreams was at last within the reach of his mind and his arm,—was almost tangible" (66). Melmoth is a suggestion of the Real that invades young Melmoth's dreams but remains tantalizingly out of reach in reality. Young Melmoth's swooning horror recalls Stanton's morbid pleasure as "he discovered the object of his search for four years" (43). But Stanton's public allegations of Melmoth's presence only lead him to the madhouse. Slavoj Žižek writes of the "point of utter madness in which fantasmatic apparitions of 'partial objects' wander around."[29] Stanton's madness occurs as a result of the "breakdown of the boundary separating reality from the Real."[30] This frame-breaking effect is disturbingly echoed in the novel's form.[31] Patrick Brantlinger engages Žižek to observe that the "multiplication of stories and texts within one main story ... gestures obsessively toward the 'traumatic kernel' of 'the Real.'"[32] The deeper level of reality established by several hypodiegetic narrative layers always converges on the ineluctable, inexorable figure of Melmoth. As Vijay Mishra argues, "[t]he many tales ... the many frames, *parerga*, delimit and make contingent what cannot be contained. It is this absence of containment, the failure of narrative to delimit and order ... that pushes Melmoth beyond the text to be 'presented' only through 'mediatizations.'"[33] In a sense, Melmoth is a representation of the abject, what Julia Kristeva argues "does not respect borders, positions, rules."[34] An intangible, un-frameable figure, he seems to exist outside the symbolic order of the novel, while nevertheless being fundamentally inescapable in it. Characters are simultaneously disgusted by his presence, and yet seek him out indefatigably. Thus, he is also a nebulous suggestion of Lacan's *objet petit a*, the "pure void which functions as the object-cause of desire."[35] Every character who encounters him describes the experience as a dream, or rather a nightmare that proves so traumatic that it irreparably disturbs reality: "not knowing whether to term it a waking dream, or a dream-like waking" (383). While his presence is a suggestion of the Real, his unexplained, impossible power *is* the Real, the horrifying remainder that escapes the process of symbolization and emerges at moments of trauma. Mladen Dolar defines the Real as "part of the individual that cannot successfully pass into the subject, an element ... that comes to haunt subjectivity once it is constituted as such."[36] Melmoth is this haunting, pre-symbolic element, as he seeks "to tempt spirits in woe, at their last mortal extremity" (435), the tipping point of the sublime when reality begins to dissolve. But the glimpse that he offers, which itself is still only words—whispered suggestions of horror that remain fundamentally unspeakable—ultimately deters each of his subjects.

In spite of his supernatural power, Melmoth remains frustratingly human, torn between reality and an inaccessible world. The conflict of his dual nature is most evident in "The Tale of the Indians," in which he seems genuinely to fall for Immalee, the sole inhabitant of a lush, tropical island. Cast as Eve to Melmoth's Satan, Immalee "tasted of the tree of knowledge, and her eyes were opened, but its fruit was bitter to her taste" (308). As the first Westerner she encounters, Melmoth also becomes a sort of Quetzalcoatl figure, and the tale, in some sense, restages the plunder of the Aztec Empire by Spanish conquistadors, who were deemed agents of a divine world. But the colonial politics in "The Tale of the Indians" are concentrated into the curious relationship between these seemingly disparate figures. While neither is an "Indian," they share the experience of being "othered" by people who regard them with fear. In their own ways, both are otherworldly, and Immalee remains so even after she is restored to her Spanish family and renamed Isidora. Alison Milbank observes that Melmoth chooses Immalee as the "tabula rasa ... for his attentions."[37] Indeed, the innocence of her primary experience becomes a palimpsest to be overwritten by Melmoth's images of horror: "You were the first human being I ever saw who could teach me language, and who taught me feeling. Your image is for ever before me, present or absent, sleeping or waking.... [T]he indelible image, is written on mine" (374–75). During his peculiar courtship, Melmoth transfixes Immalee with his stories of world suffering, which he narrates while she peers through a telescope at mainland India. The initial focus of his disturbing lessons is the hypocrisy of religion, which he confirms through a sickening panorama of mass death: "Such was the picture that presented to the strained, incredulous eyes of Immalee, those mingled features of magnificence and horror, of joy and suffering,—of crushed flowers and mangled bodies,—of magnificence calling on torture for its triumph" (293). Melmoth's next subject focuses on the misery of cities, which support a "new and singular mode of aggravating human wretchedness—that of contrasting it with the wild and wanton excess of superfluous and extravagant splendour" (302). Thus, Melmoth points to the conflict of ideology as the cause of worldwide suffering, the fundamental deadlock of social antagonism that Žižek equates with the Real. For Žižek, "class struggle" implicates the Real because it "designates the very antagonism that prevents the objective (social) reality from constituting itself as a self-enclosed whole."[38] The theological and economic antagonisms that Melmoth shows Immalee make her aware of the Real that erupts in social reality and that ceaselessly prevents its harmony. "Pain she never felt—of death she had no idea" (280), but Melmoth exposes her to both of these categories, which eventually culminate in her imprisonment and the mysterious murder of her "infant demon" (534). In some sense, then, he succeeds—not in relieving himself of his burden, but in distributing its horror.

At the conclusion of "The Tale of the Indians," Monçada "retrace[s] a short period of our narrative" (395) to follow Immalee's father, who hears "The Tale of Guzman's Family" and "The Lovers' Tale." The latter is ominously told by Melmoth himself. As with the creature's story in *Frankenstein*, however, it is mediated through several layers of narrative. After Monçada wraps up the disturbing finale to Immalee's miserable life, his narrative ends, and the novel returns to its frame. Young Melmoth has listened in rapt horror to the story that "occupied many days" (534), and requests to hear the sequel, as he is consumed with "wild hope of seeing the original of that portrait he had destroyed, burst from the walls and take up the fearful tale himself" (534). This is exactly what happens, for they have been "overheard" and "watched":

> at that moment the door opened, and a figure appeared at it, which Monçada recognized for the subject of his narrative, and his mysterious visitor in the prison of the Inquisition, and Melmoth for the original of the picture, and the being whose unaccountable appearance had filled him with consternation, as he sat beside his dying uncle's bed [535].

Melmoth's reappearance in the frame dramatically parallels *Frankenstein*. Similar to the creature, Melmoth not only appears in both the opening and the terminal frame, but he also dominates the discourse of the latter.

After some declarations of his intentions, coupled with dramatic pauses, Melmoth retires. "The Wanderer's Dream" is the last embedded tale in the novel. In the dream, Melmoth finds himself staggering on a precipice in total darkness, held by two arms, which turn out to be hands on a giant clock: "He saw the mysterious single hand revolve—he saw it reach the appointed period of 150 years ... he shrieked in his dream, and, with that strong impulse often felt in sleep, burst from the arm that held him, to arrest the motion of the hand" (539). Dropped from the giant "clock of eternity" (539), Melmoth grasps in vain at all those he tempted, falls into a Miltonic ocean of fire and awakens. Young Melmoth and Monçada return to find Melmoth, now withered, no longer resembling his portrait. He beckons them again to leave, and in the morning they see only signs of his flight from the house, footsteps that turn into marks of a dragging body that then terminate at an ocean cliff. The only indication of Melmoth's fall is a handkerchief—a loose end in more ways than one—hanging on the side of the precipice. As Ashley Marshall points out, "His final fate is inscrutable."[39]

As in *Frankenstein*, the lack of any resolution to Melmoth's fate leaves the conclusion decidedly ambiguous. Neither novel produces a body for evidence, the "cleansing violence" of death that later Gothic novelists like Dickens would take such delight in composing.[40] What is more, we are left with only a promise from Melmoth that he failed at finding a new host, which we should approach with as much reservation as we do the creature's guarantee of self-immolation. "The secret of my destiny rests with myself" (537), Melmoth remarks. Most unnerving, Melmoth's fate remains a mystery even to the frame's omniscient narrator. In contrast to the ambiguous conclusion of *Frankenstein*, which is narrated in first-person by Walton, the frame scenes featuring young Melmoth are narrated by an extradiegetic, third-person voice, who evidently remains as clueless about the mysterious figure as the characters he introduces. As Chris Baldick remarks, "[t]he whole creaky and lopsided structure ... is finally allowed to collapse."[41] Similar to the creature's jump in *Frankenstein*, the narrative structure fully breaks down when Melmoth enters the frame and then disappears from the novel, plummeting off the cliff of the narrative frame, the parergon threshold that separates fiction from reality. What is more, the implacable presence of Melmoth's Real lays bare the illusory reality of young Melmoth's frame. What he and Monçada have experienced lies beyond the symbolic register, so that the novel concludes as they "exchanged looks of silent and unutterable horror, and returned slowly home" (542).

An ambiguous Faustian pact is also a central feature of James Hogg's *The Private Memoirs and Confessions of a Justified Sinner*, but the novel's attention to the disturbing deconstruction of narrative frames is even more significant. *Confessions* is a preeminent Gothic text, featuring supernatural doppelgangers, murder mysteries, multiple and mutable perspectives and perhaps the most detestable protagonist in literature, Robert Wringhim. But the novel might best be remembered for its final moments in which a preserved corpse intensifies Radcliffe's "found manuscript" device to disturbing and disgusting ends. The triumphant appearance of Wringhim's body outside his memoir irreparably breaks the narrative frame and leaves the Editor—in a decisive moment of narrative destabilization—to admit: "I dare not venture a judgment, for I do not understand it."[42] Like Melmoth, Wringhim defies categorization and identification, and even when the Editor's biographical frame envelops and attempts to codify the mystery of his life and death, *Confessions* as a whole introduces—or rather unearths—more questions than it answers. Peter Garrett argues that the "editor becomes another protagonist in his story of discovery and another unreliable narrator in his bafflement."[43] Even readers must share the Editor's wonder: "WHAT can this work be?" (222). The ambiguity of *Confessions* is but one reason that the novel, in Penny Fielding's words, has proved both "fecund and frustrating."[44]

As with *Melmoth*, contemporary reviews of *Confessions* criticized its form and pointed explicitly to the framing structure of the novel. The *Quarterly Theological Review* contends that "[n]either the title, the subject, the frame-work, the filling up, the style, the language, nor the tendency, possesses … one single attribute of a good and useful book," and concludes that the "framework [is] disjointed and ill contrived; the filling up a heap of undigested matter."[45] The reviewer suggests not only that the frame is tenuous, but also that Wringhim's embedded manuscript is unintelligible and not fully realized. The judgment is accurate, but the reviewer fails to consider that these inconsistencies are part of Hogg's design for the novel. Other critics understandably found the dual narratives puzzling and incoherent. The *New Monthly Magazine* argues that "it is altogether unfair to treat the reader with two versions of such extraordinary trash," and the *Westminster Review* observes that the "author has managed the tale very clumsily, having made two distinct narratives of the same events; and however true it may be in mathematics, it certainly does not always hold in storytelling, that two halves are equal to one whole."[46] Once again, however, the incongruity of the sections—the often mismatched versions of Wringhim's history written by the Editor and Wringhim himself—is the novel's central theme, a challenge to both personal and editorial authority.

And the fragmented frames of *Confessions* undermine any sense of the novel being "one whole."

In a significant narrative move, Hogg dispenses with chapter distinctions. In some ways echoing the form of Thomas De Quincey's *Confessions of an English Opium-Eater* (1821), the novel refuses readers the customary pauses, the "Inn or Resting-Place" that Henry Fielding provides in *Joseph Andrews* (1742).[47] The prose, especially the embedded memoir, requires readers to participate in Wringhim's breathless adventure. As Ian Duncan argues, the novel "forges the contagious link whereby we find ourselves in Robert's situation."[48] Read linearly, *Confessions* is a triptych that consists of "The Editor's Narrative," the "Private Memoirs and Confessions of a Sinner. Written by Himself" and an unlabeled editorial return that follows the "End of the Memoir." At the conclusion of the opening frame, the Editor introduces Wringhim's text:

> I have now the pleasure of presenting my readers with an original document of a most singular nature, and preserved for their perusal in a still more singular matter. I offer no remarks on it, and make as few additions to it, leaving every one to judge for himself. We have heard much of the rage of fanaticism in former days, but nothing to this [116].

Wringhim begins his memoir by acknowledging his religious motives and calling on those who avoided his vengeance to give thanks to their "gods of silver and gold" (117). His was a life of sorrow, he records, following in the footsteps of Goethe's doomed Werther. He makes a father out of the Reverend Wringhim, who "knew the elect as it were by instinct" (120), and early on displays his proclivity towards malice. Yet Wringhim's memory is at best selective: at one point he admits, "I cannot from memory repeat his words" (144), but then at the next, "I remember my actions and words as well as it had been yesterday" (147). Wringhim's recall appears to be tied to his fatal narcissism; only his own thoughts and actions are worth remembering. More important, if Wringhim cannot remember other characters' words, then he discounts the accuracy of the oral testimony promoted by the Editor.

Wringhim's adoptive father formally appoints the boy as one of the elect, a condition that immediately heralds the appearance of the mysterious Gil-Martin. "I come now to the most important period of my existence," Wringhim ominously recalls, "the period that has modeled my character, and influenced every action of my life,—without which, this detail of my actions would have been as a tale that hath been told—a monotonous *farrago*—an uninteresting harangue—in short, a thing of nothing" (129). Read in terms of Lacan's "mirror-stage," Gil-Martin is initially Wringhim's "Ideal-I," the un-fractured image that we yearn for but never attain. That Gil-Martin does not appear in the Editor's Narrative might suggest that he cannot exist in the Editor's symbolic reality, and is instead a product of Wringhim's imagination, a residue of the imaginary order. Žižek observes that the "double embodies the phantom-like Thing in me; that is to say, the dissymmetry between me and my double is ultimately that between the (ordinary) object and the (sublime) Thing. In my double, I don't simply encounter myself (my mirror image), but first of all what is 'in me more than myself.'"[49] Put this way, Gil-Martin suggests the existence of the Real that is at the core of Wringhim's pre-symbolic existence. As in Radcliffe's novels, however, the sublime Real overwhelms reality. "[T]hey say that he whiles takes your ain shape," the servant Samuel explains, "or else enters into you, and then your turn a deil yourself" (189). Žižek writes elsewhere that "my double is not my shadow; on the contrary, its very existence reduces *me* to a shadow. In short, a double deprives me of my being.... What is so terrifying in encountering my double is that its existence makes me a copy and it the original."[50] Gil-Martin persuades Wringhim to begin purging the earth of its reprobates, but the latter takes on the burden of the crimes. Charged with multiple murders, Wringhim flees from his sanguinary double, and goes on the lam in the Scottish borderlands.

Wringhim's first stop takes him to the house of a weaver, who becomes suspicious when the former stumblingly says his name is Cowan, rather than revealing Colwan. "I was feared ye might be that waratch" (201), the weaver warns. Wringhim fails to assuage the weaver's misgivings, and he is locked inside a room with "looms, treadles, pirns, and confusion without end" (202)—the first sign of his cognitive disorientation. "[I] went doiting in amongst the weaver's looms," he recalls, "till I entangled myself, and could not get out again without working great deray amongst the coarse linen threads that stood in warp from one end of the apartment unto the other" (203). Wringhim becomes trapped within the frame of the weaver's loom, what Jason Marc Harris calls the "legendary matrix of the folk."[51] The weaver appears, calls Wringhim a devil, and asks how the unwelcome visitor became entangled. "I wanted to be at the light," Wringhim explains, "and have somehow unfortunately involved myself in the intricacies of your web" (203). Like a moth to a flame, he stumbles into a spider's threads, and the more he moves, the more stuck he becomes:

> My feet had slipped down through the double warpings of a web, and not being able to reach the ground with them, (there being a small pit below,) I rode upon a number of yielding threads, and there being nothing else that I could reach, to

> extricate myself was impossible. I was utterly powerless; and besides, the yearn and cords hurt me very much.... I determined to get out of his meshes at any risk. This effort made my case worse [204].

Wringhim's entanglement in the loom symbolizes his entrapment within the novel itself, as his memoirs are embedded within the Editor's frame narrative. As Kirsten Stirling points out, since the etymology of "text" is "that which is woven" (OED), Wringhim, "caught in the threads of the loom, is caught in the 'intricacies' of the text itself."[52] Both of these framings are only temporary, however: the weaver eventually capitulates to his wife's reasoning and "slacken[s] the web to release" (205); and the Editor ultimately relinquishes control over the subject of his narrative. In fact, the weaver's skepticism concerning Wringhim's identity and intentions parallels the Editor's confusion about the subject of his text: "I confess that I do not comprehend the writer's drift" (232). Wringhim's release from the loom, moreover, foreshadows his similar escape from the boundaries of his diegetic memoir. The Editor's narrative frame, which is meant to contain and to manage, loses its grip on Wringhim when his body miraculously appears outside the confines of his text. Like *Frankenstein* and *Melmoth*, the horror of Hogg's novel rests not only in the monstrosity's emergence in the frame, but also in its subsistence beyond the text. The distinctive horror of *Confessions*, however, is that this survival is not a potential result to be gleaned from the ambiguity of the novel's conclusion, but rather a material reality, as preserved pieces of the body escape the structural and temporal boundaries of the novel itself.

The image of Wringhim caught in the loom also highlights the novel's attention to the complex network of social ideologies that emerged within the century-wide span between Wringhim's adventures and his gruesome excavation. The dual narratives that make up the novel, the Editor's frame and Wringhim's diegetic memoir, are frustratingly discordant because they come from conflicting ideologies. The work of a staid, perplexed editorial figure overlaps jarringly with the voice of an energetic, stubborn zealot. The points at which these texts diverge are the fissures in symbolic reality that suggest the Real. But even more trenchant is the looming specter of capitalism in the novel—the increasingly dominant and unceasingly merciless ideology that motivates not only the Editor's framing, but also Wringhim's frame-breaking. For the latter admonishes those who worship "gods of silver and gold" (117). The question is, then, where does Wringhim belong in a world driven by capital? Karl Marx likened ideology to a "false consciousness" that obscures the material reality of social conditions. For

Žižek, conversely, ideology is not an "illusory representation of reality, it is rather this reality itself which is already to be conceived as 'ideological.'"[53] Thus, the conflict of ideologies is a deadlock of antagonisms—a "coincidence of opposites"—that is not a product of symbolic reality, but is instead evidence of the Real.[54] The "inexorable 'abstract,' spectral logic" of capital is the hard kernel of the Real.[55] As Žižek scathingly remarks, "if life on earth disappears, capitalism will somehow remain intact."[56] The dominant ideology, capitalism or otherwise, attempts "to render invisible the impossible/[R]eal of the antagonism" in order to endorse the vision of a comprehensive social structure.[57] Wholeness is a fantasy, however, whether social, individual, or textual. While *Confessions* appears to be a complete text(ile), it is, in fact, a network of crisscrossing ideological threads, a matrix of contradictory narratives that leaves gaps in the symbolic network. These fissures, the points at which the tapestry's conflicting strands fail to cooperate, intimate the Real. When Wringhim is introduced to the "confusion without end" (202) within the weaver's workspace, he encounters the pre-symbolic welter of the Real—a state analogous to Kant's chaotic manifold of the senses that jar together discordantly until they are organized by the understanding. But the horror of this process rests in what remains, the excess that is left out of the synthesizing formation of subjective reality. Suspended within the frame of the loom, Wringhim is momentarily absorbed in the social network, the ideological antagonisms that suggest the Real. His release from the loom, however, signifies his abject status as "an outcast and a vagabond in society" (206). It appears that he is ultimately inassimilable in the social fabric. Embedded yet rejected by the frame, he is a "jettisoned object" who turns to suicide for peace and acceptance.[58]

The principal power of the loom scene, however, lies in the weaver's anger over Wringhim being a "poor man's ruin" (204); for implicit in this event of entanglement and violence is the contemporary history of Luddism, organized efforts to destroy the frames of weaving machines. Immediately suspicious of his mysterious guest, the weaver reacts "ungraciously," but Wringhim assures his host that his "concerns were with the poor of this world" (200). Temporarily placated, the weaver locks Wringhim in a small room in which "coarse linen threads … stood in warp from one end … unto the other" (203). The weaver evidently possesses quite a large weaving frame, sizable enough that it can suspend Wringhim's entire body. This evidence suggests that the weaver's loom is distinctive or at least special enough to be kept under lock and key. The technology for improving the efficiency of weaving looms existed since at least the early seventeenth century, but these modifications were banned by city authorities. It was not until John Kay invented the flying shuttle in 1733 that mechanized looms took hold permanently. As Eric Broudy explains, Kay's invention "for the first time ... allowed a single weaver to weave cloth that exceeded the breadth of his reach."[59] By the nineteenth century, in the midst of the Industrial Revolution, fully automated looms appeared. Marx writes that when the "instrument of labour ... takes the form of a machine, [it] immediately becomes a competitor of the workman himself ... and is constantly on the point of making him superfluous."[60] Larger, more efficient machines made hand-weaving obsolete: "[h]istory discloses no tragedy more horrible than the gradual extinction of the English hand-loom weavers."[61] Nineteenth-century authors reflected on the issue regularly. In Elizabeth Gaskell's *Mary Barton* (1848), for example, Job Legh remarks: "It's true it was a sore time for the hand-loom weavers when power-looms came in: them new-fangled things make a man's life like a lottery."[62] Luddite "frame-breakers" took the matter into their own hands by engaging in the first widespread, methodical violence that targeted machines.[63] The weaver's reaction in *Confessions* to the potential damage of his looms suggests that he fears Luddite violence, which is not chronologically inconsistent with the 1712 setting of the event. Organized protests against weaving machines can be traced from at least the seventeenth century. In 1675, for example, rioters in London targeted automatic looms, arguing that "one man can do as much ... as near twenty without them."[64] Although Wringhim does not intentionally act as a Luddite, he is in the business of breaking frames. But his encounter with the weaver comes with a price, as the epigraph above from Charlotte Brontë's *Shirley* suggests. Like the Lady of Shalott, he is trapped by the design of a textual tapestry, and can only escape through death. His suspended pose in the loom, moreover, parallels the frontispiece to the first edition of *Confessions*—a handwritten facsimile of a late entry in his memoir: "hung by the locks over a yawning chasm to which [he] could perceive no bottom" (221)—which itself foreshadows his death, hanging from a hayrick.

When Wringhim's manuscript concludes, the Editor urges readers: "Attend to the sequel: which is a thing so extraordinary, so unprecedented, and so far out of the common course of human events, that if there were not hundreds of living witnesses to attest the truth of it, I would not bid any rational being believe it" (222). The Editor quickly subverts any chronological uniformity, however, by inserting an actual letter from *Blackwood's* signed by "JAMES HOGG," which "bears the stamp of authenticity in every line" (225–26). The Editor regularly appears to ignore the letter's "traditionary facts," even though it is in his possession. Yet Hogg begins the fiction even earlier, by writing to William Blackwood on 7 August 1823: "I send you in for Maga the particulars of a curious incident that has excited great interest here."[65] The letter, importantly, is only an extract, demonstrating again the Editor's proclivity to cut before pasting. Wringhim not only appears in the Editor's narrative as a preserved corpse, but he also becomes part of the world outside the novel in *Blackwood's*. Hogg accomplishes the inverse, traveling from completely outside the text and into it as a character—and an unhelpful one at that. A wonderful example of Derrida's parergon as an area of synthesis, Hogg jumps from the reality of his readership into his own fiction to interact not only with his Editor, but also with the body of his troubled protagonist.

Hogg's letter describes the location of a suicide's grave that comes with some "traditionary history" (222). The grave contains the remains of an "unfortunate youth" (223) who died one hundred years earlier. The day of his death, the despondent youth pleaded with a companion to stay with him: "Then if ye winna stay wi' me, James, ye may depond on't I'll cut my throat afore ye come back again" (223). This dialect is the first indication that Hogg has had a hand in fictionalizing the oral tale. At no point in Wringhim's memoir does he speak in Scots; rather, he explicitly sets his educated vernacular against that of people like the weaver. Hogg's characterization makes Wringhim sympathetic, a youth "remarkable for a deep, thoughtful, and sullen disposition. There was nothing against his character that anybody knew of" (223). There are no references in the letter to Wringhim's religious extremism, his murders, or Gil-Martin. In fact, Hogg never mentions Wringhim's name, as if it was lost through the many transmissions of the "disgusting oral tale" (224). The only allusion that might indicate Wringhim's appearance is when Hogg reports the grave to be located at "Cowanscroft," meaning a tenant farm run by the Cowan family—the name Wringhim adopted at the weaver's. The youth fails to return home, and a passerby finds him hanging by the neck against a hayrick. Even the death is a "singular circumstance" (224), for the youth hangs himself with a brittle hay rope that should not have held his weight. The next morning, servants wrap the body in a blanket, and bury it with the rope still intact. Over one hundred years pass when two men, "casting peats," find the grave and open it halfway, noting that the body has remained remarkably preserved. Seventeen-twelve meets 1823 in the grave.

Wringhim's journey into the nineteenth century echoes Melmoth's semi-immortality, the period of approximately 150 years that brings

Maturin's character into the 1816 frame. Whereas Melmoth's expiration leaves him haggard and (apparently) suicidal, Wringhim's exhibition is a disturbingly violent act that leaves him in pieces. The Editor and his accomplices disinter Wringhim's corpse and make note of its remarkable preservation. They remove portions of the body, bit by bit, noting that a "number of the bones came up separately," and then "[s]oon afterwards we found the skull, but it was not complete" (229). The men pick through Wringhim's clothes, which are especially well preserved. "I brought samples of all along with me" (230), the Editor boasts. During this part of the excavation, they notice "a leathern case" that "contained a printed pamphlet" (230). The Editor takes possession of Wringhim's preserved memoir and "let[s] it stand as it is" (232) for publication. Thus, Hogg inverts the found manuscript device by placing it in the terminal frame. In this sense, we might follow one early reviewer's words: "In order to make the 'Private Memoirs' which are subjoined to this *narrative* in any degree intelligible, it will be necessary to treat them as if they were written in Hebrew, and to begin at the end."[66] Although the Editor claims to have taken great pains in examining the manuscript and gathering sources to reconstruct Wringhim's life, he is left perplexed: "I confess that I do not comprehend the writer's drift" (232). Wringhim's confessions about his crimes are paralleled by the Editor's confessions about his failure. As Ian Duncan observes, "[r]ead but not understood, the fanatic's memoir recedes into the darkness from which it was exhumed."[67] As in *Melmoth*, any sense of conclusion surrenders to confusion. But Melmoth's ambiguous disappearance cannot measure up to the horror of Wringhim's preserved remains, which not only appear in the Editor's frame, but also in a *Blackwood's* letter.

The breakdown of frames in *Confessions* becomes even more disturbing if we are to believe the 1895 account of William Amos: "The Suicide's grave was no myth, but a reality which I have visited several times."[68] In addition, David Groves has examined the testimony of John Burnett, who knew Hogg in the 1820s. According to Burnett, Hogg set off one day to confirm a story told by his grandfather, which concerned a suicide's grave. Burnett alleges that Hogg came back with some clothes of a body that "had been buried in the moss just as he was, with the hay-rope still round his neck, and the moss had preserved them from decay."[69] If Hogg actually did unearth a grave and came away with clothes from the body, then he is represented in the novel not only by the Scots-speaking "James Hogg," but also by its bumbling Editor. What is more, the actual suicide's grave suggests that Wringhim has passed through several frames—from the novel, to the *Blackwood's* letter, and finally into reality. There is perhaps no more unsettling example in Gothic literature of reality being permeated by the Real, and it comes at a fitting moment, when the Romantic-era Gothic appears to have been absorbed by the purportedly more realistic Victorian novel.

Interlude

The Fabric of Reality

Sartor Resartus

> The true Romance ... is not merely a conjurer's trick box, full of flimsy quackeries, tinsel and clap traps, meant only to amuse, and relying upon deception to do even that. Is it not something better than this? Can we not see in it an instrument, keen, finely tempered, flawless—an instrument with which we may go straight through the clothes and tissues and wrappings of flesh down deep into the red, living heart of things?
>
> —Frank Norris, "A Plea for Romantic Fiction" (1901)[1]

> I think also that our bodies are in truth naked. We are only lightly covered with buttoned cloth; and beneath these pavements are shells, bones and silence.
>
> —Virginia Woolf, *The Waves* (1931)[2]

In December 1839, Mary Shelley wrote to Thomas Carlyle requesting assistance to identify a Goethe quotation she hoped to use for Percy Shelley's posthumous *Essays, Letters from Abroad, Translations and Fragments* (1840). Carlyle could not recall the exact words but made arrangements to forward Shelley a copy of his translation of *Wilhelm Meister's Apprenticeship* (1824).[3] At this point in her career, Shelley had focused her efforts on editing her late husband's works, a project that had been delayed for well over a decade.[4] Although Shelley planned initially to use a quotation from Goethe, she ultimately favored two other authors for her epigraphs—Friedrich Schiller and Carlyle.[5] That Shelley not only sought out Carlyle's guidance, but also gave his words such a prominent place in the text, is not surprising. By late 1839, Carlyle was one of the world's most influential voices. What is perhaps more unexpected, however, is the debt that Carlyle owed to Shelley. Indeed, his *Sartor Resartus* (1833–34) is a direct descendant of the Gothic novel that Shelley had such an integral hand in forging.

For Carlyle's masterpiece not only gestures back to the formal innovations of the early Gothic, but also lays a foundation for new explorations of the Gothic in the period that followed. Its stunning frame narrative—articulated through the metaphor of clothes—borrows most conspicuously from Shelley and Hogg, and its thematic logic is the product of a writer studied in the Gothic vision. Thus, *Sartor Resartus* not only ushers in Victorian values by engaging Romantic tropes, but it also bridges periods of the Gothic. Its prophetic philosophy, which blends natural and supernatural by manipulating the frame between reality and the Real, readies the Gothic for its transition into the Victorian novel. Perhaps most surprising, the spectacular energy of its frame narrative reveals that *Sartor Resartus*—like its stormy, misunderstood author—has its demons.

Carlyle's reading of the Gothic novel is well worth documenting, for his alleged antipathy toward the genre has been generally overstated. In 1817, he suggests the powerful draw of the Gothic: "The other night I sat up till four o'clock, reading Matthew Lewis's Monk."[6] The novel was evidently engrossing, but Carlyle was left disturbed and unimpressed. In an 1818 letter, he asserts that the recently published *Frankenstein* "seems to be another unnatural disgusting fiction," and in 1846 he refers to the "Millocracy" in Lancaster as "rising like a huge hideous Frankenstein."[7] He mentions poring through Horace Walpole's works in late 1838 ("not a fibre of him is duncish"), though he does not specifically mention *The Castle of Otranto* (1764).[8] Carlyle's most significant exposure to the Gothic, however, came via his wife, Jane Welsh, who routinely reminisced on her reading of Ann Radcliffe as an adolescent, and even cast herself as a Gothic heroine during anxious nights in unfamiliar lodgings.[9] During a summer of oppressive heat in 1826, Jane writes to Carlyle's brother: "I dread we are going to see Mrs Shelly's [*sic*] 'Last Man' transacted in good earnest."[10] There is little doubt that Gothic novels, especially Shelley's, were a routine subject of conversation for the Carlyles during their years in the remote, wuthering environs of Craigenputtock, where Carlyle composed *Sartor Resartus*.[11]

Carlyle began writing *Sartor Resartus* in 1830, and by 1833 he had exhausted his search for potential vehicles for publication. In a 27 May 1833 letter to James Fraser, he writes: "I have determined to slit it up into stripes, and send it forth in the Periodical way."[12] Dividing the manuscript into portions fit for *Fraser's Magazine* is a wonderful reversal of the stitchwork that the novel's "Editor" must undertake. What was a complete garment Carlyle instead brings forth in periodical patches. He explains to Fraser that *Sartor Resartus* is "put together in the fashion of a Didactic

Novel; but indeed properly like nothing extant."[13] The formal "put-together" of the novel has baffled critics, which was doubtless Carlyle's intention. J. Hillis Miller attempts to unravel the text's "complex narrative machinery" by focusing on Carlyle's reasons for employing a "fantastic mode of indirection."[14] And Geoffrey Hartman points out the "book's crazy, mockingbird style," and attributes its "*bottomless* style" to sentences that are "themselves little abysses."[15] Indeed, through the distinctive effect of the text's challenging frame narrative, Carlyle does lead readers into an abyss, the Real infinity that lies within finite reality.

As with the Gothic novels that preceded it, *Sartor Resartus* requires readers to pass through a series of frames—or, to use Carlyle's metaphor, to strip off layers of clothing. The novel's first frame begins in Chapter 1 under the title "Preliminary." The introductory voice comes from the novel's "Editor," whose capitalized title immediately positions him as a character within the text that he edits.[16] "[T]he main Actor in the business," Carlyle explains to Fraser, "assumes a kind of Conservative (tho' Anti-quack) character."[17] Teufelsdröckh initially catches the Editor's attention through a "Presentation Copy" of his book, *Die Kleider ihr Werden und Wirken*. That Teufelsdröckh's book bears a publication date of 1833 suggests that Carlyle desires the Editor's work to appear ambitiously current, if not anxiously rushed, as *Sartor Resartus* began its serial run in November 1833. The Editor is baffled by Teufelsdröckh's mysterious book, an "'extensive Volume,' of boundless, almost formless contents, a very Sea of Thought," but he sees the importance of introducing it to his native readership, and then "through England to the distant West."[18] The manifest destiny that the Editor desires was realized in 1836 when the first complete edition—a fully tailored book—was published in Boston, through the diligent needling of Ralph Waldo Emerson.

In what is properly the first frame of the novel, the Editor travels to Weissnichtwo ("know-not-where"), where he gains partial access to Teufelsdröckh's domestic life, and soaks up many aphorisms, but leaves with little grasp on the furtive author. Upon returning to England, the Editor receives a parcel—the "found manuscript" of *Sartor Resartus*—from Teufelsdröckh's confidant, Hofrath Heuschrecke: "Six considerable PAPER-BAGS, carefully sealed, and marked successively, in gilt China-ink, with the symbols of the Six southern Zodiacal Signs, beginning at Libra; in the inside of which sealed Bags lie miscellaneous masses of Sheets, and oftener Shreds and Snips" (59). The loose leaves of Teufelsdröckh's papers echo the opening frame of Mary Shelley's *The Last Man* (1826). As with Lionel Verney's manuscript, Teufelsdröckh's memoirs "fly loosely on separate slips, like Sibylline leaves" (59).[19] The chaos of the papers only adds to the obscurity of Teufelsdröckh's book, and finding substance will require "unheard-of efforts, partly of intellect, partly of imagination, on the side of Editor and of Reader" (60). Carlyle adds another piece to the puzzle, however. Whereas Shelley's editorial figure in *The Last Man* acts as a "decipherer," who has "been obliged to add links, and model the work into a consistent form," Carlyle assigns not only his Editor as an interpreter, but also the reader.[20] And it is a process that requires both erudition and imagination. The Editor explains his responsibility: "To pick out the choicest Plums, and present them separately on a cover of our own" (214). The "cover" not only represents the Editor's narrative frame that attempts to envelop Teufelsdröckh's work and life, but also functions as metaphorical clothing, the fabric of the Editor's "phantasm world" (14). *Sartor Resartus* exposes, like no other nineteenth-century novel, the roles of every actor involved in shaping the text's meaning, but it challenges the work of these figures, who search for truth unequipped with Teufelsdröckh's vision.

As several critics have pointed out, the puzzling structure of the text invites readers to participate in Teufelsdröckh's "Philosophy of Clothes."[21] The strands of metaphor and allusion, theory and biography, must be patterned, cut, and stitched-together by a series of tailors. While the Editor arranges the loose leaves of Teufelsdröckh's life, retailoring the tailor, readers must repeat the act, retailoring the retailor. The issue, however, is that *Sartor Resartus* vehemently argues for a removal of clothes, a disrobing of deceptive vestments. Any attempt to tailor means participating in the artifice that Teufelsdröckh hopes to challenge. Through the very act of reading, of attempting to weave the threads into a comprehensive outfit, we only create more illusion. In this way, *Sartor Resartus* follows the Gothic mode by suggesting that the search for material truth is futile. The novel is a loose, baggy monster in more ways than just Teufelsdröckh's autobiographical zodiac papers. The Gothic monstrosity is, in a sense, the novel itself. Unruly and obscure, like Frankenstein's creature, it is a lettered representation of its powerful central figure. That Teufelsdröckh remains a mystery, "not so much a Man as a Thing" (14), casts him partially in the darkness of the Gothic figures that preceded him. Like the creature, Melmoth, and Robert Wringhim, Teufelsdröckh, "the Wanderer" (59), resists frames, and his ambiguous disappearance at the end of the text indicates that he has jumped beyond the Editor's frame of reference. "Teufelsdröckh, is actually in London!" (218), the Editor surmises, but as the Professor draws closer to the Editor's geographic sphere, he is nevertheless "lost in

Space!" (216). Teufelsdröckh was easy to locate in the fantasy village of Weissnichtwo, but in the reality of London he vanishes. He has managed, in a sense, to outstrip the Editor's tailoring. This effect of metalepsis echoes the movement of earlier Gothic villains into extradiegetic frames, but it perhaps most eerily anticipates Dracula's relocation from the foreign landscape of Transylvania into the readerly space of London, where "he might, amongst its teeming millions, satiate his lust for blood."[22] In any case, the Editor's desire to see the text move from "England to the distant West" (10) suggests the uncontrollable spread of the novel's subversive vision. Although not as outwardly ominous as the plague in *The Last Man* or the vampire blood in *Dracula*, it is no less disturbing. For Teufelsdröckh's philosophy rests in shattering the illusory vestments of reality and uncovering the Real—in all its horror—that lurks behind.

Teufelsdröckh's resistance to being framed within his biography makes him an embodiment of his own philosophy. Since the "[s]hows of things oppress him, withstand him, threaten him with fearfullest destruction" (152), he accomplishes a "complete rending and burning" of the Editor's flashy dream-coat by providing materials (through his equally devious proxy Heuschrecke) that defy comprehensive reconstruction. Carlyle's project in great part rests on a destabilization of narrative authority, which resembles Hogg's *The Private Memoirs and Confessions of a Justified Sinner* (1824) and Radcliffe's *Gaston de Blondeville* (1826). The question mark that concludes the novel epitomizes the Editor's failure.[23] Carlyle acknowledges that the text has likely irritated many readers, most of all the editors at *Fraser's*: "have we not existed together, though in a state of quarrel?" (218). To read *Sartor Resartus* effectively requires readers to follow Teufelsdröckh by "look[ing] through the Shows of things into Things themselves" (152). Carlyle's concept of the true "Thing" explicitly channels Immanuel Kant. As an avid reader of German Idealism, Carlyle would have been familiar with Kant's *das Ding an Sich* ("the thing in itself"), which exists in an inaccessible realm beyond the reach of our sense-experience. "I still understand Kant to be the grand novelty," Carlyle writes in 1841, "the prime author of the new spiritual world."[24] *Sartor Resartus* urges readers to remove the illusory vestments of reality to access deeper truth, and Carlyle constructs the text in such a way that they may practice this performance through the very act of reading, deciphering, and discarding. For the Editor's frame is the novel's clothing, "the fair tapestry of human Life" (50), which must be stripped off in layers until the kernel of Carlyle's vision is revealed. In the "stupendous Section, headed *Natural Supernaturalism*," the Editor correctly explains: "the Professor first becomes a Seer," and his philosophy "attains to Transcendentalism" (187). At "this last leap" we remove the final textile frame and arrive at heart of the matter, the uninterrupted, naked words that "grow clear, nay radiant, and all-illuminating" (187). But this is a disturbing process, as Teufelsdröckh admits: "these considerations … fill me with a certain horror at myself and mankind" (44).

Yet this effect still fails fully to resolve Carlyle's system of frames that constitute the novel's "fantastic mode of indirection," in Miller's words.[25] One possible answer is that the Editor's narrative provides a frame that ensures readers a passageway from their reality into the Real abyss of Carlyle's visionary philosophy. "Society sails through the Infinitude on Cloth," Teufelsdröckh observes, "and without such Sheet or Mantle, would sink to endless depths, or mount to inane limbos, and in either case be no more" (40). The Editor's narrative is a cover that keeps readers from descending too suddenly, from being absorbed too violently into the disturbing Real. Jacques Derrida asserts that the parergon "economize[s] on the abyss … [and] save[s] oneself from falling into the bottomless depths by weaving and folding back the cloth to infinity."[26] The frame of the parergon provides a seemingly secure position from which to view the abyss without falling directly into it. As with previous Gothic novels, however, the concluding disappearance of the shadowy central figure suggests not only irresolution, but also indicates that the frame has collapsed. The Editor muses on the incomplete record of Teufelsdröckh's later travels: "is it not strange that … there exists nothing like an authentic diary of this his sojourn in London" (179). It is strange, indeed, that the novel's central figure manages to vanish from the text. As with Shelley's creature and Maturin's Melmoth, Teufelsdröckh escapes the limits of the extradiegetic narrative and perhaps enters the reality of the reader. The horror of *Sartor Resartus* is that "safe-moored in some stillest obscurity, not to lie always still, Teufelsdröckh, is actually in London!" (218).

Although Teufelsdröckh spends his early years in the Editor's reality, heartbreak lifts the veil and "thick curtains of Night rushed over his soul, as rose the immeasurable Crash of Doom; and through the ruins as of a shivered Universe, was he falling, falling, towards the Abyss" (111). He is cast into the dark vacuum of the Everlasting No, where his experience mirrors Percy Shelley's "one who had lifted it," the lone brightness among shadows. "[I]t was a strange isolation I then lived in," Teufelsdröckh recalls: "The men and women around me, even speaking with me, were but Figures" (124). He looks at the world from the dark side of the tapestry and sees the people woven there as mere apparitions. Eventually, he experiences a "conversion" through the Centre of Indifference and into the Everlasting Yea, a state in which he sees "all Matter and Material things as Spirit" (23). He comes to understand the world of reality as a "phantasy of our Dream" (43), and the Editor's frame becomes one of the "fantastic Dream-Grottoes through which ... he must wander" (152). The "boundless Phantasmagoria and Dream-grotto" is a "[c]anvas ... whereon all our Dreams and Life-visions are painted" (42). The hegemony of custom masks the miracle of everyday events, for custom "is the greatest of Weavers; and weaves air-raiment for all the Spirits of the Universe" (190). Teufelsdröckh leads readers "into the true Land of Dreams; and through the Clothes-Screen" to experience the "region of the Wonderful" (198). Yet the Everlasting Yea is itself only a fantasy, an illusory screen that covers the horror of the Everlasting No, the hard kernel of the Real. Like Shelley's "bright blot," who walks among shadows fruitlessly searching for truth, Teufelsdröckh cannot fully shake off the experience of the Everlasting No—the horror that lurks behind the painted veil and shivers beneath the fabric of reality. At one point, he ruminates on the curious capacity of humankind to "live at ease in the midst of Wonders and Terrors" (44), for we get the feeling that it is impossible for Teufelsdröckh to re-experience this "ease," to return to reality.

In the "stupendous" chapter on "Natural Supernaturalism," we follow Teufelsdröckh, who "severs asunder the confusion; sheers down, were it furlongs deep, into the true centre of the matter" (187, 23), by weaving through the Editorial banter and biographical chaos to arrive at the surprisingly Gothic heart of the novel's philosophy:

> Witchcraft, and all manner of Spectre-work, and Demonology, we have now named Madness, and Diseases of the Nerves. Seldom reflecting that still the new question comes upon us: What is Madness, what are Nerves? Ever, as before, does Madness remain a mysterious-terrific, altogether *infernal* boiling-up of the Nether Chaotic Deep, through this fair-painted Vision of Creation, which swims thereon, which we name the Real.... In every the wisest Soul lies a whole world of internal Madness, an authentic Demon-Empire; out of which, indeed, his world of Wisdom has been creatively built together, and now rests there, as on its dark foundations does a habitable flowery Earth rind [191].

Carlyle's conception of Gothic madness is an astounding antecedent to Lacanian psychoanalytic theory. The Gothic Real boils and bubbles behind the fantasmatic frame until it bursts "through this fair-painted vision" and manifests itself in the outward signs of madness. Slavoj Žižek writes of the "barrier separating the Real from reality" and asserts that "madness—psychosis—sets in when this barrier falls down and the Real either overflows into reality … or is itself included in reality."[27] This madness is embodied by Gothic creatures that escape the abyss and challenge the authority, if not sanity, of frame narrators. We might consider Teufelsdröckh, then, as a complex reproduction of these creatures, as he similarly disrupts the very existence of the Editor's world through his manipulation of frames. "We stand in a region of conjectures," the Editor concludes, "where substance has melted into shadow, and one cannot be distinguished from the other" (218). It seems that the professor's life and work have caused the fabric of reality to begin to unravel, and the enduring horror of the novel is that Teufelsdröckh holds the thread as he walks away.

In his essay "The Diamond Necklace" (1837), Carlyle remarks: "Romance exists … in Reality alone."[28] Yet to enter this hidden world, to transcend the limits of reality, requires great sacrifice. As with Shelley's "one who had lifted it," once Teufelsdröckh accesses the Real truth behind the veil, his contact with reality may yield only illusion. He interacts with figures in the Editor's frame with a "strange scientific freedom; like a man unversed in the higher circles" (23). As a result of his encounter with the Everlasting No, he irrevocably becomes a kernel of truth hiding out in a world of lies, a "bright blot" wandering in a sea of shadows; he is, paradoxically, the natural among the supernatural, the horror of the Gothic Real passing through the fabric of reality and shattering the hegemonic frames of symbols and sensations. In this sense, reality is romance and the Real is real. Early Victorian authors carried out this prophecy by finding in the Gothic particular forms and fashions to weave into the tapestry of everyday life. Martin Willis's recent argument is crucial: "Realism's invocation of the Gothic mode … is central to the creation of meaning."[29] But we would be remiss to ignore that this effect is a realization of Carlyle's vision: Natural Supernaturalism is Gothic realism.

4

The "science of human brutality"

Wuthering Heights *and* The Tenant of Wildfell Hall

> [O]ver much of "Wuthering Heights" there broods "a horror of great darkness."
>
> —Charlotte Brontë (1850)[1]

> The darkness drops again but now I know
> That twenty centuries of stony sleep
> Were vexed to nightmare by a rocking cradle,
> And what rough beast, its hour come round at last,
> Slouches towards Bethlehem to be born?
>
> —W. B. Yeats, "The Second Coming" (1920)[2]

In an 1848 review, G. W. Peck observes that *Wuthering Heights* "lifts the veil and shows boldly the dark side of our depraved nature."[3] By evoking Percy Shelley's "Lift not the painted veil," Peck suggests the existence of a deeper level of reality, the Real that operates as the chaotic register of pre-symbolic existence. The intricately layered narratives in Emily Brontë's *Wuthering Heights* (1847) and Anne Brontë's *The Tenant of Wildfell Hall* (1848) function as symbolic veils between the reader's reality and the "depraved nature" featured within—the heredity horror that can be neither extinguished nor controlled. In the pre-genetic scientific landscape of the Brontës' 1840s, the biological elements that span generations intimate the Real because they are similarly inconceivable yet inescapable.[4] As in previous Gothic novels, the framing devices in *Wuthering Heights* and *Wildfell Hall* ultimately fail to prevent the Real from escaping the diegetic narrative. Yet this invasion of the Real is not only the result of narrative metalepsis, but also a product of genetic transmission, as dangerous biological traits pass through reproductive lines. Thus, the novels naturalize the anxiety addressed by the potential "race of devils" in Mary Shelley's *Frankenstein* (1818), "who might make the very existence of the species of man a condition precarious and full of terror."[5] The respective antagonists, Heathcliff and Arthur, possess what Slavoj Žižek would call the "horror of addiction and consumption"—an unbridled passion for emotional and physical excess, which suggests the Real and disturbs symbolic reality.[6] And what is most troubling is that these destructive qualities are not extinguished with the death of the host, but instead spread into the next generation, "second comings" who survive beyond the terminal frame. The Brontës suggest that monsters are neither made in labs nor molded in nightmares, but rather are formed through the implacable hand of nature. It is, as one reviewer remarks, a "science of human brutality."[7]

Lines of inheritance are linked to the novels' frames through the condition of tenancy. The characters who are tenants in the titular houses themselves play host to biological tenants that control appearances, attitudes, and behaviors. In an 1841 poem, Emily Brontë muses: "What tenants haunt each mortal cell / What gloomy guests we hold within."[8] By the time she wrote *Wuthering Heights*, Brontë understood that "gloomy guests" are traits inherited by offspring that inevitably transfer through reproduction into new generations. The narrative frames of *Wuthering Heights* and *Wildfell Hall* fail to restrict the passage of traits to new offspring, who survive beyond the limits of the text. While the novels' narrators move inside the frame and become characters in the diegetic world, dangerous descendants escape the "mortal cell" of the fiction and become part of the reader's reality. In her preface to the 1850 edition of *Wuthering Heights*, Charlotte Brontë remarks: "Whether it is right or advisable to create beings like Heathcliff, I do not know: I scarcely think it is."[9] As in Shelley's novels, we should be wary that the Brontës' new generations of creatures, loaded with their parents' destructive traits, have been permitted to "go forth and prosper." The monstrous horror that is born and bred within *Wuthering Heights* and *Wildfell Hall* spreads through reproductive lines and survives beyond the text—in spite of the narrators' concluding guarantees of "quiet slumbers" and "invigorating relaxation."[10]

Theories on the transfer of traits from parents to offspring are evident since at least classical Greece. In the early modern period, reproduction began to be understood as the "transmission and redistribution of a more or less atomized biological substance," but it was not until the early nineteenth century that the concept of heredity "began to gain currency in respect to organic reproduction."[11] French naturalist Jean-Baptiste Lamarck

(1744–1829) theorized that organisms pass traits to their offspring and became an early advocate for organic evolution. By the late nineteenth century, heredity "moved into the center of the life sciences."[12] But the Brontës were writing in earlier decades that saw concepts of heredity being applied to campaigns that were more social and occupational in nature. In the 1830s, activists presaged the deterioration of the human race that would result from unregulated hours, hazardous work conditions, and the influx of machines in labor. The defects would pass from generation to generation, becoming increasingly detrimental to the body of the nation at large. The phrase "Like begets like; each after its kind" was used liberally in these early essays, which suggested that nefarious biological characteristics proliferating through reproductive lines were the foundation of social suffering. In *The Manufacturing Population of England* (1833), Peter Gaskell argues:

> Bodily deformity, bodily defect, or ugliness, may not, nay, in general, will not be transmitted. But an universal weakness and want of tone in all organs, a disposition little able to resist disease, sufficiently prove, that although the child has not inherited the peculiar failings of its parents,—yet it has, as an heir-loom, their weakened constitution, attended with all its liabilities to physical inferiority.[13]

Activist pamphlets, statistical journals, and growing support for the Chartist Movement urged officials to pass laws to regulate working conditions, but it is important to consider the charged rhetoric that writers like Gaskell used, which suggests that the physical and mental deterioration of the social body was a matter of not just industrial conditions, but also hereditary transmission. Orson Squire Fowler, an American phrenologist, was a leading figure in the debate, and published *Hereditary Descent* in 1847—a productive year as well for the Brontës. Claiming that he possessed the "laws" and "facts" to promote "human improvement," Fowler warns his readers:

> Behold, O parents! … The destinies of your DEAR PROSPECTIVE CHILDREN are thus placed completely within your control. Nay, willing or unwilling, you are COMPELLED to wield them, or else not to become parents. A NECESSITY exists. Your children are OBLIGED to be what you are, and cannot help themselves.[14]

Fowler argues that children are guaranteed to be copies of their parents' dispositions, that the "physical and mental capabilities of mankind are INNATE, not created by education … [and] have a CONSTITUTIONAL character inherited from parents."[15] Perhaps the most influential voice in the debate was Robert Chambers, whose *Vestiges of the Natural History of Creation* caused a sensation when it was published anonymously in 1844. "What is a habit in parents becomes an inherent quality in children,"

Chambers observes: "sometimes not one, but several generations, may be concerned in bringing up the result to a pitch which produces crime."[16] It is likely that the Brontës either had access to Chambers' text or had read the meticulous and quotation-heavy review that appeared in *Blackwood's Magazine*.[17]

Issues of heredity appear to have been a routine topic of discussion in the Brontë household, best evidenced by the thematic focus on familial madness in Charlotte's *Jane Eyre* (1847). Theories on the possible inheritability of madness had been a charged debate in the early nineteenth century. In 1834, for example, George Parkman observed that insanity "belong[s] to the set of diseases which are generally considered to be hereditary."[18] Jane's description of Bertha Mason suggests that the latter is an implication of the Real in line with previous Gothic monstrosities: "I never saw a face like it! It was a discolored face—it was a savage face. I wish I could forget the roll of the red eyes and the fearful blackened inflation of the lineaments!"[19] In fact, Jane's horror at Bertha's "swelled and dark" lips, "bloodshot eyes," and "bloated features" (284) echoes Victor Frankenstein's revulsion at his creature's "watery eyes," "straight black lips," and taut, tenuous skin.[20] Žižek argues that "it is not possible to pass directly from the purely 'animal soul' immersed in its natural life-world to 'normal' subjectivity dwelling in its symbolic universe—the vanishing mediator between the two is the 'mad' gesture of radical withdrawal from reality."[21] That Jane cannot decide whether Bertha is a "beast or human being" (293) suggests that the boundary between reality and the Real has broken down for Rochester's troubled wife. When she is locked in a "wild beast's den—a goblin's cell" (309)—to be guarded by the intemperate Cerberus-figure, Grace Poole—Bertha is effectively removed from reality, which only encourages her return to the primal, animal state of the Real. Yet quarantine only exacerbates Bertha's madness, which results in her fatal plunge, the ruin of Thornfield Hall, and Rochester's disfigurement—all traumas of the Real that irrupt in Jane's reality.

When Rochester finally reveals the terms of his earlier marriage, he narrates a history of hereditary transmission: "Bertha Mason is mad; and she came of a mad family:—idiots and maniacs through three generations! Her mother, the Creole, was both a mad woman and a drunkard!—as I found out after I had wed the daughter: for they were silent on family secrets before. Bertha, like a dutiful child, copied her parent in both points" (292). Readers have explored Rochester's claims extensively and imaginatively—look no further than Jean Rhys's haunting Gothic novel *Wide Sargasso Sea* (1966)—yet there is no research that ties these issues of heredity to *Wuthering Heights* and *The Tenant of Wildfell Hall*. Bertha's death is a tragedy in *Jane Eyre* because "she cannot help being mad" (301), but it does ensure that her tainted bloodline is cut off. There is no threat of reproduction, no danger of hereditary transmission. Following Bertha's most savage attack, Rochester laments: "Such is the sole conjugal embrace I am ever to know" (293). The ideal fantasy of marital copulation becomes the Real horror of physical violence. At Bertha's death, however, the Real of her madness is extinguished, and the reality of Jane and Rochester may continue in the peaceful environs of Ferndean. The novel's only lasting unease may be the continued wanderings of the troublesome St. John Rivers. While *Jane Eyre* suggests that the Real of hereditary madness vanishes with the death of its host, *Wuthering Heights* and *Wildfell Hall* explore the terrifying possibility of reproductive transmission, of a ceaselessly proliferating biological horror that cannot be contained by narrative boundaries. The destructive traits exhibited by Heathcliff and Arthur survive through "second comings," who escape the narrative frame and enter the world beyond the text.

A reviewer for the *Atlas* accurately observes that *Wuthering Heights* is a "*sprawling* story, carrying us, with no mitigation of anguish, through two generations of sufferers."[22] But to arrive at the central story readers must first negotiate a series of disorienting narrative frames. The formal makeup of *Wuthering Heights*, which is so remarkable as to be one of its most defining and memorable elements, has proved both fascinating and frustrating to critics.[23] Early reviewers found the novel's structure muddled and outdated. The *Examiner* asserts that it is "wild, confused, disjointed, and improbable," and concludes: "It is not easy to disentangle the incidents and set them forth in chronological order"; the *Literary World* criticizes the "improbabilities and incongruities of the plot"; and the *Britannia* contends it was "very unskilfully constructed."[24] J. Hillis Miller excoriates scholarship on *Wuthering Heights* that fails to read its diversity of meaning, and argues that it is "not incoherent, confused, or flawed. It is a triumph of the novelist's art."[25] Lockwood's outermost narrative embeds Nelly's central story, yet because Nelly can report only what she witnesses, other narratives, in Beth Newman's words, "keep the story going."[26] The novel's intricate frames wrench chronology and insist on multiple readings, which may never account for the absence of narrative reliability. As a result, adaptations regularly opt for linear retellings, in spite of the fact that the novel "would be unimaginable without … framing."[27] As Michael S. Macovski argues, "interpretive valuations … distort almost every episode of the story."[28] While the several frames seem to screen readers from

Heathcliff's monstrous Real, they instead break down as the result of the diminishing authority of their narrators. This effect is perhaps most evident in Lockwood's attempt to become part of the horrifying reproductive transmissions of the very story he records.

Wuthering Heights begins with Lockwood's portentous first journal entry: "I have just returned from a visit to my landlord—the solitary neighbor that I shall be troubled with.... In all England, I do not believe that I could have fixed on a situation so completely removed from the stir of society" (3). The first line not only sets the stage for the novel's thematic concern with tenancy, but it also suggests that Lockwood has entered a disorienting alien world, a "misanthropist's heaven" (3) that is removed from symbolic social structures. As in *Melmoth the Wanderer* (1820) and "The Fall of the House of Usher" (1839), the environment outside the house both forewarns the horrors within, and also suggests that this horror has seeped through architectural boundaries and has begun to transform reality. Lockwood makes note of the sharp, deathly landscape and the "quantity of grotesque carving" on the building's exterior, which includes the unsettling combination of "crumbling griffins and shameless little boys" (4). Heathcliff reluctantly invites his overeager tenant inside, and the moment Lockwood "pass[es] the threshold" (4) into the Heights, he enters a space of the Real. It is a jarring entrance, "without any introductory lobby or passage" (4). The snarling, undomesticated animals that mirror the sneering inmates again suggest that Wuthering Heights is a primal space, a kernel of the Real rudely buried in the Yorkshire moors. Although he is unsuccessful at engaging its fiercely taciturn inhabitants, Lockwood nevertheless invites himself back. On his next visit, rather than being ushered in by Heathcliff, he trespasses the house by "jump[ing] over" the gate (7). Brontë implicitly evokes Satan's "slight bound" in *Paradise Lost*, but muddles the roles and the setting.[29] Milton's anti-hero is here the novel's narrator, and Eden is the Heights of hell. During this subsequent visit, Lockwood encounters Hareton and Cathy—the nightmarish Adam and Eve of *Wuthering Heights*—who prove as aggressively unwelcoming as their glowering landlord. "You should not have come out" (9), Cathy declares—as if recalling the "Abandon all hope" warning inscribed above Dante's gates of hell. Poor weather prevents Lockwood's escape, however, and he is forced to spend the night at the Heights. The space that he was so impatient to enter turns into a prison, defended by its Cerberus-like canine guards.

Without Heathcliff's approval, the servant Zillah deposits Lockwood in Catherine's old room, which functions as the haunted nucleus of the house. Enclosed within the frame of the bed, where he "fe[els] secure against the vigilance of Heathcliff, and every one else" (15), Lockwood reads diary-annotations scribbled in Catherine's books and notices different versions of her name etched into the window ledge. Dosing off, Lockwood recalls that the "air swarmed with Catherines," as potential permutations of her names become "vivid as spectres" (16), and haunt him before her ghost appears in a subsequent dream. We later learn that she chose the last of these possibilities as Catherine Linton, temporarily establishing a secure sense of reality as Edgar's wife. But Heathcliff's return from exile quickly shatters this identity. The mental and physical anguish she endures as a result of this re-emergence of the Real is evidence of the violent wrenchings between her mental registers. She is ripped from the reality of Edgar and reabsorbed in Heathcliff's Real. In their final encounter, Nelly recalls that they were "locked in an embrace from which I thought my mistress would never be released alive" (125). Thus, Catherine's earlier loaded admission, "I *am* Heathcliff" (64), indicates that she never fully moved on from the Real. Yet, as the ghost that haunts Lockwood's second dream, she identifies herself as Catherine Linton, suggesting that she remains part of the symbolic order, and cannot complete a reunion with Heathcliff's Real. Her desperate pleas, "Let me in—let me in!" (20), demonstrate her longing to return, but Lockwood denies this entrance, sliding her terrifyingly material wrists along the broken shards of the window pane. This corporeal violence perhaps releases her from Lockwood's dream, a kind of symbolic purgatory, and readies her for a grave-site rendezvous with Heathcliff—a putrid blurring of identities that signals abjection and suggests the Real.

Lockwood's eventual asylum at Thrushcross Grange marks the terminus of the novel's stunning opening frame and permits the introduction of the diegetic narrator Ellen Dean. The majority of Nelly's narrative not surprisingly focuses on Heathcliff, whose entrance into the Heights, embarrassed escape, and systematic revenge might be considered as a narrative of the Real overwhelming reality. As with the titular figure in *Melmoth the Wanderer*, Heathcliff permeates every part of the novel's atmosphere. The *Athenaeum* observes that he "so entirely fill[s] the canvas that there is hardly a scene untainted by his presence."[30] And in a 14 August 1848 letter, Charlotte Brontë asserts: "The worst of it is, some of his spirit seems breathed through the whole narrative in which he figures: it haunts every moor and glen, and beckons in every fir-tree of the Heights."[31] Dropped into the narrative as a foreign "other," he is an abjection that disturbs the insular sanctuary of the Heights and the

Grange. His violent drives and aggressive emotions suggest the pre-symbolic welter of the Real. Following Frederic Jameson, Žižek argues that Heathcliff "is not one among the novel's characters but a kind of zero-element."[32] "Rough as a saw-edge, and hard as whinstone" (28), he is a kernel of the Real that cannot be cracked, but that nonetheless proves simultaneously magnetic and repellent. Žižek writes that the Real is the "point of resistance, the traumatic 'indivisible remainder' that resists symbolization."[33] Heathcliff is just this sort of excess that distorts reality, an orphan who irrevocably destabilizes family structures. Charlotte Brontë perhaps puts it best: "a sentiment fierce and inhuman: a passion such as might boil and glow in the bad essence of some evil genius; a fire that might form the tormented centre—the ever-suffering soul of a magnate of the infernal world."[34]

Heathcliff's entrance into the Earnshaw household comes with significant context. As Nelly recalls, the Earnshaw patriarch departed one day to Liverpool and returned swaddling a ragged boy "as dark almost as if it came from the devil" (29). That the circumstances of Earnshaw's journey remain unexplained might lead us to question his motivations. His account of finding the urchin wandering the streets seems random, at best, and the fact that Heathcliff is named after a son that had died as a child suggests that Earnshaw knew all along what he would bring back from his journey—a replacement that he may favor over his other son, Hindley. Maja-Lisa Von Sneidern has pointed out that Liverpool was a thriving commercial port, especially during the slave trade, and that Heathcliff's "bloodline is unambiguously tainted by color."[35] When Heathcliff enters the Earnshaw household "social equilibrium is upset."[36] As Nelly remarks, "from the very beginning, he bred bad feeling in the house" (30). The symbolic order of the Heights and the Grange is shattered by the arrival of the Real, which is suggested through the threat of Heathcliff "breeding" with Catherine, mixing the blood of the foreign "other" into the secure domestic pedigree. We must question, however, just how stable these families were to begin with, for Heathcliff seems to aggravate the destructive traits latent in the Earnshaw bloodline. What is more, Heathcliff's momentous entrance into the family obscures another curious arrival. Hindley brings his new wife, Frances, to his father's funeral, but her background remains as mysterious as Heathcliff's: "What she was, and where she was born he never informed us" (35). It is crucial, as well, to remember that Frances reignites Hindley's hatred of Heathcliff, which might have died out with Earnshaw, whose favoritism for his adopted son sparked the initial antagonism.

As much as he is loathed by Hindley, Heathcliff becomes a favorite of Catherine, and the pair embark on an obsessive and destructive romance. Terry Eagleton argues that "[t]heir frenzied need for one another is a passion for the Real."[37] When compared to the reality of the more tepid relationships in the novel, the sheer aggressiveness of their love suggests the Real. As Gavriel Reisner observes, "[t]he visionary-spiritual passion between Catherine and Heathcliff is Real in its erotic ferocity and Imaginary in its relentless invasion of the self."[38] It is a pairing that retreats from the symbolic and flourishes in the Real—"the senseless amorphousness," Jerrold E. Hogle writes, "where … there is no separating subjectivities from the welter of physical elements blurring violently into and out of each other."[39] As Catherine puts it, "he's more myself than I am. Whatever our souls are made of, his and mine are the same" (63). But their union is forbidden by the reality of symbolic boundaries. When the Lintons usher the injured Catherine inside the Grange and banish Heathcliff outside, they create a social, racial, and economic barrier against the Real. Heathcliff relates that a servant "dragged me into the garden … and, bidding me march directly, secured the door again. The curtains were still looped up at one corner; and I resumed my station as spy" (40). The scene is an intriguing reversal of Shelley's "painted veil" metaphor: literally abjected from the symbolic world of the Grange, Heathcliff looks from the other side of the veil. And, certainly, his systematic ruin of the novel's two families suggests that he "weave[s] … shadows, o'er the chasm, sightless and drear."[40]

Catherine's spa-day at the Lintons persuades her to acknowledge the benefits of a life with Edgar, which should involve a complete (re)entrance into the symbolic order. However, when Catherine is restored to the Heights, she negotiates the architectural framework of the house, crawling out of skylights and along the roof to be with Heathcliff. She is at the point of no return; her famous words "I *am* Heathcliff" (64) suggest that she has already been integrated into the Real. Her repeated attempts at staying within the symbolic order, exemplified by her marriage to Edgar and her relocation to the Grange, only serve to hasten her death. She is torn between two forces, but there is no going back to reality. Indeed, Catherine embodies Freud's death drive, a desire to return to a pre-symbolic state, to re-experience the comparative comfort of the Real and its unstructured, primordial chaos. When Heathcliff prepares the coffins to open into one another, he ensures the moldering union of their two bodies. It is the utmost of the abject, a disgusting reminder of the materiality of human existence, which shatters the symbolic marriage that Catherine shares with Edgar: "I've no more business to marry Edgar Linton than I have to be in heaven" (63). In the grave, the rotting bodies meld together, blurring their identities into a material emblem of their united souls. They become the "eternal rocks" (64) that form the foundation of nature, the inalterable kernel of the Real that is the horror of reality.

As in earlier Gothic novels, the distinct dynamic of the layered narratives in *Wuthering Heights* brings out the seemingly concealed horror. The novel's innermost narrative, told in a letter by Isabella, is an important place to begin to articulate the effect of these permeable frames. Soon after her marriage to Heathcliff, Isabella reflects on her new husband's condition: "Is [he] a man? If so, is he mad? And if not, is he a devil?" (106). We might trace one of the origins of Heathcliff's madness to the event of his marriage. Žižek writes that the "true point of 'madness' is … imposing a symbolic order onto the chaos of the Real."[41] Heathcliff's symbolic marriage to Isabella wars with his Real passion for Catherine, which results in a fractured identity and irreversible psychosis. It is a condition that he ultimately cannot endure, and his remaining existence is a narrative of bodily decay and mental dissolution. Heathcliff's potential madness ought to be connected to Bertha's familial madness in *Jane Eyre*, for the horror is not only that Heathcliff may be mad, but also that he plans to pass his traits on to his offspring. He chooses Isabella as his partner for this transmission, and the narrative of their marriage plays out entirely within her two hypodiegetic stories—the letter to Nelly and a short narrative that follows her flight from the Heights. The product of this unsettling union, Linton Heathcliff, is born outside the narrative confines of the text, but emerges in Nelly's diegetic tale following Isabella's death. Thus, the new host for Heathcliff's destructive traits becomes part of the diegetic world of the novel and threatens to move beyond it via a marriage to Edgar and Catherine's child, Cathy. While Linton's fatal frailty ultimately foils Heathcliff's designs, Isabella's letter confirms that he, perhaps unconsciously, has made alternate arrangements for spreading his malignance. The forced pairing of Hareton and Cathy serves as a threat for a new host to transgress yet another frame, and the novel concludes before we are able to confirm the results of their relationship. Echoing the ambiguity of previous Gothic novels, especially *Frankenstein* and *Melmoth the Wanderer*, *Wuthering Heights* ends with few answers, as its complex narrative structure yields to implacable monstrous forces. Perhaps most disturbing, the novel's framework shows its vulnerability initially in Isabella's letter—what Nelly calls a "relic of the dead" (106)—which would appear to be the point at which readers are the most distant from the narrative horrors.

To borrow again from Yeats's apocalyptic vision: "Things fall apart; the centre cannot hold."[42]

Isabella's letter also provides crucial information to characterize the growing malignance of Heathcliff's protégé, Hareton. Speaking in his offensive "jargon," Hareton cautions Isabella to "frame off" (107). The distinctly Yorkshire term means "[t]o shape one's course; to go" (OED), and John T. Matthews reads it as suggesting the "sense of ceasing or vanishing."[43] Yet it seems even more crucial to the dynamics of the novel as a whole. At the very least, it presages the novel's collapsing framework, which relies not only on Hareton's assimilation of Heathcliff's monstrous energy, but also on the threat that he will reproduce. A permanent inmate at the Heights, Hareton never experiences the reality of the Grange, which should lead us to accept Von Sneidern's assertion that he is "Heathcliff's 'immaculate' creation."[44] In a typical fit of alcohol-fueled rage, Hindley yells, "By God, as if I would rear such a monster!" (58). Shortly thereafter, Hindley drops his son from a balcony and into Heathcliff's waiting arms. Once Nelly is banished from the Heights, Hareton becomes Heathcliff's "second coming," an aggressive, abusive brute, who revitalizes Heathcliff's Real. But we should also take seriously Q. D. Leavis's bold claim that "Heathcliff was originally the illegitimate son."[45] If accurate, this argument complicates reading Heathcliff as an outsider, for it could be that Heathcliff's destructive traits are not maternal, but rather come from the Earnshaw line. This would suggest that the Real is not a foreign power that destroys the families, but instead that it was a latent part of the family all along. Heathcliff's entrance into the narrative may only bring out the Real that exists within Catherine and Hindley. What is more, since Cathy is her mother's double in both name and behavior, she too may possess malicious Earnshaw traits, which would only become more dominant in her potential offspring with Hareton.

We might ultimately attribute the enduring horror of the novel to the work of its narrators, who encourage the transmission of the Real beyond the boundaries of the text. Bernard Duyfhuizen argues that Lockwood's active participation in the story "blurs [the] embedding structure" and renders the "threshold separating the levels extremely narrow."[46] When Walton meets the creature in the terminal frame in *Frankenstein*, the encounter conspicuously exhibits his passivity. Loaded emotions are buried beneath the creature's resonant words, and Walton fails to realize Victor's only desire—to see the creature dead. And the bumbling Editor of James Hogg's *The Private Memoirs and Confessions of a Justified Sinner* (1824) concludes the novel with confusion, his only means of narrative interference the pilfering of the sinner's preserved corpse. Lockwood, on the other hand, actively attempts to become part of the story, to affect its very trajectory. Indeed, we should not take lightly his later words that he has come to "devastate the moors" (232). The novel's several narratives blur as a result of Lockwood's refusal to remain separate from what he introduces, so that the embedded horror confronts readers head on, immediately and irreversibly. His most conspicuous attempt to interject in the story comes via his initial, and surprisingly lasting, attraction to Cathy. While Lockwood's curious desire remains unsettling, its results might have ensured that destructive Earnshaw traits were diminished, if not eventually extinguished altogether. And Hareton, the de facto offspring of Heathcliff's horror, would have been left in solitude without a reproductive partner. Yet Lockwood's intentions quickly cool, perhaps due to Nelly's subtle deterrents. Indeed, her remark that the "crown of all my wishes will be the union those two" (241) is a crucial acknowledgment that she wishes to see Earnshaw traits survive. By discouraging Lockwood's "susceptible heart" (9), she promotes the development of a new Real that will survive beyond the text. While Lockwood blurs the boundaries between the narratives, Nelly ensures the novel's horror endures.

Nevertheless, in the dark world of *Wuthering Heights*, the final coupling appears comforting. Cathy's rough exterior begins to chip away as she helps Hareton with his reading by using more gentle and flirtatious barbs. Sandra M. Gilbert and Susan Gubar call the conclusion a move "away from nature and toward culture."[47] We might also consider it a progression from the Real into reality. The pair move to Thrushcross Grange, a site of storytelling and recuperation that had mostly succeeded as a symbolic barrier against Heathcliff's Real. Lockwood's final words at the graves, as he "wonder[s] how any one could ever imagine unquiet slumbers for the sleepers in that quiet earth" (258), appear to wrap a tidy bow around the novel. Indeed, Miriam Allott has argued that a "certain equilibrium has been achieved ..., a balance effected by a new combination of Earnshaws and Lintons, with Earnshaw energy modified by Linton calm."[48] Yet Heathcliff's ominous declaration, "I'm seeking a tenant for the Grange" (219), is a never-ending prophecy, an acknowledgment of the basic biological truths of reproduction and transmission. In 1849, George Bacon Wood warned of the "danger of constant intermarriages between near connexions, who may be supposed to have the same defects of constitution."[49] Allott's "new combination" ignores the fact that Hareton possess no Linton traits and that Cathy herself is half Earnshaw. Cathy and Hareton may create a new generation, one whose biology unites the pernicious traits of their ancestors. In this sense, the novel's Real escapes the boundary of Lockwood's frame. The Earnshaws claimed the Heights in 1500, and their bloodline seems prepared to survive for another three hundred years. In a sense, Nelly's exaggerated fear that Heathcliff is a "ghoul or a vampire" (252) is ultimately realized through the Real horror of biological transmission.

Anne Brontë would borrow from *Wuthering Heights* both structurally and thematically, but her novel—on the surface less atmospherically dark—traces lines of inheritance to more threatening levels. The frame narrator of *The Tenant of Wildfell Hall* inserts himself into the story with more unsettling vigor than Lockwood, thus fully blurring the boundaries between narrative layers. Most disturbing, however, is that the biological transmission of the Real, rather than being a potential threat, becomes an actual horror with the birth and survival of a "second coming" burdened with destructive traits. Often noted for its implausibly long central-narrative letter, *Wildfell Hall* consists of a protracted missive from the frame-narrator, Gilbert Markham, to his friend Halford, who remains a silent interlocutor in the vein of Margaret in *Frankenstein*.[50] Gilbert's narrative embeds a transcription of Helen Graham's diary, a formal move that Garrett Stewart reads as the "frailest and most bizarre of provocations."[51] Gilbert explains that his letter will level a debt to his friend, who married Gilbert's sister, Rose. In a previous meeting to which readers are never privy, Halford provided Gilbert with a "very particular and interesting account of the most remarkable occurrences of [his] early life" (5). That Gilbert was unable to repay the debt immediately with a story of his own soured Halford's recent correspondence. In what becomes an explicit allusion to the found manuscript trope, however, Gilbert relates: "I am alone in my library, and have been looking over certain musty old letters and papers, and musing on past times; I am now in a very proper frame of mind for amusing you with an old world story" (6). He subsequently transcribes his history from a "faded old journal" because his "memory alone—tenacious as it is," proves too weak "to depend upon" (6).

As with *Wuthering Heights*, contemporary critics found the form of *Wildfell Hall* distracting. A reviewer for the *Examiner* contends: "[o]wing to the faulty construction of the tale, it is scarcely possible to analyze it."[52] The editors of the Parlour Library edition, which appeared in 1854, excised the entire opening frame of the novel. Many subsequent English editions were based on this corrupt version, which begins: "You must go back with me to the autumn of 1827."[53] In an October 1848 review, E. P. Whipple backhandedly compliments the novel for being a "less unpleasing story" than *Wuthering Heights*.[54] In spite of its generally unfavorable reviews, *Wildfell Hall* is a bold novel that reveals the unsavory, the dangerous, and the libidinal. As a triple-decker, it stands alone, unlike Anne Brontë's previous novel, *Agnes Grey*, which was packaged with (or perhaps framed by) *Wuthering Heights* the previous year. The structure of *Wildfell Hall* leads to a heart of darkness; as we move inward—from Gilbert's letter-writing frame, to his letter-story of meeting Helen, to Helen's diary—the Gothic becomes increasingly powerful. The *Examiner* complained: "Just at the time when we begin to feel some interest about Markham and the lady, we are thrown back upon her previous history, [and] we cannot go back and recover the enthusiasm which we have been obliged to dismiss."[55] This is precisely the point: Helen's diary irrevocably darkens the novel. Situational humor and pastoral romance collapse as the core erupts with Gothic intrigue.

In spite of the dark resonances at the center of *Wildfell Hall*, categorizing it as a Gothic novel seems a stretch, if not solely because it follows in the wake of the seemingly more disturbing *Wuthering Heights*. Yet this titular edifice even more explicitly echoes the Radcliffean Gothic. Gilbert observes that Wildfell Hall is "in ruins," and that there were only "two or three rooms made habitable" (10) in the "superannuated mansion of the Elizabethan era" (18). The windows of the uninhabitable portion of the house "were in darkness, and many exhibited their black, cavernous gulfs, entirely destitute of glazing or framework" (51). The house and its inhabitants become part of local legend, stories that are passed "respecting the haunted Hall and its departed occupants" (19). The difference here is that the mysterious tenant lives in the habitable portion, unlike the mother in Radcliffe's *A Sicilian Romance* (1790). Brontë transforms the genre by focusing on the mystery of Helen's life, not her death, and the secret of Helen's arrival, not her disappearance. Gilbert's voracious behavior manifests itself in an unhealthy curiosity about Helen's situation. While the other country-folk gossip, Gilbert turns to invasion and violence in his role as amorous detective. Similar to Lockwood's repeated intrusions into Wuthering Heights, he makes no secret of his "pretext for invading [Helen's] sanctum" (70).

Gilbert's immersion into the story that he introduces undermines his authority as an objective voice and blurs the boundaries between narratives. At the conclusion of Helen's hypodiegetic diary, she refers to the contacts she has made in the neighborhood, including the "fine gentleman and beau of the parish and its vicinity" (401). The diary cuts off with an ellipsis, however, and Gilbert's diegetic narrative returns with the claim: "Here it ended. The rest was torn away. How cruel, just when she was going to mention me!" (401). The consequences of Helen's brief mention, however, are irreversible. Gilbert becomes a character in the deep, dark core of the novel with the result that the extradiegetic frame merges with the hypodiegetic tale. Thus, the Real of novel's story of addiction, adultery, and abuse comes into unsettling proximity with the reader's reality. Even more disturbing, the same textual boundary that permits Gilbert's entrance as a character also allows biological horror to pass freely into other narratives. Arthur Huntingdon, the novel's monstrous implication of the Real, transfers his biological horror to his "second coming," a child who bears both his name and his demons. Gilbert's romantic pursuit of Helen ensures that young Arthur, the troubled offspring of a disastrous marriage, has a place not only in the diegetic narrative, but also in the frame, where he becomes a member of the new family at Wildfell Hall who survive beyond the limits of the text.

Helen first encounters Arthur at a dance when he saves her from the advances of a boorish suitor. "Come," Helen recalls him saying, "I'll preserve you from that infliction" (132). Although her aunt warns her that Arthur is a "bit wildish.... So I'd have you beware" (132), Helen is incredulous, reasoning that there is no "harm in those laughing blue eyes" (133). Unfortunately, Helen does not learn until too late the scope of Arthur's dissipation. But Brontë provides clues in onc of their early meetings. During an intensely flirtatious encounter, Arthur stumbles upon his own likeness among Helen's paintings, which she had abandoned and recycled for use as another canvas. "[H]orror, beheld him complacently gazing at the *back* of the picture," Helen laments: "it was his own face that I had sketched there and forgotten to rub out!" (152). From this point, Arthur's transformation from suitor into villain is rapid. "I must look at *both* sides now" (152), he ominously remarks. The unconscious act of making Arthur's portrait the reverse side of a picture is symbolic of Helen hiding the Real of his malevolence from her reality. In a passage that clearly draws upon Shelley's "painted veil," Helen records: "where hope rises fear *must* lurk behind" (240). Arthur becomes the dark side of the tapestry, the Real horror behind the lifted veil. Once Helen has a child with Arthur, her husband's traits become a permanent part of her reality, which his protracted death will not extinguish.

Arthur's struggles in *Wildfell Hall* may have been modeled on Branwell Brontë's dissolution from alcoholism, which contributed to his early death in September 1848, just two months after the novel was published.[56] In addition to the first-hand experience of Branwell's downfall, the Brontë sisters had access to a range of temperance pamphlets that their father, Patrick, a minister and a local philanthropist, used in his own work.[57]

Wildfell Hall marks a bold entry into a recent history of linking alcoholism with heredity in the early nineteenth century. In a note to his poem *The Botanic Garden* (1791), Erasmus Darwin writes: "It is remarkable, that all the diseases from drinking spirituous or fermented liquors are liable to become hereditary, even to the third generation, gradually increasing, if the cause be continued, till the family becomes extinct."[58] Darwin's observation of hereditary alcoholism is revolutionary, if not borderline sensationalist. Nonetheless, his words—which also provide an early theory of evolutionary "survival of the fittest"—had a profound impact on early nineteenth-century tracts on alcohol, often driven by temperance leagues. "[I]t is conceded on all hands," one temperance organization concluded, "that there are many persons who from constitutional peculiarities or hereditary tendencies can take absolutely no alcohol at all without narcotism."[59] In *The Anatomy of Drunkenness* (1827), Robert MacNish suggests that a dependence on alcohol "appears to be in some measure hereditary. We frequently see it descending from parents to their children. This may undoubtedly often arise from bad example and imitation, but there can be little question that, in many instances at least, it exists as a family predisposition."[60] A reviewer for *Blackwood's*, a magazine that the Brontës treasured, found MacNish's argument flawed: "The distinction here made between choice and necessity, seems to us scarcely justifiable.... We never shall believe, that whole classes of men have ... an innate and constitutional fondness for liquor."[61] Beth Torgerson notes that literature on intemperance in the 1830s and 40s focused on the lower classes and argues that Anne Brontë "bring[s] the issue of alcoholism much closer to home" by showing its effects on wealthier families.[62] "Let it not be imagined," Brontë writes in the 1848 preface to the second edition of *Wildfell Hall*, "that I consider myself competent to reform the errors and abuses of society, but only that I would fain contribute my humble quota towards so good an aim" (xxxvii). By subtly suggesting the spread of Arthur's destructive traits beyond the text, Brontë highlights the relentless horror of biological transmission, and demonstrates that the Real cannot be controlled by environmental treatment.

Arthur's struggle with alcohol occupies the majority of Helen's diary. He several times leaves his wife for months on end to debauch in London, but when he brings the drinking party inside his home Helen fully realizes the deleterious effects of alcohol. He invites his friends for hunting trips and social gatherings, the latter of which lead to his brazen adultery and steady physical decline. Helen addresses the latent trouble early on: "His very heart ... is, I fear, less warm and generous than I thought it" (187).

The alleged rehabilitation of Lord Lowborough, one of Arthur's former drinking buddies, urges Helen to be even more wary of the virulence of Arthur's increasingly uncontrollable addiction. Nevertheless, at the very center of the novel (as with Cathy in *Wuthering Heights*) young Arthur is born. Her husband's constant inebriety leads Helen to fear for young Arthur's life: "He may live to curse his own existence" (240). Young Arthur is doomed from the start as he is but a "tiny epitome of [his] father" (241). Helen's flight from Arthur means that she may immediately commence her project of rehabilitation on her son's constitution in a desperate effort to prevent his alcoholism, to subdue young Arthur's troubled disposition through environmental discouragements aimed at counteracting his father's biological traits. But the question remains whether the environmental stimuli will work, or whether young Arthur is biologically doomed to be his father's "second coming."

Helen appears to understand the competing effects of biology and environment on a developing character, far before Francis Galton would coin the term nature vs. nurture in the late nineteenth century. Environment for Helen is a factor in changing condition. "I am familiarized with vice and almost a partaker in his sins," she admits: "Things that formerly shocked and disgusted me, now seem only natural" (263). Her husband is a "contaminating influence" (307), which only exacerbates her child's connection to a deranged "spirit and temperament" (327). Arthur and his drunkard friends "delighted to encourage in all the embryo vices a little child can show, and to instruct in all the evil habits he could acquire," and most distressingly young Arthur "learnt to tipple wine like papa" (354). Helen calls her husband's intemperance "monstrous," but the horror of the novel is that Helen and Arthur may have produced their own monster through *both* families' lines, as Helen's father was also a drunk.[63] As George Bacon Wood argues in 1849, "when both [parents] are diseased … the chances of escape on the part of the children are greatly diminished."[64] Still, Helen attempts to assuage young Arthur's growing dependence through a sort of proto-Pavlovian conditioning. Her endeavor to rehabilitate young Arthur involves "giving him an absolute disgust for all intoxicating liquors, which I hope not even his father or his father's friends will be able to overcome. He was inordinately fond of them for so young a creature, and, remembering my unfortunate father as well as his, I dreaded the consequences of such a taste" (374). Helen acknowledges that the monster is "grounded in his nature" (375), and that no amount of environmental punishment or stimulus will completely break young Arthur's condition. Yet she institutes a "regime of regulation and training."[65] Eventually, all alcoholic beverages become "objects of terror"

(375) for young Arthur. She turns fear into a force for good. Josephine McDonagh argues that the novel's moral ground lies in an "ideology of self-help through regulation and training of the body's appetites and passions."[66] Certainly, this is what Helen hopes for her son, "to obviate his becoming such a gentleman as his father" (372). Reforming young Arthur requires making alcohol an "aversion" (375). The traits he inherited from his father grow inside the boy like a parasite, but Helen works to stifle the disease and to promote new traits in its stead: "I exerted all my powers to eradicate the weeds that had been fostered in his infant mind, and sow again the good seed they had rendered unproductive. Thank heaven, it is not a barren or a stony soil; if weeds spring fast there, so do better plants" (374). Yet, in the terminal frame, Gilbert gives no indication concerning the result of Helen's undertaking, and young Arthur's place among the "promising young scions that are growing up about us" (498) remains unstated and uncertain.

The Gothic ambiguity of *Wuthering Heights* and *The Tenant of Wildfell Hall* rests in the questionable efficacy of environmental refashioning, whether the biological monsters escape the boundaries of the narrative frame. In *Wuthering Heights*, Lockwood overtly blends biological and textual production: "if I surrendered my heart to that young person, and the daughter turned out a second edition of the mother!" (121). His fear is that the plight of the first generation will be copied into the second, that a marriage to Cathy means a new story in which he will become a character. It is no wonder that he ultimately disappears from a text that he was previously so eager to enter. In *Wildfell Hall*, however, there is no escape. We should take note of the Markham family's blatant and pushy fondness for alcohol, not to mention Gilbert's voracious appetite and propensity towards violence. Could Helen have entered into another disastrous marriage in which her subsequent children are as doomed as young Arthur? Or is it telling that Gilbert's family home is named Linden Grange, a clear analogue to Thrushcross Grange in *Wuthering Heights*? The reality of the novels' granges opposes the Real of the "wild" hall and the "wuthering" heights. When Helen finally permits Gilbert to share her tenancy at Wildfell Hall, he moves in the opposite direction as Hareton and Cathy—from reality into the Real. This possibility darkens Gilbert's invitation to Halford to spend a "season of invigorating relaxation and social retirement with us" (498). In the end, the implacable forces of biological transmission allow Real horror to escape the novels' complex frameworks, leaving readers to be "vexed to nightmare by a rocking cradle."

5

The "romantic side of familiar things"

The Old Curiosity Shop *and* Bleak House

The waxwork, clockwork, all the marvellous craft
Of modern Merlins, wild beasts, puppet-shows,
All out-o'-th'-way, far-fetched, perverted things
All freaks of Nature, all Promethean thoughts
Of man—his dulness, madness, and their feats
All jumbled up together to make up
This parliament of monsters.

—William Wordsworth,
The Prelude (1805, 1850)[1]

[The] line of descent ... [is] like the course of a busy man moving about a great city. Sometimes it goes underground, sometimes it doubles and twists in tortuous streets, now it rises far overhead along some viaduct, and, again, the river is taken advantage of in these varied journeyings to and fro.

—H. G. Wells, "Zoological Retrogression" (1891)[2]

Writing of Charles Dickens's affection for the *Arabian Nights*, George Gissing observes that the author "made acquaintance with the dazzling Eastern fables and took them alternately with that more solid nutriment of the eighteenth-century novel."[3] Gissing reads in Dickens a mix of fantasy and reality, the latter supplied by the familiar canon of Richardson, Fielding, and Sterne. While Dickens's investment with eighteenth-century novels has been regularly addressed, it is instead ingredients of fancy that shape two of his most celebrated novels, *The Old Curiosity Shop* (1840–1) and *Bleak House* (1852–3). The Gothic themes of Dickens's novels—the almost ubiquitous presence of mystery and the macabre—have been routinely mined and examined, but his debt to the formal makeup of the Gothic has remained largely unexplored. Most notably, *The Old Curiosity Shop* and *Bleak House*, two novels brimming with Gothic matter, are frame narratives. Unlike previous Gothic novelists, however, Dickens does not raise horrifying specters of the Real to invade our fabricated reality, but instead suggests that the veil has already been lifted, that the Gothic is the backdrop and energy of everyday Victorian reality—what he calls in *Bleak House* "the romantic side of familiar things."[4]

Through his engagement with narrative frames, Dickens demonstrates that a single perspective, even an omniscient one, cannot adequately articulate the fluid and diverse world. The frame narrative allows Dickens to occupy the perspectives of multiple subjects (and sometimes objects) to interrogate the conventions of realism. As George Levine observes, Dickens "was less easy with the limits of realism than most of his contemporaries."[5] Recent studies of Dickens's aesthetic have motivated a reconsideration of his engagement with the Gothic. The apparent decline of the Romantic-era Gothic has traditionally been considered as a process through which it was displaced and then eventually replaced by Victorian realism. However, as Robert Mighall notes, "no writer has a greater claim to importance in the history of the Gothic during its supposed sabbatical than Dickens."[6] In fact, the omnipresence of the Gothic in the novels of the Brontës and Dickens—not to mention a wealth of other sources ranging from the Newgate novel to sensation fiction—only proves that the Gothic had not disappeared, but instead was a keystone in the formation of new approaches to representing the human experience.

Bleak House exemplifies the subgenre of the "Urban Gothic."[7] Indeed, London is not just the novel's setting, but also its most complex and nuanced character. Dickens's fascination with the city is well noted by both critics and the author himself. In 1867, he boasted: "I know London better than any other man of all its millions."[8] But to know Victorian London was to be simultaneously charmed and horrified. To borrow Dickens's own words, London possessed an "attraction of repulsion" unmatched by any other city.[9] As Wordsworth suggests, London is teeming with abjections—objects, substances, and sensations that rupture the symbolic order and disturb subjective identity. The city is a cauldron of dark matter so overwhelming that it "draws [one] toward the place where meaning collapses."[10] In its abjection, London becomes a space of the Real, a deeper, darker level of reality where primordial chaos reigns supreme. The ubiquitous melding of man and beast in Victorian literature, which includes

Dickens's feline Carker in *Dombey and Son* (1846–48) and the canine Magwitch in *Great Expectations* (1860–61), is perhaps evidence of the urban invasion of the animalistic Real—the "parliament of monsters" that Wordsworth describes. Dickens exploits the distinctive features of narrative frames to lead readers into this uncanny world, full of both the familiar (realism) and the romantic (the Gothic). Through the perspectives of multiple narrators, Dickens explores the heights and the depths of the urban world, suggesting that reality is constantly and unavoidably assailed by implications of the Real. Echoing previous Gothic novelists, Dickens undermines the narrative boundaries established by these diverse voices, allowing characters and even narrators to pass through them unrestricted, with the result that figures of authority betray our trust by becoming potential villains.

Comparing the dual narratives in *Bleak House* to Dickens's earlier experiment with voices in *The Old Curiosity Shop* suggests that the former is a highly dynamic frame narrative, one that continues to borrow thematically and formally from the Gothic tradition, but that reinvests the genre with a vibrant and complex energy. Jonathan Grossman argues that the narrative division between city and country in *The Old Curiosity Shop* "is as serious a formal experiment as that of the more famously split narrative of *Bleak House*."[11] The system of framing devices that introduces and concludes *The Old Curiosity Shop*, however, is even more germane to Dickens's project in *Bleak House*. Both novels employ two narrative voices—distinct in perspective, purpose, and power—that frame one another. This dynamic, in which the embedded or secondary narrative also functions to frame the first, suggests the welter of social antagonisms raging in Dickens's London. The novels' differing narrative voices represent the conflicting ideologies whose fundamental deadlock implicates the Real. Slavoj Žižek argues that "the ultimate paradox of the notion of 'class struggle' is that society is 'held together' by the very antagonism, splitting, that forever prevents its closure in a harmonious, transparent, rational Whole."[12] Thus, we may read the dual, often dueling, voices in both novels as highlighting the fundamental impossibility of totality, the fissures in reality that indicate the Real. The points at which the narratives diverge denote the gaps in the symbolic order where fantasmatic monstrosities emerge. This effect is especially evident in *The Old Curiosity Shop*, which features a dynamic villain who moves freely between narratives and places the Real in disturbing proximity to the reader's reality.

The Old Curiosity Shop begins with a frame narrative in which a first-person encounter with a wandering child acts as a sort of adaptation of the found-manuscript device. However, the novel's complex system of narrative frames makes this curious meeting the second instance of a found manuscript. In another narrative layer that Dickens constructs, the story itself had to be found among the manuscripts tucked away in the "dark closet" of a favorite old clock.[13] The novel began its serial run three weeks into Dickens's short-lived periodical *Master Humphrey's Clock* (4 April 1840–4 December 1841). Dickens included not only a preface for the periodical, but also two different prefaces for the novel when it was printed in full in 1841 and in cheap edition in 1848. In the 1840 preface to *Master Humphrey's Clock*, Dickens explains that he never intended for the group of friends who frame the periodical's tales to become "active agents in the stories they are supposed to relate."[14] This preface is the first in a series of apologies Dickens makes for the failings of *Master Humphrey's Clock*. The product of an overactive imagination, Dickens explains, the periodical was the result of an author "conjuring up bright figures where there is nothing but empty space."[15] Dickens's 1848 preface makes more explicit his initial plans for the periodical and the thematic inspiration for the novel. He conceived *Master Humphrey's Clock* as "detached papers," which were "to include one continuous story," that of Humphrey and his friends at the Clock club.[16] As John Bowen observes, the tales in the periodical are mostly Gothic in nature, and they are presided over by the "ghost," Humphrey, who "exists in a world that treads the boundaries of life and death."[17] This is an important distinction, for it suggests that one of the novel's most disturbing Gothic elements is its focalizer, the trusted voice of its extradiegetic narrative.

Once the novel was published outside the periodical, Dickens "freed [it] from the incumbrance of associations and interruptions with which it had no kind of concern," and canceled Humphrey's opening frame, its pages now the "property of the trunkmaker and butterman" (7). As G. K. Chesterton observes, Dickens "liked to have story within story, like room within room of some labyrinthine but comfortable castle. In this spirit he wished 'Master Humphrey's Clock' to begin, and to be a big frame or bookcase for numberless novels. The clock started; but the clock stopped."[18] This editorial excision might have resulted from harsh reviews of the periodical. Thomas Hood reviewed the text for the *Athenaeum* in November 1840. "The main fault of the work is in its construction," Hood writes, in an illuminating and biting critique that compares the novel to previous frame narratives:

> [I]t was assumed that the Reader would be interested in the interest taken by those shadowy Personages, in the narratives brought forward at their Club-meetings. This was a mistake. In the Arabian Nights, indeed, we take an interest in the interest

> excited in the Sultan, by each of the Thousand and One Tales; because a yawn from Shahriyar would be the story-teller's death warrant; but the auditors of Master Humphrey possess no such despotic power—his head does not hang by its tale; and accordingly, whilst interested ourselves at first hand,—say by the history of the Old Curiosity Shop and its inmates,—we think no more of the gentle Hunchback, his friend, and the Old Clock, than of as many printing-house readers and an Editor's box.[19]

For Hood, the periodical's framing device fails to excite enough interest to justify its existence against the texts it introduces, and Humphrey perishes under the audience's knife because his adventures do not elicit the required amount of reader-investment. Yet Hood could not yet have known that it is Humphrey who wields a "despotic power," not only during the events in the frame, but also when he becomes a character in the narrative he introduces. Nonetheless, Dickens felt it necessary to respond to Hood's review with a personal letter, and the pair engaged in a spirited correspondence. In the face of reviews like Hood's, Dickens dispensed with the frame of Humphrey's "horological predilections," to use the words of one reviewer.[20]

Master Humphrey's back story provides the opening fictional frame for the novel and its successor, *Barnaby Rudge* (1841). Humphrey begins a storytelling club, in which individual members write stories and place the manuscripts in the chamber of Humphrey's "cheerful companionable Clock."[21] On a strict schedule, Humphrey chooses from the "piles of dusty papers" hidden in the clock, so that the members may "draw means to beguile time from the heart of time itself."[22] *The Old Curiosity Shop* comes from Humphrey's hand as the novel is introduced as the "Personal Adventures of Master Humphrey."[23] The subtitle is the first subtle indication that Humphrey may have more involvement in the novel than he earlier lets on. What is more, Humphrey describes himself as a "mis-shapen, deformed, old man," which connects him not only to Nell's duplicitous grandfather, but also to the villain of *The Old Curiosity Shop*, the dwarf Daniel Quilp.[24] The uncanny link between the narrator and the novel's antagonists collapses the narrative boundaries between them so that the Real spreads into the frame world that resembles the reader's reality. This effect is further demonstrated by another of Humphrey's descriptions of his life and character. He recollects a scene from his youth in which a group of children sit huddled around his mother, who shows them a picture of angels. As a "poor crippled boy," Humphrey cannot find himself in the image, but he does "point out which of [the angels] represented each child there."[25] The scene foreshadows Nell's death in the novel, which is accompanied by a George Cattermole illustration that depicts the child being carried off by angels. In this sense, Nell becomes the last casualty of a narrator who presages the premature deaths of other children. She is not a victim of Quilp's malevolent machinations, but rather of Humphrey's morbid mind. Thus, the Real in *The Old Curiosity Shop* is initially produced in the frame of the periodical, as the monstrous figures embedded within might only embody the horrors that already exist in Humphrey's disabled body and disturbed imagination.

In the frame narrative of *The Old Curiosity Shop*, Humphrey appears as one of Dickens's roaming flâneurs, echoing the author's previous alter-ego, Boz. "Night is generally time for walking," Humphrey explains: "a glimpse of passing faces ... is often better for my purpose than their full revelation in the daylight" (9). Humphrey speaks of a "never-ending restlessness" (9), but his jaunts through London speculate rather than interrogate. Nell Trent quickly becomes the "found manuscript" of the novel, which transforms Humphrey from imaginative bystander into active agent. "An adventure which I am about to relate," Humphrey writes, "arose out of one of these rambles, and thus I have been led to speak of them by way of preface" (11). It is a chance encounter, and the most salient example that makes *The Old Curiosity Shop*, as Richard Maxwell asserts, "the most accidental of Dickens's novels."[26] Chesterton notes that the novel's "opening and original framework express the idea of a random experience, a thing come across in the street; a single face in the crowd, followed until it tells its story."[27] Since Humphrey is himself "arrested by an inquiry" (11), it is Nell, in fact, who does the finding. Her night-rambles are equally as important as Humphrey's in making the connection that sparks the novel. In this sense, Nell is Humphrey's double: she replaces him early on as the novel's emotional focus. During their walk, linked hand in hand, observer becomes observed: "she stole a curious look at [his] face" (12). Still, in their journey to her grandfather's shop, each beguiles the other; Nell refuses to reveal the secret of her dangerous wanderings, and Humphrey purposefully protracts the walk by leading Nell through streets she cannot recognize—yet another early example of his potential duplicity. Humphrey is "motivated solely by curiosity," Audrey Jaffe argues.[28] It is a devious trick by our narrator, ensuring that she leads him all the way to the door of the shop and eventually inside; and it undermines his earlier contention that his practice is only in "speculating on the characters and occupations of those who fill the streets" (9). Nell's appearance changes the game. Unlike Boz, who remains almost entirely a detached observer from the scenes he describes, Humphrey makes himself part of the action, not just a first-person narrator, but also a character in the novel he frames.

This blurring of narrator and character becomes more explicit in the novel's terminal frame, which, as with the opening sheets, Dickens abandons. Like little Nell, Humphrey has a secret, one that he "all along with difficulty repressed"—and it is a disturbing secret, indeed.[29] He reveals to the other members of the clock-group:

> You will one and all forgive me … if, for the greater convenience of the story, and for its better introduction, that adventure was fictitious. I had my share indeed—no light or trivial one—in the pages we have read, but it was not the share I feigned to have at first. The younger brother, the single gentleman, the nameless actor in this little drama, stands before you now.[30]

Humphrey undermines the entire authority of his opening frame, which he exposes as a fiction, and he does so by retrospectively breaking the frame from the outside in.[31] He never met Nell wandering London's streets, and he was never inside her grandfather's shop. He appears in *The Old Curiosity Shop*, instead, as the unnamed "single gentleman," who enters the novel as a tenant at the Brasses' business, and is apparently only referred to as such because the room advertises to be "let to a single gentleman" (250). Anticipating both Emily Brontë's Lockwood and Anne Brontë's Gilbert Markham, the narrator becomes a tenant in the novel, housed within the diegetic story rather than being the landlord of it. The mysterious single gentleman traces Nell's movements in the countryside through the forced testimonies of various characters she has encountered. As with Bucket's detective work in *Bleak House*, however, the single gentleman's efforts prove too little, too late. His search turns up a dead body. In May 1841, Edgar Allan Poe criticized Humphrey's revelation and puzzling character-transformation:

> [I]n "The Old Curiosity Shop," we feel displeased to find Master Humphrey commencing the tale in the first person, dropping this for the third, and concluding by introducing himself as the "single gentleman" who figures in the story. In spite of all the subsequent explanation we are forced to look upon him as two. All is confusion, and what makes it worse, is that Master Humphrey is painted as a lean and sober personage, while his second self is a fat, bluff and boisterous old bachelor.[32]

Poe's criticism nearly arrives at what is at stake in the novel. Dickens wraps the text in several frames that undermine rather than support one another. There is no authoritative voice if the master of ceremonies lies to his audience. It is an unsettling revelation that builds upon the disingenuous, bumbling editors notably introduced in James Hogg's *The Private Memoirs and Confessions of a Justified Sinner* (1824) and Ann Radcliffe's *Gaston de Blondeville* (1826). Perhaps more significant, the crumbling structure of the novel's frames allows its horror to escape the embedded text. Humphrey's threefold identity blurs narrative boundaries to the point that the Real, which is most explicitly suggested by Quilp's depravity, invades the reader's reality. This effect becomes even more disturbing when we acknowledge the similarities between Humphrey and Dickens. While the former dreams of Nell "holding her solitary way among a crowd of wild grotesque companions" (22), the latter writes in the 1848 preface: "I had it always in my fancy to surround the lonely figure of the child with grotesque and wild" (8). The single gentleman's inability to save Nell is the result of not only Humphrey's macabre sensibilities, but also Dickens's commercial acumen. As John Ruskin remarks, Nell "was simply killed for the market, as a butcher kills a lamb."[33]

Ultimately, Dickens was given the opportunity "to wind up my *Clock*."[34] Humphrey disappears in much the same way that Walter Scott's Jedediah Cleishbotham "melted into thin air" in the frame narrative of *Tales of My Landlord*.[35] *Barnaby Rudge* appeared in uninterrupted installments following the terminal frame to *The Old Curiosity Shop*, and the periodical concluded thereafter. Yet, when Dickens oversaw the publication of *The Old Curiosity Shop* as a complete edition, he declined either to revise or to abandon Humphrey's first-person opening frame, which occupies the first three chapters of the novel. While this narrative transfer is the most challenging part of the text, it nevertheless supports, as Grossman observes, "a shift that definitively indicates to readers that the tale had metamorphosed into a novel."[36] The frame concludes at the end of Chapter 3: "And now that I have carried this history so far in my own character and introduced these personages to the reader, I shall for the convenience of the narrative detach myself from its further course, and leave those who have prominent and necessary parts in it to speak and act for themselves" (35). Here, as Michael Slater argues, Dickens was forced "to disembarrass himself" of the first-person narration.[37] Jaffe reads the event as a "displacement rather than a disappearance—the hiding, but not the removal, of the self."[38] The narrator moves from somebody to nobody, but this transformation bears residual effects. Humphrey never totally disappears; the third-person narrator that takes his place remains oddly personal, offering to take readers by the hand to conduct them from one plot to the next. Maria K. Bachman argues that this "abrupt shift in perspective ... not only reveals the multi-layered complexity of focalization in the novel, but also shifts the burden of story world stewardship, of curiosity about others, onto the reader."[39] Since readers are led into the novel by Humphrey and then abandoned, they must adopt the residue of his vision, closing in on the diegetic world of the novel that exists in the exact time and space of the frame. Unlike previous Gothic novels, in which the frame is displaced chronologically and geographically from the embedded text, *The Old Curiosity Shop* transitions between narratives with uncanny efficiency, adhering to established moods and themes, while merely replacing the lens through which the story is told. As in Radcliffe's *The Mysteries of Udolpho* (1794) and Poe's "The Fall of the House of Usher" (1839), however, the true horror of the novel lies in what has already escaped the diegetic narrative, the Real that has invaded the frame.

When Humphrey "detaches" himself from the narrative, he leaves Nell alone and vulnerable. Although Kit claims in the frame, "I'd have found her. I'd bet that I'd find her if she was above ground, I would, as quick as anybody" (17), Nell must instead approach Humphrey for safe passage. But abandoning his involvement in the narrative sets the stage for Quilp's terror. Indeed, the third-person section of the novel begins in chapter four at the residence Quilp shares, or rather presides over, with his troubled wife; and when Nell reappears it is not within the pseudo-sanctuary of the shop, but rather out delivering a letter from her grandfather to Quilp at the dwarf's other, more fittingly Spartan, abode. She thus enters Quilp's narrative territory, an invasion that the villain turns into the terms for a loathsome, perhaps bigamous, future pairing: "see if one of these days you don't come to be Mrs Quilp of Tower Hill" (53). Yet the novel's most disturbing narrative dynamic recalls the formal methods of its Gothic predecessors, especially *The Italian* (1797), *Frankenstein* (1818), and *Melmoth the Wanderer* (1820). By appearing in Humphrey's first-person frame, Quilp enters a narrative level closer to the reader's reality. We experience the horror of the dwarf's appearance through Humphrey's familiar perspective well before the third-person narrator provides an omniscient, if not disconnected, view. Humphrey's frame, in other words, resembles the everyday reality of readers, and Quilp, with all his physical and internal suggestiveness of the Real, emerges as part of this world. He is neither composed in a lab nor formed in hell, but rather is a horrifying attraction of the urban exhibition.

Quilp makes his brief but intense appearance in Humphrey's narrative at the beginning of chapter three, when he shadows Nell through the front door of the Curiosity Shop. The dwarf's expository survey of the characters in the shop is particularly disturbing, especially once he arrives at Humphrey: "'And that?' inquired the dwarf, wheeling round and pointing straight at me" (30). To this point, Humphrey had been, at most, a bystander in the scene, recording the dialogue and mannerisms of its actors. When he is detected by Quilp, however, the thin wall between the first-person narrator and the characters he observes breaks down, and Humphrey is forced to abandon his body and subjectivity to escape the dwarf's oppressive vision. The scene epitomizes Jacques Lacan's theory of the gaze, in which we are reminded of our precarious objectivity through the anxiety of being constantly watched: "I see only from one point, but in my existence I am looked at from all sides."[40] Humphrey's transformation from first- to third-person had been gradual: although he speaks directly to Nell and her grandfather in chapter one, he is absent from dialogue thereafter, blending in with the shop's curiosities by twice pretending to be a patron. In fact, the other characters in the opening frame—Fred, Dick, and Kit—never acknowledge Humphrey's existence. But Quilp immediately exposes our narrator. The figure whose concern for Nell's wellbeing prompted his return to the shop absconds with the disingenuous excuse of contributing to the "convenience of the narrative" (35). For it is Quilp, sneaking, darting, and hovering, seeing but unseen, hearing but unheard, who challenges the first-person narrator, making his role ineffectual, if not dangerous. Quilp is too erratic to be contained by an embodied perspective, too dynamic to be framed. His textual pervasiveness—seen not just in his movement between frames, but also in his "fantastic" (30) energy within frames—indicates the implacable spread of horror beyond textual boundaries. Indeed, he is the "prime mover of the whole diabolical device" (497). Anticipating threats by Stevenson's Hyde and Stoker's Dracula, Quilp's omnipresence suggests that the Real has found permanent footing in the nineteenth-century metropolis.

Quilp was not Dickens's only big character in a small package, of course (the eponymous Little Dorrit and Jenny Wren in *Our Mutual Friend* come to mind), but he is unique in his villainy. In a November 1840 review of *The Old Curiosity Shop*, Thomas Hood calls Quilp a "Little Enormity," but questions whether "such beings exist in real life."[41] Since financial pressures forced Hood to reside in two comparatively bucolic continental cities from 1835 to 1840, it seems that he had temporarily forgotten the fantastic and terrifying characters of London life—including "those abridgments of human nature, called Dwarfs."[42] For Quilp, however monstrous his aspect, is not necessarily a unique urban sight. In 1846, for example, *Punch* satirically noted the "glut of dwarves that have lately been thrown upon the English market."[43] In some sense, Victorian London exemplifies Mikhail Bakhtin's concept of the carnivalesque, the chaotic festival environment where ideological and material categories dissolve and coalesce. Indeed, Bakhtin's description of medieval illuminated manuscripts could also express Dickens's London: "The free designs represent chimeras (fantastic forms combining human, animal, and vegetable elements), comic devils, jugglers performing acrobatic tricks, masquerade figures, and parodical scenes—that is, purely grotesque, carnivalesque themes."[44] Dickens several times refers to Quilp as grotesque, calling to mind Bakhtin's definition of "grotesque realism," which displaced classical realism by highlighting the base materiality of human existence. As the novel's sinister jester, Quilp is one of Bakhtin's clowns or fools that "represented a certain form of life, which was real and ideal at the same time. They stood on the borderline between life and art, in a peculiar mid-zone as it were."[45] It appears that Quilp's liminal uncertainty is what makes him such a terrifying force. "Monstrous head and little body" (30), Quilp amalgamates deformities. One could say he is a figure of abjection, a hideous collection of attributes and emotions that we cast off to form and maintain our place in the symbolic order. Julia Kristeva might say that he "does not respect borders, positions, rules," and that he represents the "in-between, the ambiguous, the composite."[46] In this sense, he suggests the Real—all that refuses assimilation, all that mocks order and prevents structure.

Worst of all, Quilp is a "parody of a child," a horrifying double—or perhaps the dark side of the tapestry—of the novel's other permanently diminutive figure, Nell.[47] As Lillian Craton remarks, he "clearly belongs in the freak show."[48] He is a descendent of the "Parliament of monsters" that terrorize Wordsworth in Bartholomew Fair. In response to Kit's berating, Quilp silently muses: "Ugliest dwarf that could be seen anywhere for a penny—monster—ah!" (365). His relative financial success, however, suggests that he is an active participant in the urban economic system, rather than one of its commodities. That is, in spite of his monstrousness, he is every bit a viable cog in the commercial machine—acquiring properties, making loans, and chasing down debtors. In 1859, Henry Morley offers evidence of why Bartholomew Fair's attractions no longer appealed to contemporary audiences: "Monsters became a disease; of which the nation has in our own day recovered with a wonderful rapidity in presence of events that force on the development of all its powers."[49] Published in the same year as Charles Darwin's *On the Origin of Species*, Morley's text invites readings that consider the "development" of the nation in terms of evolution. Subjects featured in the Fair were no longer supernatural creatures, but instead biological aberrations that indicated blips in the code of human progress. The lessening interest that Victorian Londoners paid to carnival attractions may be a result of the city's industrial melting pot making monstrous figures mainstays of the metropolitan experience, rather than temporary sideshows. Scientific breakthroughs encouraged Victorians to acknowledge the humanity in figures like Quilp. One writer in 1887 concludes that "[c]onsiderable differences will be found to exist, when we compare the statures of the various races of mankind; and it is the exaggeration of this fact that has given rise to the legends of dwarf and giant peoples."[50] In his portrayal of Quilp, Dickens toys with this very practice of exaggeration, regularly approaching the point at which his antagonist becomes fully otherworldly. Yet he ultimately pulls back from this characterization, especially in representing the dwarf's violent, corporal death that results from his fateful human error—a stumble amid the darkness, and a fall into unforgiving waters. That Quilp could possibly exist in the reader's reality, however, makes his Real actions and motivations all the more disturbing.

Perhaps most significant, when Quilp assumes control of The Old Curiosity Shop, he also usurps authority of *The Old Curiosity Shop*. "[T]here are new masters down stairs," Kit warns Nell: "It's a change for you" (96). Quilp's abrupt recognition of Humphrey in the novel's frame encourages the latter to escape the text. But the dwarf's extraordinary ability to see everything and to be anywhere in London also challenges the authority of the omniscient narrator. Nell's flight from Quilp's gaze is an attempt to escape the terrorizing omniscience that takes over after Humphrey disconnects. Since "[n]othing escaped the hawk's eye of the ugly little man" (45), Quilp's vision is not only acute, but also high and hovering. His oppressive vision embodies the "conscious and permanent visibility" of Michel Foucault's panopticon.[51] London is Quilp's frame, and Nell's escape to the countryside with her grandfather suggests an endeavor to locate a new geographical frame where she can reside in safety and security. Grossman observes that "Nell's journey ... initiates a division between a single-focused narrative plot thread and the multistranded plot activity in London."[52] It seems that Quilp, as a consummate urbanite, is better suited to negotiate the complex cityscape than he is the sparse countryside. Nevertheless, Quilp boasts: "I'm upon the old gentleman's track and have got a new light" (59)—but the track proves difficult to follow in the country, and, eventually, even his city light expires. However, the villain's unmistakable death, which contrasts the ambiguous fates of Shelley's creature, Maturin's Melmoth, and even Hogg's Wringhim, provides little justice for Nell, whose constant worry and perpetual flight ultimately exhaust her vitality. In Dickens's Gothic, no one is safe from the horror of the Real—least of all, as he demonstrates in *Bleak House*, children.

What was a pragmatic method to follow the strands of multiple plots in *The Old Curiosity Shop* became the formal crux of *Bleak House*, which invests the Gothic frame narrative with a new, complex energy—one that remains unmatched in the history of the novel. The unique, dual-narrative form of *Bleak House* invites rich criticism. Elizabeth Deeds Ermarth argues that the "powers of historical Nobody narrative are divided between two separate narrations, one with a capacity for oversight but no memory, and the other with a memory but insufficient oversight."[53] The third-person narrative in *Bleak House* seems to be a product of Dickens's developing conception of omniscience. It is a hovering, darting, and urgent voice; but, as many have pointed out, it is also often subjective, judgmental, and angry. It has the capacity not only to observe, but also to inhabit. In contrast, Esther's narrative remains grounded, serene, and ingenuous. For this reason, productively or not, the third-person narrator has often been gendered male. Indeed, it is difficult—and perhaps intentionally so—to read the third-person narrator as anything but "him," especially because Dickens used male pronouns for his earlier semi-omniscient "shadow" proposal for *Household Words*.[54] In the sense that the narratives are gendered, we might read their pattern within the space of the novel as a marriage, but one that "paradoxically offers both an enactment and a critique of the sexual division into separate spheres."[55]

Significantly, contemporary readers seemed neither surprised nor disturbed by the dual narrative. The *Eclectic Review* observes: "One part of [Dickens's] method in 'Bleak House' seems to have imposed a special difficulty in the way of preserving the unity of the work. As though it were not enough to break it up into pieces, ... he has given to it the character of a double narrative. The tale is told by two parties, or rather is distributed to the share of two parties."[56] Instead of drawing attention to the novelty of the narrative structure, reviewers were generally irritated at the contrivance. The *Illustrated London News* complained that "Mr Dickens fails in the construction of a plot"; the *Spectator* notes that the novel suffers from "absolute want of construction"; and *Bentley's Miscellany* argued that the "story has not been carefully constructed."[57] But not all reviews were critical of the structure. "[T]he conduct of the story appears to us singularly skilful," John Forster writes in the *Examiner*: "The studied and elaborate care bestowed upon the construction of *Bleak House* is very manifest."[58] Still, there is a surprising lack of Victorian-era discourse that refers specifically to the dual narration. T. S. Eliot was one of the first to alter the critical dialogue, calling the novel Dickens's "finest piece of construction."[59] Thinking of *Bleak House* as experimental or meta-fictional seems a modern reaction, perhaps one that underestimates Victorian readers, or that fails to acknowledge its Gothic roots.

As with previous Gothic novels, the narrative frames in *Bleak House* provide false boundaries that are transgressed by narrators, characters, and objects. Wherever narrative separation appears to be present, there is union; whoever promotes disassociation in fact practices collusion. As Graham Storey observes, the narratives "show the ultimate connectedness of the apparently unconnected."[60] This engagement is what lies at the heart of Dickens's famous digression, "What connexion can there be"—though it is not just characters, but also narratives that are "curiously brought together" (197). The novel is a bridge between the "innumerable histories of this world … from opposite sides of great gulfs" (197)—gulfs of gender, time, geography, and ontology. Grossman observes that, "[i]n Dickens's hands, the novel as an art … could enable his community, whose individuals were increasingly atomized, to come to know their manifold unseen connectedness."[61] But the secret of Esther's ancestry and the mystery of Tulkinghorn's murder are but small plot-specific pieces in the novel's greater formal puzzle. Like the "cartloads of paper" (88) that make up the Chancery case, *Bleak House* must be brought together, litigated, and solved. We might consider this mass of paper, perhaps best expressed through Krook's hoarding, through Immanuel Kant's concept of the understanding, which attempts to synthesize the subject's chaotic manifold of sensations through the frame of *a priori* categories. But the horror lies in what escapes this process, what refuses to be collected or assimilated. With this formula in mind, we may investigate what slips through the cracks in *Bleak House*—the figures that trespass the novel's framework and disturb the reader's reality.

Two schools of thought dominate scholarship on the novel's form and differ mainly in allowing one voice authority over the other. Merritt Moseley, for example, contends that the "narrators in *Bleak House* are not coordinate; Esther is *subordinate*."[62] John McBratney conversely argues that the existence of Esther's narrative proves that the "third-person narrator's story is only part of the total story that can be told."[63] And Joan Douglas Peters goes as far as to argue that Dickens himself was "privileging" Esther's narrative by "suggesting that the qualities associated with that voice are those most conducive to producing a novelistic text."[64] Hilary M. Schor even asserts that Esther's narrative "thrives on the contrast between that magisterial … third-person narrator."[65] I would argue, instead, that the two narratives thrive on one another. More symbiotic than hegemonic, one narrative cannot exist without the other; the many contrasts seemingly dwell beneath the countless points at which the voices converge and cooperate. W. J. Harvey considers Esther's narrative as a "brake, controlling the runaway tendency of Dickens's imagination," which creates the "effect of *pulsation*, of constant expansion and contraction, radiation and convergence."[66] But this reading, intriguing as it may be, fails to consider that the third-person narrator's first two chapters, "In Chancery" and "In Fashion," are stuck in quagmires of stalled circulation, whereas Esther's first chapter, "A Progress," concentrates an entire *Jane Eyre–like* Bildungsroman of Esther's childhood and entrance into adulthood at Chancery—and this is not to mention the chaotic subsequent chapter "Telescopic Philanthropy." As Schor states, Esther's "'I' shatters the complacency of those initial chapters."[67]

By beginning the first installment of *Bleak House* with the third-person narrator, Dickens suggests that the novel will continue the model established in *Dombey and Son* (1846–48). When Esther introduces herself in the third chapter, however, it seems as if another novel has begun entirely, one that will follow in the footsteps of *David Copperfield* (1849–50). This disjointed initial installment inaugurates the novel's complex structural dynamic, in which the dual narratives frame one another in sequence. While the third-person narrator frames Esther's narrative, in other words, the details that emerge in the latter retroactively frame the former. The tension created by this back-and-forth reframing suggests the level of social antagonisms fermenting in Dickens's London. The dual narratives represent conflicting ideologies—of gender, of class, of nation—whose fundamental incapacity to coalesce demonstrates the impossibility of wholeness. The antagonisms in the novel are, in Žižek's words, "a kind of opening, a hole in the field of the symbolic Other, a void of an unanswered, unresolved question."[68] The inconsistencies and disagreements between the narratives suggest that "reality" is merely a screen of subjective impressions that markedly differs depending on the perspective. Žižek elsewhere writes that "the very splitting into the two 'relative' perceptions implies the hidden reference to a constant—not the objective, … [but] the real of social antagonism, the non-symbolizable traumatic kernel that found expression in the very distortions of reality."[69] The alternate reality of Esther's narrative forces us to question the authority of the omniscient narrator, who is expected to be the voice of objective reality. When our connection to objectivity breaks down, we are left with a gap in the symbolic order that signals the Real.

Dividing the narratives to examine them as separate texts uncovers surface-level differences that affect a complete reading. Where Moseley, Jaffe, and others fail is in considering *Bleak House* as split into halves. This is far from the truth. Esther's narrative contains almost 30,000 more words than the third-person narrator's, amounting to nearly twelve percent more space in the novel. In terms of sheer word count, then, Esther dominates. The most important perspective that this sort of analysis demonstrates, however, is how much characters move between the narratives, and what happens to them when they trespass these narrative boundaries. The first move from Esther's narrative back to the third-person narrator involves a transition wherein Esther figures: "While Esther sleeps, and while Esther wakes, it is still wet weather down at the place in Lincolnshire" (76). The scene is what Grossman would call "simultaneous circulation; a coordinating 'Meantime …' logic bound together community."[70] Thereafter, Esther is rarely referred to in the third-person narrative, and only by Mrs Chadband, Guppy, and finally the detective, Bucket. The second of the orphaned triumvirate, Ada, appears only once in the third-person narration, and remains unnamed as one of the "two young people … directed to be in attendance" at Chancery (9–10). Her partner, Richard, makes a far more profound narrative jump. He is the only one of the three to achieve a speaking role in the third-person narration. Richard's appearances in chapters that feature Vholes are harbingers of his demise. His dealings with the vampiric lawyer prove to be the precipice of his steep pecuniary and physical demise. However, it is novel's eccentric family-philanthropists, the Jellybys and the Pardiggles, who substantiate an implicit connection between Esther and the narrator.

Esther's famous first line—"I have a great deal of difficulty in beginning to write my portion of these pages, for I know I am not clever"—not only immediately establishes a curious disingenuousness that her thoughtful and careful prose constantly undermines, but it also suggests that she has been assigned—or "obliged" as she later puts it—to provide her "portion" of the story (17). While Peters argues that Dickens "constructs in dialogical juxtaposition two different modes of representing the same social ideology," she does not point out that the comic injustices of "telescopic philanthropy" remain entirely confined to Esther's narrative but for one crucial instance.[71] Woodcourt finds Jo momentary refuge at George's Shooting Gallery: "Jo is brought in. He is not one of Mrs Pardiggle's Tockahoopo Indians; he is not one of Mrs Jellyby's lambs, being wholly unconnected with Borrioboola-Gha; he is not softened by distance and unfamiliarity; he is not a genuine foreign-grown savage; he is the ordinary home-made article" (564). Only Esther has encountered the Pardiggles and Jellybys; they never make their way to the other narrative. One of two explanations is thus possible: Either the narrator is flexing his omniscient muscles, tracking Esther's movements among these families, or he is working in concert with his counterpart; together they form the whole argument for focusing attention on domestic philanthropy.

The most significant discrepancy between the two narratives may prove to be what binds them so intimately together. Esther becomes the "mistress of Bleak House," its key-holder and manager. Jarndyce frees Esther to marry Woodcourt and provides the couple with a second Bleak House, what Schor describes as a "doll's house version."[72] Eventually, Jarndyce installs Ada, widowed, but with her own sequel-child named Richard, as the new mistress of the old Bleak House. (As in *Wuthering Heights* and *The Tenant of Wildfell Hall*, we should be wary of this "second coming" who inherits the name and traits of his troubled parent.) Like the Curiosity Shop and the Brontës' houses before it, Bleak House is more than just a titular edifice; its adjectival power invests the novel with a bleakness that Esther's "summer sun" can rarely light. Dickens's working notes demonstrate that he labored over a title for the novel, moving between "Tom-All-Alone's" and "The Solitary House" (among several others), before arriving at Bleak House after ten half-sheets of manuscript paper. Bleak House, in short, is crucial to *Bleak House* and is the setting and the subject for much of Esther's narration. Yet it does not appear in the third-person narration. Nor does the word "bleak." The narrator travels from the squalid depths of Tom-all-Alone's to the fashionable heights of Chesney Wold and looms over the "heart of the fog" at Chancery (6). But Bleak House remains the one sanctuary from the narrator's sight, which makes it an interesting reversal of the conventional Gothic house. Although the labyrinth of connecting rooms leaves a visitor "wondering how you got back there, or had ever got out of it" (62), it is more asylum than prison. Jo, for example, absconds all-too-easily. Rather than a mystery of Udolpho, there is a "mistress of Bleak House," who is the chief key to the Dedlocks' secrets.

When Esther first visits the lowly brickmaker family—on a stop with Mrs Pardiggle and her despondently abstemious children—she expresses the feeling of being an outsider: "Ada and I were very uncomfortable. We both felt intrusive and out of place" (99). Certainly, visiting the decay Mrs Jellyby creates from her foreign philanthropy is a far cry from the domestic ruin Esther witnesses at the brickmaker hovel: physical abuse, alcoholism, starvation, and a dead infant (the ultimate abject, a "small waxen form" [102], which recalls not only Nell in *The Old Curiosity Shop*, but also the veiled effigy in *The Mysteries of Udolpho*). Esther feels "out of place" because she is just that. As her aunt portentously declares, "You are set apart" (19). Now ward and proxy-mistress to an aristocratic lineage, Esther enters a social sphere from which she is distinctly removed. It is a world more negotiable for the third-person narrator's eye—a world best viewed with disembodiment rather than experienced as a body. The third-person narrator can enter spaces without risk, whether corporeal or social. The reversal of this feeling comes during Jo's short stay at Bleak House. He knows, despite being near death, that he has transgressed a social boundary from which no good can come. *Bleak House* demonstrates how permeable these frames have become; how a central issue like Chancery can invade and affect the lives of anyone; how disease spreads through all bodies, rich or poor.

Sir Leicester laments this social sea-change in reference to Rouncewell's audacious attempt to remove Rosa from service at Chesney Wold: "the floodgates of society are burst open, and the waters have ... obliterated the landmarks of the framework of the cohesion by which things are held together!" (504). The novel brings these elements together, linking disparate characters and contexts within its confines. Sir Leicester's regret over the crumbling framework of society reaches its apex during his employment of Bucket: "Of all men upon earth, Sir Leicester seems fallen from his high estate to place his sole trust and reliance upon this man" (669). Bucket proves to be a particularly interesting figure in *Bleak House*, who manages, with more skill than any other character, to traverse the worlds of the two narrators. He is adept at tracking characters who also move between the narratives, locating and interviewing Jo and implicating and arresting Hortense. In fact, as Ermarth points out, "[t]he two narratives finally converge on the trail of Lady Dedlock."[73] The novel's initial transition back to the third-person narration, "While Esther sleeps, and while Esther wakes" (76), is echoed when the narratives meet: "I had gone to bed and fallen asleep, when my guardian knocked at the door of my room and begged me to get up directly" (674). Bucket enters Esther's narrative and drags her on an untimely pursuit of her mother. Travelling through London's depths, Esther loses her temporal bearings: "If I ever thought of the time I had been out, it presented itself as an indefinite period of great duration" (687). Ultimately, the interval proves too lengthy. Lady Dedlock, like Jo "moving on to the berryin ground" (559), lies dead at the gravestone of Captain Hawdon. The body-count in the novel is considerable, even for Dickens. "They dies everywheres" (383), Jo explains; and Jarndyce ominously concludes: "Bleak House is thinning fast" (616).

Yet Dickens subjects none of the novel's antagonists to the sort of grisly death that he inflicts on Quilp. In fact, *Bleak House* lacks an explicit villain: Hortense, Tulkinghorn, Vholes, and even Lady Dedlock partially fit the bill, but certainly each falls short of outright villainy. For this reason, the novel's ideological antagonisms are its most disturbing points of conflict, the horror of the Real that is the deadlock of the Jarndyce and Jarndyce case. With this in mind, we might nevertheless look elsewhere to locate the novel's hidden antagonist. Esther's dizzying trip with the enigmatic Bucket is a sequel to an even more curious traveling experience. After her aunt dies, Esther takes a carriage to boarding school at Greenleaf. "There was a gentleman in the coach," she recalls, "who sat on the opposite seat and looked very large in a quantity of wrappings" (24). The coachman, she later reveals, was Jarndyce all along. Esther's earlier disingenuousness here about his passing out of her memory in fact proves that he is very much a part of it, important enough to mention during her momentous trip from being an abject disgrace to a valued ward. But her reaction, "I never was so frightened" (60), makes the discovery a discomforting example of the Gothic uncanny. Most important are the gentleman's words aboard the coach, "Now you know you are [crying].... Don't you?" which mirror Bucket's rather disturbing attempt at comfort during the pursuit of Lady Dedlock: "Now you know me, don't you?" (690). For Esther seems to require reminding of the "now," or rather of the "then."

Given that the single gentleman in *The Old Curiosity Shop* retrospectively becomes Master Humphrey, we may read the coach-man "becoming" Jarndyce in a new light. If *The Old Curiosity Shop* is also the "Personal Adventures of Master Humphrey"—who is paradoxically himself in the opening frame, the single gentlemen throughout the central narrative, and also the narrator—then perhaps *Bleak House* is partially Jarndyce's adventures, simultaneously a character in the novel and its present-tense, omniscient voice.[74] The coach-man's acerb attitude towards Esther's servant, "Con-found Mrs Rachael! ... Let her fly away in a high wind on a broomstick!" (25), is never echoed by the magnanimous and cool-headed Jarndyce. But this split personality (Jarndyce and Jarndyce) mirrors the omniscient narrator's capricious mood swings. The novel opens "In Chancery" during proceedings (or more likely recedings) over the Jarndyce and Jarndyce case—an interminable litigation that bears Jarndyce's name, but from which he strives to remain removed. An exasperated Richard tells Vholes:

> If any man had told me when I first went to John Jarndyce's house that he was anything but the disinterested friend he seemed—that he was what he has gradually turned out to be—I could have found no words strong enough to repel the slander; I could not have defended him too ardently. So little did I know of the world! Whereas now I do declare to you that he becomes to me the embodiment of the suit; that in place of its being an abstraction, it is John Jarndyce [486–87].[75]

Jarndyce may be at the center of both the case and the novel—a body on one hand and an abstraction on the other. If the novel's main conflict is the deadlock of the Jarndyce suit, then the man who is the "embodiment of the suit" represents the Real of social antagonism. That the omniscient narrator refuses to refer to Bleak House only highlights his involvement. Jarndyce's name in the case attracts litigants in the novel in much the same manner as the omniscient narrator brings characters together. Perhaps, following Master Humphrey, Jarndyce has decided to let Esther "speak and act for" herself. But for what purpose?

In a novel obsessed with litigation, Esther's narrative reads like an eye-witness testimony to corroborate the claims of the third-person narrator. In reference to Jarndyce, Richard observes that the case "taints everybody," but then wonders, "why should *he* escape?" (463). Esther's answer, meant to be supportive, instead proves unsettling: "he is an uncommon character, and he has resolutely kept himself outside the circle" (463). As a "superior being" (769), Jarndyce escapes the frame of the first-person narrative to be its omniscient narrator, the alleged voice of objective truth, whose story may merely be a deposition to be cleared from culpability for a case that has ruined countless lives: "Innumerable children have been born into the cause; innumerable young people have married into it; innumerable old people have died out of it" (8). Jarndyce's dual identity as an objective narrator and a subjective character makes him a monstrous fusion of categories in line with previous Gothic villains. "Jarndyce and Jarndyce" symbolizes the irreparable fracture of identity of its principal litigant, a condition as horrifying as Hogg's Wringhim/Gil-Martin and Stevenson's Jekyll/Hyde. Moreover, the secret of his dual role makes him ultimately responsible for keeping the narratives separate, for maintaining the Real of conflicting ideologies, which is best evidenced by the interminable, deadly case that he embodies. For the novel itself is composed of two Jarndyces—the angry activist and the benevolent guardian. In the end, we might ask whether Esther, Ada, and Richard are adopted to act as wards or as character witnesses. Significantly, Esther's last words are cut off in a dash ("even supposing—" [770]), which echoes Jo's unfinished recitation of the Lord's Prayer at his death ("Hallowed be—thy—" [572]). The similarity here might suggest Esther's untimely demise, perhaps just after she began, like Richard, to make connections about the Jarndyce case and her association with it. In another sense, the curious ending resembles the fate of several Gothic creatures who apparently turn to suicide rather than living in torment—Schedoni, Frankenstein's creature, Melmoth, Wringhim, and even Heathcliff. (Recall that "old Tom Jarndyce in despair blew his brains out" [8].) But on a less morbid level, Esther's final dash merely echoes the ambiguity with which so many Gothic novels conclude. It is no surprise that Dickens wrote in his notes, "Wind up. End (?)" (799)—words that echo the "winding up" of *Master Humphrey's Clock.* For "to wind up" simultaneously suggests resolution and revolution, termination and renewal.

6

The Descent of Man

Jekyll and Hyde *and* Dracula

> [W]ith all his noble qualities, with sympathy which he feels for the most debased, with benevolence which extends not only to other men but to the humblest living creature, with his god-like intellect which has penetrated into the movements and constitution of the solar system—with all these exalted powers—Man still bears in his bodily frame the indelible stamp of his lowly origin.
>
> —Charles Darwin (1871)[1]

> Evolution ever climbing after some ideal good,
> And Reversion ever dragging Evolution in the mud.
>
> —Alfred, Lord Tennyson (1886)[2]

Tennyson's speaker in "Locksley Hall Sixty Years After" counsels his grandson to be wary of the alleged progress of the modern world. While the "watchword, 'Evolution,'" has deceived people into thinking of humanity as becoming gradually more civilized, we must ask: "Have we risen from out the beast, then back into the beast again?"[3] Tennyson responds to contemporary debates over the terms of Darwinian evolution by suggesting not only that the species remains intimately connected to its base primitivism, but also that the plight of modern culture is evidence of its degeneration: "Forward then, but still remember how the course of Time will swerve, / Crook and turn upon itself in many a backward streaming curve."[4] Robert Louis Stevenson's *The Strange Case of Dr Jekyll and Mr Hyde* (1886) and Bram Stoker's *Dracula* (1897) similarly take up the issue of degeneration by introducing monsters that highlight the brutal primitiveness of humanity and challenge evolutionary models. As H. G. Wells writes, "[t]he Coming Beast must certainly be reckoned in any anticipatory calculations regarding the Coming Man."[5] Through the deeper reality established by the novels' framing devices, however, Stevenson and Stoker also explore the ontological threats of degeneration. Not merely a cognitive and corporeal issue, degeneration is a breakdown of symbolic reality that results from an invasion of the Real. Thus, the "reversion" that Tennyson identifies is also a return to the primordial chaos of the Real, a horror that is suggested by the monstrous figures of Hyde and Dracula.

Jekyll and Hyde and *Dracula* mark an imaginative return to the Romantic-era Gothic, a late nineteenth-century restoration of monster-driven horror that has endured today. Like Shelley's creature in *Frankenstein* (1818), the novels' monsters remain the stuff of nightmares and the subjects of relentless adaptations. Stevenson and Stoker not only visit the charnel houses of the Romantic Gothic to recall to life the passions of its troubled antagonists, but they also synthesize the mid-century Gothic of the Brontës and Dickens by exploring the threat of biological transmission in a teeming urban environment. Yet the novels do not recall former modes to ignore contemporary exigencies. For *Jekyll and Hyde* and *Dracula*, though indebted to the past, are leaders in the Gothic's newly restored voice as a genre. We might consider the novels as dynamic accumulations of Gothic matter—baggy monsters engorged with a century's worth of blood and blasphemy that pave new paths for the Gothic, worn but still walked today. In our continued obsession with irrepressible alter-egos and insatiable vampires, we reproduce the horror of ontological degeneracy founded by Stevenson and Stoker. That we remain as concerned with cultural degeneration and as skeptical of evolutionary models as the Victorian *fin de siècle* might suggest that we have come no further as a species in making sense of the world. Our fascination with figures that implicate the primordial welter of the Real demonstrates a morbid desire to see beyond the scope of symbolic structures, to experience Gothic realism.

The Victorian period was defined by progress. "It is the Age of Machinery," Thomas Carlyle cautiously asserted in 1829, at the dawn of a new era.[6] Following the Industrial Revolution, technology became the new frontier, as trains transformed the landscape, telegraph wires spanned the Atlantic, and electricity lit the streets. With these material advances came investigations into biological nature. Darwin's *On the Origin of Species* (1859) demonstrated that humankind was a story of evolutionary progress. Yet there was a dark side to this narrative. As Daniel Pick points out, Darwin "warn[ed] that there was no absolute evolutionary separation from the world of the animals, no escape from the stigma of that descent."[7] Increased attention to crime, prostitution, and alcoholism led to fears of social and biological degeneration that presaged the dissolution of the species. As Kelly Hurley observes, "the nineteenth-century imagination was preoccupied with the prospect of the reversal of evolution."[8] This anxiety was brought to a fever pitch by Max Nordau's *Degeneration* (1892), which warns of "bodily modifications" wherein "the entire being presents a strange and repulsive mixture of incompleteness and decay."[9] The Victorian city teemed with distorted bodies and deranged minds that implicated the decline of modern society. Pick argues that degeneration was a "process which could usurp all boundaries of discernible identity, threatening the very overthrow of civilization and progress."[10] Degeneration was not just a concern of the "bodily frame," to use Darwin's words, but also an ontological issue that disturbed symbolic reality by exhibiting monstrosities that suggest the Real. Jerrold E. Hogle points to "late-Victorian variants on the theory of evolution that picture modern man as struggling to separate the fully civilized from the still-primitive tendencies in himself."[11] Hyde and Dracula suggest the dark foundation of human existence, the inescapable yet indescribable core of being. To arrive at this deeper level of reality, Stevenson and Stoker manipulate framing devices. As in previous Gothic novels, these frames prove permeable, an effect most evident through the gaps in information that are an indictment of the novels' narrators. The implicit horror of *Jekyll and Hyde* and *Dracula* is that the Real is neither confined in monsters, nor restricted to aberrations that threaten the structures of civilization, but is instead the monster that lurks inside us all.

Jekyll and Hyde stages a conflict between Jekyll's reality and Hyde's Real. In Freudian terms, while Jekyll's ego is constrained by social decorum (super-ego), Hyde's id frolics in a "sea of liberty."[12] In his confession, Jekyll explains that he has been "sold a slave to my original evil" (50). He becomes an implication of the Real, evidence of the inscrutable horror that disturbs the symbolic order. Hyde's instinctual dissipations, what Jekyll calls "the horror of my other self" (60), soon begin "to turn towards the monstrous" (63). The eventual murder of the local official Danvers Carew demonstrates that Hyde has come entirely unhinged from Jekyll's reality. As Steven Arata argues, Hyde "embodies a bourgeois readership's worst fears about both a marauding and immoral underclass and a dissipated and immoral leisure class."[13] Since he occupies more than one position on the social hierarchy, Hyde shows that degeneration is a concern for both the poor and the privileged. Stevenson's play on names suggests that he conceived Hyde not only as a figure that "hides" from the novel's detectives, but also as a sort of "hide," a bestial skin that conceals the horror of the Real while simultaneously suggesting its existence. That Hyde emerges from an outwardly kind and well-respected man indicates that there is a dark drive for murder and mayhem churning within us all. Freud writes that "the more a man checks his aggressiveness towards the exterior the more severe—that is aggressive—he becomes in his ego ideal ..., the more intense becomes his ideal's inclination to aggressiveness against his ego."[14] This formula suggests that Hyde's extreme violence is, in great part, the consequence of the strict social pressures to which Jekyll must adhere. His symbolic shield against the Real was perhaps too impenetrable. What is more, the "[c]ertain agents" (49) that trigger Hyde's emergence remain horrifyingly vague, the product of an occupational experiment gone awry. Hyde's (re)surfacing "sh[akes] the very fortress of identity" (49) because it suggests the existence of a world beyond the scope of reality that is indefinable, impervious, and uncontrollable. More effectively than any other Gothic creature, Hyde embodies the fantasmatic frame that keeps readers from getting "too close" to the Real, while nevertheless constantly assailing them with its existence.

Hyde's monstrous frame gives shape to some of the amorphous welter of the Real—a process that resembles Immanuel Kant's concept of the understanding, in which the chaotic manifold of the subject's sensations are synthesized with *a priori* categories. Yet all that Hyde draws forth and projects is vile and violent; he conjures elements from the depths of an inaccessible world—Kant's realm of *das Ding an sich* ("the thing in itself")—and overwhelms Jekyll's reality with the horror of the Real: "that which stood within ran forth" (52). Žižek writes of the "subject's double who accompanies him like a shadow and gives body to a certain surplus, to what is 'in the subject more than subject himself'; this surplus represents what the subject must renounce, sacrifice even, the part in himself that the subject must murder in order to start to live as a 'normal' member of the community."[15] At the beginning of Jekyll's experiment, Hyde is just this surplus, an emergent embodiment of the Real that Jekyll abjected to become part of symbolic reality. In Julia Kristeva's words, Jekyll "finds the impossible within; when [he] finds that the impossible constitutes [his] very *being*, that it *is* none other than abject."[16] Initially, Jekyll is able to "throw off the body of Jekyll," but this process of abjection becomes impossible after he is "incorporated with [his] second and worse [self]" (55). The horrifying primal remainder overwhelms its subject, surfacing with unexpected and uncontrollable energy. From this point forward, *Jekyll and Hyde* becomes a narrative of irreversible madness, which sets in when "the Real either overflows into reality ... or is itself included in reality."[17] But the novel's distinctive frame narrative ensures that the Real has already invaded reality via the dark drives of its seemingly benign protagonist, the lawyer Gabriel Utterson.

Jekyll's concluding "Full Statement" provides a crucial third-person description of the "phenomena of consciousness" that he shares with Hyde: "[Jekyll] thought of Hyde, for all his energy of life, as of something not only hellish but inorganic. This was the shocking thing; that the slime of the pit seemed to utter cries and voices; that the amorphous dust gesticulated and sinned; that what was dead, and had no shape, should usurp the offices of life" (60). Jekyll's second descriptor of his counterpart as "inorganic" is especially interesting. That Hyde is not of organic composition suggests that he is born from non-living elements—the "slime of the pit" and the "amorphous dust." Stephan Karschay observes that Hyde's "opaque apishness gestur[es] towards a radical dissolution of the evolved human subject, even to the point of lifeless inorganity."[18] In *The Descent of Man*, Darwin writes of the "long line of progenitors" that have preceded humanity, and argues that the "most humble organism is something much higher than the inorganic dust under our feet."[19] Stevenson adds some measure of horror to Darwin's theory of evolution by suggesting that the origin of the human species was founded in the muck and mire of lifeless nature—that civilization, with all its proud progress, is inextricably tied to, and indeed controlled by, the dark depths of a chaotic, inaccessible world.[20] What is more, we might read the cries and cringes of the slime and the dust as Kant's noumenal "Thing" emerging in reality. Whereas Frankenstein revitalizes divergent parts of organic material, Jekyll conceives a creature out of inorganic matter, the turmoil of horror hidden in the nether regions of his mind. The figure of Hyde suggests that humanity perpetually stands at the precipice of horror, ready to plummet into the abyss of the Real. It is worth repeating Darwin's remarkable conclusion: "Man still bears in his bodily frame the indelible stamp of his lowly origin."[21] Stevenson appears to respond to Darwin directly in *Jekyll and Hyde*, as his troubled doctor remarks that the "second form" he was able to assume "bore the stamp of the lower elements of [his] soul" (50).[22] Thus, Stevenson explores the true depths of this "lowly origin," and finds that the link between humanity and its horrifying genesis is not only outwardly material, but also inwardly psychological—what we might call the Real register that precedes, and irrevocably disturbs, symbolic life.

In yet another sense of Hyde as a "hide," a membrane that conceals the depths beyond symbolic reality, Stevenson evokes the clothes-theory found in Carlyle's *Sartor Resartus* (1833–34). Like Enfield and Utterson, Lanyon struggles to describe precisely what bothers him about Hyde's appearance. "He must be deformed somewhere," he relates: "he gives a strong feeling of deformity, although I couldn't specify the point" (11). What Lanyon can articulate, however, is the oddity of Hyde's appearance in Jekyll's clothes. It is perhaps the novel's one comic aspect, but it also suggests the role of clothes in forming character. That "ludicrous accoutrement" (45) spurs Lanyon's "interest in the man's nature and character, ... his life, his fortune and status in the world" (53). That the clothes are ill-fitting and must be rolled and adjusted is the "fresh disparity" (45) that proves abhorrent to Lanyon, not any definable or specific corporeal disfigurement. Not only is the will regarded through the metaphor of clothes—"Edward Hyde should step into the said Henry Jekyll's shoes" (13)—but Jekyll also explains his early experiments in terms of clothes: "I began to perceive more deeply than it has ever yet been stated, the trembling immateriality, the mist-like transience, of this seemingly so solid body in which we walk attired" (49). Jekyll is able "to doff at once the body of the noted professor, and to assume, like a thick cloak, that of Edward Hyde" (52). Ingesting the potion gives Jekyll "the power to shake and to pluck back that fleshly vestment, even as a wind might toss the curtains of a pavilion" (49). This vestiary metaphor not only evokes Percy's Shelley's "lifted veil," but also rather overtly recalls Carlyle's claim: "Round his mysterious ME, there lies, under all those wool-rags, a Garment of Flesh."[23] In *Sartor Resartus*, clothes act as a metaphor for the fantasmatic screen that separates symbolic reality from the true divinity of the world. Stevenson adapts the darker elements of the metaphor to suggest that the difference between Jekyll and Hyde is merely a pulling aside of the veil. The reality of Jekyll is an illusion that the potion works to expose. Hyde's Real was present all along, hidden under the vestments of social structures, kept at bay by Jekyll's fragile ego. That Hyde is "[p]articularly small" (22) further suggests that he exists in some primordial state, if not an echo of Dickens's Quilp in *The Old Curiosity Shop* (1840–41), then a sort of presymbolic infant bursting with implacable drives and draped in his Oedipal father's oversized clothes.

Perhaps the most important formal elements in *Jekyll and Hyde* are its thresholds, evidenced not only in the novel's psychological and physiological line between Jekyll and Hyde, but also in its narrative structure. The first chapter, "Story of the Door," begins during one of Utterson's weekly rambles with his friend Enfield. Predictably, a strange door prompts the latter to narrate a "very odd story" (8) concerning its mysterious owner. That the solitary door is "equipped with neither bell nor knocker" (8) suggests that entry is permitted to its tenant only, and recalls the sealed-off buildings in previous Gothic novels, including Ann Radcliffe's *A Sicilian Romance* (1790). In the later chapter, "Incident at the Window," Utterson and Enfield return to the door, and the latter remarks with relief, "that story's at an end" (31). Nevertheless, they proceed into the court and observe Jekyll through a partially open window. While Utterson urges the "disconsolate prisoner" (31) to join them on a walk, Jekyll ominously declines: "the smile was struck out of his face and succeeded by an expression of such abject terror and despair, as froze the very blood of the two gentlemen below. They saw it but for a glimpse for the window was instantly thrust down; but that glimpse had been sufficient" (32). Slavoj Žižek's analysis of *La lunette d'approche*, a 1963 painting by René Magritte, is worth comparing to the scene. The painting features a partially open window; the panes reflect blue skies, but the small opening reveals total blackness. "[T]he frame of the windowpane is the fantasy frame that constitutes reality," Žižek writes, "whereas through the crack we get an insight into the 'impossible' Real."[24] We might consider this "crack" in the window as a visual metaphor for the formal dynamic of Gothic frame narratives, which reflect the comforting reality of the everyday world, but ultimately disjoint, unhinge, or otherwise unlock to expose the dark void of the Real. In Stevenson's novel, Jekyll begins his transformation spontaneously but manages to conceal the view of the entire horrid act. The door and the window function as thresholds between the reality of Utterson's perspective and the Real world of Hyde. Even Hyde's worst (if not only) crime, the murder of Carew, is observed through the framework of a window, as if he remains tantalizingly beyond the scope of the maid's eye-witness reality. With this effect in mind, we might read the systematic disclosures of the novel's narrative frames as permitting, if not emphasizing, the entrance of its concluding horror—the amorphous, disembodied narratorial entity that is ultimately neither Jekyll nor Hyde.

The transgression of the novel's thresholds indicates a passage into a deeper level of reality. Jekyll gives Lanyon permission to break into his laboratory cabinet, which the latter accomplishes with the assistance of a locksmith and a carpenter—a scene that Stoker would overtly echo when his heroes surreptitiously enter one of Dracula's residences in London. Utterson, in contrast, resorts to force to enter Hyde's narrative space. He enlists the aid of Jekyll's butler, Poole, who arms himself with an axe. Once sure that the voice coming from the laboratory door is not Jekyll's, Poole strikes:

> [T]he blow shook the building, and the red baize door leaped against the lock and hinges. A dismal screech, as of mere animal terror, rang from the cabinet. Up went the axe again, and again the panels crashed and the frame bounded; four times the

blow fell; but the wood was tough and the fittings were of excellent workmanship; and it was not until the fifth, that the lock burst and the wreck of the door fell inwards on the carpet [38].

The destruction of the door signals the passage into the novel's next narratives, the found manuscripts that bring readers into disturbing intimacy with Hyde's Real. Thus, Utterson's lengthy narrative acts as an extradiegetic opening frame that embeds the diegetic texts that follow. We might consider this narrative structure through the framing device in *Frankenstein*. Both Utterson and Walton are restless spirits, whose narratives introduce first-person accounts concerning an ambitious scientific experiment gone wrong. In *Jekyll and Hyde*, however, the two embedded texts usurp control of the novel, and the extradiegetic frame vanishes. A short note from Jekyll instructs Utterson to read Lanyon's narrative, the disturbing report of the doctor's fatal encounter with Hyde, and then to proceed with his confession, "Henry Jekyll's Full Statement of the Case," which is contained among other papers in a large envelope in Jekyll's cabinet study. The play on words here suggests that Utterson's narrative acts as an envelope, the text's vessel for its passage into the reader's hands, but the problem is that his narrative fails fully to envelop the charged stories that follow, as the two letters appear thereafter without Utterson's interruption or return.[25]

What makes *Jekyll and Hyde* a "strange case" when compared to *Frankenstein* or even *Wuthering Heights* is that a third person narrator conducts readers through Utterson's extradiegetic story. This voice, moreover, is neither omniscient nor interfering, but rather omnipresent at Utterson's side, for the disturbing conclusion of the novel requires readers to be kept in as much mystery as Utterson. We follow him and learn only what he learns until Stevenson introduces two first-person narratives to conclude the novel. The different voices become, as one contemporary reviewer observes, "parts of an intricate and inscrutable puzzle," which concludes with the revelation that "man is not truly one, but truly two" (48).[26] As Roger Luckhurst notes, *Jekyll and Hyde* "starts out like a detective fiction but … transmogrifies into something far more Gothic and unnerving."[27] Although the novel takes its generic cues from Edgar Allan Poe and Wilkie Collins, it ultimately chronicles a devastating series of events that cannot be prevented or solved. Once Utterson's narrative gives way to Lanyon's letter and then to "Henry Jekyll's Full Statement of the Case," it cannot return; the secret that has been revealed proves too horrifying for a terminal frame. As in Radcliffe's *The Italian* (1797), Utterson's world is lost; the familiar realism of London that Stevenson takes such care to develop disappears under the weight of the Gothic confession. The lack of a terminal frame suggests that the novel bears no "hide" between the reader's reality and the implications of the Real. When Stevenson leaves Utterson's frame open, he lifts the veil of reality, and brings readers "too close" to the Real within.

The novel's concluding confession has inspired rich commentary as a "troublesome metaphysical conundrum."[28] As Gordon Hirsch notes, Stevenson neither "enable[s] the reader to feel mastery over the book's mysteries," nor does he "permit the reader to work back to some absolute truth, presence, or sense of closure."[29] Utterson's failure to solve the mystery casts a shadow on the reliability of the omniscient voice that follows him. But the most significant challenge to omniscience arrives in the novel's concluding letter. Peter K. Garrett argues that "the 'I' who judiciously describes Jekyll's pleasures modulates into an unmarked 'omniscient' voice that judicially condemns Hyde's."[30] The "dismal screech, as of mere animal terror" (38) that Utterson reports suggests that the figure within is torn between two states—subjective confessor and objective narrator, Jekyll and Hyde, human and beast, reality and the Real. The confident "I" that begins the story undergoes a dramatic change when the narrative comes to the first transformation: "it came about that Edward Hyde was so much smaller, slighter and younger than Henry Jekyll" (51). This is the first instance of the narrator referring to himself in the third-person, and he quickly realizes: "I had lost my identity beyond redemption" (51). From this moment, the narrator steps outside himself so that the first-person pronouns "I" and "me" in fact paradoxically indicate a presence that is neither Jekyll nor Hyde. "Between these two," he remarks, "I now felt I had to choose" (55). But for some time the narrator does not choose, and prefers instead to live the double life, to enjoy both the infirm hospitality of Jekyll and the vibrant dissipations of Hyde. Eventually, the narrator loses control and runs out of the adulterated ingredient that effected the transformation. He ends his confession, "bring[ing] the life of that unhappy Henry Jekyll to an end" (62). Utterson stumbles upon the convulsing body of Hyde and concludes by sight and smell that "he was looking on the body of a self-destroyer" (39).

The ambiguity of the novel's conclusion rests in the fact that the narrator of the "Full Statement" leaves no hint that suicide is his last recourse. Indeed, he ends his confession with the implication that Hyde will return permanently. The question is, then, who poisons whom? If Hyde is the manifestation of the unbridled drives emerging from Jekyll's unconscious, then it is difficult to believe that he would have a hand in his own death.

Yet we could consider it evidence of Freud's "death drive," a fatal longing for the comforting chaos of pre-symbolic existence. Using Lacanian models, Richard Boothby regards the death drive as "the return of the [R]eal against the defensive organization of the ego that excludes it."[31] To seek death is to seek the Real. Hogle reads the event of Hyde's suicide through the liminal disjoining of the infant at birth and notes that the "commitment to death is coincident with the separation process (and the consequent want) inaugurating existence."[32] Thus, we may read the murder/suicide as Hyde's final and most brazen act of the Real. He fully and irreversibly immerses Jekyll in the pre-symbolic register, dragging his counterpart into the Real dissolution that accompanies death. Since Utterson's narrative does not return, Hyde's suicide seems to draw the text itself into an abyss from which there is no return. As Katherine Linehan observes, the novel is constructed of "simple-seeming surfaces and uncertain depths."[33] This rupture of form is seemingly the most disturbing effect of the novel's distinctive narrative frame. The third-person narrative, via its hovering detachment from the novel's events, provides a sense of security to readers who never fully step into Utterson's shoes. When the lawyer and his narrator retreat, however, readers are forced to confront the horrors of the subsequent letters on more intimate, first-person terms. The reality of Utterson's extradiegetic frame never returns, and the novel concludes with Jekyll, awaiting the "throes of change" (61), hurriedly scribbling his parting words.

Perhaps most important, Jekyll records that Hyde had been "scrawling in my own hand blasphemies on the pages of my book" (61). What evidence, then, should lead us to trust that the "Full Statement" is Jekyll's? In spite of the explicit physical difference between the figures, their handwriting is identical. Indeed, Hyde's attempt to disguise his own pen proves ineffective, as the novel's graphology expert, Utterson's head clerk Mr Guest, identifies it as only "differently sloped" (28). The out-of-body transformation that Jekyll endures over the course of his letter suggests that he is slowly losing grip on his identity as either man or monster. Given that both Jekyll and Hyde seem unable or unwilling to coexist without the structural effects of the "impure" drug (61), we might look elsewhere to expose the beneficiary of the suffering. Indeed, the character with the most to gain in Jekyll's death is Utterson, whose name curiously replaces Hyde's in the final draft of the doctor's dubious will. Carol Margaret Davison argues that Utterson "not only vies for and successfully obtains Jekyll's inheritance but is, ultimately, indictable for his murder."[34] The circumstantial evidence is damning, indeed. Utterson returns home to read the letters in privacy, but we can never be sure whether he hands the evidence over to the authorities. Utterson's story comes through the voice of a third-person narrator precisely because the mysteriously taciturn and morally suspicious lawyer would know better than to implicate himself in any way through writing. He not only instructs the obsequious Poole to "say nothing of this paper," but he also leaves the scene of crime, "locking the door of the theatre behind [him]" (41), which leaves the textual production without an audience, and suggests a censorship of the novel's events.[35]

We should recall that Utterson has the habit of being the "last reputable acquaintance and the last good influence in the lives of down-going men" (7). An "ambulance-chaser," in a sense, he approaches the desperate in much the same way as Maturin's Melmoth and Hogg's Gil-Martin. Moreover, his fixation with the "strange case" signals darker drives than the meager glory of solving the crime. Like Poe's vain detective C. Auguste Dupin, Utterson is in it for the money. He obsesses over Jekyll's will, which "had long been the lawyer's eyesore" (13), and he refuses to rest until his name replaces Hyde's. Thus, the novel stages a struggle between not only Jekyll and Hyde, but also Hyde and Utterson—and the lawyer emerges as the sole survivor and the victor of the significant spoils.[36] While Hyde suggests the physical and psychological horror of the Real, Utterson might implicate its more concealed, yet equally disturbing, attributes. Hyde is a horrifying symbol of degeneration, a primal force that emerges from the gulfs of pre-symbolic chaos. Utterson, in contrast, seems solely motivated by a "specifically financial preoccupation," which suggests the potential evil of evolution—the allegedly civilized fervor over monetary gain.[37] Žižek writes of the "fundamental systemic violence of capitalism" and notes that "the Real is the inexorable 'abstract' spectral logic of Capital."[38] Utterson embodies the ghostly Real of capitalistic obsession, which is driven by opportunism, leverage, and exploitation. The inspector's words concerning Hyde more fittingly apply to Utterson: "Money's life to the man" (24). Whereas Hyde promises decay and dissolution, Utterson practices growth and collusion. By securing Jekyll's inheritance, Utterson profits from suffering; the deaths of Carew, Lanyon, and Jekyll ultimately factor into his own financial benefit. Thus, the novel's most enduring horror is that the Real existed all along in the opening frame, that the man who tracks the monster is a monster himself. The structure of the framing device compels readers to focus their disgust on Hyde, the novel's scapegoat antagonist, while simultaneously championing Utterson, its ostensible hero. But all along readers identify with the lawyer's Real motivations—the restless and resistless drive for money that is the impenetrable kernel of horror that drives the modern world. As in previous Gothic novels, the Real that appears to be contained within the embedded text is also firmly located in the extradiegetic frame. What is more, since the inspiration for the novel had purportedly "come to [Stevenson] in a dream," the Real has existed all along beyond the boundaries of the text, deep within the author, whose "cries of horror" came from dreaming "a fine bogey tale."[39]

Jekyll and Hyde locates its horror in suggesting that the "primitive duality of man" (49) is a universal concern. Yet its central monster emerges via an experimental error that may never be replicated. The lasting unease that the novel inspires, then, may lie with Utterson, whose capitalistic greed suggests an expression of the Real that may be even more threatening than Jekyll's marauding counterpart. In *Dracula*, Stoker raises the stakes, so to speak, by introducing a degenerative force that seeks to spread the horror of the Real through the diffusion of a monstrous bloodline. In this sense, the novel reengages concerns over biological transmission that the Brontës addressed half-a-century earlier. What *Dracula* further shares with its Gothic ancestors, not to mention the more attendant sensation novels of Wilkie Collins, is an insistence on first-person narration. For *Dracula* is made up of a dizzying assortment of firsthand accounts, from journals and letters to newspaper clippings and phonograph recordings. In addition, it is remarkably attuned to its historical moment. In 1897, the *Spectator* noted the "up-to-dateness of the book—the phonograph diaries, typewriters, and so on," and more recently Jennifer Wicke has called *Dracula* the "first great *modern* novel in British literature."[40] A significant part of the novel's unsettling energy, then, is a result of its contemporary urgency. As with previous Gothic novels, however, its lasting horror is an effect of the distinctive interaction of its narrative frames, which allow monstrous suggestions of the Real to escape textual boundaries.

Dracula doubles down on the Gothic frame narrative by featuring not only a complex textual frame, but a more conspicuous geographic one, as well. Offering a return to the form of Radcliffe's frame narratives in *A Sicilian Romance* and *The Italian*, the opening portion of *Dracula*'s outermost frame not only appears in the interstitial space that precedes chapter one, but also becomes very much part of the fiction. The passage is written by an unnamed voice, apparently never heard from again, whose position in the novel's hierarchy is disturbingly indeterminate. Although Stoker's name appears prominently on both the cover and the title page, we might nevertheless assign other editorial tasks to this mysterious figure, including the subsequent table of contents, which provides some spoilers, including the Harkers' marriage and perhaps even Lucy Westenra's death, as her contributions to the narrative disappear after chapter twelve. At any rate, the opening statement provides several crucial stipulations concerning the transcription and presentation of the text:

> How these papers have been placed in sequence will be made clear in the reading of them. All needless matters have been eliminated, so that a history almost at variance with the possibilities of latter-day belief may stand forth as simple fact. There is throughout no statement of past events wherein memory may err, for all the records chosen are exactly contemporary given from the standpoints and within the range of knowledge of those who made them.[41]

This loaded paratext makes claims for the novel's authenticity, as if it was inserted by an anonymous editor, worried that his readership would approach the unsubstantiated patchwork accounts with skepticism. The editor also admits that the text will not appear in its original form, transcribed and arranged by Mina Murray (Harker), but instead will feature passages that have been "chosen" to reduce "needless matters." What we have, then, is an adulterated product, rather than a series of authentic documents. In some sense, this editorial labor mirrors the goals of the novel's titular villain, who ensures throughout that no original records survive. More than anything, however, the statement seems bent on accounting for the damaging misgivings expressed by Jonathan Harker in the terminal frame—the brief "Note" that acknowledges the futility of textual authenticity: "in all the mass of material of which the record is composed, there is hardly one authentic document.... We could hardly ask any one, even did we wish to, to accept these as proofs of so wild a story" (378). With his typical flair for the dramatic, Van Helsing earns the novel's closing words: "We want no proofs; we ask none to believe us!" (378). Taken together, these passages form a curiously self-aware framework that recognizes the lack of credible sources in a modern world of copies, facsimiles, and reproductions.

In a similar sense, the fear that Dracula inspires lies primarily in the threat of his reproductive power, which erases subjectivities and fashions monstrous replicas. The Count acts as a sort of biological palimpsest, rewriting the subject's genetic code with his own. And he invades the seat of modern civilization with a primitive imperial force that suggests degeneration rather than progress. Wicke observes that the novel stages a "collision of ancient mythologies with contemporary modes of production."[42] The wide-ranging state-of-the-art devices that the vampire hunters employ are seemingly instrumental in vanquishing the villain. Yet Dracula's ancient power also has modern implications, ones that reflect emergent technologies. "Dracula's individual powers," Wicke argues, "all have their analogue in the field of the mass cultural," with the result that the novel locates its horror in the "mass cultural vampire."[43] But a potential addendum to this innovative reading might be that the novel, as an aesthetic form, is fundamentally vampiric; it spreads as a purchasable commodity, but it can also be borrowed from circulating libraries and consumed in serialized installments. In 1840, one writer worried that "[n]o age of the world was ever cursed with such swarms of fictitious writers as now feast like vampires upon the very vitals of our literature. Their flimsy frost work has already produced a famine and spread a dire contagion throughout every department of science."[44] Yet another writer in 1852 accused American novels of "conjur[ing] up ... a group of ugly and fantastic shadows, without a wholesome touch of nature about them—a species of vampires, who exist upon the blood of good taste and common sense."[45] The Gothic novel is especially guilty of spreading its horror through its singular themes and forms. Like no other genre, it subsumes other modes into its textuality, feeding off their vitality, and growing into a disturbing and enticing aesthetic monstrosity.

Dracula's outermost frame narrative embeds diverse media, bleeding them of their original form during their transmogrification into text. In this sense, Mina acts very much like a novel writer, transcribing and copying assorted records into a consumable product. Her labor, then, is fundamentally vampiric, suggesting that novel writing is voracious in its consumption of divergent forms. One could say that the novel is imperialistic, assimilating "other" genres and modes into its chosen medium. As in previous Gothic novels, however, *Dracula*'s editorial framework complicates the authority of the embedded text. By acknowledging the reader's skepticism, Harker's "Note" undermines the authenticity of Mina's work. Thus, Van Helsing's final words that "some men ... did dare much for her sake" (378) proves disingenuous, at best. The anonymous opening frame, then, seemingly attempts to restore Mina's credibility. Yet it reveals that "needless matters have been eliminated," suggesting that Mina's collation of materials was, somehow, even more unruly than the edited version, that her finished product would have strained the credulity of readers. The frame narrative in *Dracula*, though brief and easy to disregard, is a crucial piece to the novel's puzzle. Moreover, it is a unique example in the history of the Gothic, as it is composed by two different figures making contradictory claims. This ideological antagonism, conflicting perspectives concerning the validity and reception of the product, suggests the fundamental deadlock of the Real, and challenges any reading that understands the novel as a whole artifact. Thus, Dracula's aggressive vampirism does not settle into dust, but rather spreads virulently into the frame, draining the text of its coherence and message.

Dracula's geographic frame narrative explicitly recalls several of the novel's Gothic ancestors. Harker's journey to Transylvania, for example, echoes Emily's Alpine passage into Italy in *The Mysteries of Udolpho* (1794). However, Stoker inverts Radcliffe's formal method, as Harker enters the Carpathians immediately, and the middle portion of the novel is set in England. When the group of heroes leaves London to pursue Dracula, the frame returns. In fact, roughly the same number of pages constitutes Harker's stay at Dracula's castle and the group's adventures outside England in pursuit. That Harker's journal occupies the first four chapters of the novel also echoes the four letters that make up Walton's introductory frame in *Frankenstein*. Both men, moreover, write in increasing trepidation to loved ones, though Stoker ultimately gives an essential voice to Harker's addressee, Mina, whereas Shelley's Margaret remains silent. Harker's journal begins as a travelogue of his business trip to a mysterious client in Transylvania, but quickly becomes a frenzied account of his imprisonment at Dracula's castle—a textual conversion that again recalls *Frankenstein*, in which Walton's letters transform into journal entries. As in Radcliffe's *The Italian*, the details of an Englishman's journey are arrested by the appearance of a shadowy figure—tall, thin, and draped in black. The journey leaves Harker in a literal and metaphorical fog, as if he has entered Dickens's Court of Chancery, "simply going over and over the same ground again" (11). Indeed, Esther's short experience in *Bleak House* (1852–53) with the mysterious figure in the cab in some ways anticipates Harker's first meeting with Dracula. While the gruff man Esther encounters is later revealed to be her benefactor Jarndyce, Dracula turns out to be the coach-driver during the last leg of the journey to the castle.

Harker begins his trip with the foreknowledge that his destination lies in the "midst of the Carpathian mountains; one of the wildest and least known portions of Europe" (1). There he finds himself at the "centre of some sort of imaginative whirlpool" (2). The bewildering environment that leads up to Dracula's castle acts as a threshold between Harker's symbolic reality and his entrance into the Real. Similar to the "sea of liberty" that Jekyll experiences as Hyde (62), Harker finds himself "in a sea of wonders" (18). Dracula resides on the dark side of the tapestry, behind the veil, and Harker twice makes note of the effect: the "horrible net of gloom and mystery which seemed closing round me" (33), and the "net of doom was closing round me more closely" (52). When Dracula leaves his castle, he must travel through a "dreadful abyss" (34), which Mina later describes as a "great gap between [the castle] and the steep of the adjacent mountain on any side" (372). Žižek writes of the "gap that for ever separates the fantasmatic kernel of the subject's being from the more 'superficial' modes of his or her symbolic and/or imaginary identifications," and notes that coming "too close" to this kernel causes "the aphanisis of the subject: the subject loses his or her symbolic consistency, it disintegrates."[46] Harker's stay in the castle brings him "too close" to the Real suggested by Dracula, who is one of the "spectral apparitions" that surface in the "very gap that for ever separates reality from the [R]eal."[47] The profound disorientation that Harker feels inside the castle suggests that his identity is fracturing under the threat of the Real. The horrors that Harker abjected to enter the symbolic order re-emerge in the company of Dracula, who blurs several categories that remain precariously distinct in reality: he is "Un-Dead" (life/death); he transforms into and controls animals (human/beast); and he demonstrates both hypnotic charm and barbaric violence (sexuality/brutality). Harker begins to lose his grip on reality, as the horrors of his unconscious materialize outside his dreams.

Harker's eventual freedom from Dracula's hold at the conclusion of chapter four proves so detrimental to his identity that it costs him his primary narrative position. In fact, his pen remains silent for ten chapters, and his anxious return to the narrative is forced by urgent circumstances: "I thought never to write in this diary again, but the time has come" (187). The conclusion of Harker's Transylvanian frame permits the introduction of a wealth of other voices and sources. In contrast to the textual layering of *Frankenstein* and *Wuthering Heights*, in which narratives multiply inwards, *Dracula*'s narrative unfolds in pieces that build chronologically upon one another. Critics have read the novel's narrative structure as repeated attempts to gain control of the story. For example, Alison Case argues that *Dracula* "stages a struggle between Mina and the men for narrative mastery."[48] Mina is afforded the first voice at the conclusion of Harker's frame, and hers is the final entry before her husband's "Note" in the terminal frame. But if we were to examine the narrative based on sheer word count, Dr Seward controls the story by a significant margin.[49] This is not surprising, given his Carlylean drive to "Work! work!" (71), but we may also speculate that Stoker had in mind Seward's means of recording the story when he allocated the doctor the most narrative space. For most of the novel, Seward employs a phonograph to record his notes, a technology that permits efficient reproduction, even better than Mina and Jonathan's shorthand. After Dracula destroys the phonograph's cylinders, however, Seward is forlorn: "How I miss my phonograph! To write diary with a pen is irksome to me" (335).

In spite of the novel's clear geographic distinctions—not to mention the way that Harker's long journal introduces several first-person accounts—few critics have thought of the *Dracula* as a frame narrative.[50] However, David Seed's examination of Stoker's initial notes for the novel further suggests the author's plan for frames. *Dracula* was to consist of four books, "To London," "Tragedy," "Discovery," and "Punishment."[51] If we follow the trajectory of the narrative, the majority of the first and fourth books would have been set in Transylvania. Still, as neither a frame nor a portrait appears in the novel, another metaphor may be in order, one that better engages the novel's thematic elements. Evidence of Dracula's feeding appears on his victims in the form of "white dots with red centres" (95). These marks effectively describe the villain himself, who is "deathly pale" (376), but with red eyes and "very red lips" (10)—not to mention that he is "simply gorged with blood" (51). Dracula's bite and image might be considered emblems of the novel's structure. Dracula leaves Transylvania, we must assume, because he has exhausted its resources. Indeed, the trio of vamps must feed on babies, and Dracula is so famished during his journey that the ship's entire crew becomes his nourishment. London, however, is bloated with blood. The novel's Transylvanian frame is the white circle, and its chapters in England the red passageway to immeasurable sustenance, a "bountiful wine-press" (288). Dracula portentously declares his motivation for moving: "I long to go through the crowded streets of your mighty London, to be in the midst of the whirl and rush of humanity, to share its life, its change, its death, and all that makes it what it is" (20). As Renfield declares, "The blood is the life! the blood is the life!" (141).

One early reviewer observes that Stoker "makes a bold departure, and at a single stroke transfers" Dracula from Transylvania to the "very streets of London itself."[52] The novel articulates a central concern of the "imperial Gothic"—the threat of foreign evil invading English soil.[53] In what Stephen Arata calls a "narrative of reverse colonization," *Dracula* instills the fear that the Count's foreign and primitive bloodline will taint English civilization and bring about its speedy ruin.[54] Daniel Pick observes that Harker "journeys from specific images of deformity … towards the citadel of full-blown degeneracy."[55] The animalistic vampires that Harker meets in the castle signal the "two-way traffic between human and beast," which seeks to invade and transform the civilization of London.[56] Dracula ominously remarks: "We are in Transylvania; and Transylvania is not

England" (21). But his goal is to merge the two through his monstrous, degenerate bloodline, to taint London's symbolic reality with the vampiric Real. The *Saturday Review* observes that Stoker "was not content with the small honour he could have gained by leaving [Dracula] in an out-of-the-way corner of Europe. That would have been merely to revert to the Mrs Radcliffe style of fiction. So Count Dracula is brought to London."[57] Harker early on expresses the threat: "This was the being I was helping to transfer to London, where, perhaps for centuries to come, he might, amongst its teeming millions, satiate his lust for blood, and create a new and ever widening circle of semi-demons to batten on the helpless" (51). Although not as culpable as Victor Frankenstein, Harker nonetheless is party to Dracula's relocation scheme, the delivery and the shelter of the Count's life-sustaining dirt-boxes. The transfer of soil from Transylvania to London overtly suggests transplantation. The Count puts down roots in England, quite literary creating a new family tree to branch off from his trunks.[58]

Dracula's first step is to acquire a house that serves as a suitable counterpart to his Transylvanian manor. Harker describes the listing for Carfax: "surrounded by a high wall, of ancient structure, built of heavy stones, and has not been repaired for a large number of years. The closed gates were of heavy old oak and iron, all eaten with rust" (23). The ancient vampire picks an antique and crumbling building for his residence, and not surprisingly jumps at the opportunity to be in close proximity to a "private lunatic asylum" (23), one of the sanctuaries of the Real in London. Seward diagnoses the asylum's principal patient Renfield as a "zoophagous (life-eating) maniac" (70). Dracula bonds himself intimately to Renfield, who presages the impending danger: "It is coming—coming—coming!" (103). It is only too late that Seward acknowledges the "clues from the conduct of the patient" and realizes that Renfield "has been a sort of index to the coming and going of the Count" (225). Renfield bridges the gap between Seward's reality and Dracula's Real; he is the "sanest lunatic" (248), in Quincey Morris's words. And he is an echo of Stevenson's Jekyll/Hyde, embodying Van Helsing's theory on madness: "All men are mad in some way or the other; and inasmuch as you deal discreetly with your madmen, so deal with God's madmen, too—the rest of the world" (118). Jacques Lacan writes that madness is not the result of a "contingent fact," but rather the "permanent virtuality of a gap opened up in his essence."[59] In this sense, the breakdown between reality and the Real that produces madness is a latent aspect of the human experience that requires a traumatic agent to emerge. Dracula is just this agent for Renfield. When under the spell of the Count, and invaded by the Real, Renfield is incoherent and irreverent, but at one crucial point he becomes lucid, speaking with a "courtly air of conviction" (244). He converses on equal terms with Van Helsing and introduces himself to the group of men like he is one of their own in the fight against Dracula: "Don't you know that I am sane and earnest now; I am no lunatic in a mad fit, but a sane man fighting for his soul?" (247). Seward refuses Renfield's measured supplications to be removed from the asylum, and the latter ends up being perhaps the most tragic figure in the novel. In an attempt to save Mina from another feeding, Renfield is bludgeoned to death by Dracula in a manner reminiscent of Hyde's violent murder of Danvers Carew. Renfield dies because he cannot become a permanent actor in either the symbolic reality of the novel's narrators or Dracula's Real.

Žižek's definition of the Real as a "monstrous Thing, too traumatic for our eyes," warrants some analysis in terms of how Dracula specifically suggests the inscrutable Lacanian order.[60] Dracula is the perfect example of a "monster that gives body to the surplus that escapes the vicious circle of the mirror relationship."[61] One contemporary reviewer notes that Stoker "has been at pains to get up very carefully all that can be gathered of vampire lore, and has made his book a complete treatise on the habits and customs of these strange beasts."[62] One of these famously enduring traits is that vampires cause no reflection in mirrors. For Harker, the lack of mirrors in Dracula's castle is one of its defining curiosities. Dracula shatters Harker's shaving glass and remonstrates: "It is a foul bauble of man's vanity. Away with it!" (26). The mirror is indeed a tool for vanity, but it is also a crucial component of human development. That Dracula has no reflection suggests that he cannot have experienced Lacan's "mirror stage," the fundamental infant event that permits a realization of the self as other and triggers maturity into the imaginary and the symbolic orders. On one hand, Dracula remains part of the primordial Real (Van Helsing regularly refers to the Count's "child-brain"), but on the other, he is stuck in a late mirror stage in which he comes to know himself as a subject through perpetual identification with others. "This man belongs to me!" (39), he famously bellows. Dracula, like an infant lacking motor skills, perceives himself as a fractured body (which is literalized by his ability to transform into beasts and to dissolve into mist), and the images with which he identifies are whole, the "Ideal-I" that we always grasp for, but can never reach. Yet Dracula's "jubilant assumption of his specular image," to use Lacan's words, manifests itself in vampirism, a power to replicate his own fractured image, to make humanity his vampiric clones.[63] It is a "transcendence of the mirror stage," Maria Beville notes.[64] Dracula makes an "I" out of everyone because he cannot recognize his own identity. As Van Helsing remarks, "[i]t is that we become as him" (237). In this reading, Dracula becomes one of the pathetic villains of the Gothic (the creature, Melmoth, Wringhim, and Heathcliff), whose wretched existence is a result of being different—the curse of the "super" natural.

Dracula's power permits him to slink in secrecy throughout London for the majority of the novel, taking the shape of animals and dissolving into lights and vapors. When Harker first spots his adversary in human form in London, his shock prevents him from articulating the threat. Harker's inability to narrate his adventures or to warn Mina of the danger in her mi(d)st is evidence of the breakdown of his symbolic reality. To this point, Harker had repressed his Transylvanian experience as a nightmare, but Dracula's foreign Real becomes part of Harker's domestic reality, and systems of language break down. Recall, for example, Emily's incapacitation after lifting the black veil at Udolpho—though in this case it is the "waxen image" (378) of the undead Dracula that immobilizes Harker. During the next confrontation with Dracula, Harker is again left in a stupor and relegated a static observer of the abuse of his wife. The remaining men stumble upon Dracula committing an "act of maternal aggression," as he forces Mina to feed from a wound in his breast.[65] Nancy Armstrong reads this scene as an "inversion" in which the Gothic "simply dramatizes the magical thinking that inhabits the heart of realism."[66] This scene represents Mina consuming the vampiric essence of the Real, and from then on straddling the border between the Real and reality in much the same way as Renfield. Ironically, Dracula's impulse to make Mina "my companion and my helper" (288) ends up costing him his life. Anticipating an answer to W. B. Yeats's question in "Leda and the Swan" (1925), Mina acquires knowledge and power from the brutal scene.[67] Via Van Helsing's hypnosis, she is able partially to experience the world through Dracula's senses—to become a semi-omniscient narrator—and the party may thus trace the timing and the method of his flight back to Transylvania. Dracula escapes London with the plan to reenter the Real, the Transylvanian frame "full of caverns and fissures that reach none know whither" (319), but Mina's vampiric omniscience prevents his homecoming.

As the group meticulously sanctifies the boxes, Dracula loses his power. Thus, during his one true fight with his heroic nemeses, Dracula is very much a material body, though still in possession of superhuman physicality. The scene not only recalls the creature's jump aboard Walton's ship and narrative in *Frankenstein*, but also Satan's "slight bound" into

Eden in *Paradise Lost*.[68] "Suddenly with a single bound [Dracula] leaped into the room, winning a way past us before any of us could raise a hand to stay him. There was something so panther-like in the movement—something so unhuman, that it seemed to sober us all from the shock of his coming" (304). After some knife-play, Dracula leaps through a window to the ground below. In contrast to the creature's promise of self-immolation, an assurance made just before he "sprung from the cabin-window," Dracula's exit from the house comes with an impotent warning that his "revenge has just begun!" (306).[69] Whereas the creature departs Walton's frame, Dracula seeks to reenter his own. London has not been as hospitable as the Count's cartographic books and travel literature had made it out to be. Yet he may depart knowing that he has left an indelible mark on the "little band" of hunters, the scar that he shares with Mina—a scarlet letter that is symbolic of their overtly sexual encounter, if not the "indelible stamp of [her] lowly origin." In any case, the "red scar" is intimately linked to the vampire blood circulating within, which might survive Dracula's alleged death, and pass into young Quincey Harker—fated to join the list of potentially dangerous "second comings" who endure beyond the frame.

Van Helsing makes clear Dracula's motivations for flight: "He meant escape.… He saw that with but one earth-box left, and a pack of men following like dogs after a fox, this London was no place for him" (312). While the analogy maintains that domesticated animals triumph over feral ones, it nevertheless suggests that the heroes must adopt primal instincts to vanquish their enemy. "[H]e have gone back to his Castle in Transylvania," Van Helsing boasts: "This very creature that we pursue, he take hundreds of years to get so far as London; and yet in one day, when we know of the disposal of him, we drive him out" (315). Dracula's glacial movement succumbs to the rapid technologies of communication; evolution trumps degeneration. A reviewer for the *Academy* notes: "Vampires need a Transylvanian background to be convincing. The witches in 'Macbeth' would not be effective in Oxford-street."[70] Even Mina participates in the celebratory show: "So he came to London to invade a new land. He was beaten" (342). But the conclusion of *Dracula* is laced with a disturbing ambiguity that echoes previous Gothic novels. When the vampire hunters are forced to destroy the undead Lucy, they follow Van Helsing's specific instructions: plunge a stake through the heart and remove the head. During the climactic final scene, however, the Count, lying incapacitated in his coffin, receives the simultaneous blows of Harker's "great knife … shear[ing] though the throat" and Quincey's "bowie knife plung[ing] into the heart," which cause him to "crumble into dust" (337). Several questions remain: Did Harker's blow entirely remove the head? Is Quincey's knife a suitable replacement for a wooden stake? And why the disintegration when Lucy's body earlier remains intact? What is more, just before the assault, Dracula's "eyes saw the sinking sun, and the look of hate in them turned to triumph" (337). When he leaves them in the dust, then, he has not necessarily died, but rather disappeared, recalling the ambiguous fates of Shelley's creature and Maturin's Melmoth.

Although Harker insists that Dracula has been "blotted out" (378), the latter perseveres in the textual reproductions of his story, not only in the typewritten copies that Mina produces, but also in the mass-produced novels that the editor implicitly markets in the opening frame. But the possibility that he survives the "moment of final dissolution" indicates the gaps in the narrators' accounts.[71] As Harker reveals, "there is hardly one authentic document" (378) that remains, which further suggests that the novel's evidence is dubious. By implicitly highlighting the potential inaccuracy of transliteration and transcription, *Dracula* echoes the distrust that previous Gothic novels express over editorial control. Mina's copywork takes on the impossible task of reproductive fidelity. While she "knit[s] together in chronological order every scrap of evidence they have" (225), the tapestry she creates is permeable, if not sometimes threadbare. The hurried, anxious marks of Harker's stenography and the delicate wax cylinders of Seward's phonograph must experience some measure of loss when transformed into typewritten text. We learn early on that Mina has been "practicing shorthand very assiduously" (53), but has she perfected the art? Moreover, can she accurately hear Seward's voice through the crackling static of the early phonograph? And most disturbing, what "needless matters" have been removed by the anonymous editor?

In some sense, Dracula embodies this translative loss through his vague reproductive power. Van Helsing describes the traits of vampires: "they cannot die, but must go on age after age adding new victims and multiplying the evils of the world; for all that die from the preying of the Un-Dead become themselves Un-Dead, and prey on their kind. And so the circle goes on ever widening, like as the ripples from a stone thrown in the water" (214). Yet this mythological definition does not necessarily match the empirical evidence. Lucy becomes a vampire following Dracula's feedings, but the children she feeds on bear no reported vampiric effects. Dracula's victims appear to be diluted copies, compressed files that have lost their original bite.[72] He is the urtext whose facsimiles weaken the original power. This analogy should not lessen Dracula's threat as a monstrous figure of abjection. But it does suggest that the novel's primary implication of the Real is the antagonism located in its outermost frame narrative—the conflict between Harker's "so wild a story" and the anonymous editor's "simple fact." *Dracula* exemplifies what is at stake in the history of the Gothic novel: its lasting horrors, the specters of the Real that continue to haunt readers today, are products of the explosive interaction of monstrous antagonists and dynamic frames.

Coda

Glory in a Gap

The Turn of the Screw *and* Heart of Darkness

> O God, I could be bounded in a nutshell and count myself a king of infinite space—were it not that I have bad dreams.
>
> —Shakespeare, *Hamlet*[1]

> I had begun to taste something of the horror that belongs to the lot of a human being whose nature is not adjusted to simple human conditions.
>
> —George Eliot, "The Lifted Veil" (1859)[2]

"The Lifted Veil" stands out in George Eliot's catalogue. The short story appeared in *Blackwood's* just six months after Eliot's first novel, *Adam Bede*, which features the famous digression that articulates the author's definition of realism—a perspective that seems a far cry from the supernatural Gothicism of "The Lifted Veil." What is more, the robust omniscient narrator featured in each of Eliot's subsequent novels conspicuously contrasts the tenuous first-person voice of Latimer, the troubled protagonist of "The Lifted Veil." Latimer holds the gift of both foresight and insight; he can look into the future and can read others' thoughts. In a sense, then, he is the story's omniscient narrator, accessing scenes and perspectives outside the purview of normal first-person narration.[3] But Eliot suggests that Latimer's "abnormal power of penetration" is a curse.[4] As most Gothic novels demonstrate, to possess the supernatural is to live in horror. Latimer's omniscience makes him a monster; the veil of reality lifts, and he peers through to the Real. "The Lifted Veil" suggests that even Eliot, long the figurehead of high Victorian realism, could be troubled by the power of omniscience—an effect made possible through the story's structure. For "The Lifted Veil" is a framed flashback narrative modeled overtly on the Gothic.[5] Eliot's story is thus solidly part of the Gothic frame narrative's history, and it likely informed the device's move to sensation novels and "scientific romances." But it was Henry James and Joseph Conrad who refreshed the frame narrative in its Gothic mode, employing it as a vehicle for interrogating omniscience. James and Conrad found in the Gothic frame narrative the resources to explode the conventions of Victorian realism and to initiate a new period of novel writing that would refuse to hang its hat on the fiction of omniscient narration.[6] It would be an age of Gothic realism.

In his preface to *Roderick Hudson*, James muses on the craft of the novelist: "Really, universally, relations stop nowhere, and the exquisite problem of the artist is eternally but to draw, by a geometry of his own, the circle within which they shall happily *appear* to do so."[7] The struggle for the novelist, according to James, is to provide narrative boundaries: "The prime effect of so sustained a system, so prepared a surface is to lead on and on; while the fascination of following resides, by the same token, in the presumability *somewhere* of a convenient, of a visibly-appointed stopping-place."[8] James's "canvas of life" requires a difficult process of focus and inclusion measured against marginalization and exclusion. This methodology in some ways echoes Edgar Allan Poe's 1846 remarks on the "close *circumscription of space*" he created when writing "The Raven."[9] Whereas Poe achieves Gothic effects by confining his subject inside a haunting chamber of voices, James was able to engage narrative framing to create disturbing effects of irresolution. In a 1905 essay on James's style, Conrad speaks to the rejection of finality in terms of its production of realism:

> [I]t is obvious that a solution by rejection must always present a certain lack of finality.... Why the reading public which, as a body, has never laid upon a storyteller the command to be an artist, should demand from him this sham of Divine Omnipotence, is utterly incomprehensible. But so it is; and these solutions are legitimate inasmuch as they satisfy the desire for finality, for which our hearts yearn, with a longing greater than the longing for the loaves and fishes of this earth. Perhaps the only true desire of mankind, coming thus to light in its hours of leisure, is to be set at rest. One is never set at rest by Mr Henry James's novels. His books end as an episode in life ends. You remain with the sense of the life still going on.[10]

At stake here for Conrad is a readership that insists on experiencing an ending, an outcome that requires omniscience, an objective power that mounts the world into a manageable frame. For Conrad, the world is made up of subjective experiences, perspectives colored by bias and human limitations. Thus, fiction should never end with objective resolution manufactured by a voice that cannot possibly exist.

This effect, though Conrad fails to acknowledge it, is decidedly Gothic. That late-Victorian writers refused objective finality demonstrates a debt to the Gothic novel. Does the creature immolate himself at the end of *Frankenstein*? Does Melmoth cast himself off a cliff? James expressed the struggle of crafting indeterminate realism in his notebooks while he was writing *What Maisie Knew* (1897):

> I have brought this little matter of Maisie to a point at which a really detailed scenario of the rest is indispensable for a straight and sure advance to the end. Let me not, just Heaven—not, God knows, that I *incline* to!—slacken in my deep observance of this strong and beneficent method—this intensely structural, intensely hinged and jointed preliminary frame. In proportion as this frame is vague do I directly pay for the vagueness; in proportion as it is full and finished do I gain, do I rejoice in the strength.[11]

James explains that he must avoid an unfocused frame, one that is either obscure in its language or that fails precisely to form the informational edges of the central story. Ultimately, he achieved this clarity in the frame to *Maisie*, a novel of childhood experience and adult self-absorption. As in Ann Radcliffe's *The Italian* (1797) and Robert Louis Stevenson's *The Strange Case of Dr Jekyll and Mr Hyde* (1886), the introductory frame for *Maisie* never returns, and readers, like the governess Mrs Wix, are left to "wonder at what Maisie knew."[12] James's haunting Gothic masterpiece *The Turn of the Screw* (1898) similarly fails to return to the frame, but in this case readers are left wondering what anyone knew—whether child, governess, storyteller, or narrator.[13]

The Turn of the Screw opens upon a group of partygoers who have just finished listening to a chilling ghost story that involves a child. Douglas, a particularly shadowy member of the group, boasts that he knows a story that ups the ante, for it involves ghosts and "*two* children"—another turn of the screw.[14] An unnamed narrator, with the support of the equally enthralled listeners, prods Douglas to tell his story, but he prefers to read it directly from an original manuscript. "The story's written," he explains: "It's in a locked drawer—it has not been out in years" (23). Douglas sends away for the manuscript, and some time later he begins by way of a "prologue," which is "required for a proper intelligence" (26). Douglas's words, which provide the "found manuscript" some introductory context—and function as another frame—come through the voice of the narrator, who promises to have taken them "from an exact transcript of my own made much later" (26). The manuscript is written in the hand of an unnamed governess, who had answered an advertisement to care for the nephew and niece of a "gentleman, a bachelor in the prime of life, such a figure as had never risen, save in a dream or an old novel" (26), at an Essex manor named Bly. The frame concludes with the narrator offering a suggestion for a title (which is ignored), and the governess's manuscript begins at chapter one.

Bly is a veritable Gothic edifice, which houses the main characters—the governess, the two children, Miles and Flora, and Mrs Grose, another caretaker. Returning from a walk in the gardens, the governess notices the figure of a man standing at one of the manor's towers, as "definite as a picture in a frame" (40). This marks the governess's first allusion to framing when describing the apparitions she sees. As with many of Radcliffe's heroines, the governess routinely frames her views through windows, creating picturesque borders for her potential imaginings. The figure she views atop the house leads her to question: "Was there a 'secret' at Bly—a mystery of Udolpho or an insane, an unmentionable relative kept in unsuspected confinement?" (41). Referring to both *The Mysteries of Udolpho* (1794) and *Jane Eyre* (1847) positions the governess as an avid reader of Gothic fiction and thus, like Austen's Catherine Morland, a potential victim of its snares. Her next encounter with the figure, however, proves far more distinctive and disturbing. She sees it staring in at a window and surmises that it must be looking for Miles. She later describes its features and dress to Mrs Grose, who confirms that it is Peter Quint, a servant who had earlier died. Although Quint is the central terror of the story, he is only a fleeting symbol, a fantasmatic frame for the more disturbing events of the novel that remain shrouded in secrecy.

Mrs Grose reveals that Quint and another servant, Miss Jessel, who previously held the governess position, "were both infamous" (58). Quint reportedly had been inappropriate with many of Bly's inmates, but the implication of an illicit sexual relationship with Jessel makes her a partner in his crimes. Thereafter, the governess begins to see the ghostly figure of the woman, dressed in black, apparently attempting to haunt Flora. But it is Quint who continues to appear, and eventually he makes his way into the house, where the governess has an intense encounter with him. "They're seen only across, as it were, and beyond," the governess concludes, "in strange places and on high places, the top of towers, the roof of houses, the outside of windows, the further edge of pools; but there's a deep design, on either side, to shorten the distance and overcome the obstacle" (77). These geographic and architectural barriers appear to function as frames between the governess's reality and the world of the ghostly figures, which, in James's words, are "coming over to where they are."[15] In fact, however, the ghosts are themselves the governess's fantasy frame, which separates the reality of the children from the Real of her erotic desires.

This secret proves too much for the governess to manage, as she "felt the importance of giving the last jerk to the curtain" (61). She desires access to the Real truth hidden behind the false veil of reality. Since she has read *The Mysteries of Udolpho*, however, the governess knows that the corpse Emily thinks she sees behind the veil in Radcliffe's novel proves to be nothing but a waxen effigy, and the Real is the horror of Emily's imagination. Thus, the ghosts are fantasy figures painted on the veil that screens the reality of Bly from the Real of the governess's desires. Quint and Jessel are scapegoats that the governess creates to distract from her own traumatic thoughts. Before Flora leaves Bly, she challenges the governess's authority: "I don't know what you mean. I see nobody. I see nothing. I never *have*. I think you're cruel. I don't like you!" (103). Flora cannot see, in the governess's words, "the hideous author of our woe—the white face of damnation" (116). In the novella's momentous final scene, the governess smothers Miles as she sees Quint looking in at the window. She asserts that his heart has stopped, but the cause of the shock is never divulged. Instead of Quint's ghost, Miles finally sees the Real of the governess's illicit passion. Miles's "cry of a creature hurled over an abyss" (120) instantaneously transports him from innocence to experience, transforms him from a boy into a troubled Gothic creature.

The governess's magnetic attraction to Miles and his adult manner, which includes the scandalous words he tells his friends that get him expelled from school, is perhaps the salacious secret of the novel. What the governess sees in Quint and Jessel is a manifestation of her guilt over her own forbidden desire for a young boy. The governess one day sees Miles facing a window and

> an extraordinary impression dropped on me as I extracted a meaning from the boy's embarrassed back—none other than the impression that I was not barred now. This inference grew in a few minutes to sharp intensity and seemed bound up with the direct perception that it was positively *he* who was. The frames and squares of the great window were a kind of image, for him, of a kind of failure. I felt that I saw him, at any rate, shut in or shut out. He was admirable, but not comfortable: I took it in with a throb of hope. Wasn't he looking, through the haunted pane, for something he couldn't see? [114].

The window frames Miles's reflection, a portrait not of a ghost outside, but of a child trapped inside, consumed by his oppressive protector. The governess sees Miles and Quint, the cause and representation of her guilt, framed in the same window. She wants the children to blame the dead, to pass her sins to the ghosts of lascivious servants past, but Miles is too innocent to understand, too young for his heart to beat for her love. "I caught him, yes, I held him," the governess reveals: "it may be imagined with what a passion" (120). His "little heart" stops, "dispossessed," but not from ghosts—instead from a forbidden love. The novel ends—ambiguous, frustrating, and Gothic—the villain alive and the blame securely passed to the voiceless dead. As in previous Gothic novels, the conclusion is disturbingly equivocal. What on the surface appears to be the death of a child in fact could be the story of a governess's love. The woman who sent Douglas the manuscript story "before she died" (24) may have finally found the courage to admit her wrongdoings, however tacitly.[16]

The story's emergence in the extradiegetic frame earns it a greater degree of reality than had it simply been issued as a freestanding text. Douglas relates that the writer of the manuscript was also his sister's governess and that she revealed the story because she was in love. Although Douglas only remarks that she "liked" him, the gossipy group infers love, at least on his end. There is a possibility that she loved another, namely the mysterious, aristocratic figure who advertised the position, but the truth is never explicitly stated. Whatever the case, James establishes an intimacy between Douglas and the governess, which connects the diegetic and extradiegetic narratives.[17] This parergon-like blurring of boundaries becomes disturbing, however, if we acknowledge the governess's prurient desires. Douglas reveals that the governess was twenty-years-old during the time of the story, and we later learn that Miles was ten. Since the governess is ten years older than Douglas, then the latter is the same age as Miles. We might wonder, then, whether she enacted her illicit desires on the young man, freshly home from university, who might resemble a decade-older Miles. Regardless, ghosts from the embedded narrative, implications of the Real that result from any number of textual interpretations, invade the world closer to the reality of the reader. It is no surprise that the party calls Douglas's storytelling an "outbreak."

Five years after he reframed his novels with new prefaces for the *New York Edition* (1907–09), and almost a decade after Conrad's laudatory "Henry James: An Appreciation," James wrote an essay, "The New Novel," in which he examined Conrad's storytelling frame narratives:

> Mr Conrad's first care … is expressly to posit or set up a reciter, a definite responsible intervening first person singular, possessed of infinite sources of reference, who immediately proceeds to set up another, to the end that this other may conform again to the practice, and that even at that point the bridge over to the creature, or in other words to the situation or the subject, the thing "produced," shall, if the

> fancy takes it, once more and yet once more glory in a gap. It is easy to see how heroic the undertaking of an effective fusion becomes on these terms, fusion between what we are to know and that prodigy of our knowing which is ever half the very beauty of the atmosphere of authenticity.[18]

Whether or not James intended it to do so, this passage illuminates a new approach to reading Gothic novels, especially *Frankenstein*. The "creature" that Victor produces is yet another storyteller who himself introduces Safie's story. Each of the frames in *Frankenstein* reveals a gap in knowledge even more than it builds a bridge. As Slavoj Žižek has observed, the gaps in the symbolic order are evidence of the Real.[19] For James, however, the ultimate "fusion" of Conrad's disparate voices makes the narrative authentic. We might think of this effect as a disingenuous veiling of the Real, an insistence that gaps do not exist in order to establish a homogenous reality that was never present in the first place. The same phenomenon applies to several of Conrad's novels, where Charles Marlow's "prolonged hovering light of the subjective over the outstretched ground of the case exposed" constructs story within story—connected by crumbling, perilous, and apocryphal bridges of information.[20]

Heart of Darkness (1899) begins aboard the "*Nellie*" (the last of the nineteenth-century Nells), a ship anchored in the Thames, awaiting a tidal change to carry it out to sea. Five characters are on the ship, including an unnamed narrator and Marlow. Although the narrator asserts that the sea has made the group "tolerant of each other's yarns—and even convictions," he expresses targeted annoyance at Marlow, who demonstrates the "weakness of many tellers of tales who seem so often unaware of what their audience would best like to hear."[21] The narrator immediately undermines Marlow's authority as a storyteller, but, like Coleridge's Wedding Guest, "cannot choose but hear."[22] The narrator does, however, supply a vital argument concerning narrative structure:

> The yarns of seamen have a direct simplicity ... the whole meaning of which lies within the shell of a cracked nut. But Marlow was not typical (if his propensity to spin yarns be excepted), and to him the meaning of an episode was not inside like a kernel but outside, enveloping the tale which brought it out only as a glow brings out a haze, in the likeness of one of these misty halos that sometimes are made visible by the spectral illumination of moonshine [5].

For most tales, the narrator suggests, meaning lies in the core, but for Marlow it appears in the framework. The connotation of the word "within" complicates the quote: meaning could be found *inside* the shell or *in* the shell itself. Moreover, the nut is "cracked," which suggests an incomplete, if not broken, framework—a metaphor that recalls the ambiguous conclusions of earlier Gothic novels. The narrator's assertion has at least two other implications. The first is that Marlow's tale is itself framed, and we can perhaps see this effect if the scenes outside Africa frame his river adventures and meeting with Kurtz. Although he barely survives the journey, Marlow does manage to return to London and to settle Kurtz's business. Thus, the frame outside Africa should be the hazy, "misty halo" that surrounds the distinct and defined interior. But it is rather the opposite; the central passages in Africa, the kernel, the heart of darkness, are a nebulous dreamscape, which in fact bewilders Marlow in his return to England, and frustrates any coherent reading. The second implication of the narrator's shell metaphor is even more significant: if the narrator follows Marlow in believing that meaning is located in the frame, then he implicitly suggests that the framework he provides is more relevant than Marlow's story. Perhaps it is.

The narrator complains that the group aboard the ship is fated "to hear about one of Marlow's inconclusive experiences" (7). Yet again this undermines Marlow's authority by drawing immediate attention to the fact that it will provide no resolution. Indeed, as with Esther Summerson's final dash in *Bleak House* (1852–53), Marlow's story trails off mid-sentence: "It would have been too dark—too dark altogether" (77). The novel's avoidance of finality, however, reiterates Conrad's praise of James. *Heart of Darkness* purposefully frustrates readers who desire conclusiveness, which only becomes available, courtesy of the narrator, in the frame. Like Fielding's biographer-host in *Tom Jones* (1749), the narrator breaks in for points of rest, several times noting Marlow's intervals of silent reflection. The most dramatic of these pauses comes nearly halfway through the text:

> It had become so pitch dark that we listeners could hardly see one another. For a long time already he, sitting apart, had been no more to us than a voice. There was not a word from anybody. The others might have been asleep, but I was awake. I listened on the watch for the sentence, for the word that would give me the clue to the faint uneasiness inspired by this narrative that seemed to shape itself without human lips in the heavy night-air of the river [27].

The narrator becomes a reader, experiencing Marlow through a disembodied voice, and participating in a fruitless search for meaning, for structure, for resolution. Marlow fails to help his cause when he undermines his own authority: "You know I hate, detest, and can't bear a lie.... There is a taint of death, a flavour of mortality in lies" (27). Yet his last act is a lie: he tells Kurtz's "Intended" that the dead man's last words were her name, rather than the disturbing "The horror! The horror!" (69). This scene completes what is perhaps the most disturbing example of metalepsis in literature. Kurtz's horror, the unexplained Real of his affairs, infects Marlow and travels with him back to London and then into the frame on the Thames. Even more unsettling, the meaning of *Heart of Darkness* is the Real. There are so many holes in the story, so many gaps in knowledge, that it is impossible to construct complete meaning. Marlow's story, like his sunken ship, is missing its rivets. In the frame, the sea and the river are "welded together without a joint" (3), which recalls the "intensely structural, intensely hinged and jointed preliminary frame" of James's *What Maisie Knew*.[23] The meaning comes through the interstitial space between frame and framed, between Africa and London, between the "heart of darkness" (35) and "one of the dark places of the earth" (5). The points at which the narratives meet provide the structure and finality that Marlow (and perhaps Conrad) sought to deny: at the joints we see that the "thing monstrous" (365) and the "monstrous town" (5) present the same horrors. But these gaps also function as Real fissures in the symbolic order. "[F]or Lacan," Žižek writes, "the Real ... is not an external thing that resists being caught in the symbolic network, but the crack within the symbolic network itself."[24] Our "glory in the gap," in other words, is an attraction to the Real, a fascination with the traumatic, the uncanny, the incomplete—a desire to fall down the rabbit hole, to lift the veil, to break the frame, to experience Gothic realism.

I would like to conclude by examining a late-Victorian Gothic text that provides a useful bookend, or terminal frame, for this study's claims—Arthur Machen's *The Great God Pan* (1894). The bubbling concoction of its twisting, incomplete narratives and ominous, obscure atmosphere makes the text a prototype for new, modernist forms of the Gothic that would be exemplified by H. P. Lovecraft's cosmicist writing on the occult. *The Great God Pan* features a distinctive frame narrative: the characters in the opening frame, Clarke and Raymond, appear together again in the terminal frame, though over two decades have passed since their initial encounter.[25] In the opening frame, Raymond readies himself to perform a surgical experiment on a young woman, Mary, and explains to Clarke that the scenes of reality

> are but dreams and shadows; the shadows that hide the real world from our eyes. There is a real world, but it is beyond this glamour and this vision, ... beyond them all as beyond a veil. I do not know whether any human being has ever lifted that veil; but I do know, Clarke, that you and I shall see it lifted this very night from before another's eyes. You may think this all strange nonsense; it may be strange, but it is true, and the ancients knew what lifting the veil means. They called it seeing the god Pan.[26]

The operation is evidently a success, but it causes Mary to experience violent convulsions, and she is left mentally incapacitated from the experience. Machen subsequently introduces several other, often fragmentary, narratives that eventually coalesce around a mysterious woman, primarily known as Helen Vaughan, who has been linked to several deaths.[27] We learn in the terminal frame that Helen is Mary's daughter, and that her father is the titular Pan, who was able to pass through the "unutterable, the unthinkable gulf that yawns profound between two worlds, the world of matter and the world of spirit" (85).

Helen's path of destruction begins in rural Wales, spreads to South America, and eventually settles in London's high society. Christine Ferguson observes that Helen "remakes herself and continues, neither progressing nor degenerating but continually becoming something that is never quite finished enough to be absorbed into the logic of her surrounding culture."[28] We might expand on this idea by thinking of Helen as a Gothic monster who implicates the existence of the Real by refusing to be assimilated into symbolic reality.[29] Similarly, those who fall into her snares can no longer be part of reality; children are traumatized into psychic paralysis, and men hang themselves.[30] Although the exact circumstances surrounding the deaths are never revealed, Machen implies that Helen reveals Pan (with all its sybaritic implications) to her victims. The tale's amateur detective, Villiers, manages to turn the table on Helen, presenting her a rope with which she hangs herself. The scene of her death is recorded in a fragmentary note written in Latin by an attendant doctor:

> The skin, and the flesh, and the muscles, and the bones, and the firm structure of the human body that I had thought to be unchangeable, and permanent as adamant, began to melt and dissolve.... I saw the form waver from sex to sex, dividing itself from itself, and then again reunited. Then I saw the body descend to the beasts whence it ascended, and that which was on the heights go down to the depths, even to the abyss of all being.... I watched, and at last I saw nothing but a substance as jelly [228–29].

Although the traumatic scene of Helen's death might seem to implicate the Real, it is instead the climax of release—the gruesome termination of a miserable life. Helen's suicide demonstrates that she seeks to escape from her demon, and we should feel relief rather than horror at her fatal liquefaction. The Real, instead, is suggested exclusively within the tale's frame. Whereas the circumstances of Helen's crimes remain entirely hearsay, Machen actually raises the Great God Pan in Clarke's dream—a fantasy that takes place in the outwardly everyday world of the opening narrative. There is perhaps no better literary attempt to represent the Real, as Clarke seems to be drawn, by an inexpressible force, into an abyss, where the symbolic order of language breaks down in the unwieldy final sentence:

> [F]or a moment in time he stood face to face there with a presence, that was neither man nor beast, neither the living nor the dead, but all things mingled, the form of all things but devoid of all form. And in that moment, the sacrament of body and soul was dissolved, and a voice seemed to cry "Let us go hence," and then the darkness of darkness beyond the stars, the darkness of everlasting [188].

Chapter Notes

Introduction

1. Quoted in Nikolai Pan'kov, "'Everything else depends on how this business turns out…': Bakhtin's Dissertation Defence as Real Event, as High Drama and as Academic Comedy," in Ken Hirschkop and David Shepherd (eds.), *Bakhtin and Cultural Theory* (Manchester: Manchester University Press, 2001), 52.

2. Mikhail Bakhtin, *Rabelais and His World*, trans. Hélène Iswolsky (Bloomington: Indiana University Press, 1984), 38–39.

3. *Ibid.*, 44.

4. Mikhail Bakhtin, "Discourse in the Novel," in Michael Holquist (ed.), *The Dialogic Imagination*, trans. Caryl Emerson and Michael Holquist (Austin: University of Texas Press, 1981), 269.

5. Horace Walpole, *The Castle of Otranto* and *The Mysterious Mother*, ed. Frederick S. Frank (Peterborough, Ontario: Broadview, 2003), 65.

6. Samuel Taylor Coleridge, *Biographia Literaria*, in H. J. Jackson (ed.), *The Major Works* (Oxford: Oxford University Press, 2008), 314, 194.

7. Bakhtin, *Rabelais and His World*, 24.

8. Carol Margaret Davison, *Gothic Literature, 1764–1824* (Cardiff: University of Wales Press, 2009), 21.

9. Scholarship on Gothic frame narratives is valuable. Elizabeth MacAndrew writes: "Such complex structures show how these works are to be read. They are variations of a technique for establishing the sense of a fiction that cannot be taken at face value, so that the reader will indeed apprehend the closed world as the isolated world of the self" (*The Gothic Tradition in Fiction* [New York: Columbia University Press, 1979], 119); Peter Brooks observes that the "nineteenth century's frequent use of the framed tale … reveal[s] … a deep anxiety about the possibility of transmission" (*Reading for the Plot: Design and Intention in Narrative* [Cambridge: Harvard University Press, 1992], 28); Fiona Robertson argues that "instances of early Gothic usages of frames and authenticating interventions by editors and narrators suggest that Gothic was developing a complex and self-conscious relationship to its historical materials, and to different types and levels of authority within its narrative schema" (*Legitimate Histories: Scott, Gothic, and the Authorities of Fiction* [Oxford: Clarendon Press, 1994], 89); and Anne Williams notes that frame narratives "dramatize both the materiality of writing and its implicit inadequacies: its discontinuities, ambiguities, unreliabilities, silences" (*Art of Darkness: A Poetics of Gothic* [Chicago: University of Chicago Press, 1995], 67).

10. One such limitation is the breadth of novels. Although I have attempted to provide examples of frame narratives throughout the Gothic canon, I have admittedly neglected some important texts. Clara Reeve's *The Champion of Virtue* (1777) and Sophia Lee's *The Recess* (1783–85) warrant analysis on how their prefatory materials function as narrative frames. In addition, I have ignored some important Gothic novels from the 1790s, including Mary Wollstonecraft's *Maria: or, The Wrongs of Woman* (1798) and Charles Brockden Brown's *Ormond; or, The Secret Witness* (1799) and *Arthur Mervyn; or, Memoirs of the Year 1793* (1799–1800). Perhaps most regrettably, three quintessential Gothic texts—M. G. Lewis's *The Monk* (1796), J. W. Polidori's *The Vampyre* (1819), and Sheridan Le Fanu's *Carmilla* (1871–72)—have met the cutting-room floor, although each features formal de-

vices that resemble narrative frames. Finally, I have not included epistolary collections in this study. Since they are not framed in the paratextual and geographical fashion of Bram Stoker's similarly arranged *Dracula* (1797), Wilkie Collins's *The Woman in White* (1859) and *The Moonstone* (1868) and Richard Marsh's *The Beetle* (1897) do not appear.

11. Cultural studies, which includes theoretical approaches ranging from feminist and Marxist to Postcolonial and Foucauldian, have led the way in recent Gothic criticism. But the latest shift, arguably, has been towards queer studies. For example, George E. Haggerty's *Queer Gothic* argues that a "wide range of writers, dispersed historically and culturally, use 'gothic' to evoke a queer world that attempts to transgress the binaries of sexual decorum" ([Urbana: University of Illinois Press, 2006], 2); and Ardel Haefele-Thomas notes that the "strength of Gothic rests upon its being a liminal genre; it allowed many nineteenth-century authors to look at social and cultural worries consistently haunting Victorian Britain even as the official discourse worked tirelessly to silence those concerns" (*Queer Others in Victorian Gothic: Transgressing Monstrosity* [Cardiff: University of Wales Press, 2012], 3). See also Max Fincher's *Queering the Gothic in the Romantic Age: The Penetrating Eye* (New York: Palgrave Macmillan, 2007), Paulina Palmer's *The Queer Uncanny: New Perspectives on the Gothic* (Cardiff: University of Wales Press, 2012), and the collection of essays *Queering the Gothic* (eds. Andrew Smith and William Hughes [Manchester: Manchester University Press, 2011]).

12. Dale Townshend's *The Orders of the Gothic: Foucault, Lacan, and the Subject of Gothic Writing, 1764–1820* argues that "[i]n order to account for the complex relations of Gothic to modernity, Foucauldian new historicism needs a Lacanian supplement" ([New York: AMS Press, 2007], 11). And Ed Cameron's *The Psychopathology of the Gothic Romance: Perversion, Neuroses and Psychosis in Early Works of the Genre* draws attention to the "psychopathological structure of the Gothic," which is "tied to the Gothic's inherent and incessant haunting by its lost past" ([Jefferson, NC: McFarland, 2010], 2).

13. Steven Jay Schneider asserts that "psychoanalysis … *succeeds* in providing insight into many of the figures of horror—not so much into what they metaphorically *mean* as into what they literally *say*" (Introduction to *Horror Film and Psychoanalysis*, ed. Steven Jay Schneider [Cambridge: Cambridge University Press, 2004], 9).

14. William Patrick Day, *In the Circles of Fear and Desire: A Study of Gothic Fantasy* (Chicago: University of Chicago Press, 1985), 179. Allan Lloyd-Smith similarly argues that Jacques Lacan's "language is *already* Gothic" (*American Gothic Fiction: An Introduction* [New York: Continuum, 2005], 142). Malcolm Bowie makes this connection explicit: "The self-division of the subject, first revealed to Freud by dreams, is here being re-imaged by Lacan as nightmare" (*Lacan* [Cambridge: Harvard University Press, 1991], 26).

15. Samuel Taylor Coleridge, "The Rime of the Ancyent Marinere," in Paul H. Fry (ed.), *The Rime of the Ancient Mariner* (Boston: Bedford/St Martin's, 1999), 72, ll. 625–28.

16. Recent studies have attempted to establish new metaphors for conceptualizing frame narratives, which include stacks from the computer field and the gutters and panels of comic books (see Marie-Laure Ryan, "Stacks, Frames, and Boundaries," in Brian Richardson [ed.], *Narrative Dynamics: Essays on Time, Plots, Closure, and Frames* [Columbus: Ohio State University Press, 2002], 366–86; and Eric Berlatsky, "Lost in the Gutter: Within and Between Frames in Narrative and Narrative Theory," *Narrative* 17.2 [May 2009], 162–87). Still, as William Nelles observes, "there is no generally accepted model or terminology for the analysis or even discussion of the structure" ("Stories within Stories: Narrative Levels and Embedded Narrative," in Brian Richardson [ed.], *Narrative Dynamics: Essays on Time, Plots, Closure, and Frames* [Columbus: Ohio State University Press, 2002], 339). This study continues to envision framing devices through the metaphor of pictorial frames, and it does so in great part because nineteenth-century authors and critics employed this aesthetic rhetoric. The earliest critical engagement with narrative frames appears in John Colin Dunlop's widely read 1814 text *The History of Fiction*, and critics throughout the nineteenth century drew on the metaphor of frames to conceptualize layered narratives.

17. Werner Wolf, "Framing Borders in Frame Stories," in Werner Wolf and Walter Bernhart (eds.), *Framing Borders in Literature and Other Media* (Amsterdam: Rodopi, 2006), 180.

18. William Wordsworth, "Advertisement,"

in Michael Gamer and Dahlia Porter (eds.), *Lyrical Ballads 1798 and 1800* (Peterborough, Ontario: Broadview, 2008), 48.

19. Paul H. Fry, "Biographical and Historical Contexts," in *The Rime of the Ancient Mariner* (Boston: Bedford/St Martin's, 1999), 12.

20. Jerome J. McGann, "The Meaning of the Ancient Mariner," *Critical Inquiry* 8.1 (Autumn 1981), 41. See also Huntington Brown, "The Gloss to the Ancient Mariner," *Modern Language Quarterly* 6 (1945), 319–24.

21. The gloss could alternatively be seen as a paratext, which Gérard Genette defines as "those liminal devices and conventions, both within and outside the book, that form part of the complex mediation between book, author, publisher, and reader" (*Paratexts: Thresholds of Interpretation* [Cambridge: Cambridge University Press, 1997], i). Mieke Bal argues that once embedded texts meet the "criteria for narrativity" they can "be considered as a narrative text" (*Narratology: Introduction to the Theory of Narrative* [Toronto: University of Toronto Press, 1997], 52); and John Frow contends that the "frame can be anything that acts as a sign of a qualitative difference," which includes not only paratexts, but also such seemingly extraneous features as the date, the author's name, and the publisher ("The Literary Frame," in Brian Richardson [ed.], *Narrative Dynamics* [Columbus: Ohio State University Press, 2002], 333–34).

22. MacAndrew, *The Gothic Tradition in Fiction*, 110.

23. Coleridge, "Ancient Mariner," p. 28, ll. 22.

24. *Ibid.*, 74, ll. 671–72.

25. *Charles Lamb: Selected Writings*, ed. J. E. Morpurgo (New York: Routledge, 2003), 158.

26. Coleridge, "Ancient Mariner," p. 28, l. 17.

27. John Spencer Hill, *A Coleridge Companion: An Introduction to the Major Poems and the* Biographia Literaria (London: Macmillan, 1984), 121.

28. These new supernatural explanations include "*A spirit had followed them; one of the invisible inhabitants of this planet, neither departed souls nor angels*" (37); "*a blessed troop of angelic spirits, sent down by the invocation of the guardian saint*" (55); and "*The Polar Spirit's fellow-dæmons, the invisible inhabitants of the element*" (59).

29. Quoted in McGann, "The Meaning of the Ancient Mariner," p. 39.

30. William Shakespeare, *Macbeth*, ed. Kenneth Muir (London: Arden Shakespeare, 1984), 81, 3.2.16.

31. Edgar Allan Poe, "The Philosophy of Composition," *Graham's Magazine*, 28.4 (April 1846), 166.

32. Edgar Allan Poe, "The Raven," in G. R. Thompson (ed.), *The Selected Writings of Edgar Allan Poe* (New York: Norton, 2004), 61, l. 108.

33. Frow, "The Literary Frame," p. 336.

34. Edgar Allan Poe, "The Fall of the House of Usher," in G. R. Thompson (ed.), *The Selected Writings of Edgar Allan Poe* (New York: Norton, 2004), 199.

35. *Ibid.*, 201–02.

36. Jacques Derrida, "Force and Signification," in *Writing and Difference*, trans. Alan Bass (Chicago: University of Chicago Press, 1978), 4–5.

37. Immanuel Kant, *Critique of the Power of Judgment*, ed. Paul Guyer (Cambridge: Cambridge University Press, 2000), 109.

38. *Ibid.*, 110–11.

39. Immanuel Kant, *Critique of Judgement*, ed. Nicholas Walker (Oxford: Oxford University Press, 2007), 60.

40. Jacques Derrida, *The Truth in Painting*, trans. Geoff Bennington and Ian McLeod (Chicago: University of Chicago Press, 1987), 54.

41. *Ibid.*, 61.

42. *Ibid.*, 63.

43. Poe, "The Fall of the House of Usher," 199–201.

44. Derrida, *The Truth in Painting*, 59. David Wills calls on readers to imagine a "series of paintings with frames that 'face' outward, whose corners have had their means of support dislocated from them; paintings exposed in all their vulnerability to what lies outside them, flimsily or impossible held together by the four imaginary apices of the open half-crochets" (*Matchbook: Essays on Deconstruction* [Stanford: Stanford University Press, 2005], 27).

45. Poe, "The Fall of the House of Usher," 211.

46. *Ibid.*, 215.

47. *Ibid.*, 200.

48. *Ibid.*, 211.

49. Samuel Taylor Coleridge, "The Eolian Harp," in H. J. Jackson (ed.), *The Major Works* (Oxford: Oxford University Press, 2008), 28–29, ll. 44–48.

50. Percy Bysshe Shelley, "A Defence of Po-

etry," in Bruce Woodcock (ed.), *The Selected Poetry and Prose of Shelley* (Hertfordshire: Wordsworth, 2002), 635.

51. Shelley writes that "there is a principle within the human being, and perhaps within all sentient beings, which acts otherwise than in the lyre, and produces not melody alone, but harmony, by an internal adjustment of the sounds or motions thus excited to the impressions which excite them" (*Ibid.*, 635).

52. William Wordsworth, "Expostulation and Reply," in Michael Gamer and Dahlia Porter (eds.), *Lyrical Ballads* (Peterborough, Ontario: Broadview, 2008), 135, ll. 25–26.

53. Immanuel Kant, *Critique of Pure Reason*, ed. Marcus Weigelt (London: Penguin, 2007), 258.

54. Stephen Houlgate, *The Opening of Hegel's Logic: From Being to Infinity* (West Lafayette: Purdue University Press, 2006), 131.

55. *Kant: Philosophical Correspondence, 1759–99*, ed. Arnulf Zweig (Chicago: University of Chicago Press, 1967), 103.

56. Jonathan Bennett, *Kant's Analytic* (Cambridge: Cambridge University Press, 1966), 57.

57. Kant, *Critique of Pure Reason*, 437, 80. Andrew L. Cooper succinctly states that "[o]bjective reality is only accessible as a consensus of subjectivities.... All realities come from reflections on representations" (*Gothic Realities: The Impact of Horror Fiction on Modern Culture* [Jefferson, NC: McFarland, 2010], 19).

58. Marcus Weigelt, Introduction to *Critique of Pure Reason*, by Kant (London: Penguin, 2007), xxxiv. Slavoj Žižek argues that G. W. F. Hegel intervenes between Kant and Lacan: "The Kantian Real is the noumenal Thing beyond phenomena whereas the Hegelian Real is the gap itself between the phenomenal and the noumenal, the gap that sustains freedom" (*Organs without Bodies: On Deleuze and Consequences* [New York: Routledge, 2004], 38).

59. William Patrick Day remarks that "[n]o discussion of the Gothic can avoid discussing Freud" (*In the Circles of Fear and Desire*, 177). Yet this book perhaps unwisely takes Freud for granted by assuming some amount of general knowledge about his central concepts. However, two concepts worth recording here are repression and the unconscious, the latter of which Freud delineates as follows: "the essence of the process of repression lies, not in putting an end to, in annihilating, the idea which represents an instinct, but in preventing it from becoming conscious. When this happens we say of the idea that it is in a state of being 'unconscious,' and we can produce good evidence to show that even when it is unconscious it can produce effects, even including some which finally reach consciousness" ("The Unconscious," in Peter Gay [ed.], *The Freud Reader* [New York: Norton, 1989], 573).

60. Jacques Lacan, *The Four Fundamental Concepts of Psycho-Analysis*, ed. Jacques-Alain Miller, trans. Alan Sheridan (London: Karnac, 2004), 167.

61. *Ibid.*, 55.

62. Slavoj Žižek, *The Sublime Object of Ideology* (London: Verso, 1989), xxv. Žižek delineates "three modalities" of the Real—the real Real, the symbolic Real, and the imaginary Real (*For They Know Not What They Do: Enjoyment as a Political Factor* [New York: Verso, 1991], xii).

63. *Ibid.*, xxviii.

64. *Ibid.*, 193.

65. "Terrorist Novel Writing," *Spirit of the Public Journals for 1797*, vol. 1 (London: James Ridgeway, 1799), 225.

66. Lacan, *Four Fundamental Concepts*, 167. Žižek writes that the "traumatic event is ultimately just a fantasy-construct filling out a certain void in a symbolic structure" (*Sublime Object of Ideology*, 191).

67. Lacan, *Four Fundamental Concepts*, 55. "[T]he Lacanian [R]eal," Žižek notes, "erupts in the form of a traumatic return, derailing the balance of our daily lives" (*Looking Awry: An Introduction to Jacques Lacan through Popular Culture* [Cambridge, MA: MIT Press, 1992], 29). Elsewhere Žižek writes of "the place, in which this Real interferes: it irrupts on the very boundary separating the 'outside' from the 'inside'" ("The Undergrowth of Enjoyment: How Popular Culture Can Serve as an Introduction to Lacan," in Elizabeth Wright and Edmond Wright [eds.], *The Žižek Reader* [Oxford: Blackwell, 1999], 19).

68. Slavoj Žižek, *The Abyss of Freedom/Ages of the World* (Ann Arbor: University of Michigan Press, 1997), 23.

69. Slavoj Žižek, "General Introduction," in Slavoj Žižek (ed.), *Jacques Lacan: Critical Evaluations in Cultural Theory*, vol. 1 (New York: Routledge, 2003), 2. Žižek makes an important distinction: "if what we experience as 'reality' is structured by fantasy, and if fantasy serves as the screen that protects us from being directly overwhelmed by the raw Real,

then *reality itself can function as an escape from encountering the Real.* In the opposition between dream and reality, fantasy is at the side of reality, and it is in dreams that we encounter the traumatic Real. It is not that dreams are for those who cannot endure reality; reality itself is for those who cannot endure (the Real that announces itself in) their dreams" ("Psychoanalysis and the Lacanian Real: 'Strange shapes of the unwarped primal world,'" in Matthew Beaumont [ed.], *A Concise Companion to Realism* [Malden, MA: Wiley-Blackwell, 2010], 240).

70. Jerrold E. Hogle, "The Gothic Ghost of the Counterfeit and the Progress of Abjection," in David Punter (ed.), *A New Companion to the Gothic* (Malden, MA: Blackwell, 2012), 499.

71. Richard Boothby, "The Psychical Meaning of Life and Death: Reflections on the Lacanian Imaginary, Symbolic, and Real," in David Pettigrew and François Raffoul (eds.), *Disseminating Lacan* (Albany: State University of New York Press, 1996), 347.

72. Julia Kristeva, *Powers of Horror*, trans. Leon S. Roudiez (New York: Columbia University Press, 1982), 2, 4. Kristeva's model of the abject in many ways parallels Freud's concept of the uncanny, which is "nothing else than a hidden, familiar thing that has undergone repression and then emerged from it" ("The Uncanny," in David Sander [ed.], *Fantastic Literature: A Critical Reader* [London: Praeger, 2004], 94).

73. *Ibid.*, 3.

74. Joan Copjec, "Vampires, Breast-Feeding, and Anxiety," *October* 58 (Autumn 1991): 34.

75. Jerrold E. Hogle, "The Struggle for a Dichotomy: Abjection in Jekyll and His Interpreters," in William Veeder and Gordon Hirsch (eds.), *Dr Jekyll and Mr Hyde After One Hundred Years* (Chicago: University of Chicago Press, 1988), 174.

76. Kristeva, *Powers of Horror*, 208.

77. Slavoj Žižek, *For They Know Not What They Do*, 220.

78. Kristeva, *Powers of Horror*, 1.

79. John Milton, *Paradise Lost*, ed. John Leonard (London: Penguin, 2000), 78, ll. 4.178–83.

80. *Ibid.*, ll. 4.174–75.

81. *Ibid.*, ll. 4.181, 187, 191.

82. In the eighteenth century, the novel of sensibility used frame narratives in innovative and energetic ways, ranging from Henry Mackenzie's *The Man of Feeling* (1771) to Johann Wolfgang von Goethe's *The Sorrows of Young Werther* (1774). However, there is no novelist so invested in narrative frames as Walter Scott, whose *Magnum Opus* editions (1829–33) layered editorial frames on novels that already featured fictional frames. Scott's career-long engagement with frame narratives exemplifies how different the form was when used by genres other than the Gothic. For Scott's layers of narrative shielded his identity, and, after he came public as the Author of Waverley in 1827, the *Magnum Opus* editions highlighted the genius of his craft.

83. Coleridge, *Biographia Literaria*, 314.

84. William Wordsworth, "Preface to *Lyrical Ballads*, with Pastoral and Other Poems," in Stephen Gill (ed.), *The Major Works* (Oxford: Oxford University Press, 2008), 599.

85. Coleridge, *Biographia Literaria*, 314. Wordsworth himself writes that his poems would feature "ordinary things ... presented to the mind in an unusual way" ("Preface to *Lyrical Ballads*," 97).

86. Poe, "The Fall of the House of Usher," 199–200.

87. Genette defines metalepsis as "any intrusion by the extradiegetic narrator or narratee into the diegetic universe (or by diegetic characters into a metadiegetic universe, etc.), or the inverse" (*Narrative Discourse: An Essay on Method* [Ithaca: Cornell University Press, 1990], 234–35).

88. Debra Malina, *Breaking the Frame: Metalepsis and the Construction of the Subject* (Columbus: Ohio State University Press, 2002), 4. Brian McHale describes the effect as a "short-circuit of the ontological structure" (*Postmodernist Fiction* [London: Routledge, 1987], 213).

89. Coleridge, "Ancient Mariner," p. 28, ll. 3, 9.

90. Malina, *Breaking the Frame*, 2. William Nelles notes that "narrative embedding often has the paradoxical effect not only of producing the illusion of a more profound realism or aesthetic unity ... but also of undercutting that illusion at the same time" (*Frameworks: Narrative Levels and Embedded Narrative* [New York: P. Lang, 1994], 150). John T. Matthews asserts that "[t]he literary frame exists as a function which enables a relation between differentiated realms (the reader and author, the world and the artwork, reality and imagination, and so on)" ("Framing in *Wuthering Heights*," *Texas Studies in Literature and Language* 27.1 [1985], 26). Robyn Warhol argues that "[a]n engaging narrator ... uses

the [frame narrative] to suggest that the characters are possibly as 'real' as the narrator and narratee, who are, in these cases, to be identified with the actual author and actual reader" ("Toward a Theory of the Engaging Narrator," *PMLA* 101 [1986], 814).

91. Kristeva, *Powers of Horror*, 4. Genette observes that "[t]he most troubling thing about metalepsis ... [is] that the extradiegetic is perhaps always diegetic and that the narrator and his narratees—you and I—perhaps belong to some narrative" (*Narrative Discourse*, 236).

92. Percy Shelley, "Lift not the painted veil," in Kelvin Everest and Geoffrey Matthews (eds.), *The Poems of Shelley*, vol. 2 (Harlow, UK: Pearson, 2000), 414, ll. 1–6. The lines quoted above are from the 1839 edition of Percy Shelley's poems. In the 1824 edition, Mary Shelley appears to have revised line 6 to read "The shadows, which the world calls substance, there."

93. Shelley's sonnet also adapts Plato's "The Allegory of the Cave." In the text, the character of Socrates states: "[T]he prison-house is the world of sight, the light of the fire is the sun.... [T]hose who attain to this beatific vision are unwilling to descend to human affairs; for their souls are ever hastening into the upper world where they desire to dwell" (in *The Classical Greek Reader*, ed. Kenneth J. Atchity [Oxford: Oxford University Press, 1996], 191).

94. Ann Radcliffe, *The Mysteries of Udolpho*, ed. Bonamy Dobrée (Oxford: Oxford University Press, 1998), 248–49.

95. Shelley, "Lift not the painted veil," 414–15, ll. 7, 13–14.

96. Emily's encounter with the illusory effigy might be considered through Lacan's reading of *trompe l'oeil* (optical illusion) and "anamorphosis" (a distorted image that becomes normal when viewed at a particular angle or with a certain device) in painting. For Lacan, all paintings possess vestiges of the gaze, but paintings that employ *trompe l'oeil* or anamorphosis especially disturb the subject's reality by demonstrating the limitations and vulnerability of our sight. It is a "triumph of the gaze over the eye" (*Four Fundamental Concepts*, 103). Anne Trubek observes that "the lack of perspective in *trompe l'oeil* leads to an uncanny sense of immanence, a *merging* of subject and object" ("American Literary Realism and the Problem of *Trompe l'Oeil* Painting," *Mosaic* 34.3 [Sept. 2001]: 43). In *Udolpho*, the effigy's blurring of boundaries and manifestation of the gaze make it serve as an example of Lacan's *objet petit a*—"a privileged object, which has emerged from some primal separation, from some self-mutilation induced by the very approach of the real" (83).

97. In *Northanger Abbey*, Isabella Thorpe enquires whether Catherine Morland is "wild to know" what lies behind the black veil in *The Mysteries of Udolpho*, which the latter had been reading all morning. Catherine replies: "Oh! Yes, quite; what can it be? But do not tell me—I would not be told upon any account. I know it must be a skeleton, I am sure it is Laurentina's [*sic*] skeleton" (ed. Marilyn Butler [London: Penguin, 2003], 38–39).

98. Jacques Lacan, *The Ethics of Psychoanalysis: Book VII*, ed. Jacques-Alain Miller (New York: Norton, 1992), 118.

99. Kristeva, *Powers of Horror*, 4.

100. Bakhtin, *Rabelais and His World*, 40.

101. Edgar Allan Poe, "The Masque of the Red Death," in G. R. Thompson (ed.), *The Selected Writings of Edgar Allan Poe* (New York: Norton, 2004), 304.

102. Žižek, *For They Know Not What They Do*, 112.

103. It is important to address the possibility that readers knowingly enter into the fictional world with the *intent* of being scared. The potential result is that the frame world of the novel remains ontologically separate from the readers' reality. However, narrative frames, paratextual or otherwise, are fundamentally employed to advance the text's claims to realism, regardless of the genre. So readers who begin a Gothic novel with the understanding that they will be frightened are nonetheless lulled into a false sense of security by the seeming comfort and familiarity of the frame world. The Gothic monstrosities embedded within the diegetic narrative thus become all the more horrifying, especially when they enter extradiegetic or even paratextual spaces.

104. Arthur Symons, *The Symbolist Movement in Literature* (London: Constable, 1908), 4.

105. *Horace Walpole's Correspondence*, vol. 28, eds. W. S. Lewis, Grover Cronin, Jr, and Charles H. Bennett (Oxford: Oxford University Press, 1955), 114.

106. Walpole, *The Castle of Otranto*, 59.

107. Peter K. Garrett, *Gothic Reflections: Narrative Force in Nineteenth-Century Fiction* (Ithaca: Cornell University Press, 2003), 48.

108. *Ibid.*, 48.

109. Walpole, *The Castle of Otranto*, 59.

110. *Ibid.*, 59.

111. *Ibid.*, 65. Walpole's dual prefaces complicate Lennard J. Davis's conception of authorial distance and the mode of the novel. Davis uses the metaphor of frames to argue that the "author displaces himself from the central, creative role, and by so doing denies his connection to the work. This act of disownment shifts the focus of narrative to the being of the protagonist, to the authenticity of the document, to the verisimilar human life itself. Such a shift, and the distance created by the removal of the author, is uniquely novelistic" (*Factual Fictions: The Origins of the English Novel* [Philadelphia: University of Pennsylvania Press, 1996], 16). *Otranto* challenges the parameters of "displacement" and "disownment" that Davis observes.

112. John Langhorne, *Monthly Review*, in Peter Sabor (ed.), *Horace Walpole: The Critical Heritage* (New York: Routledge, 1999), 72.

113. Walpole, *The Castle of Otranto*, 70. Walpole declares that his goal was "to blend the two kinds of romance, the ancient and the modern" (65).

114. *Ibid.*, 164.

115. Not surprisingly, *Otranto*'s prefaces have been the subject of rich critical debate. In addition to chapters 3 and 4 of Clery's *Rise of Supernatural Fiction* (Cambridge, 1999), see chapter 1 of James Watt's *Contesting the Gothic* (Cambridge, 1999); chapter 4 of Edward H. Jacobs's *Accidental Migrations* (Bucknell, 2000); chapter 2 of Peter K. Garrett's *Gothic Reflections* (Cornell, 2003); chapter 1 of Angela Wright's *Gothic Fiction* (Palgrave Macmillan, 2007); and chapter 3 of Ed Cameron's *The Psychopathology of Gothic Romance* (McFarland, 2010).

116. E. J. Clery, *The Rise of Supernatural Fiction, 1762–1800* (Cambridge: Cambridge University Press, 1999), 69.

117. E. J. Clery, Introduction to *The Castle of Otranto*, by Horace Walpole (Oxford: Oxford University Press, 1998), xxx.

118. Slavoj Žižek, *Less than Nothing: Hegel and the Shadow of Dialectical Materialism* (London: Verso, 2012), 959.

119. Walpole, *The Castle of Otranto*, 86. Ruth Bienstock Anolik observes that the "breaching of the walls of church and state (the abbey and the castle) is echoed by the Gothic tendency to subvert conceptual boundaries" (Introduction to *Demons of the Body: Essays on Disability in Gothic Literature*, ed. Ruth Bienstock Anolik [Jefferson, NC: McFarland, 2000], 2).

120. Slavoj Žižek, "The Spectre of Ideology," in Elizabeth Wright and Edmond Wright (eds.), *The Žižek Reader* (Oxford: Blackwell, 1999), 74.

121. Clery, *The Rise of Supernatural Fiction*, 61.

122. Walpole, *The Castle of Otranto*, 60.

123. Walter Scott remarks in his 1811 introduction to the novel that "[t]here are few who have not felt, at some period of their childhood, a sort of terror from the manner in which the eye of an ancient portrait appears to fix that of the spectator from every point of view" (Introduction to *The Castle of Otranto*, in Peter Sabor [ed.], *Horace Walpole: The Critical Heritage* [New York: Routledge, 1999], 95).

124. Walpole, *The Castle of Otranto*, 81.

125. Clery, *The Rise of Supernatural Fiction*, 74.

126. *Ibid.*, 79.

127. Walpole, *The Castle of Otranto*, 70.

Chapter 1

1. Alfred, Lord Tennyson, "The Gardener's Daughter," in Christopher Ricks (ed.), *The Poems of Tennyson* (London: Longmans, 1969), 521, ll. 264–69.

2. G. K. Chesterton, *The Return of Don Quixote* (Cornwall, UK: House of Stratus, 2008), 120.

3. Horace Walpole, *The Castle of Otranto* and *The Mysterious Mother*, ed. Frederick S. Frank (Peterborough, Ontario: Broadview, 2003), 59.

4. Thomas Talfourd, "Memoir of the Life and Writings of Mrs Radcliffe," in *Gaston de Blondeville*, vol. 1 (Philadelphia: H. C. Carey, 1826), 75.

5. Walter Scott, "A Memoir of the Life of the Author," in *The Novels of Mrs Ann Radcliffe* (Edinburgh: Ballantyne, 1824), xiv–xv.

6. Salvator Rosa (1615–73), Claude Lorrain (1600–82), Nicolas Poussin (1594–1665) and Gaspard Dughet (Poussin) (1615–75). Gaspart Dughet (also known as Gaspard Poussin) was a landscape painter and Nicholas Poussin's student and brother-in-law.

7. William Hazlitt, *Lectures on the English Comic Writers* (London: Taylor and Hessey, 1819), 250.

8. David Marshall, *The Frame of Art: Fictions of Aesthetic Experience 1750–1815* (Baltimore: Johns Hopkins University Press, 2005), 39.

9. "A Journey Made in the Summer of 1794," *Critical Review* 14 (July 1795), 241.

10. William Gilpin, *Three Essays: on Picturesque Beauty; on Picturesque Travel; and on Sketching Landscape* (London: R. Blamire, 1792), 3; William Gilpin, *An Essay on Prints* (London: T. Cadell, 1802), xii.

11. Nancy Armstrong, *Fiction in the Age of Photography: The Legacy of British Realism* (Cambridge: Harvard University Press, 1999), 33.

12. Uvedale Price, *Essay on the Picturesque* (London: J. Robinson, 1796), 82.

13. Mary Wollstonecraft, "The Italian, or the Confessional of the Black Penitents. A Romance," *Analytical Review* 25 (May 1797), 516.

14. Edmund Burke, *A Philosophical Enquiry into the Origin of Our Ideas of the Sublime and Beautiful*, ed. Paul Guyer (Oxford: Oxford University Press, 2015), 33.

15. *Ibid.*, 33–34.

16. Immanuel Kant, *Critique of the Power of Judgment*, ed. Paul Guyer (Cambridge: Cambridge University Press, 2000), 129–30.

17. Slavoj Žižek, *Interrogating the Real* (London: Bloomsbury, 2006), 131.

18. Julia Kristeva, *Powers of Horror*, trans. Leon S. Roudiez (New York: Columbia University Press, 1982), 11.

19. *Ibid.*, 12.

20. Slavoj Žižek, *The Sublime Object of Ideology* (London: Verso, 1989), 229.

21. Žižek, *Interrogating the Real*, 132.

22. Slavoj Žižek, *The Abyss of Freedom/Ages of the World* (Ann Arbor: University of Michigan Press, 1997), 22.

23. Žižek, *The Sublime Object of Ideology*, 192. Žižek's words uncannily echo the opening of Radcliffe's essay "On the Supernatural in Poetry" (1826): "an object often flatters and charms at a distance, which vanishes into nothing as we approach it" (*New Monthly Magazine* 16 [1826], 145–52).

24. Žižek, *Interrogating the Real*, 239–40.

25. *Ibid.*, 240.

26. *Ibid.*, 355.

27. Ann Radcliffe, *A Sicilian Romance*, ed. Alison Milbank (Oxford: Oxford University Press, 2008), 1. All further references to this edition will be given in the text.

28. For more on veils and the Gothic, see Elizabeth P. Broadwell, "The Veil Image in Ann Radcliffe's *The Italian*," *South Atlantic Bulletin* 40.4 (November 1975), 76–87; and Eve Kosofsky Sedgwick, "The Character in the Veil: Imagery on the Surface in the Gothic Novel," *PMLA* 96.2 (1981), 255–70.

29. Slavoj Žižek, "The Undergrowth of Enjoyment: How Popular Culture Can Serve as an Introduction to Lacan," in Elizabeth Wright and Edmond Wright (eds.), *The Žižek Reader* (Oxford: Blackwell, 1999), 14. Lacan notes that "[t]he gaze may contain in itself the *objet a* of the Lacanian algebra where the subject falls" (*The Four Fundamental Concepts of Psycho-Analysis*, ed. Jacques-Alain Miller, trans. Alan Sheridan [London: Karnac, 1977], 76).

30. Joan Copjec, "Vampires, Breast-Feeding, and Anxiety," *October* 58 (Autumn 1991): 38.

31. Kristeva, *Powers of Horror*, 4.

32. *The Romance of the Forest* (1791) begins *in medias res* as characters enter a carriage and flee from Paris. Although the novel does not feature a frame narrative, Radcliffe does experiment with the "found manuscript" device by making it an integral element of the main narrative. Two hypodiegetic stories (Adeline's autobiographical tale and the fragmented central manuscript she discovers) prove so crucial that they powerfully frame the other events in the novel as they are gradually revealed.

33. *The Mysteries of Udolpho* also pauses for the hypodiegetic stories: "The Provençal Tale" and "a brief history of Laurentini di Udolpho." The former, Radcliffe writes, "is strongly tinctured with the superstition of the times" (552).

34. Scott, "A Memoir of the Life of the Author," vii.

35. Elizabeth A. Bohls, *Women Travel Writers and the Language of Aesthetics, 1716–1818* (Cambridge: Cambridge University Press, 1995), 210.

36. Terry Castle, *The Female Thermometer: Eighteenth-Century Culture and the Invention of the Uncanny* (Oxford: Oxford University Press, 1995), 121, 124.

37. *Ibid.*, 122–23.

38. *Ibid.*, 124, 133.

39. Ann Radcliffe, *The Mysteries of Udolpho*, ed. Bonamy Dobrée (Oxford: Oxford University Press, 1981), 226. All further references to this edition will be given in the text.

40. Edgar Allan Poe, "The Fall of the House of Usher," in G. R. Thompson (ed.), *The Selected Writings of Edgar Allan Poe* (New York: Norton, 2004), 199.

41. Castle, *The Female Thermometer*, 129.

42. Anthony Trollope, *Barchester Towers*,

eds. Michael Sadleir and Frederick Page (Oxford: Oxford University Press, 1996), 143.

43. Lacan, *Four Fundamental Concepts*, 112.

44. Slavoj Žižek, *The Parallax View* (Cambridge, MA: MIT Press, 2006), 304.

45. Lacan, *Four Fundamental Concepts*, 112.

46. Slavoj Žižek, *The Sublime Object of Ideology* (London: Verso, 1989), 163.

47. *Ibid.*, 163.

48. Jane Austen, *Northanger Abbey*, ed. Marilyn Butler (London: Penguin, 2003), 38–39.

49. Anna Laetitia Barbauld, "Mrs Radcliffe," in *The British Novelists*, vol. 43 (London: F. C. and J. Rivington, 1820), 5–6.

50. Scott, "A Memoir of the Life of the Author," ix. Talfourd similarly notes that the opening frame "impresses the reader with awe" ("Memoir of the Life and Writings of Mrs Radcliffe," 82).

51. E. J. Clery, Introduction to *The Italian*, by Ann Radcliffe (Oxford: Oxford University Press, 1998), xiii; Rictor Norton, *Mistress of Udolpho* (Leicester: Leicester University Press, 1999), 128.

52. Liz Bellamy, *Commerce, Morality and the Eighteenth-Century Novel* (Cambridge: Cambridge University Press, 1998), 163; Cannon Schmitt, "Techniques of Terror, Technologies of Nationality: Ann Radcliffe's *The Italian*," *ELH* 61.4 (1994), 852.

53. Michel Foucault, *The History of Sexuality*, vol. 1 (New York: Vintage, 1978), 59.

54. Žižek, *The Parallax View*, 304.

55. *Ibid.*, 304.

56. Foucault, *The History of Sexuality*, 18.

57. Ann Radcliffe, *The Italian*, ed. Frederick Garber (Oxford: Oxford University Press, 1998), 2. All further references to this edition will be given in the text.

58. Jerrold E. Hogle, "Recovering the Walpolean Gothic: *The Italian: Or, the Confessional of the Black Penitents* (1796–1797)," in Dale Townshend and Angela Wright (eds.), *Ann Radcliffe, Romanticism and the Gothic* (Cambridge: Cambridge University Press, 2012), 167, 153.

59. E. J. Clery, *The Rise of Supernatural Fiction, 1762–1800* (Cambridge: Cambridge University Press, 1999), 54.

60. Clery, Introduction to *The Italian*, xiii.

61. *A Sicilian Romance* is set at the "close of the sixteenth century" (3), and *Gaston de Blondeville* during the reign of Henry III (1207–72), or, as Willoughton can "make out" from the manuscript, "twelve hundred and something" ([Chicago: Valancourt, 2006], 18).

62. Talfourd, "Memoir of the Life and Writings of Mrs Radcliffe," 82.

63. Clara Frances McIntyre, *Ann Radcliffe in Relation to Her Time* (New Haven: Yale University Press, 1920), 70.

64. Clery, Introduction to *The Italian*, xv.

65. "Mrs Radcliffe's *The Italian*," *Anti-Jacobin Review and Magazine* 7 (1801), 28.

66. Gilpin, *Observations on the River Wye*, 31.

67. Kant, *Critique of the Power of Judgment*, 128.

68. Norton, *Mistress of Udolpho*, 193. Both the *Ladies' Monthly Museum* (24 [1826], 45) and *The New Monthly Magazine* (16 [1826], 533) specifically contend that the novel was withheld.

69. "Review of New Books," *London Literary Gazette* 488 (May 1826), 321; "Novelists," *La Belle Assemblée* 3 (July 1826), 303; "Mrs Radcliffe's Posthumous Romance," *New Monthly Magazine* 16 (1826), 532.

70. Norton, *Mistress of Udolpho*, 194–95.

71. "Review of New Books," 322.

72. Ann Radcliffe, *The Italian*, ed. Robert Miles (London: Penguin, 2004), 479, note 1.

73. Ann Radcliffe, *Gaston de Blondeville* (Chicago: Valancourt, 2006), 7. All further references to this edition will be given in the text.

74. "Gaston de Blondeville," *The Port Folio* 1 (1826), 101.

75. "Gaston de Blondeville: With an Essay on the Life and Writings of Mrs Radcliffe," *London Magazine* 6 (1826), 39.

76. Terry Castle, Introduction to *The Mysteries of Udolpho*, by Ann Radcliffe (Oxford: Oxford University Press, 1998), xiv.

77. Žižek, *The Sublime Object of Ideology*, 182.

78. Dale Townshend, "Gothic Shakespeare," in David Punter (ed.), *A New Companion to the Gothic* (Malden, MA: Wiley-Blackwell, 2012), 48.

79. Norton, *Mistress of Udolpho*, 197. "On the Supernatural in Poetry" appears with a footnote that explains its origin: "Having been permitted to extract the above eloquent passages from the manuscripts of the author of the 'Mysteries of Udolpho,' we have given this title to them, though certainly they were not intended by the writer to be offered as a

formal or deliberate essay, under this, or any other denomination. They were, originally, part of an INTRODUCTION to the Romance, or Phantasie, which is about to appear" (145).

80. Radcliffe, "On the Supernatural in Poetry," 149.

81. *Ibid.*, 150.

82. *Ibid.*, 149.

83. Kant, *Critique of the Power of Judgment*, 151–52.

84. Radcliffe, "On the Supernatural in Poetry," 152.

Chapter 2

1. William Wordsworth, "Ode: Intimations of Immortality from Recollections of Early Childhood," in *The Major Works*, ed. Stephen Gill (Oxford: Oxford University Press, 2008), 301, ll. 144–48.

2. Robert Frost, "Mending Wall," in Edward Connery Lathem (ed.), *The Poetry of Robert Frost* (London: Jonathan Cape, 1971), 33, ll. 1–4.

3. Mary Shelley, *The Last Man*, ed. Morton D. Paley (Oxford: Oxford University Press, 2008), 462. All further references to this edition will be given in the text.

4. Shelley read *The Italian* in 1814 and *The Mysteries of Udolpho* in 1815.

5. In a 28 January 1826 letter, Shelley writes of *The Last Man*: "You can form no idea of the difficulty of the subject—the necessity of making the scene universal to all mankind and of combining this with a particular interest which must constitute the novel" (*The Letters of Mary Wollstonecraft Shelley*, vol. 1, ed. Betty T. Bennett [Baltimore: Johns Hopkins University Press, 1980], 510).

6. Mary Shelley, *Frankenstein*, ed. Marilyn Butler (Oxford: Oxford University Press, 1998), 10–11. All further references to this edition will be given in the text.

7. Shelley's historical novel *Valperga* was published in 1823. She also employs frame narratives in short tales that appeared in *The Keepsake*: "The Mourner" (1830), "The Evil Eye" (1830), and "The Mortal Immortal: A Tale" (1834), and two unpublished tales, "Valerius: The Reanimated Roman" and "An Eighteenth-Century Tale: A Fragment."

8. Slavoj Žižek, "Grimaces of the Real, or When the Phallus Appears," *October* 58 (Autumn 1991), 63; Slavoj Žižek, *The Abyss of Freedom/Ages of the World* (Ann Arbor: University of Michigan Press, 1997), 60.

9. *Frankenstein* had evolved from an apparent ur-text in the summer of 1816, to a substantially longer Draft (structured in two volumes and thirty-three chapters), and finally to a Fair Copy (three volumes and twenty-three chapters). Shelley probably added Walton's introductory letters in October 1816. That is, they apparently were not part of the nonextant 1816 ur-text that Robinson conjectures was composed during the famous Geneva summer, and they are not extant in the 1816–17 manuscript Draft.

10. Mieke Bal, *Narratology: Introduction to the Theory of Narrative* (Toronto: University of Toronto Press, 1997), 58.

11. "Frankenstein; or, the modern Prometheus," *Literary Panorama and National Register* 8 (1 June 1818), 412.

12. "Frankenstein; or the Modern Prometheus," *British Critic* 9 (April 1818), 432–33.

13. In the frame to Shakespeare's *The Taming of the Shrew*, a nobleman tricks a drunken Christopher Sly into thinking he is a lord. The central play serves as a distraction for Sly, especially so that a male page, disguised as his "wife," will not have to sleep with him. Although Sly's frame does not return in *The Taming of the Shrew*, another quarto that was published in 1594 called *The Taming of a Shrew* restores Sly's narrative in a terminal frame.

14. Mary Poovey, "My Hideous Progeny: Mary Shelley and the Feminization of Romanticism," *PMLA* 95.3 (May 1980), 339.

15. Anne Mellor, *Mary Shelley: Her Life, Her Fiction, Her Monsters* (New York: Routledge, 1989), 57.

16. Beth Newman, "Narratives of Seduction and the Seductions of Narrative: The Frame Structure of *Frankenstein*," *ELH* 53.1 (Spring 1986), 159.

17. Jacques Derrida, *The Truth in Painting*, trans. Geoff Bennington and Ian McLeod (Chicago: U of Chicago P, 1987), 61.

18. Criscillia Benford, "'Listen to my tale': Multilevel Structure, Narrative Sense Making, and the Inassimilable in Mary Shelley's *Frankenstein*," *Narrative* 18.3 (October 2010), 327.

19. Mellor, *Mary Shelley*, 54; Marc Rubenstein, "'My Accursed Origin': The Search for the Mother in *Frankenstein*," *Studies in Romanticism* 15 (Spring 1976), 178.

20. Maggie Kilgour observes that the form of the Gothic novel "is itself a Frankenstein's

monster, assembled out of bits and pieces of the past" (*The Rise of the Gothic Novel* [London: Routledge, 1995], 4).

21. Joseph W. Lew, "The Deceptive Other: Mary Shelley's Critique of Orientalism in *Frankenstein*," *Studies in Romanticism* 30 (Summer 1991), 271.

22. According to Susan Wolfson, "Colburn amplified the buzz" of a new edition of *Frankenstein* "by pre-publishing Shelley's 'new Introduction'" in his *Court Journal* on 22 October 1831 (Introduction to *Frankenstein*, by Mary Shelley [New York: Longman, 2006], 183).

23. *The* Frankenstein *Notebooks*, ed. Charles E. Robinson (New York: Garland, 1996), 2:639. The quote is from p. 189 of Butler's edition of *Frankenstein*. This line is also extant in the Fair Copy (*The* Frankenstein *Notebooks*, 2:775).

24. The creature enters the symbolic world of words, that "godlike science" (88), before he passes through the mirror stage. Thus, Žižek argues, he remains a "monster that gives body to the surplus that escapes the vicious circle of the mirror relationship" ("Grimaces of the Real," 66).

25. Slavoj Žižek, *The Abyss of Freedom*, 21, 23.

26. Walton admits that his designs "want (as the painters call it) *keeping*" (9), that he lacks the harmony of proportion. Yet Walton's frame is proportionate. Both the opening and terminal frames contain roughly 5,000 words.

27. Shelley, *Frankenstein* (1831), 201–02.

28. Joan Copjec, "Vampires, Breast-Feeding, and Anxiety," *October* 58 (Autumn 1991): 31.

29. Benford, "Listen to my tale," 327.

30. Walter Scott, "Remarks on Frankenstein, or The Modern Prometheus; a Novel," *Blackwood's Edinburgh Magazine* 2 (March 1818), 619.

31. Garrett Stewart, *Dear Reader: The Conscripted Audience in Nineteenth-Century British Fiction* (Baltimore: Johns Hopkins University Press, 1996), 117.

32. Mary A. Favret, "The Letters of *Frankenstein*," *Genre* 20 (Spring 1987), 3. Eleanor Salotto similarly observes that the structure of the novel "indicate[s] a resistance to closure of the self and story" ("*Frankenstein* and Dis(re)membered Identity," *The Journal of Narrative Technique* 24.3 [Fall 1994], 200).

33. Reviewers were interested in the dynamics of this scene. John Wilson Croker remarks that the creature, "notwithstanding his huge bulk, jumps in at Mr Walton's cabin window" ("Frankenstein, or the Modern Prometheus," *Quarterly Review* 18 [January 1818], 381–82); the *British Critic* notes that the creature "most unceremoniously climbs in at [Walton's] cabin window" (437); and *La Belle Assemblée* observes that the creature "comes in at the cabin-window of Captain Walton's ship … and then plunges into the icy waves, the same way as he entered" ("Frankenstein; or, The Modern Prometheus," *La Belle Assemblée, or Bell's Court and Fashionable Magazine* 108 [March 1818], 141).

34. "The Cave of Fancy" introduces a sage, aptly named Sagestus, who returns home one day after a terrible storm to find a shipwreck, its dead crew washed up and scattered about the shore. Sagestus ambles about reading the occupations and personalities of the dead through their physiognomies. Eventually he comes upon a young girl who has survived. He names her Sagesta and decides to educate her through the tales of dead spirits he conjures from purgatory. Thus, the story of Sagesta's education would have acted as the frame for the several tales within. Wollstonecraft finished only one tale.

35. Elizabeth Nitchie, Introduction to *Mathilda*, by Mary Shelley (Chapel Hill: University of North Carolina Press, 2008), 11.

36. Margaret Davenport Garrett, "Writing and Re-Writing Incest in Mary Shelley's *Mathilda*," *Keats-Shelley Journal* 45 (1996), 50.

37. Pamela Clemit argues that Shelley's "abandonment of the frame narrative indicates her rejection of overtly didactic fiction in favor of the indirect educative purpose of the Godwinian confessional mode" ("*Frankenstein*, *Mathilda*, and the Legacies of Godwin and Wollstonecraft," in Esther Schor [ed.], *Cambridge Companion to Mary Shelley* [Cambridge: Cambridge University Press, 2003], 38).

38. Autobiographical readings began with Shelley herself. "Mathilda fortells even many small circumstances most truly," she writes in 1823, "& the whole of it is a monument of what now is" (*The Letters of Mary Wollstonecraft Shelley*, 336).

39. Percy Bysshe Shelley, *Essays, Letters from Abroad, Translations and Fragments*, ed. Mary Shelley (London: Edward Moxon, 1845), x.

40. *Maria Gisborne and Edward E. Williams, Shelley's Friends: Their Journals and*

Letters, ed. Frederick L. Jones (Norman: University of Oklahoma Press, 1951), 44.

41. *Ibid.*, 44.

42. "*Frankenstein; or, The Modern Prometheus*," 139.

43. Mary Shelley, *Mathilda*, ed. Elizabeth Nitchie (Chapel Hill: University of North Carolina Press, 2008), 109. All further references to this edition will be given in the text.

44. In the final manuscript, Mathilda's mother dies after giving birth, and Mathilda's father, overcome by grief, flees to the East. Mathilda is raised under the cold care of her aunt, and after sixteen years, her father returns. As the smooth reunion sours into silence, jealousy, and animosity, Mathilda persuades him to reveal his deep secret. He painfully admits a romantic attachment to his daughter, writes a farewell letter, and again flees. Mathilda chases him to the coast but finds him dead. After staging her own death, Mathilda moves to a solitary cottage where she later meets Woodville, a young poet who has recently lost his lover. Mathilda realizes the impossibility of their stable romantic union, and attempts to form a suicide pact. Woodville refuses, Mathilda falls mortally ill, and her narrative ends abruptly and ambiguously.

45. Charlene Bunnell, "*Mathilda*: Mary Shelley's Romantic Tragedy," *Keats-Shelley Journal* 46 (1997), 87.

46. *Maria Gisborne and Edward E. Williams*, 44.

47. *Mathilda* is part of a corpus of (pre-)Romantic texts that treat the subject of incest. In Horace Walpole's *The Castle of Otranto* (1764), the marriage of Manfred and Hippolita is, at least partially, incestuous, and Manfred's pursuit of his would-be daughter-in-law, Isabella, is a form of matrimonial incest. In addition, Walpole's *The Mysterious Mother* (1769) features a child born to mother-son incest, who then unintentionally becomes the wife of the father. In M. G. Lewis's *The Monk* (1796), Ambrosio unknowingly rapes his sister Antonia; Lord Byron's *Manfred* (1817) directly refers to incestuous relations between the titular Count and his sister Astarte; and Percy Shelley's *The Cenci* (1819) discusses the implied rape of Beatrice by her father Count Cenci. For more on *Mathilda*'s treatment of incest, and also Mathilda's reading of incest literature, see Frederick Burwick's "*Mathilda*—Who Knew Too Much" (in *Master Narratives: Tellers and Telling in the English Novel*, ed. Richard Gravil [London: Ashgate, 2001], 69–81).

48. Slavoj Žižek, *Less Than Nothing: Hegel and the Shadow of Dialectical Materialism* (London: Verso, 2012), 952.

49. Jacques Lacan, *The Ethics of Psychoanalysis: Book VII*, ed. Jacques-Alain Miller (New York: Norton, 1992), 68.

50. Slavoj Žižek, *Interrogating the Real* (London: Bloomsbury, 2006), 64.

51. Slavoj Žižek, "Fantasy as a Political Category: A Lacanian Approach," in Elizabeth Wright and Edmond Wright (eds.), *The Žižek Reader* (Oxford: Blackwell, 1999), 97.

52. Charles E. Robinson, "Mathilda as Dramatic Actress," in Betty T. Bennett and Stuart Curran (eds.), *Mary Shelley in Her Times* (Baltimore: Johns Hopkins University Press, 2000), 78.

53. Shelley read *The Decameron* in 1819 and in 1820 and refers to it in both *Mathilda* and *The Last Man*.

54. Barbara Johnson, "*The Last Man*," in Audrey A. Fisch, Anne K. Mellor, and Esther H. Schor (eds.), *The Other Mary Shelley: Beyond* Frankenstein (Oxford: Oxford University Press, 1993), 264.

55. Charlotte Sussman, "'Islanded in the World': Cultural Memory and Human Mobility in *The Last Man*," *PMLA* 118.2 (March 2003), 286–87.

56. Mark Canuel, "Acts, Rules and *The Last Man*," *Nineteenth-Century Literature* 53.2 (Sept. 1998), 168.

57. William Shakespeare, *Macbeth*, ed. Kenneth Muir (London: Arden Shakespeare, 1984), 132, 135.

58. Quoted in Bernice W. Kliman, *Macbeth: Shakespeare in Performance* (Manchester: Manchester University Press, 1995), 19.

59. Edmund Burke, *A Philosophical Enquiry into the Origin of Our Ideas of the Sublime and Beautiful*, ed. Paul Guyer (Oxford: Oxford University Press, 2015), 48.

60. Slavoj Žižek, *The Plague of Fantasies* (London: Verso, 1997), 66.

61. Jacques Lacan, *The Four Fundamental Concepts of Psycho-Analysis*, ed. Jacques-Alain Miller, trans. Alan Sheridan (London: Karnac, 1977), 60.

62. Peter Melville, "The Problem of Immunity in *The Last Man*," *SEL* 47.4 (2007), 825.

63. Morton D. Paley, Introduction to *The Last Man*, by Mary Shelley (Oxford: Oxford University Press, 1998), xx.

64. Ann Radcliffe, *The Mysteries of Udolpho*, ed. Bonamy Dobrée (Oxford: Oxford University Press, 1981), 248.

65. Perdita's words echo Shelley's 26 October 1824 journal entry: "Shelley had said Lift not the painted veil w[hich] call life—mine is not painted—dark & enshadowed it curtains out all of happiness—all of hope" (*The Journals of Mary Shelley 1814–1844*, vol. 2, eds. Paula R. Feldman and Diana Scott Kilvert [Oxford: Clarendon Press, 1987], 485).

66. "Sullen it plunged, and slowly sank, / The calm wave rippled to the bank; / I watch'd it as it sank" (Lord Byron, *The Giaour*, in Jerome McGann [ed.], *Lord Byron: The Major Works* [Oxford: Oxford University Press, 2008], 217, ll. 374–76).

67. The epigraph is from Milton's *Paradise Lost* (Book XI, ll. 770–72) and concerns Adam's regrets over having seen a vision of the flood as presented by the archangel Michael.

Chapter 3

1. Alfred, Lord Tennyson, "The Lady of Shalott," in Christopher Ricks (ed.), *The Poems of Tennyson* (London: Longmans, 1969), 359, ll. 109–17.

2. Charlotte Brontë, *Shirley*, eds. Andrew and Judith Hook (London: Penguin, 1988), 72.

3. The poem's Gothic themes are many: the imprisoned heroine yearning for freedom; the "helmet" and "plume" that recall the giant armor in *The Castle of Otranto*; and the "found manuscript" death-note in the 1832 version.

4. Slavoj Žižek, *For They Know Not What They Do: Enjoyment as a Political Factor* (New York: Verso, 1991), lxxvii.

5. One nineteenth-century writer describes the process: "the artisans do not see the effect of their work until the piece is finished—tapestry being all wrought on the wrong side, so that the weaver works, as it were, blindfold" (Caroline A. Halsted, *Investigation; or, Travels in the Boudoir* [London: Smith, Elder and Co., 1837], 44).

6. Percy Shelley, "Lift not the painted veil," in Kelvin Everest and Geoffrey Matthews (eds.), *The Poems of Shelley*, vol. 2 (Harlow, UK: Pearson, 2000), 414, ll. 5–6.

7. André Breton, Preface to *Melmoth, L'Homme Errant*, by Charles Robert Maturin, trans. Jean Cohen (Paris: Jean-Jacques Pauvert, 1954), v; my translation.

8. *Ibid.*, v.

9. *Melmoth* has been called the "last and greatest expression of its kind" (William F. Axton, Introduction to *Melmoth the Wanderer*, by Charles Robert Maturin [Lincoln: University of Nebraska Press, 1966], xii), and the "Gothic romance to end all Gothic romances" (Victor Sage, Introduction to *Melmoth the Wanderer*, by Charles Robert Maturin [London: Penguin, 2000], viii).

10. "Melmoth the Wander; a Tale," *London Literary Gazette* 200 (November 1820), 737.

11. "Maturin's Melmoth," *Eclectic Review* 14 (1820), 554.

12. *Melmoth* features not only a preface by Maturin, but also many parenthetical remarks and footnotes, which appear sometimes to be part of different diegetic levels. As Victor Sage observes, "[a]t times, the Editor will jump tactlessly into the frame whose stability he guarantees" ("The Author, the Editor, and the Fissured Text: Scott, Maturin and Hogg," in Kyriaki Hadjiafxendi and Polina Mackay [eds.], *Authorship in Context: From the Theoretical to the Material* [Basingstoke, England: Palgrave Macmillan, 2007], 23).

13. Charles Robert Maturin, *Melmoth the Wanderer*, ed. Douglas Grant (Oxford: Oxford University Press, 1968), 76. All further references to this edition will be given in the text.

14. Mary Shelley, *Frankenstein*, ed. Marilyn Butler (Oxford: Oxford University Press, 2008), 11.

15. Maturin's first published fiction was the self-financed Gothic thriller *Fatal Revenge; or, the Family of Montorio* (1807). Long considered an unnecessary imitation of Radcliffe, whose novels Maturin called "irresistibly and delightfully dangerous," *Fatal Revenge* in fact proves innovative and reveals Maturin's early interest in formal complexity (Charles Robert Maturin, "Novel-writing," *British Review* 11 [1818], 48).

16. Sage, Introduction to *Melmoth the Wanderer*, xi.

17. The *Quarterly Review* quipped: "Mr Maturin has contrived … to unite in this work all the worst particularities of the worst modern novels" ("Melmoth, the Wanderer," *Quarterly Review* 24 [1821], 303). "Compared with it," the review continues, "Lady Morgan is almost intelligible—The Monk, decent—The Vampire, amiable—and Frankenstein, natural" (303). The *Edinburgh Review* was particularly harsh in its remarkably accurate summary, which concludes that the figures are "all opposed to each other in glaring and violent contrast, and all their adventures nar-

rated with the same undeviating display of turgid, vehement, and painfully elaborated language. Such are the materials, and the style of this expanded nightmare" ("Melmoth, the Wanderer," *Edinburgh Review* 35 [1821], 354).

18. "Melmoth, the Wanderer," 354; "Melmoth, the Wanderer," *Ladies' Monthly Museum* 13 (1821), 95; "Remarks on "Melmoth," *New Monthly Magazine* 14 (1820), 663.

19. "Melmoth, the Wanderer," *Quarterly Review* 24 (1821), 304. Catherine Lanone considers the novel a "fractal set of Chinese boxes" ("Verging on the Gothic: Melmoth's Journey to France," in Avril Horner [ed.], *European Gothic: A Spirited Exchange 1760–1960* [Manchester: Manchester University Press, 2002], 75). Using similar metaphors, William Axton describes the novel as a "system of interpolated tales nested one within another like the boxes of a child's toy" (Introduction to *Melmoth the Wanderer*, xv); and Joseph Lew notes: "structurally it resembles a series of Russian dolls, each containing a smaller one inside" ("'Unprepared for sudden transformations': Identity and Politics in *Melmoth the Wanderer*," *Studies in the Novel* 26 [1994], 176). G. St John Stott provides the most intricate metaphor for the novel: "Just as images seen in two mirrors set to face one another seem to be infinitely multiplied, so the violence, evil, and despair in Melmoth seem multiplied and intensified by their juxtaposition in the interpolated tales" ("The Structure of *Melmoth the Wanderer*," *Etudes Irlandaises* 12.1 [1987], 50).

20. Immanuel Kant, *Critique of Pure Reason*, ed. Marcus Weigelt (London: Penguin, 2007), 23.

21. *Ibid.*, 260.

22. Percy Shelley, "Lift not the painted veil," in Kelvin Everest and Geoffrey Matthews (eds.), *The Poems of Shelley*, vol. 2 (Harlow, UK: Pearson, 2000), 414, ll. 12–13.

23. Edgar Allan Poe, "Stanley Thorn," *Graham's Magazine* 20.1 (January 1842), 70.

24. Robert E. Lougy, *Charles Robert Maturin* (Cranbury, NJ: Associated, 1975), 67.

25. *The Correspondence of Sir Walter Scott and Charles Robert Maturin*, eds. Fannie E. Ratchford and William H. McCarthy (New York: Garland, 1980), 14.

26. Sage, "The Author, the Editor, and the Fissured Text," 86.

27. Alfred, Lord Tennyson, "Mariana," in Christopher Ricks (ed.), *The Poems of Tennyson* (London: Longmans, 1969), 206–07, ll. 6, 20.

28. Horace Walpole, *The Castle of Otranto* and *The Mysterious Mother*, ed. Frederick S. Frank (Peterborough, Ontario: Broadview, 2003), 81.

29. Slavoj Žižek, *The Abyss of Freedom/ Ages of the World* (Ann Arbor: University of Michigan Press, 1997), 9.

30. Slavoj Žižek, "The Undergrowth of Enjoyment: How Popular Culture Can Serve as an Introduction to Lacan," in Elizabeth Wright and Edmond Wright (eds.), *The Žižek Reader* (Oxford: Blackwell, 1999), 23.

31. Lanone observes that Melmoth is a "character whom no walls can stop," which promotes the "dreamlike, bewildering erasure of all spatial boundaries" ("Verging on the Gothic: Melmoth's Journey to France," 72). Sage envisions the novel's frames on a vertical hierarchy that is a "paradoxical act" because "the framed will escape into the frame and appear higher up" ("The Author, the Editor, and the Fissured Text," 23). It is, Sage posits elsewhere, part of a 'frame-breaking' principle" ("Irish Gothic: C. R. Maturin and J. S. Le Fanu," in David Punter [ed.], *A New Companion to the Gothic* [Malden, MA: Blackwell, 2012], 140).

32. Patrick Brantlinger, *The Reading Lesson: The Threat of Mass Literacy in Nineteenth-Century British Fiction* (Bloomington: Indiana University Press, 1998), 31.

33. Vijay Mishra, *The Gothic Sublime* (Albany: State University of New York Press, 1994), 246.

34. Julia Kristeva, *Powers of Horror*, trans. Leon S. Roudiez (New York: Columbia University Press, 1982), 4.

35. Slavoj Žižek, *The Sublime Object of Ideology* (London: Verso, 1989), 184.

36. Mladen Dolar, "Beyond Interpellation," *Qui Parle* 6.2 (Spring/Summer 1993): 77.

37. Alison Milbank, "Sacrificial Exchange and the Gothic Double in *Melmoth the Wanderer* and *The Picture of Dorian Gray*," in Victor Morgan and Clare Williams (eds.), *Shaping Belief: Culture, Politics and Religion in Nineteenth-Century Writing* (Liverpool: Liverpool University Press, 2008), 117.

38. Slavoj Žižek, *Interrogating the Real* (London: Bloomsbury, 2006), 349.

39. Ashley Marshall, "Melmoth Affirmed: Maturin's Defense of Sacred History," *Studies in Romanticism* 47.2 (2008), 144.

40. Jon Mee, *The Cambridge Introduction to Charles Dickens* (Cambridge: Cambridge University Press, 2010), 45. M. G. Lewis pro-

vides this violence through the death of Ambrosio in *The Monk* (1896): "Headlong fell the monk through the airy waste; the sharp point of a rock received him; and he rolled from precipice to precipice, till, bruised and mangled he rested on the river's banks" (ed. Christopher MacLachlan [London: Penguin, 1998], 376).

41. Chris Baldick, Introduction to *Melmoth the Wanderer*, by Charles Robert Maturin (Oxford: Oxford University Press, 1989), xi.

42. James Hogg, *The Private Memoirs and Confessions of a Justified Sinner*, ed. Adrian Hunter (Peterborough, Ontario: Broadview, 2001), 232. All further references to this edition will be given in the text.

43. Peter K. Garrett, *Gothic Reflections: Narrative Force in Nineteenth-Century Fiction* (Ithaca: Cornell University Press, 2003), 66.

44. Penny Fielding, "*The Private Memoirs and Confessions of a Justified Sinner*: Approaches," in Ian Duncan and Douglas S. Mack (eds.), *The Edinburgh Companion to James Hogg* (Edinburgh: Edinburgh University Press, 2012), 132.

45. "The Private Memoirs and Confessions of a Justified Sinner," *Quarterly Theological Review* 1 (1825), 99–100.

46. "Private Memoirs and Confessions of a Justified Sinner," *Westminster Review* 2 (October 1824), 560. Critics still find the novel's form jarring. The narrative doubling, Catherine Spooner notes, "profoundly destabilizes notions of unitary meaning" ("Crime and the Gothic," in Charles J. Rzepka and Lee Horsley [eds.], *A Companion to Crime Fiction* [Malden, MA: Wiley-Blackwell, 2010], 250); Susan Manning observes that "[t]he languages, suppositions and intentions of these narrators are utterly opposed; both are, finally, found wanting as complete or objective accounts" (*The Puritan-Provincial Vision: Scottish and American Literature in the Nineteenth Century* [Cambridge: Cambridge University Press, 1990], 80); and Ian Duncan points out chronological discrepancies between the narratives, which create a "general disorder that undoes the work's insistence on an apparent formal symmetry" ("Fanaticism and Enlightenment in *Confessions of a Justified Sinner*," in Sharon Alker and Holly Faith Nelson [eds.], *James Hogg and the Literary Marketplace: Scottish Romanticism and the Working-Class Author* [Burlington, VT: Ashgate, 2009], 60).

47. Henry Fielding, *Joseph Andrews* and *Shamela*, ed. Judith Hawley (London: Penguin, 1999), 119.

48. Ian Duncan, *Scott's Shadow: The Novel in Romantic Edinburgh* (Princeton: Princeton University Press, 2007), 272.

49. Slavoj Žižek, *Enjoy Your Symptom! Jacques Lacan in Hollywood and Out* (New York: Routledge, 1992), 124–25. Mladen Dolar similarly notes that "the double is that mirror image in which the object a [Lacan's *objet petit a*] is included. So the imaginary starts to coincide with the [R]eal, provoking a shattering anxiety. The double is the same as me plus the object a, that invisible part of being added to my image" ("'I Shall Be with You on Your Wedding-Night': Lacan and the Uncanny," *October* 58 [Autumn 1991]: 13).

50. Slavoj Žižek and Mladen Dolar, *Opera's Second Death* (New York: Routledge, 2002), 183–84.

51. Jason Marc Harris, *Folklore and the Fantastic in Nineteenth-Century British Fiction* (Burlington, VT: Ashgate, 2009), 106.

52. Kirsten Stirling, "The Devil in the Printing Press," in Kirsten Stirling and Martine Hennard Dutheil de la Rochère (eds.), *After Satan: Essays in Honour of Neil Forsyth* (Newcastle upon Tyne: Cambridge Scholars, 2010), 123.

53. Žižek, *The Sublime Object of Ideology*, 15.

54. Slavoj Žižek, *Less than Nothing: Hegel and the Shadow of Dialectical Materialism* (London: Verso, 2012), 480.

55. Slavoj Žižek, *Violence* (New York: Picador, 2008), 13.

56. Slavoj Žižek, "Attempts to Escape the Logic of Capitalism," review of John Keane, *Vaclav Havel: A Political Tragedy in Six Acts*, *London Review of Books* 21.21 (28 October 1999), 6.

57. Slavoj Žižek, *Living in the End of Times* (London: Verso, 2010), 420.

58. Kristeva, *Powers of Horror*, 2. Wringhim's suicide is also the result of the shadowing pursuit of his double, Gil-Martin. As Mladen Dolar writes, "[t]he double, retaining the object [Lacan's *objet petit a*], also immediately introduces the death drive" ("'I Shall Be with You on Your Wedding-Night': Lacan and the Uncanny," *October* 58 [Autumn 1991]: 14).

59. Eric Broudy, *The Book of Looms: A History of the Handloom from Ancient Times to the Present* (Hanover: University Press of New England, 1979), 148.

60. Karl Marx, *Capital I*, in Jon Elster (ed.), *The Karl Marx Reader* (Cambridge: Cambridge University Press, 1986), 94, 98.

61. *Ibid.*, 94.

62. Elizabeth Gaskell, *Mary Barton*, ed. Thomas Recchio (New York: Norton, 2008), 332.

63. E. J. Hobsbawm calls Luddite efforts "collective bargaining by riot" and notes not only the organization and diversity of the executions, but also their success ("The Machine Breakers," in *Uncommon People: Resistance, Rebellion and Jazz* [London: Weidenfeld & Nicolson, 1998], 7).

64. Hobsbawm, "The Machine Breakers," pp. 10–11.

65. James Hogg, *The Collected Letters of James Hogg* (Edinburgh: Edinburgh University Press, 2004), 193.

66. *British Critic* 12 (1824), in Adrian Hunter (ed.), *The Private Memoirs and Confessions of a Justified Sinner* (Peterborough, Ontario: Broadview, 2001), 303.

67. Ian Duncan, "Fanaticism and Enlightenment in *Confessions of a Justified Sinner*," 59.

68. Quoted in Douglas Mack, "The Suicide's Grave in *The Confessions of a Justified Sinner*," *Newsletter of the James Hogg Society* 1 (1982), 9.

69. Quoted in David Groves, "James Hogg's *Confessions*: New Information," *Review of English Studies* 40.158 (May 1989), 241.

Interlude

1. Frank Norris, "A Plea for Romantic Fiction," in Donald Pizer (ed.), *McTeague* (New York: Norton, 1997), 277–78.

2. Virginia Woolf, *The Waves* (London: Hogarth Press, 1931), 81.

3. Carlyle's translation had recently gone into a second edition (see Rodger L. Tarr's *Thomas Carlyle: A Descriptive Bibliography* [Charlottesville, VA: UP of Virginia, 1976], 15). Shelley's original letter to Carlyle has not been identified, and whether the authors met in person is still up for debate.

4. Mary Shelley published an edition of Percy's works in 1824, but it was quickly pulled from the shelves following legal threats from her father-in-law, Sir Timothy Shelley.

5. The second epigraph to *Essays* is a quotation from Carlyle's "Varnhagen von Ense's Memoirs" (*London and Westminster Review* 32 [December 1838], 60–84).

6. *The Carlyle Letters Online*, ed. Brent E. Kinser (Durham: Duke University Press, 2007), DOI: 10.1215.lt-18170925-TC-JJ-01. Carlyle also read Walter Scott's Gothic novel, *The Black Dwarf* (1816). In addition, Carlyle and Jane Welsh several times obliquely refer to Scott's Gothic novel *The Bride of Lammermoor* (1819) through the character Caleb Balderstone.

7. *CLO*, DOI: 10.1215.lt-18180430-TC-JJ-01; *CLO*, DOI: 10.1215.lt-18460203-TC-RWE-01.

8. *CLO*, DOI: 10.1215.lt-18381202-TC-RWE-01.

9. In a 19 July 1846 letter to Carlyle, written during a stay at Speke Hall, Jane writes: "I was sure there must be a secret door behind this tapestry, and after I had gone to my room for the night I began to tap and feel all about, like the Heroine of the [*M*]*ysteries of Udolpho* and Oh joy! I actually found one!" (*CLO*, DOI: 10.1215.lt-18460719-JWC-TC-01). And not two years later she records: "seeking thro the books I came upon *The Romance of the Forrest* which I seized on with avidity, remembring [*sic*] the 'tremendous' emotions with which I read it in my night-shift, by the red light of our dying schoolroom fire, nearly half a century ago.... I decidedly like the dear old book" (*CLO*, DOI: 10.1215.lt-18480413-JWC-TC-01).

10. *CLO*, DOI: 10.1215.lt-18260626-JBW-JAC-01.

11. The Carlyles lived at Craigenputtock from 1828 to 1834.

12. *CLO*, DOI: 10.1215.lt-18330527-TC-JFR-01. In *The Life of John Sterling* (1851), Carlyle calls *Sartor Resartus* "a mere aggregate of Magazine Articles; having at last been slit into that form, and lately completed so, and put together into legibility" ([London: Chapman and Hall, 1851], 108).

13. *CLO*, DOI: 10.1215.lt-18330527-TC-JFR-01.

14. J. Hillis Miller, "'Hieroglyphical Truth' in *Sartor Resartus*," in John Clubbe and Jerome Meckier (eds.), *Victorian Perspectives* (London: Macmillan Press, 1989), 3, 5.

15. Geoffrey Hartman, *Criticism in the Wilderness* (New Haven: Yale University Press, 1980), 152.

16. Carlyle elsewhere writes that "[e]very work ... is embaled in some fantastic wrappage, some mad narrative accounting for its appearance, and connecting it with the author, who generally becomes a person of the drama himself, before all is over" ("Jean Paul

Friedrich Richter," *Critical and Miscellaneous Essays* [Boston: Phillips, Sampson and Company, 1857], 10–11).

17. *CLO*, DOI: 10.1215.lt-18330527-TC-JFR-01.

18. Thomas Carlyle, *Sartor Resartus*, ed. Rodger L. Tarr (Berkeley: University of California Press, 2000), 8, 10. All further references to this edition will be given in the text.

19. Teufelsdröckh's papers also recall Samuel Taylor Coleridge's 1817 collection of poetry, *Sibylline Leaves*. In the preface, Coleridge explains that he chose the title as "an allusion to the fragmentary and widely scattered state in which they have been long suffered to remain" ([London: Rest Fenner, 1817], i).

20. Mary Shelley, *The Last Man*, ed. Morton D. Paley (Oxford: Oxford University Press, 1998), 5–6.

21. For example, Rodger L. Tarr observes that the "reader must look at the text as if it were a tapestry in the making. Cords must be connected to cords; knots must be tied, only to be retied. The text challenges the reader to string together discordant allusions (sartor) and thereby to (re)weave transcendent harmony (resartus)" (Introduction to *Sartor Resartus*, by Thomas Carlyle [Berkeley: University of California Press, 2000], xxvii).

22. Bram Stoker, *Dracula*, ed. Maud Ellman (Oxford: Oxford University Press, 2008), 51.

23. Anne Mellor notes that *Sartor Resartus* "exhibit[s] a structure that is deliberately open-ended and inconclusive" (*English Romantic Irony* [Cambridge: Harvard University Press, 1980], 6); and Tarr argues: "in spite of its apparent dogmatism, *Sartor Resartus* does not pretend to contain any ultimate truth, evidence formally be the question mark that ends the text" (Introduction to *Sartor Resartus*, xxvi).

24. *CLO*, DOI: 10.1215.lt-18410828-TC-FEHD-01.

25. Miller, "'Hieroglyphical Truth' in *Sartor Resartus*," 5.

26. Jacques Derrida, *The Truth in Painting*, ed. Geoff Bennington and Ian McLeod (Chicago: University of Chicago Press, 1987), 37.

27. Slavoj Žižek, "The Undergrowth of Enjoyment: How Popular Culture Can Serve as an Introduction to Lacan," in Elizabeth Wright and Edmond Wright (eds.), *The Žižek Reader* (Oxford: Blackwell, 1999), 23.

28. Thomas Carlyle, "The Diamond Necklace," *Fraser's Magazine* 85.15 (January 1837), 3.

29. Martin Willis, "Victorian Realism and the Gothic: Objects of Terror Transformed," in Andrew Smith and William Hughes (eds.), *The Victorian Gothic: An Edinburgh Companion* (Edinburgh: Edinburgh University Press, 2012), 18. Willis examines "not *where* the Gothic might be found …, but *why* it is found there, what it is employed to do, and under what conditions it achieves this" by "illuminating the Gothic mode from realism's perspective" (17).

Chapter 4

1. Charlotte Brontë, "Editor's Preface to the New Edition of *Wuthering Heights*," in Richard J. Dunn (ed.), *Wuthering Heights* (New York: Norton, 2003), 315. Charlotte Brontë also uses this phrase from *Genesis* 15:12 in her posthumously published novel *The Professor* (1857), which she had written before *Jane Eyre*.

2. William Butler Yeats, "The Second Coming," in Richard J. Finneran (ed.), *The Collected Poems of W. B. Yeats* (New York: Scribner, 1996), 187, ll. 18–22.

3. G. W. Peck, *American Review* (June 1848), in Miriam Allott (ed.), *The Brontës: A Critical Heritage* (London: Routledge, 1974), 240.

4. The work of Gregor Mendel (1822–84), not fully appreciated until the early twentieth century, provided concrete evidence for theories on heredity and the transmission of traits that many earlier scholars, including John-Baptist Lamarck (1744–1829) and Charles Darwin (1809–82), had theorized.

5. Mary Shelley, *Frankenstein*, ed. Marilyn Butler (Oxford: Oxford University Press, 2008), 138.

6. Slavoj Žižek, *The Year of Living Dangerously* (London: Verso, 2012), 93.

7. E. P. Whipple, *North American Review* (October 1848), in *The Brontës: A Critical Heritage*, 247.

8. Emily Brontë, *The Complete Poems of Emily Jane Brontë*, ed. C. W. Hatfield (New York: Columbia University Press, 1995), 167, ll. 18–19.

9. Charlotte Brontë, "Editor's Preface to *Wuthering Heights*," 316.

10. Emily Brontë, *Wuthering Heights*, ed. Richard J. Dunn (New York: Norton, 2003),

258. All further references to this edition will be given in the text; Anne Brontë, *The Tenant of Wildfell Hall*, ed. Herbert Rosengarten (Oxford: Clarendon, 1992), 498. All further references to this edition will be given in the text

11. Staffan Müller-Wille and Hans-Jörge Rheinberger, *A Cultural History of Heredity* (Chicago: University of Chicago Press, 2012), xl; Staffan Müller-Wille and Hans-Jörge Rheinberger, *Heredity Produced: At the Crossroads of Biology, Politics, and Culture, 1500–1987* (Cambridge: MIT Press, 2007), 4.

12. Müller-Wille and Rheinberger, *A Cultural History of Heredity*, xl.

13. Peter Gaskell, *The Manufacturing Population of England* (London: Baldwin and Cradock, 1833), 169–70.

14. Orson Squire Fowler, *Hereditary Descent* (New York: Fowlers and Wells, 1847), 21.

15. Fowler, *Hereditary Descent*, 5.

16. Robert Chambers, *Vestiges of the Natural History of Creation* (London: John Churchill, 1844), 357–58.

17. The review was published in the April 1845 issue *Blackwood's* (vol. 57, 448–60). Long reviews also appeared in the *Examiner* and the *Athenaeum*. Janis McLarren Caldwell points out that the "source and impetus for much of the Brontë family medical theorizing" was Thomas John Graham's *Modern Domestic Medicine* (1826), which Patrick Brontë heavily annotated, including underlining a "pertinent passage" on the inheritability of alcoholism ("Physical Health," in Marianne Thormählen [ed.], *The Brontës in Context* [Cambridge: Cambridge University Press, 2012], 337).

18. "Evidences of Insanity," *Boston Medical and Surgical Journal* 11.23 (14 January 1835), 367. Parkman is perhaps best known for being the victim of a grisly murder in Boston on 23 November 1849.

19. Charlotte Brontë, *Jane Eyre*, ed. Margaret Smith (Oxford: Oxford University Press, 2000), 283. All further references to this edition will be given in the text.

20. Shelley, *Frankenstein*, 39.

21. Slavoj Žižek, *The Abyss of Freedom/Ages of the World* (Ann Arbor: University of Michigan Press, 1997), 9.

22. *Atlas* (22 January 1848), in *The Brontës: A Critical Heritage*, 231.

23. Sandra M. Gilbert and Susan Gubar, for example, read the frames of *Wuthering Heights* as a "Romantic storytelling method that emphasizes the ironic disjunctions between different perspectives on the same events" (*The Madwoman in the Attic: The Woman Writer and the Nineteenth-Century Literary Imagination* [New Haven: Yale University Press, 2000], 249); Helen Small observes that the "embedding of narratives within narratives involves an acute, and at times comedic, willingness to invoke and disturb expectations of genre, above all of sentimental romance" (Introduction to *Wuthering Heights*, by Emily Brontë [Oxford: Oxford University Press, 2009], ix); and J. Hillis Miller argues that the novel "produces its effect on its reader through the way it is made up of repetitions of the same in the other which permanently resist rational reduction to some satisfying principle of explanation" (*Fiction and Repetition: Seven English Novels* [Cambridge: Harvard University Press, 1982], 52).

24. *Examiner* (January 1848), *Literary World* (April 1848), and *Britannia* (15 January 1848), in *The Brontës: A Critical Heritage*, 220, 231, 234, and 224.

25. Miller, *Fiction and Repetition*, 52.

26. Beth Newman, "The Situation of the Looker-On: Gender, Narration, and Gaze in Wuthering Heights," *PMLA* 105.5 (1990), 1033.

27. John T. Matthews, "Framing in *Wuthering Heights*," *Texas Studies in Literature and Language* 27.1 (1985), 56.

28. Michael S. Macovski, "*Wuthering Heights* and the Rhetoric of Interpretation," *ELH* 54.2 (1987), 364.

29. John Milton, *Paradise Lost*, ed. John Leonard (London: Penguin, 2000), 78, ll. 4.181.

30. *Athenaeum* (25 December 1847), in *The Brontës: A Critical Heritage*, 218.

31. *Charlotte Brontë: Selected Letters*, ed. Margaret Smith (Oxford: Oxford University Press, 2010), 117.

32. Slavoj Žižek, *Organs without Bodies* (New York: Routledge, 2004), 100.

33. Slavoj Žižek, "General Introduction," in Slavoj Žižek (ed.), *Jacques Lacan: Critical Evaluations in Cultural Theory* (London: Routledge, 2003), 2.

34. Charlotte Brontë, "Editor's Preface to *Wuthering Heights*," 315.

35. Maja-Lisa Von Sneidern, "*Wuthering Heights* and the Liverpool Slave Trade," *ELH* 62 (1995), 172.

36. *Ibid.*, 175.

37. Terry Eagleton, "Fictions on the Real: 'All truth with malice in it,'" in Matthew Beaumont (ed.), *A Concise Companion to Realism* (Malden, MA: Wiley-Blackwell, 2010), 76.

38. Gavriel Reisner, *The Death-Ego and the Vita Self: Romances of Desire in Literature and Psychoanalysis* (Cranbury: Associated University Press, 2003), 154.

39. Jerrold E. Hogle, "The Gothic Ghost of the Counterfeit and the Progress of Abjection," in David Punter (ed.), *A New Companion to the Gothic* (Malden, MA: Blackwell, 2012), 498.

40. Percy Shelley, "Lift not the painted veil," in Kelvin Everest and Geoffrey Matthews (eds.), *The Poems of Shelley*, vol. 2 (Harlow, UK: Pearson, 2000), 414, ll. 5¬–6.

41. Slavoj Žižek, "*Cogito*, Madness, and Religion: Derrida, Foucault, and Then Lacan," in Creston Davis, Marcus Pound, and Clayton Crockett (eds.), *Theology after Lacan: The Passion for the Real* (Cambridge: James Clarke, 2015), 25.

42. Yeats, "The Second Coming," 187, l. 3.

43. Matthews, "Framing in *Wuthering Heights*," 58.

44. Von Sneidern, "*Wuthering Heights* and the Liverpool Slave Trade," 187.

45. Q. D. Leavis, "A Fresh Approach to *Wuthering Heights*," in G. Singh (ed.), *The Collected Essays*, vol. 1 (Cambridge: Cambridge University Press, 1983), 231.

46. Bernhard Duyfhuizen, *Narratives of Transmission* (Rutherford: Fairleigh Dickinson University Press, 1992), 219.

47. Gilbert and Gubar, *The Madwoman in the Attic*, 301.

48. Miriam Allott, "The Rejection of Heathcliff," in Miriam Allott (ed.), *Emily Brontë:* Wuthering Heights: *A Casebook* (London: Macmillan, 1970), 187.

49. George Bacon Wood, *A Treatise on the Practice of Medicine*, vol. 1 (Philadelphia: Grigg, Elliot, and Co., 1849), 157.

50. Jane Gordon describes *Wildfell Hall* as the "longest single-narrative enclosing epistolary novel of the nineteenth century" ("Gossip, Diary, Letter, Text: Anne Brontë's Narrative Tenant and the Problematic of the Gothic Sequel," *ELH* 51.4 [Winter 1984], 719).

51. Garrett Stewart, *Novel Violence: A Narratology of Victorian Fiction* (Chicago: University of Chicago Press, 2009), 91.

52. *Examiner* (29 July 1848), in *The Brontës: A Critical Heritage*, 255–56.

53. This quote appears in the Clarendon edition on page 7.

54. Whipple, *North American Review*, in *The Brontës: A Critical Heritage*, 261.

55. *Examiner* (29 July 1848), in *The Brontës: A Critical Heritage*, 255.

56. As Sally Shuttleworth notes, "Far from being a wild 'gothic' excess, insanity, in all its forms from nervous disorder through to drunkenness and drug addiction, formed part of Brontë's own experience of the everyday" (Introduction to *Jane Eyre*, by Charlotte Brontë [Oxford: Oxford University Press, 2000], xxi).

57. Patrick Brontë founded the Haworth Temperance Society in November 1834.

58. Erasmus Darwin, *The Botanic Garden* (London: J. Johnson, 1799), 156. In his 1621 *The Anatomy of Melancholy*, Robert Burton quotes Plutarch: "*Ebrii gignunt Ebrios*, one drunkard begets another" [London: Chatto & Windus, 1891], 138).

59. Daniel Merriman, *A Sober View of Abstinence* (Andover, MA: Warren F. Draper, 1881), 718

60. Robert MacNish, *The Anatomy of Drunkenness* (New York: D. Appleton, 1835), 16.

61. "The Anatomy of Drunkenness," *Blackwood's Edinburgh Magazine* 23 (April 1828), 483.

62. Beth Torgerson, *Reading the Brontë Body: Disease, Desire, and the Constraints of Culture* (New York: Palgrave Macmillan, 2005), 21.

63. During an argument, Arthur asks Helen whether her father "has thought proper to drink himself to death?" (269).

64. Wood, *A Treatise on the Practice of Medicine*, 157.

65. Josephine McDonagh, Introduction to *The Tenant of Wildfell Hall*, by Anne Brontë (Oxford: Oxford University Press, 2008), xvii.

66. *Ibid.*, xvii.

Chapter 5

1. William Wordsworth, *The Prelude 1799, 1805, 1850*, eds. Jonathan Wordsworth, M. H. Abrams, and Stephen Gill (New York: Norton, 1979), 7.688–94.

2. H. G. Wells, "Zoological Retrogression," *Gentleman's Magazine* 271 (1891), 247.

3. George Gissing, *Charles Dickens: A Critical Study* (New York: Dodd, Mead, and Company, 1912), 31–32.

4. Charles Dickens, *Bleak House*, eds. George Ford and Sylvère Monod (New York: Norton, 1977), 4. All further references to this edition will be given in the text.

5. George Levine, *The Realistic Imagination: English Fiction from* Frankenstein *to*

Lady Chatterley, in Michael McKeon (ed.), *Theory of the Novel: A Historical Approach* (Baltimore: Johns Hopkins University Press, 2000), 622.

6. Robert Mighall, "Defining the Gothic," in David Paroissien (ed.), *A Companion to Charles Dickens* (Malden, MA: Blackwell, 2008), 82. Judith Halberstam observes: "Although the Gothic itself after Shelley seems to disappear for eighty years as a distinct genre, it lives on throughout the nineteenth century as the dark heart of a realism that is always, to some degree, Gothic" (*Skin Shows: Gothic Horror and the Technology of Monsters* [Durham: Duke University Press, 2000], 52).

7. Robert Mighall contends that the novel is the "highpoint of the Urban Gothic at mid-century" (*A Geography of Victorian Gothic Fiction: Mapping History's Nightmares* [Oxford: Oxford University Press, 1999], 69). See also Allan Pritchard's "The Urban Gothic of *Bleak House*" (*Nineteenth-Century Literature* 45 [1991], 432–52).

8. Quoted in Jon Mee, *The Cambridge Introduction to Charles Dickens* (Cambridge: Cambridge University Press, 2010), 43.

9. Charles Dickens, "City of the Absent," *The Uncommercial Traveller* (Oxford: Oxford University Press, 1958), 234. John Forster also borrows the phrase, remarking that Dickens "had a profound attraction of repulsion to St Giles's" (*The Life of Charles Dickens*, vol. 1 [London: Dent, 1969], 14).

10. Julia Kristeva, *Powers of Horror*, trans. Leon S. Roudiez (New York: Columbia University Press, 1982), 2.

11. Jonathan H. Grossman, *Charles Dickens's Networks: Public Transport and the Novel* (Oxford: Oxford University Press, 2012), 107.

12. Slavoj Žižek, "Introduction: The Spectre of Ideology," in *Mapping Ideology*, ed. Slavoj Žižek (London: Verso, 2012), 21–22.

13. Charles Dickens, *Master Humphrey's Clock* (London: Chapman and Hall, 1840), 6.

14. *Ibid.*, iii.

15. *Ibid.*, iii.

16. Charles Dickens, *The Old Curiosity Shop*, ed. Norman Page (London: Penguin, 2000), 7. All further references to this edition will be given in the text.

17. John Bowen, *Other Dickens: Pickwick to Chuzzlewit* (Oxford: Oxford University Press, 2000), 144. Samuel Pickwick and Sam Weller also appear in the periodical and achieve a "strange supplementary half- or afterlife" (144).

18. G. K. Chesterton, *Charles Dickens: A Critical Study* (New York: Dodd, Mead & Co, 1906), 120.

19. Thomas Hood, *Athenæum* (7 November 1840), in Philip Collins (ed.), *Dickens: The Critical Heritage* (New York: Barnes & Noble, 1971), 95–96.

20. *Metropolitan Magazine* (June 1840), in *Dickens: The Critical Heritage*, 93. This reviewer also criticized the "want of novelty and of art in introducing" the stories in the periodical (93). Poe criticized the failings of Humphrey's frame, as well: "The design of the general work, 'Humphrey's Clock,' is simply the common-place one of putting various tales into the mouths of a social party. The meetings are held at the house of Master Humphrey—an antique building in London, where an old-fashioned clock-case is the place of deposit for the M.S.S. Why such designs have become common is obvious. One half the pleasure experienced at a theatre arises from the spectator's sympathy with the rest of the audience, and, especially, from his belief in their sympathy with him.... This is sympathy doubled-diluted—the shadow of a shade. It is unnecessary to say that the design invariably fails of its effect" (*Essays and Reviews*, ed. G. R. Thompson [New York: Viking Press, 1984], 209).

21. Dickens, *Master Humphrey's Clock*, 4.

22. *Ibid.*, 6.

23. *Ibid.*, 37.

24. *Ibid.*, 3.

25. *Ibid.*, 4.

26. Richard Maxwell, "Crowds and Creativity in *The Old Curiosity Shop*," *The Journal of English and Germanic Philology* 78.1 (January 1979), 50.

27. G. K. Chesterton, *Collected Works*, vol. 15 (San Francisco: Ignatius Press, 1989), 272.

28. Audrey Jaffe, *Vanishing Points: Dickens, Narrative, and the Subject of Omniscience* (Berkeley: University of California Press, 1991), 52.

29. Dickens, *Master Humphrey's Clock*, 224.

30. *Ibid.*, 224–25.

31. Grossman argues that Humphrey "breaks out from the tale's (diegetic) storyworld to reveal that he both exists within it and supplies a semi-omniscient viewpoint upon it" (*Charles Dickens's Networks*, 137).

32. Poe, *Essays and Reviews*, 211.

33. John Ruskin, "Fiction, Fair and Foul," in John D. Rosenberg (ed.), *The Genius of John*

Ruskin: Selections from His Writings (Charlottesville: University of Virginia Press, 1998), 442.

34. Charles Dickens, *The Speeches of Charles Dickens*, ed. K. J. Fielding (Oxford: Oxford University Press, 1960), 21.

35. Walter Scott, *A Legend of the Wars of Montrose*, ed. J. H. Alexander (Edinburgh: Edinburgh University Press, 1995), 183. Scott's *Tales of My Landlord* (1816–31) is framed by an enthusiastic compiler (Peter Pattieson) and an irascible editor (Jedidiah Cleishbotham).

36. Grossman, *Charles Dickens's Networks*, 93.

37. Michael Slater, *Charles Dickens* (New Haven: Yale University Press, 2009), 152.

38. Jaffe, *Vanishing Points*, 49.

39. Maria K. Bachman, "Who Cares? Novel Reading, Narrative Attachment Disorder, and the Case of *The Old Curiosity Shop*," *Journal of Narrative Theory* 37.2 (Summer 2007), 300.

40. Jacques Lacan, *The Four Fundamental Concepts of Psycho-Analysis*, ed. Jacques-Alain Miller, trans. Alan Sheridan (London: Karnac, 1977), 72. Lacan continues: "From the moment that this gaze appears, the subject tries to adapt himself to it, he becomes that punctiform object, that point of vanishing being with which the subject confuses his own failure" (83).

41. Hood, *Athenæum*, in *Dickens: The Critical Heritage*, 98.

42. "Dwarfs," *New Monthly Magazine* 3 (1822), 49. Hood lived in Koblenz, Germany, and Ostend, Belgium, and returned to England in late summer 1840, some months before his review of *Master Humphrey's Clock* was published.

43. "Don Roebucco, the Smallest Man in 'The House,'" *Punch* 10 (1846), 118.

44. Mikhail Bakhtin, *Rabelais and His World*, trans. Hélène Iswolsky (Bloomington: Indiana University Press, 1984), 96.

45. *Ibid.*, 8.

46. Kristeva, *Powers of Horror*, 4.

47. Michael Hollington, *Dickens and the Grotesque* (Beckenham, UK: Croom Helm, 1984), 85.

48. Lillian Craton, *The Victorian Freak Show: The Significant of Disability and Physical Differences in 19th-Century Fiction* (Amherst, NY: Cambria Press, 2009), 53.

49. Henry Morley, *Memoirs of Bartholomew Fair* (London: Chapman and Hall, 1859), 317.

50. M. Guyot Daubés, "Variations in Human Stature," *Popular Science Monthly* (July 1887), 315.

51. Michel Foucault, *Discipline and Punish: The Birth of the Prison*, trans. Alan Sheridan (New York: Pantheon, 1977), 201.

52. Grossman, *Charles Dickens's Networks*, 108.

53. Elizabeth Deeds Ermarth, *The English Novel in History: 1840–1895* (New York: Routledge, 1997), 95.

54. See Dickens's 7 October 1849 letter to Forster (*The Letters of Charles Dickens*, vol. 5, eds. Graham Storey and Kenneth Fielding [Oxford: Oxford University Press, 1981], 622–23).

55. Virginia Blain, "Double Vision and the Double Standard in *Bleak House*: A Feminist Perspective," in Jeremy Tambling (ed.), Bleak House: *Charles Dickens* (New York: St Martin's Press, 1998), 82.

56. "*Bleak House*," *Eclectic Review* 6.98 (December 1853), 666. This reviewer considers the omniscient narrator to be the "author speaking in his own person" (666).

57. *Illustrated London News* (24 September 1853); George Brimley, *Spectator* (24 September 1853); *Bentley's Miscellany* 34 (October 1853), in *Dickens: The Critical Heritage*, 281, 293, 288.

58. John Forster, *Examiner* (8 October 1853), in *Bleak House* (New York: Norton), 938.

59. T. S. Eliot, "Wilkie Collins and Dickens," in *T. S. Eliot: Selected Essays* (New York: Harcourt, Brace, 1950), 411.

60. Graham Storey, *Charles Dickens: Bleak House* (Cambridge: Cambridge University Press, 1987), 20.

61. Grossman, *Charles Dickens's Networks*, 6.

62. Merritt Moseley, "The Ontology of Esther's Narrative in *Bleak House*," *South Atlantic Review* 50.2 (May 1985), 41.

63. John McBratney, "'What Connexion Can There Be?': Secrecy and Detection in Dickens's *Bleak House*," in Albert D. Pionke and Denise Tischler Millstein (eds.), *Victorian Secrecy: Economies of Knowledge and Concealment* (Burlington, VT: Ashgate, 2010), 69.

64. Peters, *Feminist Metafiction and the Evolution of the British Novel* (Gainesville: University Press of Florida, 2002), 102.

65. Hilary M. Schor, *Dickens and the Daughter of the House* (Cambridge: Cambridge University Press, 1999), 103.

66. W. J. Harvey, "*Bleak House*: The Double

Narrative," in A. E. Dyson (ed.), *Dickens:* Bleak House—*A Casebook* (London: Macmillan, 1969), 147, 150.

67. Schor, *Dickens and the Daughter of the House*, 102.

68. Slavoj Žižek, *The Sublime Object of Ideology* (London: Verso, 1989), 177.

69. Žižek, "Introduction: The Spectre of Ideology," 26. Žižek names this distortion the "*parallax gap*, the confrontation of two closely linked perspectives between which no neutral common ground is possible" (*The Parallax View* [Cambridge, MA: MIT Press, 2006], 4).

70. Grossman, *Charles Dickens's Networks*, 6.

71. Peters, *Feminist Metafiction*, 103.

72. Schor, *Dickens and the Daughter of the House*, 119.

73. Elizabeth Deeds Ermarth, *Realism and Consensus in the English Novel* (Princeton: Princeton University Press, 1983), 191.

74. Robert Giddings observes that "[s]ometimes Esther quotes John Jarndyce as sounding a great deal like the omniscient narrator.... His description of Tom All-Alone's ... is the particular realization of the omniscient narrator's generic representation, in Chapter 1, of Chancery's holdings" (*The Changing World of Charles Dickens* [London: Vision, 1983], 192).

75. Jane M. Ford points out that "[t]here is never any indication in *Bleak House* that John Jarndyce at any time, past or present, has worked to earn the money he is so generously spending.... [T]here is an unnamed usurer in the background throughout the novel, and the blackest note in this black novel may well be that the usurer is the ostensibly 'good' man" (*Patriarchy and Incest from Shakespeare to Joyce* [Gainesville: University of Florida Press, 1998], 67).

Chapter 6

1. Charles Darwin, *The Descent of Man*, in Philip Appleman (ed.), *Darwin* (New York: Norton, 1970), 276.

2. Alfred, Lord Tennyson, "Locksley Hall Sixty Years After," in Christopher Ricks (ed.), *The Poems of Tennyson* (London: Longmans, 1969), 1367, ll. 199–200.

3. *Ibid.*, 1365, l. 148.

4. *Ibid.*, 1368, l. 236. This thesis opposes his lines in "In Memoriam" (1849) concerning humanity, "[w]ho throve and branched from clime to clime, / The herald of a higher race, / And of himself in higher place" (in Christopher Ricks [ed.], *The Poems of Tennyson* [London: Longmans, 1969], 969, ll. 110.13–15).

5. H. G. Wells, "Zoological Retrogression," *Gentleman's Magazine* 271 (1891), 253.

6. Thomas Carlyle, "Signs of the Times," in Gertrude Himmelfarb (ed.), *The Spirit of the Age: Victorian Essays* (New Haven: Yale University Press, 2007), 34.

7. Daniel Pick, *Faces of Degeneration: A European Disorder, c. 1848–c. 1918* (Cambridge: Cambridge University Press, 1989), 171.

8. Kelly Hurley, *The Gothic Body: Sexuality, Materialism, and Degeneration at the* fin de siècle (Cambridge: Cambridge University Press, 1996), 10.

9. Max Nordau, *Degeneration* (New York: D. Appleton and Company, 1895), 36.

10. Pick, *Faces of Degeneration*, 9.

11. Jerrold E. Hogle, "The Struggle for a Dichotomy: Abjection in Jekyll and His Interpreters," in William Veeder and Gordon Hirsch (eds.), *Dr Jekyll and Mr Hyde After One Hundred Years* (Chicago: University of Chicago Press, 1988), 163.

12. Robert Louis Stevenson, *The Strange Case of Dr Jekyll and Mr Hyde*, ed. Katherine Linehan (New York: Norton, 2003), 52. All further references to this edition will be given in the text.

13. Stephen Arata, *Fictions of Loss in the Victorian fin de siècle* (Cambridge: Cambridge University Press, 1996), 35.

14. Sigmund Freud, "The Ego and the Id," in Peter Gay (ed.), *The Freud Reader* (New York: Norton, 1989), 655.

15. Slavoj Žižek, *Enjoy Your Symptom!: Jacques Lacan in Hollywood and Out* (New York: Routledge, 2002), 143.

16. Julia Kristeva, *Powers of Horror*, trans. Leon S. Roudiez (New York: Columbia University Press, 1982), 4.

17. Slavoj Žižek, "The Undergrowth of Enjoyment: How Popular Culture Can Serve as an Introduction to Lacan," in Elizabeth Wright and Edmond Wright (eds.), *The Žižek Reader* (Oxford: Blackwell, 1999), 23.

18. Stephan Karschay, *Degeneration, Normativity and the Gothic at the Fin de Siècle* (London: Palgrave Macmillan, 2015), 97.

19. Darwin, *The Descent of Man*, 263.

20. Gillian Beer notes that "[e]volutionary theory implied a new myth of the past: instead of the garden at the beginning, there was the sea and the swamp. Instead of man, emptiness—or the empire of mollusks. There was no way back to a previous paradise: the pri-

mordial was comfortless" (*Darwin's Plots: Evolutionary Narrative in Darwin, George Eliot and Nineteenth-Century Fiction* [London: Routledge, 1983], 127).

21. Darwin, *The Descent of Man*, 276.

22. In a 1 September 1873 letter, Stevenson writes: "I could not settle to read anything; I bought Darwin's last book in despair, for I knew I could generally read Darwin, but it was a failure. However, the book served me in good stead" (*Selected Letters of Robert Louis Stevenson*, ed. Ernest Mehew [New Haven: Yale University Press, 1997], 38).

23. Thomas Carlyle, *Sartor Resartus*, ed. Rodger L. Tarr (Berkeley: University of California Press, 2000), 50.

24. Slavoj Žižek, "A Hair of the Dog That Bit You," in Mark Bracher, Marshall W. Alcorn, Jr., Ronald J. Corthell, and François Massardier-Kenney (eds.), *Lacanian Theory of Discourse: Subject, Structure, and Society* (New York: New York University Press, 1994), 55.

25. Roger Luckhurst observes that the sealed envelopes that contain other sealed envelopes symbolize the novel's structure as a "sequence of Russian dolls nested inside each other" (Introduction to *The Strange Case of Dr Jekyll and Mr Hyde and Other Tales*, by Robert Louis Stevenson [Oxford: Oxford University Press, 2006], xiii).

26. *Times* (25 January 1886), in *Robert Louis Stevenson: The Critical Heritage*, 205.

27. Luckhurst, Introduction to *Jekyll and Hyde*, xii.

28. *Ibid.*, xiv.

29. Gordon Hirsch, "*Frankenstein*, Detective Fiction, and *Jekyll and Hyde*," in William Veeder and Gordon Hirsh (eds.), *Dr Jekyll and Mr Hyde After One Hundred Years* (Chicago: University of Chicago Press, 1988), 236.

30. Peter K. Garrett, *Gothic Reflections: Narrative Force in Nineteenth-Century Fiction* (Ithaca: Cornell University Press, 2003), 108.

31. Richard Boothby, *Death and Desire: Psychoanalytic Theory in Lacan's Return to Freud* (New York: Routledge, 1991), 185. Žižek succinctly writes that the "main Freudian name for the Real is the 'death drive'" ("From Desire to Drive: Why Lacan Is Not Lacaniano," *Atlántica de Las Artes* 14 [Autumn 1996], 5).

32. Hogle, "The Struggle for a Dichotomy," 173.

33. Katherine Linehan, Introduction to *The Strange Case of Dr Jekyll and Mr Hyde*, by Robert Louis Stevenson (New York: Norton, 2003), xii.

34. Carol Margaret Davison, "Solving *The Strange Case of Dr Jekyll and Mr Hyde*," in Allan Hepburn (ed.), *Troubled Legacies: Narrative and Inheritance* (Toronto: University of Toronto Press, 2007), 139.

35. Mark Jancovich notes that the "final horror of the story is that, in the hands of Utterson, the episode will probably be repressed and hidden in silence for the sake of decorum" (*Horror* [London: Batsford, 1992], 48).

36. Jekyll is heir to a staggering "quarter of a million sterling" (23). Davison points out that Utterson's "specific reference to the exact amount of Jekyll's fortune again attests to the lawyer's monomania" ("Solving *The Strange Case of Dr Jekyll and Mr Hyde*," 147).

37. Davison, "Solving *The Strange Case of Dr Jekyll and Mr Hyde*," 146.

38. Slavoj Žižek, *Less than Nothing: Hegel and the Shadow of Dialectical Materialism* (London: Verso, 2012), 244.

39. Quoted in *Selected Letters of Robert Louis Stevenson*, 288, n. 3; Lloyd Osbourne, "Stevenson at Thirty-Seven," quoted in *The Strange Case of Dr Jekyll and Mr Hyde*, ed. Martin A. Danahay (Peterborough, Ontario: Broadview, 2005), 131.

40. "Recent Novels," *Spectator* 78 (31 July 1897), 151; Jennifer Wicke, "Vampiric Typewriting: *Dracula* and its Media," *ELH* 59.2 (Summer 1992), 467.

41. Bram Stoker, *Dracula*, ed. Maud Ellman (Oxford: Oxford University Press, 2008), xxxviii. All further references to this edition will be given in the text.

42. Wicke, "Vampiric Typewriting," 467.

43. *Ibid.*, 475–76.

44. "The Literary Character of the Present Age," *Monthly Magazine* 1.8 (September 1840), 245–48.

45. *The London Atlas* in "The Devil in Literature," *The National Magazine* 2 (February 1853), 128.

46. Slavoj Žižek, "Fantasy as a Political Category: A Lacanian Approach," in Elizabeth Wright and Edmond Wright (eds.), *The Žižek Reader* (Oxford: Blackwell, 1999), 97.

47. Slavoj Žižek, "The Spectre of Ideology," in Elizabeth Wright and Edmond Wright (eds.), *The Žižek Reader* (Oxford: Blackwell, 1999), 74.

48. Alison Case, "Tasting the Original Apple: Gender and the Struggle for Narrative Authority in *Dracula*," *Narrative* 1.3 (October 1993), 224.

49. Nearly forty percent of the narrative is

Seward's compared to twenty percent for Mina and almost twenty-eight percent for Harker (most of which comes in his opening frame).

50. Margot Gayle Backus makes note of the novel's "Transylvanian frame narrative" (*The Gothic Family Romance: Heterosexuality, Child Sacrifice, and the Anglo-Irish Colonial Order* [Durham: Duke University Press, 1999], 135).

51. David Seed, "The Narrative Method of *Dracula*," *Nineteenth-Century Fiction* 40.1 (June 1985), 61–75.

52. "Fiction," 662.

53. See Patrick Brantlinger, "Imperial Gothic: Atavism and the Occult in the British Adventure Novel, 1880–1914," in Lyn Pykett (ed.), *Reading* Fin de Siècle *Fictions* (London: Longman, 1996), 184–209.

54. Stephen D. Arata, "The Occidental Tourist: *Dracula* and the Anxiety of Reverse Colonization," *Victorian Studies* 33.4 (Summer 1990), 623.

55. Pick, *Faces of Degeneration*, 172.

56. Cannon Schmitt, "Evolution and Victorian Fiction," in Bernard Lightman and Bennett Zon (eds.), *Evolution and Victorian Culture* (Cambridge: Cambridge University Press, 2014), 18.

57. "New Fiction," *Saturday Review of Politics, Literature, Science and Art* 84 (3 July 1897), 21.

58. Valdine Clemens asserts that Dracula "hails from an even earlier evolutionary stage than does the apelike Hyde: the beginnings of animal life on earth.... Dracula signifies the eruption of the most primitive and elemental instinctual drives related to the struggle for species survival ... at a time when a rapidly transforming environment was making increasing demands on the human power of adaptation" (*The Return of the Repressed: Gothic Horror from* The Castle of Otranto *to* Alien [Albany: State University of New York Press, 1999], 154).

59. Jacques Lacan, "Presentation on Psychical Causality," in *Écrits*, trans. Bruce Fink (New York: Norton, 1999), 144.

60. Slavoj Žižek, "Psychoanalysis and the Lacanian Real: 'Strange shapes of the unwarped primal world,'" in Matthew Beaumont (ed.), *A Concise Companion to Realism* (Malden, MA: Wiley-Blackwell, 2010), 225.

61. Slavoj Žižek, "Grimaces of the Real, or When the Phallus Appears," *October* 58 (Autumn 1991), 66.

62. "New Fiction," 21.

63. Jacques Lacan, "The Mirror Stage as Formative of the Function of the I as Revealed in Psychoanalytic Experience," *Écrits: A Selection*, trans. Alan Sheridan (London: Tavistock, 1977), 2.

64. Maria Beville, *Gothic-Postmodernism: Voicing the Terrors of Postmodernity* (Amsterdam: Rodopi, 2009), 131.

65. Nancy Armstrong, *How Novels Think: The Limits of Individualism from 1790–1900* (New York: Columbia University Press, 2005), 147.

66. Nancy Armstrong, "Gender and the Victorian Novel," in Deirdra David (ed.), *The Cambridge Companion to the Victorian Novel* (Cambridge: Cambridge University Press, 2001), 115.

67. "So mastered by the brute blood of the air, / Did she put on his knowledge with his power / Before the indifferent beak could let her drop?" (William Butler Yeats, "Leda and the Swan," in Richard J. Finneran [ed.], *The Collected Poems of W. B. Yeats* [New York: Scribner, 1996], 214, ll. 12–14).

68. John Milton, *Paradise Lost*, ed. John Leonard (London: Penguin, 2000), 78, ll. 4.181.

69. Shelley, *Frankenstein*, 191.

70. "Dracula. By Bram Stoker," *Academy* 52 (12 June 1897), 11.

71. Carol A. Senf examines the novel's unreliable narrators and notes that Stoker "provides several clues to their unreliability and encourages the reader to see the frequent discrepancies between their professed beliefs and their actions" ("*Dracula*: The Unseen Face in the Mirror," *The Journal of Narrative Technique* 9.3 [Fall 1979], 161).

72. To hear the rather unsettling remnants left behind by MP3 and MP4 file compression, see Ryan Maguire's "The Ghost in the MP3" (<the ghostinthemp3.com>).

Coda

1. William Shakespeare, *Hamlet*, eds. Ann Thompson and Neil Taylor (London: Arden Shakespeare, 2006), 466, 2.2.253–55.

2. George Eliot, "The Lifted Veil," in Helen Small (ed.), *The Lifted Veil* and *Brother Jacob* (Oxford: Oxford University Press, 2009), 12.

3. Richard Menke argues that "The Lifted Veil" "offers a parable of the powers and limitations of depersonalized perception; a horror tale helps unveil the hidden logic, and

the suppressed alienation or violence, of realism's fantasies of information" (*Telegraphic Realism: Victorian Fiction and Other Information Systems* [Stanford: Stanford University Press, 2008], 138).

4. Eliot, "The Lifted Veil," 33.

5. The blood transfusion that briefly brings the maid Mrs Archer back to life in "The Lifted Veil" anticipates the transfusions conducted to save Lucy in *Dracula*. The story's flashback structure recalls Mary Shelley's *The Last Man* (1826) and the tale "The Mortal Immortal" (1833), and it is an uncanny echo of *Mathilda*, though Eliot could not have read it.

6. J. Hillis Miller writes that Victorian novelists who employed an omniscient narrator were "unwilling to accept the notion so prevalent in fiction after Conrad and James that no comprehensive view of society is possible" (*The Form of Victorian Fiction* [Notre Dame: University of Notre Dame Press, 1968], 119).

7. Henry James, "Preface to *Roderick Hudson*," in *The Art of the Novel* (New York: Charles Scribner's Sons, 1962), 5.

8. James, "Preface to *Roderick Hudson*," 6.

9. Edgar Allan Poe, "The Philosophy of Composition," *Graham's Magazine* 28.4 (April 1846), 166.

10. Joseph Conrad, "Henry James: An Appreciation," in *Heart of Darkness* (New York: Norton, 2006), 287–88.

11. Henry James, *The Notebooks of Henry James*, eds. F. O. Matthiessen and Kenneth Murdock (Chicago: University of Chicago Press, 1981), 257.

12. Henry James, *What Maisie Knew*, ed. Adrian Poole (Oxford: Oxford University Press, 2008), 275.

13. The novel has been called a "half-frame" (Susan Crowl, "Aesthetic Allegory in *The Turn of the Screw*," *Novel* 4 [1971], 108), "asymmetrical" (William Goetz, "The 'Frame' of *The Turn of the Screw*: Framing the Reader In," *Studies in Short Fiction* 18 [1988], 73), and "terribly unframed" (Richard Dilworth Rust, "Liminality in *The Turn of the Screw*," *Studies in Short Fiction* 25 [1988], 444). Nita Schechet observes that "[n]either male narrator resumes his opening narrative after the governess's tale, creating a layered narrative, an open-bottom frame and the source of the story's ambiguity" (*Narrative Fissures: Reading and Rhetoric* [Cranbury, NJ: Associated Press, 2005], 45); and T. J. Lustig notes that the novel "systematically blanks out beginnings and endings" (*Henry James and the Ghostly* [Cambridge: Cambridge University Press, 1994], 121). Paul G. Beidler offers a different perspective, arguing that the "Prologue is not a broken frame at all but a complete one that describes events occurring both before and after the story, thus framing the manuscript temporally and providing the closure that critics argue is missing" (*Frames in James*: The Tragic Muse, The Turn of the Screw, What Maisie Knew, *and* The Ambassadors [Victoria: University of Victoria English Literary Studies, 1993], 48).

14. Henry James, *The Turn of the Screw*, ed. Peter G. Beidler (Boston: Bedford/St Martin's, 2010), 23. All further references to this edition will be given in the text.

15. James, *The Notebooks of Henry James*, 178.

16. George E. Haggerty argues that the governess "never fully admits the implicit erotics of her intense voyeuristic pleasure in their lives.... She chooses to see ghosts—she is haunted, that is—because she is unwilling to confront the complex erotics of her position" (*Queer Gothic* [Champaign: University of Illinois Press, 2006], 140).

17. Shoshana Felman argues that the frame is a "blurring of the very difference between inside and outside" ("Turning the Screw of Interpretation," *Yale French Studies* 55–56 [1978], 123).

18. Henry James, "The New Novel," in *Heart of Darkness* (New York: Norton, 2006), 313.

19. Žižek argues that "the Real is *nothing but* the gap or antagonism that thwarts the symbolic from within" (*Less than Nothing: Hegel and the Shadow of Dialectical Materialism* [London: Verso, 2012], 959).

20. James, "The New Novel," 314.

21. Joseph Conrad, *Heart of Darkness*, ed. Paul B. Armstrong (New York: Norton, 2006), 3, 7. All further references to this edition will be given in the text.

22. Samuel Taylor Coleridge, "The Rime of the Ancyent Marinere," in Paul H. Fry (ed.), *The Rime of the Ancient Mariner* (Boston: Bedford-St Martin's, 1999), 28, l. 22.

23. James, *The Notebooks of Henry James*, 257.

24. Slavoj Žižek, "Psychoanalysis and the Lacanian Real: 'Strange shapes of the unwarped primal world,'" in Matthew Beaumont

(ed.), *A Concise Companion to Realism* (Malden, MA: Wiley-Blackwell, 2010), 233.

25. Stephen King has recently described the story's theme: "reality is thin, and the *true* reality beyond is a limitless abyss filled with monsters" ("Sunset Notes," in *Just After Sunset* [New York: Pocket Books, 2008], 534).

26. Arthur Machen, *The Great God Pan*, in Roger Luckhurst (ed.), *Late Victorian Gothic Tales* (Oxford: Oxford University Press, 2005), 184. All further references to this edition will be given in the text.

27. Villiers, who gathers evidence of the events, usefully describes the tale's structure: "A case like this is like a nest of Chinese boxes; you open one after the other and find a quainter workmanship in every box" (199).

28. Christine Ferguson, "Decadence as Scientific Fulfillment," *PMLA* 117.3 (May 2002), 475.

29. Kimberly Jackson examines how Machen's tales explore the "descent into the primordial" by arguing that his "monsters represent the imaginative possibilities that emerge from evolutionary theory but which the scientific mode of understanding cannot entertain" ("Non-Evolutionary Degeneration in Arthur Machen's Supernatural Tales," *Victorian Literature and Culture* 41 [2013], 125, 130). Susan J. Navarette argues that "[t]he narrative hesitations as well as the stylistic disruptions of 'The Great God Pan' thus serve as signposts of linguistic and structural degeneration that we might think of as being analogous to biological and cultural dissolution" (*The Shape of Fear: Horror and the Fin de Siècle Culture of Decadence* [Lexington: University Press of Kentucky, 1998], 193).

30. Žižek argues that the conditions for "the breakdown of the boundary separating reality from the Real" causes the "psychotic breakdown[s]" of autism and paranoia ("The Undergrowth of Enjoyment: How Popular Culture Can Serve as an Introduction to Lacan," in Elizabeth Wright and Edmond Wright [eds.], *The Žižek Reader* [Oxford: Blackwell, 1999], 22–23).

Bibliography

Primary Sources

Austen, Jane. *Northanger Abbey*, ed. Marilyn Butler. London: Penguin, 2003.

Brontë, Anne. *The Tenant of Wildfell Hall*, ed. Herbert Rosengarten. Oxford: Clarendon, 1992.

Brontë, Charlotte. *Jane Eyre*, ed. Margaret Smith. Oxford: Oxford University Press, 2000.

_____. *Shirley*, ed. Andrew Hook and Judith Hook. London: Penguin, 1988.

Brontë, Emily. *The Complete Poems of Emily Jane Brontë*, ed. C. W. Hatfield. New York: Columbia University Press, 1995.

_____. *Wuthering Heights*, ed. Richard J. Dunn. New York: Norton, 2003.

Burke, Edmund. *A Philosophical Enquiry into the Origin of Our Ideas of the Sublime and Beautiful*, ed. Paul Guyer. Oxford: Oxford University Press, 2015.

Burton, Robert. *The Anatomy of Melancholy*. London: Chatto and Windus, 1891.

Byron, Lord. *The Giaour*. In *The Major Works*, ed. Jerome McGann, 207–47. Oxford: Oxford University Press, 2008.

Carlyle, Thomas. "Cruthers and Jonson; or, the Outskirts of Life." *Fraser's Magazine* 2.12 (January 1831): 691–705.

_____. "The Diamond Necklace." *Fraser's Magazine* 85.15 (January 1837): 1–19.

_____. "Jean Paul Friedrich Richter." *Critical and Miscellaneous Essays*, 7–15. Boston: Phillips, Sampson and Company, 1857.

_____. *The Life of John* Sterling. London: Chapman and Hall, 1851.

_____. *Sartor Resartus*, ed. Rodger L. Tarr. Berkeley: University of California Press, 2000.

_____. "Signs of the Times." In *The Spirit of the Age: Victorian Essays*, ed. Gertrude Himmelfarb, 31–49. New Haven: Yale University Press, 2007.

_____. "Varnhagen von Ense's Memoirs." *London and Westminster Review* 32 (December 1838): 60–84.

Charles Lamb: Selected Writings, ed. J. E. Morpurgo. New York: Routledge, 2003.

Chesterton, G. K. *The Return of Don Quixote*. Cornwall, UK: House of Stratus, 2008.

Coleridge, Samuel Taylor. *Biographia Literaria*. In *The Major Works*, ed. H. J. Jackson, 155–482. Oxford: Oxford University Press, 2000.

_____. "The Eolian Harp." In *The Major Works*, ed. H. J. Jackson, 27–29. Oxford: Oxford University Press, 2008.

_____. "The Rime of the Ancyent Marinere." In *The Rime of the Ancient Mariner*, ed. Paul H. Fry, 26–74. Boston: Bedford/St Martin's, 1999.

_____. *Sibylline Leaves*. London: Rest Fenner, 1817.

Conrad, Joseph. *Heart of Darkness*, ed. Paul B. Armstrong. New York: Norton, 2006.

Darwin, Charles. *The Descent of Man*. In *Darwin*, ed. Philip Appleman, 199–276. New York: Norton, 1970.

Darwin, Erasmus. *The Botanic Garden*. London: J. Johnson, 1799.

Dickens, Charles. *Bleak House*, ed. George Ford and Sylvère Monod. New York: Norton, 1977.

_____. *Master Humphrey's Clock*. London: Chapman and Hall, 1840.

_____. *The Old Curiosity Shop*, ed. Norman Page. London: Penguin, 2000.

_____. "City of the Absent." In *The Uncommercial Traveller*, 233–40. Oxford: Oxford University Press, 1958.

Eliot, George. "The Lifted Veil." In *The Lifted Veil* and *Brother Jacob*, ed. Helen Small, 1–44. Oxford: Oxford University Press, 2009.

Fielding, Henry. *Joseph Andrews* and *Shamela*, ed. Judith Hawley. London: Penguin, 1999.

Fowler, Orson Squire. *Hereditary Descent*. New York: Fowlers and Wells, 1847.

Frost, Robert. "Mending Wall." In *The Poetry of Robert Frost*, ed. Edward Connery Lathem, 33–34. London: Jonathan Cape, 1971.

Gaskell, Elizabeth. *Mary Barton*, ed. Thomas Recchio. New York: Norton, 2008.

Gaskell, Peter. *The Manufacturing Population of England*. London: Baldwin and Cradock, 1833.

Gilpin, William. *An Essay on Prints*. London: T. Cadell, 1802.

_____. *Three Essays: on Picturesque Beauty; on Picturesque Travel; and on Sketching Landscape*. London: R. Blamire, 1792.

Hazlitt, William. *Lectures on the English Comic Writers*. London: Taylor and Hessey, 1819.

Hogg, James. *The Private Memoirs and Confessions of a Justified Sinner*, ed. Adrian Hunter. Peterborough, Ontario: Broadview, 2001.

James, Henry. *What Maisie Knew*, ed. Adrian Poole. Oxford: Oxford University Press, 2008.

_____. *The Turn of the Screw*, ed. Peter G. Beidler. Boston: Bedford/St Martin's, 2010.

Kant, Immanuel. *Critique of Judgement*, ed. Nicholas Walker. Oxford: Oxford University Press, 2007.

_____. *Critique of the Power of Judgment*, ed. Paul Guyer. Cambridge: Cambridge University Press, 2000.

_____. *Critique of Pure Reason*, ed. Marcus Weigelt. London: Penguin, 2007.

Lewis, Matthew Gregory. *The Monk*, ed. Christopher MacLachlan. London: Penguin, 1998.

Machen, Arthur. *The Great God Pan*. In *Late Victorian Gothic Tales*, ed. Roger Luckhurst, 183–233. Oxford: Oxford University Press, 2005.

Marx, Karl. *Capital I*. In *Karl Marx: A Reader*, ed. Jon Elster, 81–99. Cambridge: Cambridge University Press, 1986.

Maturin, Charles Robert. *Melmoth the Wanderer*, ed. Douglas Grant. Oxford: Oxford University Press, 1968.

Merriman, Daniel. *A Sober View of Abstinence*. Andover, MA: Warren F. Draper, 1881.

Milton, John. *Paradise Lost*, ed. John Leonard. London: Penguin, 2000.

Plato. "The Allegory of the Cave." In *The Classical Greek Reader*, ed. Kenneth J. Atchity, 187–94. Oxford: Oxford University Press, 1996.

Poe, Edgar Allan. "The Fall of the House of Usher." In *The Selected Writings of Edgar Allan Poe*, ed. G. R. Thompson, 199–216. New York: Norton, 2004.

_____. "The Masque of the Red Death." In *The Selected Writings of Edgar Allan Poe*, ed. G. R. Thompson, 299–304. New York: Norton, 2004.

_____. "The Raven." In *The Selected Writings of Edgar Allan Poe*, ed. G. R. Thompson, 58–61. New York: Norton, 2004.

Price, Uvedale. *Essay on the Picturesque*. London: J. Robinson, 1796.

Radcliffe, Ann. *Gaston de Blondeville*, ed. Frances Chiu. Chicago: Valancourt, 2006.

_____. *The Italian*, ed. Frederick Garber. Oxford: Oxford University Press, 1998.

_____. *The Mysteries of Udolpho*, ed. Bonamy Dobrée. Oxford: Oxford University Press, 1998.

_____. "On the Supernatural in Poetry." *New Monthly Magazine* 16 (1826): 145–52.

_____. *A Sicilian Romance*, ed. Alison Milbank. Oxford: Oxford University Press, 2008.

Scott, Walter. *A Legend of the Wars of Montrose*, ed. J. H. Alexander. Edinburgh: Edinburgh University Press, 1995.

Shakespeare, William. *Hamlet*, ed. Ann Thompson and Neil Taylor. London: Arden Shakespeare 2006.

_____. *Macbeth*, ed. Kenneth Muir. London: Arden Shakespeare, 1984.

Shelley, Mary. *Frankenstein*, ed. Marilyn

Butler. Oxford: Oxford University Press, 1998.

_____. *Mathilda*, ed. Elizabeth Nitchie. Chapel Hill: University of North Carolina Press, 2008.

_____. *The Last Man*, ed. Morton D. Paley. Oxford: Oxford University Press, 2008.

Shelley, Percy Bysshe. "A Defence of Poetry." In *The Selected Poetry and Prose of Shelley*, ed. Bruce Woodcock, 635–60. Hertfordshire: Wordsworth, 2002.

_____. *Essays, Letters from Abroad, Translations and Fragments*, ed. Mary Shelley. London: Edward Moxon, 1845.

_____. "Lift not the painted veil." In *The Poems of Shelley*, vol. 2, ed. Kelvin Everest and Geoffrey Matthews, 414. Harlow, UK: Pearson, 2000.

Stevenson, Robert Louis. *The Strange Case of Dr Jekyll and Mr Hyde*, ed. Katherine Linehan. New York: Norton, 2003.

Stoker, Bram. *Dracula*, ed. Maud Ellman. Oxford: Oxford University Press, 2008.

Tennyson, Alfred Lord. "The Gardener's Daughter." In *The Poems of Tennyson*, ed. Christopher Ricks, 507–21. London: Longmans, 1969.

_____. *In Memoriam*. In *The Poems of Tennyson*, ed. Christopher Ricks, 853–958. London: Longmans, 1969.

_____. "The Lady of Shalott." In *The Poems of Tennyson*, ed. Christopher Ricks, 354–61. London: Longmans, 1969.

_____. "Locksley Hall Sixty Years After." In *The Poems of Tennyson*, ed. Christopher Ricks, 1359–69. London: Longmans, 1969.

_____. "Mariana." In *The Poems of Tennyson*, ed. Christopher Ricks, 205–09. London: Longmans, 1969.

Trollope, Anthony. *Barchester Towers*, ed. Michael Sadleir and Frederick Page. Oxford: Oxford University Press, 1996.

Walpole, Horace. *The Castle of Otranto* and *The Mysterious Mother*, ed. Frederick S. Frank. Peterborough, Ontario: Broadview, 2003.

Woolf, Virginia. *The Waves*. London: Hogarth Press, 1931.

Wordsworth, William. "Expostulation and Reply." In *Lyrical Ballads*, ed. Michael Gamer and Dahlia Porter, 134–35. Peterborough, Ontario: Broadview, 2008.

_____. "Ode: Intimations of Immortality from Recollections of Early Childhood." In *The Major Works*, ed. Stephen Gill, 297–302. Oxford: Oxford University Press, 2008.

_____. *The Prelude 1799, 1805, 1850*, ed. Jonathan Wordsworth, M. H. Abrams and Stephen Gill. New York: Norton, 1979.

Yeats, William Butler. "Leda and the Swan." In *The Collected Poems of W. B. Yeats*, ed. Richard J. Finneran, 214. New York: Scribner, 1996.

_____. "The Second Coming." In *The Collected Poems of W. B. Yeats*, ed. Richard J. Finneran, 187. New York: Scribner, 1996.

Secondary Sources

Allott, Miriam. "The Rejection of Heathcliff." In *Emily Brontë:* Wuthering Heights: *A Casebook*, ed. Miriam Allott, 183–206. London: Macmillan, 1970.

"The Anatomy of Drunkenness." *Blackwood's Edinburgh Magazine* 23 (April 1828): 481–99.

Andrews, Malcolm. *The Search for the Picturesque*. Stanford: Stanford University Press, 1989.

Anolik, Ruth Bienstock. Introduction. *Demons of the Body: Essays on Disability in Gothic Literature*, ed. Ruth Bienstock Anolik, 1–20. Jefferson, NC: McFarland, 2000.

Arata, Stephen. *Fictions of Loss in the Victorian fin de siècle*. Cambridge: Cambridge University Press, 1996.

_____. "The Occidental Tourist: *Dracula* and the Anxiety of Reverse Colonization." *Victorian Studies* 33.4 (Summer 1990): 621–45.

Armstrong, Nancy. *Fiction in the Age of Photography: The Legacy of British Realism*. Cambridge: Harvard University Press, 1999.

_____. "Gender and the Victorian Novel." In *The Cambridge Companion to the Victorian Novel*, ed. Deirdra David, 97–124. Cambridge: Cambridge University Press, 2001.

_____. *How Novels Think: The Limits of Individualism from 1790–1900*. New York: Columbia University Press, 2005.

The Athenaeum (25 December 1847). In *The Brontës: A Critical Heritage*, ed. Miriam Allot, 218–19. London: Routledge, 1974.

Atlas (22 January 1848). In *The Brontës: A Critical Heritage*, ed. Miriam Allott, 230–33. London: Routledge, 1974).

Axton, William F. Introduction. *Melmoth the Wanderer*. By Charles Robert Maturin, vii–xviii. Lincoln: University of Nebraska Press, 1966.

Bachman, Maria K. "Who Cares? Novel Reading, Narrative Attachment Disorder, and the Case of *The Old Curiosity Shop*." *Journal of Narrative Theory* 37.2 (Summer 2007): 296–325.

Backus, Margot Gayle. *The Gothic Family Romance: Heterosexuality, Child Sacrifice, and the Anglo-Irish Colonial Order*. Durham: Duke University Press, 1999.

Bakhtin, Mikhail. "Discourse in the Novel." In *The Dialogic Imagination*, ed. Michael Holquist, trans. Caryl Emerson and Michael Holquist, 269–422. Austin: University of Texas Press, 1981.

_____. *Rabelais and His World*, trans. Hélène Iswolsky. Bloomington: Indiana University Press, 1984.

Bal, Mieke. *Narratology: Introduction to the Theory of Narrative*. Toronto: University of Toronto Press, 1997.

Baldick, Chris. Introduction. *Melmoth the Wanderer*. By Charles Robert Maturin, vii–xix. Oxford: Oxford University Press, 1989.

Barbauld, Anna Laetitia. "Mrs Radcliffe." In *The British Novelists*. Vol. 43. London: F. C. and J. Rivington, 1820.

Bayer-Berenbaum, Linda. *The Gothic Imagination*. Cranbury: Associated University Press, 1982.

Beer, Gillian. *Darwin's Plots: Evolutionary Narrative in Darwin, George Eliot and Nineteenth-Century Fiction*. London: Routledge, 1983.

Beidler, Paul G. *Frames in James:* The Tragic Muse, The Turn of the Screw, What Maisie Knew, *and* The Ambassadors. Victoria: English Literary Studies, University of Victoria, 1993.

Bellamy, Liz. *Commerce, Morality and the Eighteenth-Century Novel*. Cambridge: Cambridge University Press, 1998.

Bender, John. *Ends of Enlightenment*. Stanford: Stanford University Press, 2012.

Benford, Criscillia. "'Listen to my tale': Multilevel Structure, Narrative Sense Making, and the Inassimilable in Mary Shelley's *Frankenstein*." *Narrative* 18.3 (October 2010): 324–46.

Bennett, Betty T., ed. *The Letters of Mary Wollstonecraft Shelley*. Vol. 1. Baltimore: Johns Hopkins University Press, 1980.

Bennett, Jonathan. *Kant's Analytic*. Cambridge: Cambridge University Press, 1966.

Bentley's Miscellany, 34 (October 1853). In *Dickens: The Critical Heritage*, ed. Philip Collins, 287–89. New York: Barnes & Noble, 1971.

Berlatsky, Eric. "Lost in the Gutter: Within and Between Frames in Narrative and Narrative Theory." *Narrative* 17.2 (May 2009): 162–87.

Beville, Maria. *Gothic-Postmodernism: Voicing the Terrors of* Postmodernity. Amsterdam: Rodopi, 2009.

Blain, Virginia. "Double Vision and the Double Standard in *Bleak House*: A Feminist Perspective." In Bleak House: *Charles Dickens*, ed. Jeremy Tambling, 65–86. New York: St Martin's Press, 1998.

"*Bleak House*." *Eclectic Review* 698 (December 1853): 665–79.

Bohls, Elizabeth A. *Women Travel Writers and the Language of Aesthetics, 1716–1818*. Cambridge: Cambridge University Press, 1995.

Boothby, Richard. *Death and Desire: Psychoanalytic Theory in Lacan's Return to Freud*. New York: Routledge, 1991.

_____. "The Psychical Meaning of Life and Death: Reflections on the Lacanian Imaginary, Symbolic, and Real." In *Disseminating Lacan*, ed. David Pettigrew and François Raffoul, 337–63. Albany: State University of New York Press, 1996.

Bowen, John. *Other Dickens: Pickwick to Chuzzlewit*. Oxford: Oxford University Press, 2000.

Bowie, Malcolm. *Lacan*. Cambridge: Harvard University Press, 1991.

Brantlinger, Patrick. "Imperial Gothic: Atavism and the Occult in the British Adventure Novel, 1880–1914." In *Reading* Fin de Siècle *Fictions*, ed. Lyn Pykett, 184–209. London: Longman, 1996.

_____. *The Reading Lesson: The Threat of Mass Literacy in Nineteenth-Century British Fiction*. Bloomington: Indiana University Press, 1998.

Breton, André. Preface. *Melmoth, L'Homme Errant*. By Charles Robert Maturin, trans. Jean Cohen, xi–xx. Paris: Jean-Jacques Pauvert, 1954.

Brimley, George. *Spectator* (24 September 1853). In *Dickens: The Critical Heritage*, ed. Philip Collins, 283–86. (New York: Barnes & Noble, 1971.

Britannia (15 January 1848). In *The Brontës: A Critical Heritage*, ed. Miriam Allott, 223–26. London: Routledge, 1974.

The British Critic, 12 (1824). In *The Private Memoirs and Confessions of a Justified Sinner*, ed. Adrian Hunter, 303. Peterborough, Ontario: Broadview, 2001.

Broadwell, Elizabeth P. "The Veil Image in Ann Radcliffe's *The Italian*." *South Atlantic Bulletin* 40.4 (November 1975): 76–87.

Brontë, Charlotte. "Editor's Preface to the New Edition of *Wuthering Heights*." In *Wuthering Heights*, ed. Richard J. Dunn, 313–16. New York: Norton, 2003.

Brooks, Peter. *Reading for the Plot: Design and Intention in Narrative*. Cambridge: Harvard University Press, 1992.

Broudy, Eric. *The Book of Looms: A History of the Handloom from Ancient Times to the Present*. Hanover: University Press of New England, 1979.

Brown, Huntington. "The Gloss to the Ancient Mariner." *Modern Language Quarterly* 6 (1945): 319–24.

Bunnell, Charlene. "*Mathilda*: Mary Shelley's Romantic Tragedy." *Keats-Shelley Journal* 46 (1997): 75–96.

Caldwell, Janis McLarren. "Physical Health." In *The Brontës in Context*, ed. Marianne Thormählen, 335–43. Cambridge: Cambridge University Press, 2012.

Cameron, Ed. *The Psychopathology of the Gothic Romance: Perversion, Neuroses and Psychosis in Early Works of the Genre*. Jefferson, NC: McFarland, 2010.

Canuel, Mark. "Acts, Rules and *The Last Man*." *Nineteenth-Century Literature* 53.2 (Sept. 1998): 147¬–70.

Carlyle, Thomas and Jane Welsh Carlyle. *The Carlyle Letters Online* [*CLO*]. Ed. Brent E. Kinser. Durham: Duke University Press, 2007–16. <www.carlyleletters.org>

Case, Alison. "Tasting the Original Apple: Gender and the Struggle for Narrative Authority in *Dracula*." *Narrative* 1.3 (October 1993): 223–43.

Castle, Terry. *The Female Thermometer: Eighteenth-Century Culture and the Invention of the Uncanny*. Oxford: Oxford University Press, 1995.

_____. Introduction. *The Mysteries of Udolpho*. By Ann Radcliffe, vii–xxvi. Oxford: Oxford University Press, 1998.

Chambers, Robert. *Vestiges of the Natural History of Creation*. London: John Churchill, 1844.

Chesterton, G. K. *Charles Dickens: A Critical Study*. New York: Dodd, Mead & Co, 1906.

_____. *Collected Works*. Vol. 15. San Francisco: Ignatius Press, 1989.

Clemens, Valdine. *The Return of the Repressed: Gothic Horror from* The Castle of Otranto *to* Alien. Albany: State University of New York Press, 1999.

Clemit, Pamela. "*Frankenstein*, *Mathilda*, and the Legacies of Godwin and Wollstonecraft." In *Cambridge Companion to Mary Shelley*, ed. Esther Schor, 26–44. Cambridge: Cambridge University Press, 2003.

Clery, E. J. Introduction. *The Castle of Otranto*. By Horace Walpole, vii–xxxiii. Oxford: Oxford University Press, 1998.

_____. Introduction. *The Italian*. By Ann Radcliffe, xxi–xxxi. Oxford: Oxford University Press, 1998.

_____. *The Rise of Supernatural Fiction 1762–1800*. Cambridge: Cambridge University Press, 1999.

Conrad, Joseph. "Henry James: An Appreciation." In *Heart of Darkness*, 286–88. New York: Norton, 2006.

Cooper, L. Andrew. *Gothic Realities: The Impact of Horror Fiction on Modern Culture*. Jefferson, NC: McFarland, 2010.

Copjec, Joan. "Vampires, Breast-Feeding, and Anxiety." *October* 58 (Autumn 1991): 24–43.

Craton, Lillian. *The Victorian Freak Show: The Significant of Disability and Physical Differences in 19th-Century Fiction*. Amherst, NY: Cambria Press, 2009.

Croker, John Wilson. "Frankenstein, or the Modern Prometheus." *Quarterly Review* 18 (January 1818): 379–85.

Cronin, Richard. *Romantic Victorians: English Literature 1824–1840*. New York: Palgrave Macmillan, 2002.

Crowl, Susan. "Aesthetic Allegory in *The Turn of the Screw*." *Novel* 4 (1971): 107–22.

Daubés, M. Guyot. "Variations in Human Stature." *Popular Science Monthly* (July 1887): 314–23.

Davis, Lennard J. *Factual Fictions: The Origins of the English Novel*. Philadelphia: University of Pennsylvania Press, 1996.

Davison, Carol Margaret. *Gothic Literature, 1764–1824*. Cardiff: University of Wales Press, 2009.

_____. "Solving *The Strange Case of Dr Jekyll and Mr Hyde*." In *Troubled Legacies: Narrative and Inheritance*, ed. Allan Hepburn, 137–62. Toronto: University of Toronto Press, 2007.

Day, William Patrick. *In the Circles of Fear and Desire: A Study of Gothic Fantasy*. Chicago: University of Chicago Press, 1985.

Derrida, Jacques. "Force and Signification." In *Writing and Difference*, trans. Alan Bass, 1–35. Chicago: U of Chicago P, 1978.

_____. *The Truth in Painting*, trans. Geoff Bennington and Ian McLeod. Chicago: University of Chicago Press, 1987.

Dolar, Mladen. "Beyond Interpellation." *Qui Parle* 6.2 (Spring/Summer 1993): 75–96.

_____. "'I Shall Be with You on Your Wedding-Night': Lacan and the Uncanny." *October* 58 (Autumn 1991): 5–23.

"Don Roebucco, the Smallest Man in 'The House.'" *Punch* 10 (1846): 118.

"Dracula. By Bram Stoker." *Academy* 52 (12 June 1897): 620.

Duncan, Ian. "Fanaticism and Enlightenment in *Confessions of a Justified Sinner*." In *James Hogg and the Literary Marketplace: Scottish Romanticism and the Working-Class Author*, ed. Sharon Alker and Holly Faith Nelson, 57–70. Burlington, VT: Ashgate, 2009.

_____. *Scott's Shadow: The Novel in Romantic Edinburgh*. Princeton: Princeton University Press, 2007.

_____. "Walter Scott, James Hogg, and Scottish Gothic." In *A New Companion to the Gothic*, ed. David Punter, 123–34. Malden, MA: Blackwell, 2012.

Duyfhuizen, Bernard. *Narratives of Transmission*. Rutherford: Fairleigh Dickinson University Press, 1992.

"Dwarfs." *New Monthly Magazine* 3 (1822): 49–55.

Eagleton, Terry. "Fictions of the Real: 'All truth with malice in it.'" In *A Concise Companion to Realism*, ed. Matthew Beaumont, 68–85. Malden, MA: Wiley-Blackwell, 2010.

Eliot, T. S. "Wilkie Collins and Dickens." In *T. S. Eliot: Selected Essays*, 373–82. New York: Harcourt, Brace, 1950.

Ermarth, Elizabeth Deeds. *The English Novel in History: 1840–1895*. New York: Routledge, 1997.

_____. *Realism and Consensus in the English Novel*. Princeton: Princeton University Press, 1983.

"Evidences of Insanity." *The Boston Medical and Surgical Journal* 11.23 (14 January 1835): 361–72.

Examiner (January 1848). In *The Brontës: A Critical Heritage*, ed. Miriam Allott, 220–22. London: Routledge, 1974.

Favret, Mary A. "The Letters of *Frankenstein*." *Genre* 20 (Spring 1987): 3–24.

Feldman, Paula R. and Diana Scott Kilvert, ed. *The Journals of Mary Shelley 1814–1844*. Vol. 2. Oxford: Clarendon, 1987.

Felman, Shoshana. "Turning the Screw of Interpretation." *Yale French Studies* 55–56 (1978): 94–207.

Ferguson, Christine. "Decadence as Scientific Fulfillment." *PMLA* 117.3 (May 2002): 465–78.

Fielding, K. J., ed. *The Speeches of Charles Dickens*. Oxford: Oxford University Press, 1960.

Fielding, Penny. "*The Private Memoirs and Confessions of a Justified Sinner*: Approaches." In *The Edinburgh Companion to James Hogg*, ed. Ian Duncan and Douglas S. Mack, 132–39. Edinburgh: Edinburgh University Press, 2012.

Fludernik, Monika. "The Eighteenth-Century Legacy." In *A Companion to Charles Dickens*, ed. David Paroissien, 65–80. Malden, MA: Blackwell, 2008.

Ford, Jane M. *Patriarchy and Incest from Shakespeare to Joyce*. Gainesville: University of Florida Press, 1998.

Forster, John. *Examiner* (8 October 1853). In *Dickens: The Critical Heritage*, ed. Philip Collins, 290–93. New York: Barnes & Noble, 1971.

_____. *The Life of Charles Dickens*. Vol. 1. London: Dent, 1969.

Foucault, Michel. *Discipline and Punish: The Birth of the Prison*, trans. Alan Sheridan. New York: Pantheon, 1977.

_____. *The History of Sexuality*. Vol. 1. New York: Vintage, 1978.

"Frankenstein; or, The Modern Prometheus." *La Belle Assemblée, or Bell's Court and Fashionable Magazine* 108 (March 1818): 139–41.

"Frankenstein; or the Modern Prometheus." *British Critic* 9 (April 1818): 432–38.

"Frankenstein; or, the modern Prometheus." *Literary Panorama and National Register* 8 (1 June 1818): 411–14.

Freud, Sigmund. "The Ego and the Id." In *The Freud Reader*, ed. Peter Gay, 628–58. New York: Norton, 1989.

_____. "The Uncanny." In *Fantastic Literature: A Critical Reader*, ed. David Sander, 74–101. London: Praeger, 2004.

_____. "The Unconscious." *The Freud Reader*, ed. Peter Gay, 572–84. New York: Norton, 1989.

Frow, John. "The Literary Frame." In *Narrative Dynamics*, ed. Brian Richardson, 333–38. Columbus: Ohio State University Press, 2002.

Fry, Paul H. "Biographical and Historical Contexts." In *The Rime of the Ancient Mariner*. Boston: Bedford/St Martin's, 1999.

Garrett, Margaret Davenport. "Writing and Re-Writing Incest in Mary Shelley's *Mathilda*." *Keats-Shelley Journal* 45 (1996): 44–60.

Garrett, Peter K. *Gothic Reflections: Narrative Force in Nineteenth-Century Fiction*. Ithaca: Cornell University Press, 2003.

"Gaston de Blondeville." *Port Folio* 1 (1826): 99–108.

"Gaston de Blondeville: With an Essay on the Life and Writings of Mrs Radcliffe." *London Magazine* 6 (1826): 34–40.

Genette, Gérard. *Narrative Discourse: An Essay on Method*. Ithaca: Cornell University Press, 1990.

_____. *Paratexts: Thresholds of Interpretation*. Cambridge: Cambridge University Press, 1997.

Giddings, Robert. *The Changing World of Charles Dickens*. London: Vision, 1983.

Gilbert, Sandra M. and Susan Gubar. *The Madwoman in the Attic: The Woman Writer and the Nineteenth-Century Literary Imagination*. New Haven: Yale University Press, 2000.

Gissing, George. *Charles Dickens: A Critical Study*. New York: Dodd, Mead and Company, 1912.

Goetz, William. "The '*Frame*' of *The Turn of the Screw*: Framing the Reader In." *Studies in Short Fiction* 18 (1988): 71–74.

Gordon, Jane. "Gossip, Diary, Letter, Text: Anne Brontë's Narrative Tenant and the Problematic of the Gothic Sequel." *ELH* 51/4 (Winter 1984): 719–45.

Grossman, Jonathan H. *Charles Dickens's Networks: Public Transport and the Novel*. Oxford: Oxford University Press, 2012.

Groves, David. "James Hogg's *Confessions*: New Information." *The Review of English Studies* 40.158 (May 1989): 240–42.

Haefele Thomas, Ardel. *Queer Others in Victorian Gothic: Transgressing Monstrosity*. Cardiff: University of Wales Press, 2012.

Haggerty, George E. *Queer Gothic*. Champaign: University of Illinois Press, 2006.

Halberstam, Judith. *Skin Shows: Gothic Horror and the Technology of Monsters*. Durham: Duke University Press, 2000.

Halsted, Caroline A. *Investigation; or, Travels in the Boudoir*. London: Smith, Elder and Co., 1837.

Harris, Jason Marc. *Folklore and the Fantastic in Nineteenth-Century British Fiction*. Burlington, VT: Ashgate, 2009.

Hartman, Geoffrey. *Criticism in the Wilderness*. New Haven: Yale University Press, 1980.

Harvey, W. J. "*Bleak House*: The Double Narrative." In *Dickens:* Bleak House*—A Casebook*, ed. A. E. Dyson, 224–34. London: Macmillan, 1969.

Hill, John Spencer. *A Coleridge Companion: An Introduction to the Major Poems and the* Biographia Literaria. London: Macmillan, 1984.

Hirsch, Gordon. "*Frankenstein*, Detective Fiction, and *Jekyll and Hyde*." In *Dr Jekyll and Mr Hyde After One Hundred Years*, ed. William Veeder and Gordon Hirsh, 223–46. Chicago: University of Chicago Press, 1988.

Hobsbawm, E. J. "The Machine Breakers." In *Uncommon People: Resistance, Rebellion and Jazz*, 5–17. London: Weidenfeld & Nicolson, 1998.

Hogle, Jerrold E. "The Gothic Ghost of the Counterfeit and the Progress of Abjection." In *A New Companion to the Gothic*, ed. David Punter, 496–509. Malden, MA: Blackwell, 2012.

_____. "Recovering the Walpolean Gothic: *The Italian: Or, the Confessional of the Black Penitents* (1796–1797)." In *Anne Radcliffe, Romanticism and the Gothic*, ed. Dale Townshend and Angela Wright, 151–67. Cambridge: Cambridge University Press, 2012.

_____. "The Struggle for a Dichotomy: Abjection in Jekyll and His Interpreters." In *Dr Jekyll and Mr Hyde After One Hundred Years*, ed. William Veeder and Gordon Hirsch, 161–207. Chicago: University of Chicago Press, 1988.

Hollington, Michael. *Dickens and the Grotesque*. Beckenham, UK: Croom Helm, 1984.

Hood, Thomas. *Athenæum* (7 November 1840). In *Dickens: The Critical Heritage*, ed. Philip Collins, 94–98. New York: Barnes & Noble, 1971.

Houlgate, Stephen. *The Opening of Hegel's Logic: From Being to Infinity*. West Lafayette: Purdue University Press, 2006.

House, Madeline, Graham Storey, and Kathleen Tillotson, ed. *The Letters of Charles Dickens*. 12 vols. Oxford: Oxford University Press, 1965–2002.

Hughes, Gillian, ed. *The Collected Letters of James Hogg*. 3 vols. Edinburgh: Edinburgh University Press, 2004–08.

Hurley, Kelly. *The Gothic Body: Sexuality, Materialism, and Degeneration at the* fin de siècle. Cambridge: Cambridge University Press, 1996.

Hustis, Harriet. "Black and White and Read All Over: Performative Textuality in Bram Stoker's *Dracula*." *Studies in the Novel* 33.1 (Spring 2001): 18–33.

Illustrated London News (24 September 1853). In *Dickens: The Critical Heritage*, ed. Philip Collins, 280–82. New York: Barnes & Noble, 1971.

Jackson, Kimberly. "Non-Evolutionary Degeneration in Arthur Machen's Supernatural Tales." *Victorian Literature and Culture* 41 (2013): 125–35.

Jaffe, Audrey. *Vanishing Points: Dickens, Narrative, and the Subject of Omniscience*. Berkeley: University of California Press, 1991.

James, Henry. "The New Novel." In *Heart of Darkness*, 313–14. New York: Norton, 2006.

_____. *The Notebooks of Henry James*, ed. F. O. Matthiessen and Kenneth Murdock. Chicago: University of Chicago Press, 1981.

_____. "Preface to *Roderick Hudson*." In *The Art of the Novel*, 3–19. New York: Charles Scribner's Sons, 1962.

Jancovich, Mark. *Horror*. London: Batsford, 1992.

Johnson, Barbara. "*The Last Man*." In *The Other Mary Shelley: Beyond* Frankenstein, ed. Audrey A. Fisch, Anne K. Mellor and Esther H. Schor, 258–66. Oxford: Oxford University Press, 1993.

Jones, Frederick L., ed. *Maria Gisborne and Edward E. Williams, Shelley's Friends: Their Journals and Letters*. Norman: University of Oklahoma Press, 1951.

"A Journey Made in the Summer of 1794." *Critical Review* 14 (July 1795): 241–55.

Karschay, Stephan. *Degeneration, Normativity and the Gothic at the Fin de Siècle*. London: Palgrave Macmillan, 2015.

Kilgour, Maggie. *The Rise of the Gothic Novel*. London: Routledge, 1995.

King, Stephen. "Sunset Notes." In *Just After Sunset*, 529–41. New York: Pocket Books, 2008.

Kliman, Bernice W. *Macbeth: Shakespeare in Performance*. Manchester: Manchester University Press, 1995.

Kristeva, Julia. *Powers of Horror*, trans. Leon S. Roudiez. New York: Columbia University Press, 1982.

Lacan, Jacques. "Presentation on Psychical

Causality." In *Écrits*, trans. Bruce Fink, 123–60. New York: Norton, 1999.
_____. *The Ethics of Psychoanalysis: Book VII*, ed. Jacques-Alain Miller. New York: Norton, 1992.
_____. *The Four Fundamental Concepts of Psycho-Analysis*, ed. Jacques-Alain Miller, trans. Alan Sheridan. London: Karnac, 2004.
Langhorne, John. *Monthly Review*. In *Horace Walpole: The Critical Heritage*, ed. Peter Sabor, 70–72. New York: Routledge, 1999.
Lanone, Catherine. "Verging on the Gothic: Melmoth's Journey to France." In *European Gothic: A Spirited Exchange 1760–1960*, ed. Avril Horner, 71–83. Manchester: Manchester University Press, 2002.
Leavis, Q. D. "A Fresh Approach to *Wuthering Heights*." In *The Collected Essays*. Vol. 1, G. Singh, 228–74. Cambridge: Cambridge University Press, 1983.
"A Lesson from a Woman's Life: Charlotte Bronte." *Titan* 24 (May 1857): 452–62.
Levine, George. *The Realistic Imagination: English Fiction from* Frankenstein *to* Lady Chatterley." In *Theory of the Novel*, ed. Michael McKeon, 613–31. Baltimore: Johns Hopkins University Press, 2000.
Lew, Joseph W. "The Deceptive Other: Mary Shelley's Critique of Orientalism in *Frankenstein*" *Studies in Romanticism* 30 (Summer 1991): 255–83.
_____. "'Unprepared for sudden transformations': Identity and Politics in *Melmoth the Wanderer*." *Studies in the Novel* 26 (1994): 173–95.
Lewis, W. S., Grover Cronin, Jr, and Charles H. Bennett, ed. *Horace Walpole's Correspondence*. Vol. 28. Oxford: Oxford University Press, 1955.
Linehan, Katherine. Introduction. *The Strange Case of Dr Jekyll and Mr Hyde*. By Robert Louis Stevenson, xi–xv. New York: Norton, 2003.
"The Literary Character of the Present Age." *Monthly Magazine* 1.8 (September 1840): 245–48.
Literary World (April 1848). In *The Brontës: A Critical Heritage*, ed. Miriam Allott, 233–34. London: Routledge, 1974.
Lloyd-Smith, Allan. *American Gothic Fiction: An Introduction*. New York: Continuum, 2005.
The London Atlas. In "The Devil in Literature." *The National Magazine* 2 (February 1853): 124–28.
Lougy, Robert E. *Charles Robert Maturin*. Cranbury, NJ: Associated, 1975.
Luckhurst, Roger. Introduction. *The Strange Case of Dr Jekyll and Mr Hyde and Other Tales*. By Robert Louis Stevenson, vii–xxxii. Oxford: Oxford University Press, 2006.
Lustig, T. J. *Henry James and the Ghostly*. Cambridge: Cambridge University Press, 1994.
MacAndrew, Elizabeth. *The Gothic Tradition in Fiction*. New York: Columbia University Press, 1979.
Mack, Douglas S. "The Suicide's Grave in *The Confessions of a Justified Sinner*." *Newsletter of the James Hogg Society* 1 (1982): 8–11.
MacNish, Robert. *The Anatomy of Drunkenness*. New York: D. Appleton, 1835.
Macovski, Michael S. "*Wuthering Heights* and the Rhetoric of Interpretation." *ELH* 54.2 (1987): 363–84.
Malina, Debra. *Breaking the Frame: Metalepsis and the Construction of the Subject*. Columbus: Ohio State University Press, 2002.
Manning, Susan. *The Puritan-Provincial Vision: Scottish and American Literature in the Nineteenth Century*. Cambridge: Cambridge University Press, 1990.
Marshall, Ashley. "Melmoth Affirmed: Maturin's Defense of Sacred History." *Studies in Romanticism* 47.2 (2008): 121–45.
Marshall, David. *The Frame of Art: Fictions of Aesthetic Experience 1750–1815*. Baltimore: Johns Hopkins University Press, 2005.
Matthews, John T. "Framing in *Wuthering Heights*." *Texas Studies in Literature and Language* 27.1 (1985): 25–61.
Maturin, Charles Robert. "Novel-writing." *British Review* 11 (1818): 37–61.
"Maturin's Melmoth." *Eclectic Review* 14 (1820): 553–58.
Maxwell, Richard. "Crowds and Creativity in *The Old Curiosity Shop*." *The Journal of English and Germanic Philology* 78.1 (January 1979): 49–71.
McBratney, John. "'What Connexion Can

There Be?': Secrecy and Detection in Dickens's *Bleak House*." In *Victorian Secrecy: Economies of Knowledge and Concealment*, ed. Albert D. Pionke and Denise Tischler Millstein, 59–74. Burlington, VT: Ashgate, 2010.

McGann, Jerome J. "The Meaning of the Ancient Mariner." *Critical Inquiry* 8.1 (Autumn 1981): 35–67.

McHale, Brian. *Postmodernist Fiction*. London: Routledge, 1987.

McIntyre, Clara Frances. *Ann Radcliffe in Relation to Her Time*. New Haven: Yale University Press, 1920.

Mee, Jon. *The Cambridge Introduction to Charles Dickens*. Cambridge: Cambridge University Press, 2010.

Mehew, Ernest, ed. *Selected Letters of Robert Louis Stevenson*. New Haven: Yale University Press, 1997.

Mellor, Anne. *English Romantic Irony*. Cambridge: Harvard University Press, 1980.

_____. *Mary Shelley: Her Life, Her Fiction, Her Monsters*. New York: Routledge, 1989.

"Melmoth, the Wanderer." *Edinburgh Review* 35 (1821): 353–62.

"Melmoth, the Wanderer." *Ladies' Monthly Museum* 13 (1821): 95–96.

"Melmoth the Wander; a Tale." *London Literary Gazette* 200 (November 1820): 737–39.

Melville, Peter. "The Problem of Immunity in *The Last Man*." *SEL* 47.4 (2007): 825–46.

Menke, Richard. *Telegraphic Realism: Victorian Fiction and Other Information Systems*. Stanford, CA: Stanford University Press, 2008.

Metropolitan Magazine (June 1840). In *Dickens: The Critical Heritage*, ed. Philip Collins, 93–94. New York: Barnes & Noble, 1971.

Mighall, Robert. "Dickens and the Gothic." In *A Companion to Charles Dickens*, ed. David Paroissien, 81–96. Malden, MA: Blackwell, 2008.

_____. *A Geography of Victorian Gothic Fiction: Mapping History's Nightmares*. Oxford: Oxford University Press, 1999.

Milbank, Alison. "Sacrificial Exchange and the Gothic Double in *Melmoth the Wanderer* and *The Picture of Dorian Gray*." In *Shaping Belief: Culture, Politics and Religion in Nineteenth-Century Writing*, ed. Victor Morgan and Clare Williams, 113–28. Liverpool: Liverpool University Press, 2008.

Miller, J. Hillis. *Fiction and Repetition: Seven English Novels*. Cambridge: Harvard University Press, 1982.

_____. *The Form of Victorian Fiction*. Notre Dame: University of Notre Dame, Press, 1968.

_____. "'Hieroglyphical Truth' in *Sartor Resartus*." In *Victorian Perspectives*, ed. John Clubbe and Jerome Meckier, 1–20. London: Macmillan Press, 1989.

Mishra, Vijay. *The Gothic Sublime*. Albany: State University of New York Press, 1994.

Morley, Henry. *Memoirs of Bartholomew Fair*. London: Chapman and Hall, 1859.

Moseley, Merritt. "The Ontology of Esther's Narrative in *Bleak House*." *South Atlantic Review* 50.2 (May 1985): 35–46.

"Mrs Radcliffe's Posthumous Romance." *New Monthly Magazine* 16 (1826): 532–36.

Müller-Wille, Staffan and Hans-Jörge Rheinberger. *A Cultural History of Heredity*. Chicago: University of Chicago Press, 2012.

_____. *Heredity Produced: At the Crossroads of Biology, Politics, and Culture, 1500–1987*. Cambridge: MIT Press, 2007.

Navarette, Susan J. *The Shape of Fear: Horror and the Fin de Siècle Culture of Decadence*. Lexington: University Press of Kentucky, 1998.

Nelles, William. *Frameworks: Narrative Levels and Embedded Narrative*. New York: P. Lang, 1994.

_____. "Stories within Stories: Narrative Levels and Embedded Narrative." In *Narrative Dynamics: Essays on Time, Plots, Closure, and Frames*, ed. Brian Richardson, 339–53. Columbus: Ohio State University Press, 2002.

"New Fiction." *Saturday Review of Politics, Literature, Science and Art* 84 (3 July 1897): 21.

Newman, Beth. "Narratives of Seduction and the Seductions of Narrative: The Frame Structure of *Frankenstein*." *ELH* 53.1 (Spring 1986): 141–63.

_____. "The Situation of the Looker-On: Gender, Narration, and Gaze in Wuthering Heights." *PMLA* 105.5 (1990): 1029–41.

Nitchie, Elizabeth. Introduction. *Mathilda*. By Mary Shelley, vii–xv. Chapel Hill: University of North Carolina Press, 2008.

Nordau, Max. *Degeneration*. New York: D. Appleton and Company, 1895.

Norris, Frank. "A Plea for Romantic Fiction." In *McTeague*, ed. Donald Pizer, 277–80. New York: Norton, 1997.

Norton, Rictor. *Mistress of Udolpho*. Leicester: Leicester University Press, 1999.

"Novels." *Ladies' Monthly Museum* 20 (1824): 106.

"Novels." *Ladies' Monthly Museum* 24 (1826): 45–46.

"Novelists." *La Belle Assemblée* 3 (July 1826): 303–07.

Osbourne, Lloyd. "Stevenson at Thirty-Seven." In *The Strange Case of Dr Jekyll and Mr Hyde*, ed. Martin A. Danahay, 129–33. Peterborough, Ontario: Broadview, 2005.

Paley, Morton D. Introduction. *The Last Man*. By Mary Shelley, vii–xxiii. Oxford: Oxford University Press, 1998.

Pan'kov, Nikolai. "'Everything else depends on how this business turns out...': Bakhtin's Dissertation Defence as Real Event, as High Drama and as Academic Comedy." In *Bakhtin and Cultural Theory*, ed. Ken Hirschkop and David Shepherd, 26–61. Manchester: Manchester University Press, 2001.

Peck, G. W. *American Review* (June 1848). In *The Brontës: A Critical Heritage*, ed. Miriam Allott, 235–41. London: Routledge, 1974.

Peters, Joan Douglas. *Feminist Metafiction and the Evolution of the British Novel*. Gainesville: University Press of Florida, 2002.

Pick, Daniel. *Faces of Degeneration: A European Disorder, c. 1848–c. 1918*. Cambridge: Cambridge University Press, 1989.

Poe, Edgar Allan. *Essays and Reviews*, ed. G. R. Thompson. New York: Viking Press, 1984.

_____. "The Philosophy of Composition." *Graham's Magazine* 28.4 (April 1846): 163–67.

_____. "Stanley Thorn." *Graham's Magazine* 20.1 (January 1842): 69–70.

Poovey, Mary. "My Hideous Progeny: Mary Shelley and the Feminization of Romanticism." *PMLA* 95.3 (May 1980): 332–47.

Price, Leah. *The Anthology and the Rise of the Novel*. Cambridge: Cambridge University Press, 2003.

Pritchard, Allan. "The Urban Gothic of *Bleak House*." *Nineteenth-Century Literature* 45 (1991): 432–52.

"The Private Memoirs and Confessions of a Justified Sinner." *Quarterly Theological Review* 1 (1825): 99–100.

"Private Memoirs and Confessions of a Justified Sinner." *Westminster Review* 2 (October 1824): 560–62.

Ratchford, Fannie E., ed. *The Correspondence of Sir Walter Scott and Charles Robert Maturin*. New York: Garland, 1980.

"Recent Novels." *Spectator* 78 (31 July 1897): 150–51.

Reisner, Gavriel. *The Death-Ego and the Vita Self: Romances of Desire in Literature and Psychoanalysis*. Cranbury: Associated University Press, 2003.

"Remarks on 'Melmoth.'" *New Monthly Magazine* 14 (1820): 662–68.

"Review of New Books." *London Literary Gazette* 488 (May 1826): 321–25.

Robertson, Fiona. *Legitimate Histories: Scott, Gothic, and the Authorities of Fiction*. Oxford: Clarendon Press, 1994.

Robinson, Charles E., ed. *The* Frankenstein *Notebooks*. 2 parts. New York: Garland, 1996.

_____. "Mathilda as Dramatic Actress." In *Mary Shelley in Her Times*, ed. Betty T. Bennett and Stuart Curran, 76–87. Baltimore: Johns Hopkins University Press, 2000.

Rubenstein, Marc. "'My Accursed Origin': The Search for the Mother in *Frankenstein*." *Studies in Romanticism* 15 (Spring 1976): 165–94.

Ruskin, John. "Fiction, Fair and Foul." In *The Genius of John Ruskin: Selections from His Writings*, ed. John D. Rosenberg. Charlottesville: University of Virginia Press, 1998.

Rust, Richard Dilworth. "Liminality in *The Turn of the Screw*." *Studies in Short Fiction* 25 (1988): 441–46.

Ryan, Marie-Laure. "Stacks, Frames, and Boundaries." In *Narrative Dynamics: Essays on Time, Plots, Closure, and Frames*, ed. Brian Richardson, 366–86. Columbus: Ohio State University Press, 2002.

Sage, Victor. "The Author, the Editor, and the Fissured Text: Scott, Maturin, and Hogg." In *Authorship in Context: From the Theoretical to the Material*, ed. Kyriaki Hadjiafxendi and Polina Mackay, 15–32. Basingstoke, England: Palgrave Macmillan, 2007.

_____. Introduction. *Melmoth the Wanderer*. By Charles Robert Maturin, vii–xxix. London: Penguin, 2000.

_____. "Irish Gothic: C. R. Maturin and J. S. Le Fanu." In *A New Companion to the Gothic*, ed. David Punter, 81–93. Malden, MA: Blackwell, 2012.

Salotto, Eleanor. "*Frankenstein* and Dis(re)membered Identity." *The Journal of Narrative Technique* 24.3 (Fall 1994): 190–211.

Schechet, Nita. *Narrative Fissures: Reading and Rhetoric*. Cranbury, NJ: Associated Press, 2005.

Schmitt, Cannon. "Evolution and Victorian Fiction." In *Evolution and Victorian Culture*, ed. Bernard Lightman and Bennett Zon, 17–38. Cambridge: Cambridge University Press, 2014.

_____. "Techniques of Terror, Technologies of Nationality: Ann Radcliffe's *The Italian*." *ELH* 61.4 (1994): 853–76.

Schneider, Steven Jay. Introduction. *Horror Film and Psychoanalysis*, ed. Steven Jay Schneider, 1–15. Cambridge: Cambridge University Press, 2004.

Schor, Hilary M. *Dickens and the Daughter of the House*. Cambridge: Cambridge University Press, 1999.

Scott, Walter. Introduction. *The Castle of Otranto*. In *Horace Walpole: The Critical Heritage*, ed. Peter Sabor, 95. New York: Routledge, 1999.

_____. "A Memoir of the Life of the Author." In *The Novels of Mrs Ann Radcliffe*. Edinburgh: Ballantyne, 1824.

_____. "Remarks on Frankenstein, or The Modern Prometheus; a Novel." *Blackwood's Edinburgh Magazine* 2 (March 1818): 613–20.

Sedgwick, Eve Kosofsky. "The Character in the Veil: Imagery on the Surface in the Gothic Novel." *PMLA* 96.2 (1981): 255–70.

Seed, David. "The Narrative Method of *Dracula*." *Nineteenth-Century Fiction* 40.1 (June 1985): 61–75.

Senf, Carol. A. *Dracula*: The Unseen Face in the Mirror." *The Journal of Narrative Technique* 9.3 (Fall 1979): 160–70.

Shuttleworth, Sally. Introduction. *Jane Eyre*. By Charlotte Brontë, vii–xxxiii. Oxford: Oxford University Press, 2000.

Slater, Michael. *Charles Dickens*. New Haven: Yale University Press, 2009.

Small, Helen. Introduction. *Wuthering Heights*. By Emily Brontë, vii–xxi. Oxford: Oxford University Press, 2009.

Smith, Margaret, ed. *Charlotte Brontë: Selected Letters*. Oxford: Oxford University Press, 2010.

Spooner, Catherine. "Crime and the Gothic." In *A Companion to Crime Fiction*, ed. Charles J. Rzepka and Lee Horsley, 245–57. Malden, MA: Wiley-Blackwell, 2010.

Stewart, Garrett. *Dear Reader: The Conscripted Audience in Nineteenth-Century British Fiction*. Baltimore: Johns Hopkins University Press, 1996.

_____. *Novel Violence: A Narratology of Victorian Fiction*. Chicago: University of Chicago Press, 2009.

Stirling, Kirsten. "The Devil in the Printing Press." In *After Satan: Essays in Honour of Neil Forsyth*, ed. Kirsten Stirling and Martine Hennard Dutheil de la Rochère, 114–24. Newcastle upon Tyne: Cambridge Scholars, 2010.

Storey, Graham. *Charles Dickens:* Bleak House. Cambridge: Cambridge University Press, 1987.

Stott, G. St John. "The Structure of *Melmoth the Wanderer*." *Etudes Irlandaises* 12.1 (1987): 41–52.

Sussman, Charlotte. "'Islanded in the World': Cultural Memory and Human Mobility in *The Last Man*." *PMLA* 118.2 (March 2003): 286–301.

Symons, Arthur. *The Symbolist Movement in Literature*. London: Constable, 1908.

"Tales of My Landlord." *Literary Gazette*. Quoted in *Athenæum* 5 (1819): 409–15.

Talfourd, Thomas. "Memoir of the Life and Writings of Mrs Radcliffe." In *Gaston de*

Blondeville. Vol. 1, 3–83. Philadelphia: H. C. Carey, 1826.

Tarr, Rodger L. Introduction. *Sartor Resartus*. By Thomas Carlyle, xxi–xciv. Berkeley: University of California Press, 2000.

_____. *Thomas Carlyle: A Descriptive Bibliography*. Charlottesville: University Press of Virginia, 1976.

"Terrorist Novel Writing." *Spirit of the Public Journals for 1797*. Vol. 1, 223–25. London: James Ridgeway, 1799.

Thormählen, Marianne. "The Villain of *Wildfell Hall*: Aspects and Prospects of Arthur Huntingdon." *The Modern Language Review* 88.4 (October 1993): 831–41.

Times (25 January 1886). In *Robert Louis Stevenson: The Critical Heritage*, ed. Paul Maixner, 205–07. London: Routledge, 1971.

Torgerson, Beth. *Reading the Brontë Body: Disease, Desire, and the Constraints of Culture*. New York: Palgrave Macmillan, 2005.

Townshend, Dale. "Gothic Shakespeare." In *A New Companion to the Gothic*, ed. David Punter, 38–63. Malden, MA: Wiley-Blackwell, 2012.

_____. *The Orders of Gothic: Foucault, Lacan, and the Subject of Gothic Writing 1764–1820*. New York: AMS Press, 2007.

Trubek, Anne. "American Literary Realism and the Problem of *Trompe l'Oeil* Painting." *Mosaic* 34.3 (Sept. 2001): 35–54.

Von Sneidern, Maja-Lisa. "*Wuthering Heights* and the Liverpool Slave Trade." *ELH* 62 (1995): 171–96.

Warhol, Robyn. "Toward a Theory of the Engaging Narrator: Earnest Interventions in Gaskell, Stowe, and Eliot." *PMLA* 101 (1986): 811–18.

Weigelt, Marcus. Introduction. *Critique of Pure Reason*. By Immanuel Kant, xv–lxix. London: Penguin, 2007.

Wells, H. G. "Zoological Retrogression." *Gentleman's Magazine* 271 (1891): 246–53.

Whipple, E. P. *North American Review* (October 1848). In *The Brontës: A Critical Heritage*, ed. Miriam Allott, 261–2. London: Routledge, 1974.

Wicke, Jennifer. "Vampiric Typewriting: *Dracula* and its Media." *ELH* 59.2 (Summer 1992): 467–93.

Williams, Anne. *Art of Darkness: A Poetics of Gothic*. Chicago: University of Chicago Press, 1995.

Willis, Martin. "Victorian Realism and the Gothic: Objects of Terror Transformed." In *The Victorian Gothic: An Edinburgh Companion*, ed. Andrew Smith and William Hughes, 15–28. Edinburgh: Edinburgh University Press, 2012.

Wills, David. *Matchbook: Essays on Deconstruction*. Stanford: Stanford University Press, 2005.

Wolf, Werner. "Framing Borders in Frame Stories." In *Framing Borders in Literature and Other Media*, ed. Werner Wolf and Walter Bernhart, 179–206. Amsterdam: Rodopi, 2006.

Wolfson, Susan. Introduction. *Frankenstein*. By Mary Shelley. vii–xxii. New York: Longman, 2006.

Wood, George Bacon. *A Treatise on the Practice of Medicine*. Vol. 1. Philadelphia: Grigg, Elliot, and Co., 1849.

Wollstonecraft, Mary. "The Italian, or the Confessional of the Black Penitents. A Romance." *Analytical Review* 25 (May 1797): 516–20.

Wordsworth, William. "Advertisement." In *Lyrical Ballads 1798 and 1800*, ed. Michael Gamer and Dahlia Porter, 47–48. Peterborough, Ontario: Broadview, 2008.

_____. "Preface to *Lyrical Ballads*, with Pastoral and Other Poems." In *The Major Works*, ed. Stephen Gill, 595–615. Oxford: Oxford University Press, 2008.

Žižek, Slavoj. *The Abyss of Freedom / Ages of the World*. Ann Arbor: University of Michigan Press, 1997.

_____. "Attempts to Escape the Logic of Capitalism." Review of John Keane. In *Vaclav Havel: A Political Tragedy in Six Acts*. *London Review of Books* 21.21 (28 October 1999): 3–6.

_____. "*Cogito*, Madness, and Religion: Derrida, Foucault, and Then Lacan." In *Theology after Lacan: The Passion for the Real*, ed. Creston Davis, Marcus Pound, and Clayton Crockett, 19–33. Cambridge: James Clarke, 2015.

_____. "From Desire to Drive: Why Lacan Is Not Lacaniano." *Atlántica de Las Artes* 14 (Autumn 1996): 1–7.

_____. *Enjoy Your Symptom! Jacques Lacan in Hollywood and Out*. New York: Routledge, 1992.

_____. "Fantasy as a Political Category: A Lacanian Approach." In *The Žižek Reader*, ed. Elizabeth Wright and Edmond Wright, 87–101. Oxford: Blackwell, 1999.

_____. *For They Know Not What They Do: Enjoyment as a Political Factor*. New York: Verso, 1991.

_____. "Grimaces of the Real, or When the Phallus Appears." *October* 58 (Autumn 1991): 44–68.

_____. "General Introduction." In *Jacques Lacan: Critical Evaluations in Cultural Theory*. Vol. 1, ed. Slavoj Žižek, 1–3. New York: Routledge, 2003.

_____. "A Hair of the Dog That Bit You." In *Lacanian Theory of Discourse: Subject, Structure, and Society*, ed. Mark Bracher, Marshall W. Alcorn, Jr., Ronald J. Corthell, and François Massardier-Kenney, 46–73. New York: New York University Press, 1994.

_____. *Interrogating the Real*. London: Bloomsbury, 2006.

_____. "Introduction: The Spectre of Ideology," In *Mapping Ideology*, ed. Slavoj Žižek, 1–33. London: Verso, 2012.

_____. *Living in the End of Times*. London: Verso, 2010.

_____. *Looking Awry: An Introduction to Jacques Lacan through Popular Culture*. Cambridge: MIT Press, 1992.

_____. *Organs without Bodies*. New York: Routledge, 2004.

_____. and Mladen Dolar. *Opera's Second Death*. New York: Routledge, 2002.

_____. *The Parallax View*. Cambridge: MIT Press, 2006.

_____. *The Plague of Fantasies*. London: Verso, 1997.

_____. "Psychoanalysis and the Lacanian Real: 'Strange shapes of the unwarped primal world.'" In *A Concise Companion to Realism*, ed. Matthew Beaumont, 225–41. Malden, MA: Wiley-Blackwell, 2010.

_____. "The Spectre of Ideology." In *The Žižek Reader*, ed. Elizabeth Wright and Edmond Wright, 52–86. Oxford: Blackwell, 1999.

_____. *The Sublime Object of Ideology*. London: Verso, 1989.

_____. "The Undergrowth of Enjoyment: How Popular Culture Can Serve as an Introduction to Lacan." In *The Žižek Reader*, ed. Elizabeth Wright and Edmond Wright, 11–36. Oxford: Blackwell, 1999.

_____. *Violence*. New York: Picador, 2008.

_____. *The Year of Living Dangerously*. London: Verso, 2012.

Zweig, Arnulf, ed. *Kant: Philosophical Correspondence, 1759–99*. Chicago: University of Chicago Press, 1967.

Index

abjection 2, 3, 11–16, 18, 19, 20, 24, 25, 27, 28, 31, 32, 33, 34, 44, 46, 54, 70, 78, 97, 99, 110, 119, 125, 127, 133, 136, 145, 152, 169*n*72
abyss 18, 28, 46, 47, 65, 85, 88, 90, 134, 139, 144, 157, 162
ambiguous death 50, 73, 81, 86, 120, 151, 155, 158, 176*n*44, 177*n*9, 177*n*12, 177*n*17, 178*n*19, 178*n*31
antagonism 10, 12, 14, 18, 19, 20, 24, 25, 33, 35, 43, 54, 72, 78, 98, 111, 123, 127, 128, 143, 152, 189*n*19
Arabian Nights 109, 112
Arata, Steven 132, 146
Austen, Jane 16, 32, 156, 170*n*97; *see also Northanger Abbey*

Bakhtin, Mikhail 1–2, 16, 118–19; *see also* Carnivalesque; Grotesque Realism
Bal, Mieke 46, 167*n*21
Barnaby Rudge 113, 116; *see also* Dickens, Charles
Benford, Criscillia 47, 50
Bleak House 109, 110, 111, 115, 120–29; *see also* Dickens, Charles
Boccaccio: *The Decameron* 56, 176*n*53
Bowen, John 112, 184*n*17
Brontë, Anne 91, 103–104, 115; *see also The Tenant of Wildfell Hall*
Brontë, Charlotte 27, 29, 63, 79, 91, 92, 94, 97, 98, 181*n*1, 183*n*56; *see also Jane Eyre*; *Shirley*
Brontë, Emily 91–92, 115; *see also Wuthering Heights*
Brontë, Patrick 105, 182*n*17, 183*n*57
Burke, Edmund 23, 43, 59
Byron, Lord George Gordon 61, 64, 176*n*47, 177*n*66; *see also The Giaour*

capitalism 77, 78, 140, 141
Carlyle, Jane Welsh 84, 180*n*6
Carlyle, Thomas 14, 83–90, 131, 134, 135, 145, 180*n*3, 180*n*5, 180*n*6, 180*n*9, 180*n*12, 180*n*16; *see also Sartor Resartus*
Carnivalesque 1, 118–19; *see also* Bakhtin, Mikhail
The Castle of Otranto 1, 2, 3, 17–20, 21, 26, 35, 38, 41, 68, 70, 84, 171*n*111, 171*n*113, 171*n*115, 171*n*119, 176*n*47, 177*n*3; *see also* Walpole, Horace
"The Cave of Fancy" 50, 175*n*34; *see also* Wollstonecraft, Mary
Chambers, Robert 93, 94
Chesterton, G.K. 21, 112, 114
Chinese boxes 66, 178*n*19, 190*n*27
Clery, E.J. 18–20, 33, 35, 37
Coleridge, Samuel Taylor 2, 4–6, 9, 13–15, 159, 181*n*19; *see also Lyrical Ballads*; "The Rime of the Ancient Mariner"; *Sibylline Leaves*
Collins, Wilkie 137, 141, 166*n*10
confessional 33–36
Conrad, Joseph 154–55, 158–60, 161, 189*n*6; *see also Heart of Darkness*
Copjec, Joan 11, 27, 50
Critique of Pure Reason 9, 43, 66; *see also* Kant, Immanuel
Critique of the Power of Judgment 7, 23, 43; *see also* Kant, Immanuel

Darwin, Charles 119, 130, 131, 132, 134, 181*n*4, 187*n*22; *see also On the Origin of Species*
Davison, Carol Margaret 139, 187*n*36
Day, William Patrick 3, 168*n*59
Death Drive 99, 139, 179*n*58, 187*n*31; *see also* Freud, Sigmund
Derrida, Jacques 2, 7–8, 14, 22, 47, 80, 88; *see also* parergon
Dickens, Charles 73, 109–116, 118, 119–29, 131, 135, 144, 184*n*9; *see also Barnaby Rudge*; *Bleak House*; *Dombey and Son*; *Master Humphrey's Clock*; *The Old Curiosity Shop*
das Ding an sich (the thing in itself) 2, 9–10, 12, 20, 23, 31, 43, 54, 87, 133; *see also* Kant, Immanuel
Dolar, Mladen 71, 179*n*49, 179*n*58

Dombey and Son 111, 123; *see also* Dickens, Charles
double 18, 36, 39, 50, 76, 101, 114, 119, 133, 138, 179*n*49, 179*n*58
Dracula 30, 87, 118, 130–32, 136, 141–52, 166*n*10, 188*n*58, 188*n*71, 189*n*5; *see also* Stoker, Bram
Duncan, Ian 75, 81, 179*n*46

editors 6, 19, 21, 25, 26, 28, 36, 38, 39, 41–43, 56, 57, 58, 68, 74–77, 79–81, 84–90, 101, 115, 142, 143, 151, 152, 165*n*9, 169*n*82, 177*n*12, 185*n*35
Eliot, George 153–54, 189*n*5; *see also* "The Lifted Veil"
Ermarth, Elizabeth Deeds 121, 126
explained supernatural 23, 24, 29, 39, 42, 44, 45
extradiegetic 4–7, 13–14, 19, 22, 23, 28, 32–34, 36, 38, 39, 40, 41, 46, 73, 87, 88, 105, 112, 137, 139, 141, 158, 169*n*87, 170*n*91, 170*n*103
extra-extradiegetic 5

"The Fall of the House of Usher" 7–8, 13, 14, 26, 28, 30, 69, 96, 117; *see also* Poe, Edgar Allan
fantasmatic frame 11, 24, 49, 56, 89, 133, 156
"The Fields of Fancy" 50, 52, 56; *see also* Shelley, Mary
Foucault, Michel 33, 120, 166*n*12
found manuscript 14, 21, 35, 41, 42, 56, 57, 74, 81, 85, 103, 112, 114, 137, 172*n*32, 177*n*3
Frankenstein 46–51, 53, 54, 57, 60, 61, 64, 65, 72, 73, 77, 84, 86, 92, 94, 100, 101, 103, 117, 128, 131, 134, 137, 144, 145, 147, 149, 155, 159, 174*n*9, 174*n*20, 175*n*22, 175*n*24, 175*n*32, 175*n*33, 177*n*17; *see also* Shelley, Mary
Fraser, James 84, 85; *see also Fraser's Magazine*
Fraser's Magazine 84, 87; see also Fraser, James
Freud, Sigmund 3, 99, 132, 133, 139, 166*n*14, 168*n*59, 169*n*72, 187*n*31; *see also* Death Drive; uncanny; unconscious

Garrett, Peter K. 17, 74, 138
Gaston de Blondeville 38–44, 87, 115, 171, 173*n*61; *see also* Radcliffe, Ann
the gaze 27, 118, 170*n*96, 172*n*29, 185*n*40; *see also* Lacan, Jacques
Genette, Gérard 167*n*21, 169*n*87, 170*n*91
The Giaour 61, 177*n*66; *see also* Byron, Lord George Gordon
Gilbert, Sandra M. 102, 182*n*23; *see also* Gubar, Susan
Gilpin, William 22, 38
Godwin, William 2, 51, 52, 54, 67, 175*n*37
Goethe, Johann Wolfgang von 75, 83, 169*n*82
gothic realism 1, 12, 14, 60, 90, 131, 154, 161
The Great God Pan 161–163; *see also* Machen, Arthur
Grossman, Jonathan 111, 116, 120, 122, 124, 184*n*31
Grotesque Realism 1, 2, 119; *see also* Bakhtin, Mikhail
Gubar, Susan 102, 182*n*23; *see also* Sandra M. Gilbert

Hamlet 54, 153; *see also* Shakespeare, William
Heart of Darkness 153, 159–61; *see also* Conrad, Joseph
Hogg, James 64, 74, 75, 77, 79–81, 84, 87, 101, 115, 120, 128, 140; *see also The Private Memoirs and Confessions of a Justified Sinner*
Hogle, Jerrold E. 11, 35, 99, 132, 139
Hood, Thomas 112–113, 118
hypodiegetic 41, 70, 100, 104, 105, 172*n*32, 172*n*33

Ideal-I 76, 148; *see also* Lacan, Jacques
ideology 25, 72, 77, 78, 108, 124
the Imaginary 10, 76, 148, 179*n*49; *see also* Lacan, Jacques
incest 9, 13, 14, 51, 54–56, 176*n*47
Inquisition 34, 37, 65, 72
The Italian 23, 30, 32–39, 40, 41, 42, 45, 56, 61, 117, 137, 141, 144, 155; *see also* Radcliffe, Ann

Jaffe, Audrey 114, 116, 123
James, Henry 154–55, 156, 158, 159, 160, 161; *see also The Turn of the Screw*; *What Maisie Knew*
Jane Eyre 27, 29, 94, 95, 100, 123, 156, 181*n*1, 183*n*56; *see also* Brontë, Charlotte
jouissance 54; *see also* Lacan, Jacques

Kant, Immanuel 2, 7, 9–12, 14, 20, 22–24, 31, 38, 43, 66, 78, 87, 122, 133, 134, 168*n*58; *see also Critique of Pure Reason*; *Critique of the Power of Judgment*; manifold of senses; noumenon; phenomenon
Kristeva, Julia 2, 3, 11–12, 15, 24, 28, 70, 119, 133, 169*n*72; *see also* abjection; *Powers of Horror*

Lacan, Jacques 2, 3, 10, 11, 13, 16, 23, 24, 31, 54, 66, 71, 75, 89, 118, 139, 147, 148, 161, 166*n*12, 166*n*14, 168*n*58, 168*n*67, 170*n*96, 172*n*29, 179*n*49, 179*n*58, 185*n*40; *see also* the gaze; Ideal-I; the Imaginary; *jouissance*; Mirror Stage; *Objet Petit a*; the Real; the Symbolic; *trompe l'oeil*
"The Lady of Shalott" 63–64, 79; *see also* Tennyson, Alfred Lord
Lamarck, Jean-Baptiste 92, 181*n*4

Lamb, Charles 5
The Last Man 45, 46, 56–62, 85, 86, 87, 174*n*5, 176*n*53, 189*n*5; *see also* Shelley, Mary
"Leda and the Swan" 149, 188*n*67; *see also* Yeats, William Butler
Lewis, Matthew 32, 43, 84, 165*n*10, 176*n*47, 178*n*40; *see also The Monk*
"Lift not the painted veil" 15–16, 63, 67, 89, 91, 99, 105, 170*n*92, 177*n*65; *see also* Shelley, Percy Bysshe
"The Lifted Veil" 153, 188*n*3, 189*n*5; *see also* Eliot, George
Luddite 79, 180*n*63
Lyrical Ballads 2, 6, 13, 169*n*85; *see also* Coleridge, Samuel Taylor; Wordsworth, William

MacAndrew, Elizabeth 5, 165*n*9
Macbeth 6, 58, 60, 150; *see also* Shakespeare, William
Machen, Arthur 161–163, 190*n*29; *see also The Great God Pan*
madness 8, 27, 70, 89, 90 94–95, 100, 133, 147
Malina, Debra 14, 15
manifold of senses 9–11, 14, 43, 78, 122, 133; *see also* Kant, Immanuel
Marx, Karl 77, 79
Master Humphrey's Clock 112 13, 129, 184*n*20, 185*n*42; *see also* Dickens, Charles
Mathilda 46, 50–56, 60, 175*n*37, 175*n*38, 176*n*44, 176*n*47, 189*n*5; *see also* Shelley, Mary
Matthews, John T. 101, 169*n*90
Maturin, Charles Robert 64–68, 81, 88, 120, 140, 151, 177*n*12, 177*n*15, 177*n*17; *see also Melmoth the Wanderer*
Mellor, Anne 47, 181*n*23
Melmoth the Wanderer 64–74, 77, 80, 81, 86, 88, 96, 97, 100, 117, 120, 128, 140, 149, 151, 155; *see also* Maturin, Charles Robert
metalepsis 14–16, 19, 23, 25, 28, 65, 87, 91, 169*n*87, 170*n*91
Mighall, Robert 110, 184*n*7
Miller, J. Hillis 85, 88, 95, 182*n*23
Milton, John 12, 13, 14, 43, 73, 96, 150, 177*n*67; *see also Paradise Lost*
Mirror Stage 75, 148, 149, 175*n*24; *see also* Lacan, Jacques
missing frame 37, 38, 65, 159, 189
The Monk 32, 43, 165*n*10, 176*n*47, 177*n*17, 178*n*40; *see also* Lewis, Matthew
monster 2, 11, 12, 14, 16, 20, 46, 55, 61, 68, 77, 86, 92, 94, 101, 107, 108, 109, 111, 119, 130, 131, 132, 139, 140, 141, 143, 148, 153, 162, 170*n*103, 175*n*20, 175*n*24, 190*n*25, 190*n*29
The Mysteries of Udolpho 8, 15, 16, 22, 26, 28–32, 35, 37, 41, 42, 61, 69, 117, 125, 144, 149, 156, 157, 170*n*96, 170*n*97, 172*n*33, 173*n*79, 180*n*9; *see also* Radcliffe, Ann

Newman, Beth 47, 95
Northanger Abbey 16, 32, 156, 170*n*97; *see also* Austen, Jane
Norton, Rictor 33, 38, 39, 43
noumenon 20, 66, 134, 168*n*58; *see also* phenomenon

objet petit a 31, 33, 71, 170*n*96, 179*n*49, 179*n*58; *see also* Lacan, Jacques
The Old Curiosity Shop 109, 110, 111–120, 125, 127, 135; *see also* Dickens, Charles
On the Origin of Species 119, 131; *see also* Darwin, Charles
"On the Supernatural in Poetry" 39, 42–43, 172*n*23, 173*n*79; Radcliffe, Ann

Paradise Lost 12, 13, 14, 96, 150, 177*n*67; *see also* Milton, John
paratext 6, 14, 17, 19, 21, 39, 45, 46, 142, 166*n*10, 167*n*21, 170*n*103
parergon 2, 7–8, 12, 14, 22, 47, 73, 80, 88, 158; *see also* Derrida, Jacques
phenomenon 12, 20, 168*n*58; *see also* noumenon
Pick, Daniel 131, 132, 146
picturesque 22–23, 25, 26, 29, 37–39, 69, 156
The plague 56–58, 59, 60, 61–62, 87
Poe, Edgar Allan 6–8, 14, 16, 26, 28, 30, 67, 69, 115, 117, 137, 140, 154, 184*n*20; *see also* "The Fall of the House of Usher"; "The Raven"
portrait 19, 24, 30, 68, 69, 70, 72, 73, 105, 171*n*123
Powers of Horror 11, 24; *see also* Kristeva, Julia
The Prelude 109, 111, 119; *see also* Wordsworth, William
The Private Memoirs and Confessions of a Justified Sinner 64, 74–82, 86, 87, 101, 115, 120, 128, 149, 179*n*46, 179*n*58; *see also* Hogg, James

Radcliffe, Ann 8, 15, 21–44, 45, 56, 57, 61, 65, 66, 68, 69, 74, 76, 84, 87, 104, 115, 117, 136, 137, 141, 144, 147, 155, 156, 157, 172*n*23, 172*n*32, 172*n*33, 177*n*15; *Gaston de Blondeville*; *The Italian*; *The Mysteries of Udolpho*; "On the Supernatural in Poetry"; *The Romance of the Forest*; *A Sicilian Romance*
"The Raven" 6, 154; *see also* Poe, Edgar Allan
the Real 2, 10–16, 18, 19, 20, 22–34, 36, 38, 42, 43, 46–49, 51, 53–56, 58–61, 63–65, 67, 69–72, 76–78, 80, 82, 84, 85, 87–90, 91–92, 94–103, 105–106, 108, 110–11, 113, 114, 116–

20, 123, 127–28, 131–36, 138–41, 143–45, 147–49, 152, 153, 157–59, 161–62, 168*n*62, 169*n*69, 170*n*96, 187*n*31, 189*n*19, 190*n*30; *see also* Lacan, Jacques
realism 1–2, 10, 90, 110, 111, 137, 149, 153–55, 169*n*90, 170*n*103, 181*n*29, 184*n*6, 188*n*3
"The Rime of the Ancient Mariner" 4–6, 13–15, 159; *see also* Coleridge, Samuel Taylor
Robinson, Charles E. 56, 174*n*9
The Romance of the Forest 69, 172*n*32, 180*n*9; *see also* Radcliffe, Ann

Sage, Victor 65, 68, 177*n*12
Sartor Resartus 83–90, 134, 135, 180*n*12, 181*n*21, 181*n*23; *see also* Carlyle, Thomas
Schor, Hilary M. 122, 123, 125
Scott, Walter 22, 29, 32, 50, 116, 169*n*82, 171*n*123, 180*n*6, 185*n*35; *see also Tales of My Landlord*
"The Second Coming" 91, 108; *see also* Yeats, William Butler
Shakespeare, William 6, 39, 43, 47, 54, 58, 60, 150, 153, 174*n*13; *see also Hamlet*; *Macbeth*; *The Taming of the Shrew*
Shelley, Mary 45–62, 83, 84, 85, 86, 88, 92, 120, 131, 144, 151, 170*n*92, 174*n*5, 174*n*7, 174*n*9, 175*n*22, 175*n*37, 175*n*38, 177*n*65, 180*n*3, 180*n*4, 184*n*6, 189*n*5; *see also* "The Fields of Fancy"; *Frankenstein*; *The Last Man*; *Mathilda*
Shelley, Percy Bysshe 9, 15, 46, 48, 49, 51, 63, 83, 88, 91, 135, 170*n*92, 176*n*47, 180*n*4; *see also* "Lift not the painted veil"
Shirley 63, 79; *see also* Brontë, Charlotte
sibyl 57, 58, 60, 61, 69, 86
Sibylline Leaves 4–5, 181*n*19; *see also* Coleridge, Samuel Taylor
A Sicilian Romance 25–28, 32, 36, 37, 42, 56, 104, 136, 141, 173*n*61; *see also* Radcliffe, Ann
Stevenson, Robert Louis 118, 128, 130–32, 134–38, 141, 147, 155, 187*n*22; *see also The Strange Case of Dr Jekyll and Mr Hyde*
Stoker, Bram 30, 118, 130–32, 136, 141, 144, 145, 146, 147, 148, 166*n*10, 188*n*71; *see also Dracula*
The Strange Case of Dr Jekyll and Mr Hyde 128, 130–41, 144, 147, 155, 187*n*25, 187*n*36; *see also* Stevenson, Robert Louis
sublime 22–31, 34, 35, 37, 38, 39, 43, 59, 65, 71, 76
suicide 34, 55, 78, 80, 81, 128, 138, 139, 162, 176*n*44, 179*n*58
the Symbolic 10, 11, 13, 14, 18, 19, 24, 25, 28, 42, 54, 55, 67, 70, 73, 78, 97, 98, 99, 110, 111, 119, 123, 132, 145, 148, 159, 161, 163, 175*n*24, 189*n*19; *see also* Lacan, Jacques

Tales of My Landlord 116, 185*n*35; *see also* Scott, Walter
Talfourd, Thomas 22, 36, 173*n*50
The Taming of the Shrew 47, 174*n*13; *see also* Shakespeare, William
tapestry 27, 64, 65, 66, 78, 79, 87, 88, 90, 105, 119, 144, 151, 177*n*5, 180*n*9, 181*n*21
Tarr, Rodger L. 181*n*21, 181*n*23
temperance 105, 106, 107, 183*n*57
The Tenant of Wildfell Hall 91, 95, 103–108, 125; *see also* Brontë, Anne
Tennyson, Alfred Lord 21, 64, 69, 130–31, 186*n*4; *see also* "The Lady of Shalott"
Townshend, Dale 42, 166*n*12
trompe l'oeil 170*n*96; *see also* Lacan, Jacques
The Turn of the Screw 155–58, 189*n*13, 189*n*17; *see also* James, Henry

uncanny 16, 36, 41, 46, 49, 111, 113, 117, 127, 161, 169*n*72; *see also* Freud, Sigmund
unconscious 4, 16, 23, 31, 33, 54, 55, 56, 138, 145, 168*n*59; *see also* Freud Sigmund
Urban Gothic 110, 184*n*7

veils 3, 7, 15–16, 21, 23, 26, 27, 30–32, 34, 38, 41, 58, 60, 61, 63, 67, 88, 91, 99, 105, 125, 135, 144, 149, 153, 157, 161, 170*n*97, 172*n*28, 177*n*65
Von Sneidern, Maja-Lisa 98, 101

Walpole, Horace 1, 2, 3, 16, 17–20, 21, 26, 35, 38, 41, 42, 68, 70, 84, 171*n*111, 171*n*113, 171*n*119, 176*n*47; *see also The Castle of Otranto*
weaving loom 63–64, 76–79
Wells, H.G. 109, 130
What Maisie Knew 155, 161; *see also* James, Henry
Wicke, Jennifer 141, 142
Wollstonecraft, Mary 23, 50, 165*n*10, 175*n*34; *see also* "The Cave of Fancy"
Wordsworth, William 2, 4, 5, 6, 9, 13, 45, 109, 110, 111, 119, 169*n*85; *see also Lyrical Ballads*; *The Prelude*
Wuthering Heights 91–92, 95–103, 104, 107, 108, 125, 137, 145, 169*n*90, 182*n*23; *see also* Brontë, Emily

Yeats, William Butler 91, 101, 149, 188*n*67; *see also* "Leda and the Swan"; "The Second Coming"

Žižek, Slavoj 10, 11, 12, 14, 18, 20, 24, 25, 27, 31, 33, 42, 46, 49, 55, 59, 70, 72, 76, 78, 89, 92, 94, 98, 100, 111, 123, 133, 136, 140, 145, 148, 159, 161, 168*n*58, 168*n*62, 168*n*66, 168*n*67, 168*n*69, 172*n*23, 175*n*24, 186*n*69, 187*n*31, 189*n*19, 190*n*30

www.ingramcontent.com/pod-product-compliance
Lightning Source LLC
Chambersburg PA
CBHW050324110726
47899CB00007B/2358

* 9 7 8 1 4 7 6 6 6 7 4 8 5 *